OX

THE ITALIAN CARTEL #7

SHANDI BOYES

D1710331

COPYRIGHT

This work is fiction. No names, people, or places are real. It is all made up by Shandi's imagination.

Written By: Shandi Boyes

Edited by: Nicki at Swish Design & Editing

Proofread by: Kaylene at Swish Design & Editing

Cover Model: Sonny Henty

Photographer: Wander Aguiar

Cover Design: SSB Covers and Design

DEDICATION

To the Boyes Family,

You've shown such grace and dignity the past couple of weeks. Your strengths are shining even during your darkest days. You should be proud as I am sure those who passed over are.

Shandi xx

WANT TO STAY IN TOUCH?

Facebook: facebook.com/authorshandi

Instagram: instagram.com/authorshandi

Email: authorshandi@gmail.com

Reader's Group: bit.ly/ShandiBookBabes

Website: authorshandi.com

Newsletter: https://www.subscribepage.com/AuthorShandi

ALSO BY SHANDI BOYES

Perception Series

Saving Noah (Noah & Emily)

Fighting Jacob (Jacob & Lola)

Taming Nick (Nick & Jenni)

Redeeming Slater (Slater and Kylie)

Saving Emily (Noah & Emily - Novella)

Wrapped Up with Rise Up (Perception Novella - should be read after the Bound Series)

Enigma

Enigma (Isaac & Isabelle #1)

Unraveling an Enigma (Isaac & Isabelle #2)

Enigma The Mystery Unmasked (Isaac & Isabelle #3)

Enigma: The Final Chapter (Isaac & Isabelle #4)

Beneath The Secrets (Hugo & Ava #1)

Beneath The Sheets(Hugo & Ava #2)

Spy Thy Neighbor (Hunter & Paige)

The Opposite Effect (Brax & Clara)

I Married a Mob Boss(Rico & Blaire)

Second Shot(Hawke & Gemma)

The Way We Are(Ryan & Savannah #1)

The Way We Were(Ryan & Savannah #2)

Sugar and Spice (Cormack & Harlow)

Lady In Waiting (Regan & Alex #1)

Man in Queue (Regan & Alex #2)

Couple on Hold(Regan & Alex #3)

Enigma: The Wedding (Isaac and Isabelle)

Silent Vigilante (Brandon and Melody #1)

Hushed Guardian (Brandon & Melody #2)

Quiet Protector (Brandon & Melody #3)

Bound Series

Chains (Marcus & Cleo #1)

Links(Marcus & Cleo #2)

Bound(Marcus & Cleo #3)

Restrain(Marcus & Cleo #4)

Psycho (Dexter & ??)

Russian Mob Chronicles

Nikolai: A Mafia Prince Romance (Nikolai & Justine #1)

Nikolai: Taking Back What's Mine (Nikolai & Justine #2)

Nikolai: What's Left of Me(Nikolai & Justine #3)

Nikolai: Mine to Protect(Nikolai & Justine #4)

Asher: My Russian Revenge (Asher & Zariah)

Nikolai: Through the Devil's Eyes(Nikolai & Justine #5)

Trey (Trey & K)

K: A Trey Sequel

The Italian Cartel

Dimitri

Roxanne

Reign

Mafia Ties (Novella)

Maddox

Demi

Ox

Rocco

Clover

Smith

RomCom Standalones

Just Playin' (Elvis & Willow)

Ain't Happenin' (Lorenzo & Skylar)

The Drop Zone (Colby & Jamie)

Very Unlikely (Brand New Couple)

Short Stories

Christmas Trio (Wesley, Andrew & Mallory -- short story)

Falling For A Stranger (Short Story)

Coming Soon

Skitzo

1

DEMI

*W*hen my uncle's bloody knife falls to his side, I gasp in a sharp breath. I thought death would be more painful than this. Don't get me wrong, my heart is decimated, shattered from witnessing Maddox's fight to get to me, but there's a peacefulness associated with knowing my uncle isn't the ruler of my realm anymore, that he'd rather end my life than govern it. I just wish I had gotten Maddox off his radar first.

That was the term my uncle agreed to when I arrived at his private residence only an hour ago, to the house I avoided like the plague in my teens. He said if I followed the rules and gave myself wholly to him, Maddox would be free.

It was stupid of me to believe he'd keep his word. I was clearly blinded by hope.

The only good that's come from his betrayal is having more understanding of my father's decision. More respect. Heartbreak hurts but being manipulated by the people who are meant to love you is a devastating blow to overcome.

I hope Maddox is stronger than my father, and he can find it in his heart to forgive me. I had to put him first, or not a single thing I've done in my short life would have been worthwhile. Sacrificing my life for his was the easiest decision I've ever made. My father often said that the greatest sacrifice you can give is surrendering yourself for someone you love. I'm sure with time, Maddox will understand this.

Wanting my last breaths to be shared with my fifteen-year-long crush, I tilt forward until my forehead rests on the un-shadowed glass separating Maddox and me. Unlike when I pressed my hand to the two-way mirror, Maddox doesn't balance his forehead against mine. He stares up at my uncle, his eyes murderous yet stunned.

I discover the reason for his shock when I follow the direction of his gaze. My severed head isn't in my uncle's hands. Massive clumps of my hair are.

As my hand shoots up to check my neck for a life-ending gash, my uncle's victorious eyes drop to mine. "Let this be a lesson," he says, his tone slow and brimming with superiority. "The next time either of you go against me, we will return here so I can finish what I started." After smirking at my shocked expression that I don't have a fatal neck wound, he strays his eyes to Maddox. "You now know what I am capable of doing. Don't underestimate me again, or I won't stop at one member of your family next time."

While taking in the massacre behind Maddox, my uncle clicks his fingers together two times. Like magic, several men enter the room from a door in the far corner. I assume they're here to hurt Maddox but am proven wrong when they drag the deceased man into the corridor before popping bullets into the two Maddox subdued without mortally wounding them.

I stop contemplating how inhumanely my uncle treats members of his crew when the vault-like door my uncle walked me through ten minutes ago automatically opens. I scramble for Maddox, my wish to get to him having me unconcerned that I'm as naked as the day I was born.

I have no reason to fret. Maddox moves for me just as quickly, and within seconds, his shuddering frame engulfs every inch of me.

As the fast beat of his heart mollifies the fear clutching my throat, he blocks my view of the horrifying scene circling us with his hand, having no clue scenarios like this will soon become the norm for us.

Our love saw us selling our souls to the devil.

Now we're living in our own version of hell.

When I say that to Maddox, he brushes away the strands of hair my uncle's unexpected cut forced into my eyes before muttering, "If you're here, I'm right where I am meant to be."

He doesn't say it, but his eyes most certainly expose he isn't remorseful about the lengths he went to today to get to me.

That's the fear my uncle is feeding off. He used my wish not to be sexually abused by a family member to force Maddox into my life, and now he will use Maddox's anxiety about losing me to fuel his wish to rule the world. We're nothing but puppets to him, people he can manipulate to do whatever he wants, and since I'm convinced his brutality won't stop at Justine next time, I have no clue how to prevent his plans.

"He'll use this against us. He now knows how far we will go for one another, and he will milk it for all it's worth." I bang my forehead with my palm, frustrated about the naïve idiot I've portrayed the past couple of months. "I should have let him kill me."

Maddox's heart skips a beat before he snatches my hand away from my face. "Don't ever say that, Demi. *Ever.* If you die, I die." He brushes away the tears careening down my face with the back of his index finger. "Remember that the next time you want to let him win."

"I'm not letting him win. He *is* winning because he's cruel and heartless. I fucking hate him."

When my watering eyes drift across the room three men lost their lives in—four if you include Maddox's soul—Maddox grips my chin in a nonpainful manner before wordlessly demanding my eyes back to his. "Look at me, Demi." When I do as asked, he mutters, "*Truly* look at me."

I do. I take in every inch of him—the fear in his eyes that we nearly lost each other, the love a lifetime of hurt couldn't shift, and a soul that won't bend no matter how rough the conditions. I drink it all in while falling in love with him even more than I thought possible.

Confident I have the gist of what he's saying, Maddox drags his index finger down my nose. It isn't as effective today as it usually is, but it does lessen the turmoil wreaking havoc with my stomach.

"He isn't winning, Demi. We are because we have each other." The nicks his battle stabbed my heart with are filled with love when he adds, "This game will never last as long as our love. We can't lose if we remember that. It isn't possible."

We're in a house of torture, in a town I hate, but the horrors of my life fade away when I press my lips to Maddox's. My head is too hazy to conjure up meaningful, heart-stuttering words like he did, so I use my body instead. It's probably stupid of me to do, but when you sell your soul to the devil, you do anything you can to grip reality.

"I love you," I whisper over Maddox's kiss-swollen lips a couple of seconds later.

He smiles in a way that wipes the agony from my heart as quickly as his hands clear away my tears before replying, "I love you back. Never forgot that because our love is what makes *this* worthwhile."

2

DEMI

I begin to wonder how long it will be before Maddox regrets his decision to fight for me when he enters our room in my uncle's private compound. His forehead is holding the groove it only ever gets when someone's life is precariously dangling in the wind, and his eyes look lifeless. He struggled running drugs for my family's 'business,' so I'd hate to consider how dirty he feels after working directly under my uncle the past ten days. I fight the urge to shower multiple times a day, and I'm only hearing about my uncle's shady dealings from Maddox. Maddox is experiencing them firsthand.

Although the reports make my skin crawl, something still seems amiss. My uncle is being too casual about what he shares with Maddox. He's talking 'business' in the open and flaunting his lawlessness for the world to see. It's as if he's unafraid of prosecution, like not even the law is capable of bringing him down.

It isn't a far cry from his usual personality, but it is extremely off-putting. If he grows bored of puppeteering Maddox and me, we will be disposed of even sooner than we were snared by his trap. My uncle lives off fear. He feeds off it. If we're not giving him that anymore, he'll find another way to scare us.

Upon noticing I am getting dressed, Maddox shuts the door of our room, leaving his permanent shadow on the other side. My uncle is confident he scared us enough to follow his every whim, but that doesn't mean he trusts us. We're never alone for long. Even while visiting Justine in the hospital last week, he ordered three of his goons to follow us. Caidyn and Saint have mentioned similar. Maddox's entire family is being monitored by my uncle. One wrong move, and they'll be taken out in under a second.

I had hoped when news circulated that I had moved back into Col's primary residence, Dimitri would smell a rat. Regretfully, his father's unexpected return from Italy saw Dimitri go on his own vacation abroad. No one has heard from his crew in days. You'd swear he has given up on overtaking his father's reign, instead choosing to start his own empire in another country.

"Have you eaten?"

I lift my chin to Maddox's question before moving for the bag of goodies I brought back from Petretti's. I still work as a sous-chef there, but I'm no longer paid for my services. It's the same for Maddox. He fought the past two Fridays in the underground circuit the Petrettis have run for almost two decades, yet not a single denomination exchanged hands. My uncle doesn't solely want us to be his puppets. He wants us reliant on him for the most basic necessities as well.

His domineering personality makes me grateful that I work in a kitchen. Even feeling hopeless, I can ensure Maddox and his family are fed. Most are still holding a bedside vigil in Justine's hospital room. Her wounds will eventually heal, but doctors have cited concern that they're the least of their worries.

My focus shifts from Justine's mental well-being to Maddox when he says, "I'll do that." He removes a takeout container full of food from my hand before jerking his head to a dressing gown on the edge of my bed. "Then you can finish getting dressed." When his narrowed gaze swings to the security dome in the far corner of our room, the work of his jaw is quick, but I don't miss it. My uncle has sworn the cameras aren't monitored, but neither Maddox nor I believe him. "Who took you to your shift today?"

I shove my hands into the opening of my dressing gown before replying, "Mario. He stayed the entire shift." Even aware my uncle is most likely watching won't stop the roll of my eyes. "He's making everyone *really* uncomfortable. The waitstaff dropped more meals today than they served."

Maddox sighs like he understands my concerns. Everyone is getting restless—even us, two lost souls unsure how we can escape our nightmare without procuring one-way tickets to hell. The past couple of days have been tough, and I'm genuinely stumped on how to make it better. We're breathing, but we are not close to being alive, if that makes any sense.

After plopping my backside onto the mattress, I fold my legs under my bottom. "What about you? Who did you hang out with today?" I ask my questions as if he spent the day in the playground with friends in middle school instead of the underworld I swore he'd never be a part of. It's easier to act daft than remind him of all the horrid things he did today.

Being seen as an idiot is worth it when my daftness weakens the groove between Maddox's brows. He doesn't want to give me all the gory details, and in all honesty, I don't want to hear about them either.

"Ezra J—"

"Jason?" I interrupt before he can get half of Ezra's surname out.

Maddox sucks up a string of creamy linguini before nodding. "Have you heard of him?"

"Unfortunately, yes." I angle my body so my lips are hidden from the camera before explaining, "He's usually brought in to hide my uncle's messes. He isn't a hired hitman, so to speak. More a..."

"Fixer?" Maddox fills in when words elude me.

Although it would be better to voice my reply since my uncle's security system is too ancient to have sound, I nod instead. "Ezra's services range from cooked books to the dissolution of marriages."

The reminder of Ezra's last visit to my uncle's compound screws up my nose. "Why is he here? Col hasn't remarried since his fourth wife..." my stomach gurgles when I murmur, "... who hasn't been seen since their divorce."

The involuntary shiver that darts up Maddox's spine announces he is also suspicious about Samantha's disappearance, but he keeps our focus on the less gruesome parts of my uncle's life. "I don't know what he's working on. I spent most of my day in his car." He swallows a chunk of juicy chicken before dragging the back of his hand across his saucy lips. "Do you remember the camp we went to in seventh grade?"

"The one where we had pitched our own tents and were eaten alive by mosquitoes?"

The rarity of Maddox's grin makes it even more precious. I cherish it like it's the sun, and I've been locked away for twenty years. They have been far and few between the past two weeks.

As quickly as Maddox's smile arrived, it disappeared. The reason behind his sagging lips comes to light when he says, "You swore we had been there before, and when you told your mom that upon our return—"

"She slapped me in front of everyone. I remember."

With my well-being always in the forefront of his mind, Maddox tugs on my wrist until I'm sitting side-straddled on his lap. I die a little on the inside when he forgets about the pixie cut my uncle forced me to get. He can weave his fingers through my hair—*just*— but he can no longer tuck it behind my ear like he once did.

It isn't all bad. Instead of wrangling wayward strands stuck to my face into submission, he drags his index finger down my nose instead. It instantly halves my heartache, freeing him to ask, "Did you ever find out why she responded the way she did?"

I urge him to eat some more before replying, "No. But everyone was a little weird that afternoon." When Maddox slants his head to the side as if to question '*how,*' I add, "No write-ups about our camp were in the school newsletter. They were so desperate for stories back then, someone's pet having a litter was front-page news."

Maddox laughs for barely a second before he clamps his mouth shut with a grunt. "It wasn't in the yearbook either. I'd know. My mom shoves them under my nose every Thanksgiving."

Forgetting where we are and why we're here, I giggle. "She did the same to me multiple times during our prolonged sleepovers." When Maddox groans to hide his embarrassment, my grin doubles. "What would you prefer? Clothed yearbook photos or naked photos of you in the bathtub?"

"Naked pictures of me in the tub," he answers without pause for thought. "A stallion doesn't grow into his dick. He's born with it."

Even though I'm aware he's slipped back into his coping mechanism of flirting to hide his anguish, I slap his chest, playing along with his ruse. His groove has lessened the longer we talk, but it's still very much prominent. "Your bragging will get you in trouble one day, Mister."

"I fuckin' hope so." He hits me with a cocky wink before nudging his head to the top of our bed. "But for now, how about we call it a night? I'm wrecked." He doesn't need to say he means both emotionally and physically. I can see it in his eyes.

I watch him like a hawk when my slip beneath the sheets sees him removing his boots, jeans, and shirt. He has such a gorgeous body, compact yet fitted with muscles in *all* the required places.

His underwear covers the most impressive muscle on his body until he enters the bathroom attached to our room. It's basic compared to the many others in this residence, but it has the essentials you need after a hard day, such as endless hot water, and it's minus the one thing we'd happily live without—security cameras.

Our bathroom is the only room in this entire twelve-bedroom residence without monitored surveillance. This isn't a feature my uncle insisted on after demanding we stay with him. It was installed long before we moved in. Dimitri is so accustomed to being spied on, he thinks it's normal. From what I've gathered from Rocco, his newly built mansion is similarly wired. Every room has eyes in it, *except* the bathrooms.

A lack of trust is another annoying Petretti trait, but the recollection sees me slipping out of bed and tugging off my dressing gown. The amount of steam in the bathroom assures me even if my uncle could see through walls, he'd have a hard time witnessing me removing my nightie and panties.

I take a couple of seconds to relish the visual of a naked Maddox before cracking open the glass door. It releases a heap of steam. It has nothing on the sigh Maddox disperses when I band my arms around his midsection, though. I hug him fiercely, aware that this moment in time is about more than a sexual attraction. He's struggling, and it's my job as his girlfriend to help him through the darkness engulfing him. I'd rather remove him from it entirely, but since that isn't an option right now, I take what I can get.

After several heart-fixing seconds, I mumble, "Talk to me, Maddox. We'll be nothing if we lose the ability to communicate with one another."

It takes me loading up a shower puff with a scented shower gel and scrubbing half of his back before he mutters, "There was a girl today, probably a couple of years older than us." I find it odd that he calls her a girl since she's older than us, but discover why when he mutters, "She wasn't quite with it. I wouldn't say she's slow. She just..." he pauses to consider how to explain her demeanor, "... doesn't live in reality."

When he spins to face me, I commence cleaning his torso. I'm dying to prompt him, but I realize that would be wrong of me to do. He's talking, which is all I ask of him. "That's why I asked if you remembered camp. I swear I've seen her before."

"Is she from our school?" I inwardly scold myself for butting in, but it couldn't be helped. I am as curious as I am attracted to Maddox.

Reddish-blond locks fall into Maddox's eyes when he shakes his head. My uncle's bad hack of my hair could only be fixed by making my hair as short as Maddox's. He has sworn on multiple occasions that he loves my new 'do,' but I plan to grow it back. "But I think she was at camp."

My brows join as confusion makes itself known with my gut. "She couldn't have been. That was a Seaforth Academy camp. If you weren't a student, you weren't allowed to attend. My dad found that out the hard way."

Maddox plucks the shower puff out of my hand, reloads it with gel, then sets to work on getting me clean, even with me recently showering.

It dawns on me what he's doing when he says, "That's when I saw her. When your dad came to visit." He's distracting me. Under normal circumstances, it would work, but when it comes to my dad, there's no recommended form of distraction. "She was sitting in the back seat of your dad's truck."

"No... he came alone." I swallow when my memories fail me for the second time in my life. The memory is hazy, but I think Maddox is right. There was a girl in his truck the morning my father arrived at camp headquarters unannounced. I didn't pay her much attention because I was so mortified watching my father being marched off the property, I had my hand slapped over my eyes.

My lips quiver when I ask, "Do you know her name?"

It feels like minutes pass before Maddox jerks up his chin. "Megan Shroud."

My chest deflates like a balloon. I don't know why I thought the girl with mousy-brown hair would have been Kaylee. That would make my parents snatch of my memories even crueler. I guess I just don't want to believe the obvious—my sister is dead.

Ignorance seems to be a favorite pastime of mine lately.

The woes of my childhood are pushed aside for adult worries when Maddox's scrub of my torso has him taking in the sliver of silver in the middle of my breastplate. I barely felt the cut my uncle inflicted to assure Maddox knew he was serious about hurting me. The pain in Maddox's eyes that night hurt more than any knife wound ever could. He was truly gutted, unhinged, and on the verge of a mental breakdown.

Only one time previously have I seen a man on the brink like that. It was my dad the morning after my uncle took Kaylee. He didn't hear my tiptoes out of my room, meaning I not only saw the pain in his eyes when he gathered Kaylee's blanket from the floor, but I also saw the tears he shed when he brought it to his nose to smell it.

I scrub under my nose to ensure my newfound memory didn't cause anything gross to spill there before diverting my focus back to Maddox. I can't bring Kaylee nor my father back, but I can do everything in my power to ensure Maddox isn't swallowed by the same dark world that ripped my family apart.

"Still bad at multitasking, I see," I murmur with a smile, teasing Maddox about his still hands. "Can you do this?" He cocks a brow when I rub my belly and pat my head at the same time. "It's never too late to learn new tricks."

When my tease doubles the electricity crackling between us, Maddox moans like he's in pain. "Don't... please. Not here. I can't." He's so distrusting by my uncle's motives, we haven't been sexually active since we moved in. I can't say I don't understand his hesitation. I've witnessed some sick things in my life, yet I'm still aware there are many more ways my uncle can hurt me.

In an endeavor to lighten the mood, I mention the one thing capable of de-masting Maddox by the sheer mention of his name. "I saw Max today."

"Yeah?" Maddox replies with a ghost-like grin. He'll never admit it, but I'm confident he's missing Max as much as me the past ten days. "Has he bitten any of Jude's suitors on the ass yet?"

My laugh bounces around the steam-filled space. "Not yet, but Ty assures me he's willing to take one for the team if the opportunity arises."

"Of course he would," Maddox replies with a chuckle, his earlier anguish almost fully dispersed. "He has nothing to lose and—"

"Everything to gain," we say at the same time.

"Unlike me," he murmurs under his breath before he ends our conversation by requesting for me to step under the spray.

Once he's confident all the suds coating my body are circling the drain, he switches off the faucet, then steps out. I swoon like crazy when he commences drying me with the untouched towel on the rack as mine is soaked through and dumped on the floor, then blood surges through my heart when he places my nightie over my head before bobbing down to assist me into my panties. He does the same thing every time we shower together—period or not.

"You should eat some more," I say during our walk back to the main part of our room.

The container of food I made him at Petretti's is barely touched. He'll fade away to nothing if he doesn't maintain adequate nutrition. Dimitri and Rocco don't preserve their desired weight by working out in a gym. They get it from all the heavy lifting they do in this industry. Dead people weigh the same as they did before they were killed, but have you ever tried to lift a ninety-pound plank of wood? It's much harder to get off the ground than a ninety-pound person because it can't shift its weight to a central point to make it appear less heavy.

For once, I can say my family business isn't the source of my data. Seaforth Academy pushed the boundaries with its teachings, which makes me even more surprised about the Walshs' attendance. Mr. and Mrs. Walsh are as conservative as they come. They don't even talk politics, so why did they send their child to a school known for controversial practices?

My thoughts drift back to the present when Maddox shakes his head. "I'm not hungry."

"Still, you should eat—"

I take a step back when he cuts me off with a surly tone, "I said I'm not hungry." He regrets his snapped tone in an instant. While raking his fingers through his hair, he mutters more respectively, "I'm sorry. I am not angry at you. I'm just... *tired*."

He means exhausted. Not solely because of a lack of sleep, but life in general. I've often said men like Maddox aren't built for this life. His quick spiral exposes I was right. He barely had the chance to catch his breath before our uncle pitted our love against us. It's been one thing after another ever since.

I can only hope I'm strong enough to keep his head above the water still surging our way. Drowning is one of the cruelest forms of death. A bullet is instant. A knife wound is almost as quick, but drowning is long and painful, and more times than not, it doesn't just pull you under the current, it takes everyone propping you up as well.

3

DEMI

*F*our days later, it appears as if Maddox is a rejuvenated man. Excluding a brief meeting with Ezra the morning following our conversation in the shower, he's spent a majority of the past four days with me. We cooked together at Petretti's and ate our creations without the shadows we usually have. This afternoon, he even included Max in the surprise he organized in the large industrial freezer my uncle often states was used for more than the storing of meat in his heydays.

Although it isn't quite the winter wonderland he surprised me with on my birthday, the snow this time around feels real. He borrowed an ice shaver from the man who supplies the ice for the Petretti's establishments this side of the coast. When placed in front of the vents that keep the freezer at a perfect temperature, it makes it truly seem as if I walked into a snowstorm.

"Maddox..." There are so many more words in my head, but not a single one of them could be expressed without my voice cracking, so I had no choice but to keep my reply short. Furthermore, we've faced many ups and downs the past two weeks, so I refuse to ignore even the minutest moment of peace.

Maddox's smile warms my snap-frozen nose when I throw my

head back, stretch out my arms, then twirl in a circle. If I had ice skates on, the fanning of my skirt would replicate an Olympic skater in the middle of a robust routine. Even Max gets in on the act. He drags his gooey jowls along the icy floor before rolling over to make doggy angels in the splinters of ice.

It's a truly blissful moment that's cruelly torn away when reality smacks into me hard and fast. Maddox promised my next snowstorm would be real, so why is he granting wishes now like he won't be around to grant them in the future?

I drop my arms to my sides before spinning around to face Maddox. "What's going on?"

When he steps toward me, panicked about the flood of moisture bombarding my eyes, I swat him away. I can't think straight when he's close, and if the expression on his face is anything to go by, my smarts need to be fully functioning. He looks like he's about to break my heart at the same time as granting me my greatest wish.

If that's true, something is definitely amiss. My greatest wish is him. I thought he knew that.

After swishing my tongue around my mouth, hopeful some spit will deliver my next comment without angst, I say, "You said my next snowstorm would be real."

As a familiar flare darts through his eyes, Maddox replies, "I did, but I also said I'd get you as far away from this life as possible. I haven't kept that promise yet either."

This isn't the first time he's voiced annoyance about his personal pledge this week. It comes up in almost all our conversations.

"You will keep your promise, Maddox. You just need to be patient. Everything happens with time."

A tear almost falls down my face when he nods in agreement. I'm not on the verge of crying because I've helped him see sense through the madness. I'm devastated by what he says next, "Or when you devise a better plan." He steps closer to me with pleading, please-understand-me eyes. "I was offered one earlier this week. It will give us a future. You'll just need to do it without me for the first couple of years."

"What?" I query, certain I heard him wrong. Our plan was always for us to get out together, but he's talking as if his itinerary only has one ticket.

The meal we shared creeps up my throat when Maddox kicks his gym bag stuffed under the bottom shelf of the freezer. It's fatter than it was every time Rocco delivered it. Almost double in width. There must be at least two hundred thousand dollars in there.

The cracking of my heart is heard in my words. "There better be a minimum of eight tickets in there, Maddox. Six for your family, and another two for us."

The optimism in my reply is way too high for my liking. My uncle would never grant me clemency, and I share his blood, so there's no way Maddox would have gotten through to him. If he has, I'm lost as to what he offered. We're already jumping on demand. We can't give him more than we already have.

Well, so I thought.

"There's only one ticket in my bag, Demi. It has your name on it."

I shove him back two places, too angered to care my push shatters his heart as much as it does mine. "We're in this together. If you go, I go. If you die, I die. That's what we agreed upon. That's what *you* promised." My voice cracks when the reasoning behind his roller-coaster moods the past couple of days pummels into me. He wasn't tired. He was disappointed in himself. That's what morally ethical men feel when they renege on a promise.

"You went against me." When Maddox shakes his head, I shout," Yes, you did! If you sided with him, you went against me." I thrust my hand at the freezer door like my uncle is standing behind it.

Maddox uses my flung-out arm to his advantage. He curls his hand around my wrist before tugging me closer to him, where he tries to fool me like I'm not accustomed to the trickery of this horrible existence. "My deal is with Ezra. He made it impossible to give up. This will let me keep my promise, Demi. It'll keep you safe."

"Ezra *works* for my uncle! He's paid to do as he is told."

Striving to wake myself up, I yank on my hair. This can't be real. I must be having a nightmare. Nothing happening makes any sense.

Maddox only said two weeks ago that us sticking together would see us through this, so what happened to change his mind so quickly?

I'm pushed to the brink of a panic attack when Maddox says, "If I agree to a seven-year sentence with the eligibility for parole in three, your debt with your uncle and Dimitri will be wiped clean. You'll be free."

I can see why my uncle's offer has sparked an interest out of him —I would have accepted a much harsher penalty for the same result —but this isn't how it's meant to go down. I was born into this life. Maddox was forced into it, so if anyone should be freed first, it should be him.

"Tell him no."

Maddox stares at me like I am insane. "No. I can't."

"Why?" Even though I am asking a question, I don't give him the chance to answer. "We will renegotiate, come up with a better deal." When I fail to conjure up a better plan on the fly, my breaths turn ragged. The wheeze of my lungs won't stop me from announcing the obvious, though. "Inmates aren't free, Maddox, so you need to remove that suggestion from the table."

When my reply is chopped up by ragged, wheezy breaths, Maddox tries to subdue my panic by rubbing his thumbs over the veins protruding in my wrists.

I slap his hands away. I'm so mad at him, so very devastated.

"Demi—"

"No!" cracks out of my mouth like a whip. "This isn't fair. We had an agreement."

"An agreement I can't keep if I want to be the man you deserve. He's killing me, Demi. What he's getting me to do day in and day out is slowly killing me." The absolute honesty in his voice breaks my heart. "There are women, and kids... and fucking babies."

The pain in his eyes exposes I only know a fraction of the stuff he's endured the past fourteen days. My uncle has dragged him to the depths of hell, but instead of striving to help him claw his way out of the carnage, I'm selfishly arguing for him to stay there.

That makes me a terrible person, and it changes my fight in an instant.

When I band my arms around Maddox's neck to hug him tight, he pulls me in close before tucking his head into my neck. "I don't want to become him, Demi," he whispers against my sweat-slicked skin, his lips quivering. "He's changing who I am. He's killing my soul."

"It's okay. You don't have to become him. I understand." My heart is in tatters, but I still know this is the right thing to do. "Three years is nothing. We kept our crushes hidden *way* longer than that, so three years will fly by." My reply would be more convincing if it were said without a heap of tears and snot. I usually have a better hold on my emotions, but today, my heart truly feels like it's being ripped out of my chest.

I lied last night when I said drowning was the cruelest way to die.

This hurts ten times more.

4

MADDOX

One month later...

*T*he packed-to-the-rafters courtroom chamber hisses in disbelief when the judge says, "I sentence Maddox Richard Walsh to life behind bars without eligibility for parole."

When he smacks his gavel onto the podium, the lawyer Ezra assigned to my case leaps to his feet. He's as far out of the Petretti family business as you can get, so you can picture how green around the gills he got when I used attorney-client confidentiality to explain why I was confessing to a murder I didn't do.

I've seen some sick fucking shit in my life. I thought my sister being mauled by a dog, Col forcing his niece's lips to land on his, and the time he dragged the blade of his knife up Demi's chest would remain at the top of my sick list, but many things my first two weeks under Col's command gave my top contenders a run for their money.

Death was everywhere. Men, women, and children. I smelled it on my skin no matter how hard I scrubbed it, and I saw it everywhere I looked. It was getting so bad, even eating was more a chore than a pleasure. I'm not ashamed to admit I was struggling, but I am embarrassed to say Demi was subjected to my dithering moods.

The life we were living was *not* the life I had predicted for us. I was supposed to pull Demi out of the murkiness of her family business, but all I did was submerge her in it more. We were living under Col's rule, jumping on fucking cue. It wasn't living, but since it was the only way I could guarantee Demi's safety, I did everything her uncle asked.

When Ezra first came to me with his proposal, I told him no. I hated leaving Demi alone for sixteen hours a day, so there was no way I couldn't see her for years on end.

Then Col made me bury a bucket full of unborn babies.

I fucking lost it. I wanted to kill Col. I probably would have if it weren't for Ezra. He didn't just remind me that I'd have to get through the increase in security Col ordered to protect him when he moved Demi and me into his home, but he also noted that even if I succeeded in killing Col, my debt would be transferred to Demi—a debt she'd never be able to repay without going into the trade like her mother.

That dampened my desire to go on a murderous rampage, then Ezra completely smothered it.

"Col is so desperate for this matter to go away, you'll be surprised what he's willing to negotiate for it," he said that fateful day a little over four weeks ago while nudging his head to Megan Shroud, the woman we had been tailing the previous two days. "It's something worth considering. This could be your last chance to get his claws out of Demi."

I asked for a couple of days to contemplate. In other words, I wanted to run his suggestion by Demi. The decision was taken out of my hands the following day. I either accepted Ezra's proposal or force Col to be more 'inventive' on the ways Demi could repay the debt he wrongly believed she owed him.

Recalling the expression on Demi's face when she offered herself to Col to save me was one of the many reasons I agreed to his ruse. It was also why I lied to Demi when I made out serving a seven-year sentence was the perfect solution for our predicament. She was willing to face her biggest fear head-on to save me, so I knew without a doubt she'd accept anything Col threw at her to pluck me from the fire for the second time.

Don't misunderstand what I'm saying. A bit of my soul died every day I was under Col's command, but Demi repaired the damage every night. I could have survived *if* it were my choice.

Regretfully, it wasn't, and I couldn't even ask Dimitri to intervene this time around. His spontaneous trip to Italy wasn't for a business venture. Ezra let slip that he's there because when I investigated people I shouldn't have been investigating, they assumed I was working on Dimitri's behalf. That's why they flew his daughter out of the country the very night Justine was mauled. The men holding his daughter captive assumed he'd be too occupied with Justine to pay their movements any attention.

Little did they know.

Although I'm not responsible for his daughter's captivity, I don't think Dimitri would be eager to help me again if he discovers I'm the reason his daughter was taken out of the country. He may have even upped the ante, so instead of admitting to my mistake, I accepted Ezra's offer.

After a prolonged meeting between Col, Ezra, and myself, it was agreed that Megan's 'death' would be classified as manslaughter under the guise of self-defense. With a guilty plea, I'd be given a seven-year sentence that is generally reduced to three for good behavior.

Some would say I'm foolish for believing Col will abide by the terms stipulated during negotiations, but not only did Ezra and I ensure there were a handful of witnesses for the signing of our negotiation, but Dimitri's permission was also sought.

Everyone thought Ezra's plan was solid. I'll still be in debt to Col until my sentence is over, but Demi's portion was immediately wiped out. The instant I was arrested for Megan's 'murder,' Demi became a free woman. Her uncle no longer has a hold over her, and once I finish my term, my family will be free as well.

I begged for Demi to move in with Sloane, who's studying abroad in the United Kingdom, or at the very least, visit her for a couple of months to make sure Col adhered to the terms stated in our agreement, but Demi is as stubborn as she is beautiful. She won't leave my side for anything.

I wonder if her thoughts will change now that I've been sentenced to life behind bars?

"Your honor," my lawyer squawks, pulling me back from my negative thoughts. "My client was an obliging witness. He assisted the DA with their inquiries on the agreement he would be given a plea bargain. This hearing is merely to sentence my client to the *agreed* term negotiated upon his arrest."

Judge Polst glares at Owen Mitchem, third-year attorney, over the bifocal glasses balancing on his slim nose. "The presiding judge has the discretion on whether he accepts or rejects a plea agreement based on the seriousness of the charges presented before him." He shifts his narrowed eyes to me. "A seven-year sentence with eligibility for parole in three is *not* an acceptable sentence for a murderer."

"Your honor—"

The judge continues speaking as if my lawyer never interrupted him. "You admitted guilt for your crime. You confessed to the death of a young *woman* in your community." It dawns on me that we were assigned one of the vigilante judges Ezra warned us about when the judge chokes on the word 'woman.' "But you've not shown an ounce of remorse."

"Because there's nothing for him to be remorseful about," Demi shouts against the advice of my lawyer. Owen banned everyone but Demi from my court hearing today because he didn't want my argumentative family making the judge grumpy. With my arrest occurring shortly after Justine's release from the hospital, things are super tense for my family. Owen wanted to avoid more drama.

It appears as if his worries were warranted but came hours too late. Judge Polst sentenced me the instant he read the transcript I memorized long before my arrest. Col wanted it to be authentic, so he made me retell the scene he had created to him over and over again for days on end—how Megan struck me during a heated argument, that I hadn't meant to shove her as hard as I did, and that I demolished the bathroom in the cabin with my fists because I felt guilty about the mortal head injury Megan sustained from my push.

My admission of guilt would have been more authentic if I hadn't supposedly buried her body during a psychosis brought on by extreme mental exhaustion. I'm certain that was the tipping point for the judge. It was for me. Even Ezra struggled agreeing with that part of Col's terms, but we didn't have any other choice. There was no way in hell I was going to kill a random woman to authenticate Col's ruse that Megan was dead, so I had to pretend I buried her in the woods.

To this date, forensic scientists are still looking for evidence of a burial site near the cabin. After spending two weeks under Col's watch, I can assure you they will eventually find a body. It won't be Megan's, though. She's hundreds of miles from Hopeton. I dropped her off at her new residence myself.

The judge bangs down his gavel three times, silencing the chamber before he locks his eyes with Demi. The look he gives her pisses me off as do the words he speaks. "If you believe that, young lady, it's fortunate you have at least another sixty years to learn better."

He throws down his gavel another two times for good measure before he exits the chambers. I stand at the bailiff's request, but I am incapable of speaking. This was *not* how things were meant to go down. We had all our T's crossed and our I's dotted. Col was upholding his side of our agreement. Demi has been out of his clutch for a little over a month. She's finally free.

I just won't be a part of her newfound freedom.

Fuck it!

"We will appeal," Demi whispers into my ear after slinging her arms around my neck. "A second judge will overturn the verdict. I swear. Ezra is working it out now." Her words come out with a quiver when the bailiff moves to stand beside me. I'm being immediately taken away. I don't even get the chance to kiss my girl for the final time. "I'll be okay," Demi promises when I'm pulled away from her. "You've given me the strength to fight. We will get through this."

She continues shouting encouraging words until I'm pulled into a room at the back of the chambers by the bailiff. I'm re-shackled like a prisoner, then told to sit on a hard plastic chair to await transport.

It takes around ten minutes for my impatience to get the better of me. "Do you know where they're taking me?" There's a medium-security prison about fifty miles out of Hopeton, so I'm assuming that's where I'll end up.

The sole guard left to watch a murderer shakes his head. "With your sentence, it will most likely be Wallens Ridge."

"Wallens Ridge?" I parrot, shocked. Even a novice criminal like me has heard of Wallens Ridge State Penitentiary. It has one of the highest gang-related incarceration rates in the country.

My eyes shift from the murmuring guard to Owen when he joins us in the holding room. "Please tell me I haven't been sentenced to Wallens Ridge?" When his forlorn expression answers my question on his behalf, I curse. "That's hundreds of miles from Hopeton. I'll never be able to see Demi or my family. Justine hasn't left the house in a month. There's no way she'll travel three hundred miles to visit me."

Col's punishment switched Justine from a bubbly, outgoing sophomore to a depressed, suicidal woman. The only person she allows to see her scars is our mother, and that's only because she has to change her dressings or face more surgeries due to infections. Not even Dad can get through to her, and he was once the apple of her eye. I saved her from a monster, but she is still in the deep depths of hell.

My theory is even more convincing when Owen says, "The judge refuses to accept the plea of self-defense. Wallens Ridge is the only prison within a four-hundred-mile radius capable of housing life inmates."

"Then take it to trial," I argue like I should have four weeks ago. "A jury may issue a lesser sentence, one that will get me closer to Hopeton."

Dark hair falls into Owen's eyes when he shakes his head. "We can't take this to trial. You admitted guilt. You pled guilty. Our only option is to submit an appeal to have the judge's sentence overturned. We can't overturn your admission of guilt."

"Fuck!" The guard requests that I calm down when I add to my annoyance by throwing my fist into the wall next to my chair. As my knuckles throb, I suck in some big breaths before locking my eyes with Owen. "This wasn't our agreement." He knows I only admitted guilt with the agreement I'd most likely serve three years. I told him *everything* during our first meeting, and I mean everything.

"I know, Maddox, but as much as this kills me to admit, this isn't Col's doing." I can see the truth in his eyes, feel it radiating out of him, and I also agree with it, but it doesn't make it any easier to swallow. "Judge Polst is known for harsher sentences when the victim is a woman. He is an advocator of domestic violence. His life's work has been to lower the number of violent crimes against women. Lowering statistics in this region proves his theories are working. We were just unlucky when he was assigned your case."

I want to hate the judge, but Owen makes it a little hard. "What are the chances of an appeal?" My stomach gurgles when he pulls a face I don't want to see after being sentenced to life behind bars. "That bad?"

"Judge Polst is highly respected by his peers."

"And murderers aren't. I get it." I drag my fingers through my hair that's overdue for a trim while breathing out of my nose. I have to trust that Karma will eventually come into play, but I'd be a lying prick if I said I weren't struggling to believe she even exists anymore.

I guess I brought this on myself. I expected the world to be fair because I was fair to it. That's as foolish as expecting Col not to fire at me because I didn't fire at him first. There is good and bad in all of us, but it's up to the individual as to which side they harness.

Col *always* strives for the latter.

I used to crave the former.

I don't know which way the axis will tilt if Judge Polst's sentence isn't overturned. My mom often quotes that good always wins over evil, but believing you're a good person and actually being a good person are two entirely different things.

Months ago, if you had asked me if a murderer could be redeemed, I would have said no, so why should the verdict change because the accused is me?

The simple answer is love.

I'd do anything for Demi.

For her love, I'd do even more.

5

DEMI

I'm numb. I can't feel my heart, my feet, or my hands. Every part of me is shut down, so how the hell am I moving my lips? Why are they expressing the words I swore I'd never speak to the very people I swore never to hurt? I told them Maddox would come home, and the lesser verdict of manslaughter would give him a few days to pack his belongings and say his goodbyes before he was shipped off to a minimum-security prison with lenient visitation hours.

Instead, I'm standing across from the Walsh brethren alone, explaining that the son they know would never hurt another soul has been sentenced to life behind bars for murder.

"We're going to appeal," I tell Mrs. Walsh when her shuddering legs see her collapsing onto the couch in the middle of her living room with a heartbreaking sob. "Owen is filing the paperwork as we speak."

When Mr. Walsh bobs down to comfort his wife, I tug on Max's leash, silently advising him that Mr. Walsh would never hurt his wife. He just wants to cocoon her from the world of hurt that pummeled into me only hours ago, to whisper reassurances none of us are sure of anymore. He wants to keep her safe the same way Maddox did me when he accepted my uncle's terms.

The more I think about Maddox's agreement with my uncle, the more I wonder how it would ever benefit Maddox. Even if he were only sentenced to the agreed seven-year term at a minimum-security prison, their agreement stated he was to remain under my uncle's reign until the end of his sentence. Although he wouldn't be subjected to the inhumane things my uncle made him do the first two weeks under his supervision, I don't see my uncle simply walking away. He has wanted the Walshs on his payroll for years. He wouldn't give it up for anything.

I wish I had time to think it through so it could have benefited Maddox. He was arrested not even an hour after our confrontation in the freezer at Petretti's, denied bail due to the admission of guilt, and the days between his arrest and his hearing were a big hazy mess. Not solely for Maddox and me, but his entire family. Even now, during the most vital family meeting the Walshs have ever had, Justine is hearing the news from her post at the top of the stairs since she refuses to leave her room.

This family has so much on their plate, I'm once again on the verge of doing something stupid. If it weren't for Ezra asking for the chance to make things right, I might have driven straight to my uncle's residence instead of the Walshs. That's how gutted I am that Maddox was dragged out of the chambers before I could even kiss him goodbye.

I swipe at the invisible tear I swear is rolling down my cheek when Caidyn asks, "How long will the appeal take?"

"Thirty days," I answer matter-of-factly. That was the first thing I asked Owen when he returned from arranging Maddox's transfer to Wallens Ridge.

"Thirty days?" This question isn't from Caidyn. It's from Landon. And he doesn't use the same nurturing tone Caidyn used. His words blast from his throat as if I am deaf.

When I dip my chin, answering him without words, he raises his voice several more decibels. "He'll never last thirty days at Wallens

Ridge." He rips his fingers through his hair, leaving it standing on its ends. "Especially when they find out who he's associated with." He doesn't need to say my name. The disdain in his voice indicates who he means. "He didn't get handed a life sentence. He just handed over his life!"

"That's enough!" Caidyn interrupts before hitting Landon with a stern finger point. "Talking out of your ass won't change anything." Although he swivels his torso so he's facing Landon, I still hear what he mouths. "*Demi isn't the enemy.*"

"How can you say that?" Landon fires back, his voice still loud. "She may not have increased the length of his sentence, but she *is* the reason he pled guilty." When Saint tries to intervene, Landon pushes him off him. His shove pricks Max's ear as much as it does Justine's. She isn't close to descending the stairwell, but I can see her feet. "No, I'm sick of holding my fucking tongue. Maddox isn't a murderer. We all know that, and she knows it, so why the fuck is he pretending as if he is?" I feel my heart crack a little when he thrusts his index finger my way. "Because to save *her,* he had to sacrifice himself."

I stop Caidyn from ending Landon's rant with more than words by grabbing ahold of his wrist. What Landon is saying cuts through me like a knife, but it is also true, so I am deserving of his wrath.

My voiceless request for Caidyn to hold back frees Landon to continue with his belligerent tirade. "You're all a bunch of soft cocks. What happened to our family morals and putting everyone's well-being before our own? Blood before water? Family before work. Bros before hoes?"

His last comment snaps Caidyn's last nerve. He's always been more a lover than a fighter, so not even his brother who loves to brawl is anticipating for him to knock Landon's words back into his mouth with his fist.

With Saint's shock as high as mine, Landon retaliates to Caidyn's hit without interference. He pole drives him into the coffee table. The sickening thud of their collision is soon overtaken by the grunts of two men willing to fight to the death.

Even with Mr. Walsh grabbing Caidyn's shoulders and Saint

banding his arms around Landon's torso, Caidyn and Landon go punch for punch for the next several minutes. Max wants in on the action as well. His vicious, fang-bearing growl exposes how brave Justine truly is. It should have her cowering away. Instead, she stands on the landing of the stairwell, screaming for her family to stop fighting.

"Do you really think more violence will fix anything?" She doesn't fight her tears as I do. She sets them free, knowing they'll be more effective than her words. "You know Maddox picked me over himself, Caidyn. You were with him when he made his decision." My stomach gurgles at the same time Mrs. Walsh's shocked eyes snap to Caidyn. "And you..." Justine stares at Landon like she's both hurt for him and angry at him. "You should know better. Things could have been starkly different for you if you had spoken out for yourself as you're endeavoring to do for Maddox."

I'm lost as to what she is referencing, but Landon seems to understand. He un-balls his hands in an instant before he lowers his chin to rest on his chest.

With her family subdued, Justine's focus shifts to the outcast. The recluse. The woman who would have given anything to be raised in a household like hers. She locks her eyes with me. "This isn't your fault. It's mine." Her voice cracks during her last two words. "He tried to warn me." Tears roll down her cheeks unchecked when she adds, "They all did. I didn't listen, and now my brother is suffering for my stupidity."

I try to tell her no. I try to explain that nobody can predict how sadistic my uncle's rulings will be, but before I can voice either of those things, she spins on her heels and races back up the stairwell. The swish of her hair silences the room. Her attack was a little over six weeks ago, yet her wounds aren't close to being healed. They are a brutal reminder of exactly how cruel this world can be, and they have me sprinting for the closest exit before my brain clues on to the fact I have nowhere to run.

When they found out Maddox had been arrested, the first thing his family did was sell the lakeside cabin so they could fund his legal expenses. I almost offered them the two hundred thousand dollars Maddox had saved, but since I would have had to explain how he got that much money, I decided not to. I didn't want them treating him differently while he was facing the biggest battle of his life. Was it stupid of me to do? Probably. But no one could accuse me of being smart lately.

I run and run and run until Max isn't the only one whimpering in pain. I'm wheezing, out of breath, and have enough sweat running down my face I can cry without shame.

It's a heart-tugging couple of minutes that becomes even more defeating when a voice on my right says, "Maybe it's time to call it." Caidyn steps out of the shadows. The sweat marks on his shirt expose his sprint was as strenuous as mine, he just remained a few paces back to give me some much-needed privacy. "Knowing you're hurting will hurt Maddox more than any sentence. His happiness is through you, Demi. If you're not happy, he's fucking miserable."

It's the worst time for me to smile, but it can't be helped. Maddox has always said he and Caidyn have opposing personalities. I'm not close to reaching the same conclusion. If you exclude the alternative outside packaging, they're one and the same.

After lifting my shirt to clear the sweat and tears from my face, I say, "I can't give up on him, Caidyn. I don't know how to be happy without him. I existed before him, but I didn't live. He brought me to life." I could emphasize my reply, but I don't need to. Caidyn understands because he too is facing his own rebirthing.

He holds his hands in the air to ensure Max he means me no harm before he steps closer to me. "Then what's your plan? And where do I enter into it?"

My uncle has always said love and affection fixes nothing.

He's a liar.

The thank-you hug I give Caidyn mends my heart. It's still in tiny little pieces, but it's together, in one place, instead of being scattered in all directions.

We stay huddled in the middle of the street until Max gets too close to Caidyn's backside for him to feel comfortable. I'd laugh at his cowardice if Justine's wounds weren't burned into my retinas.

While inching back, I pat Max on the head. It took a lot for him to realize I needed Caidyn's support. I can only hope it won't take Maddox quite as long to realize he needs mine.

"Is it true? Did Maddox pick between Justine and himself?"

Caidyn licks his lips before halfheartedly shrugging. "It wasn't exactly like that. It was more a suggestion than an order."

My heart aches for Maddox. I fought my demons head-on just vying to keep him safe. He had more than my life on his shoulders.

No wonder he's so exhausted.

"If I tell you something, will you promise it will remain between us?"

Caidyn's delay in answering isn't surprising. You couldn't hear how much angst was in my tone when I asked my question. He knows what I want to share is big, and he needed time to prepare his stomach for the impact it would cause.

When he nods, I gather Max's leash into my hand before slowly pacing back toward his family home. "It started approximately eighteen months before Saint pulled his signature move on Sloane..."

Just like on my first 'date' with Maddox, Caidyn and I take the long route home. It gives me plenty of time to update Caidyn on everything that has happened on the whirlwind yet terrifyingly scary commencement of my relationship with his baby brother. I don't leave a single thing out. I tell him everything. My uncle's threats to sexually assault me. The outcome of Maddox's death match. Why we were living at my uncle's residence even with us having perfectly acceptable accommodations elsewhere. I even admit the shame I felt upon discovering the mortality rate of the men I recruited to my uncle's fight circuit.

"I should have stuck to my guns, but I just couldn't. Maddox was like a bull in a china shop."

Caidyn tosses back his head and laughs. In the tenseness of the situation, it's a nice thing to hear. "It isn't the first time he's been accused of that. Won't be the last." He curls his arm around my shoulders before pulling me into his side. "He wanted you to be his girl for over a decade. I understand his eagerness." After dropping his arm from my side, he climbs the front stairs of his family's home before sitting on the top step. "How much does he owe?" When my brows join, he adds, "Your uncle. If Maddox agreed to go away to pay back a debt, there has to be a monetary amount attached to it."

"There would be, but I don't know how much it is." I sound like an idiot. Rightfully, so. I feel like one as well.

"Could you find out?" Caidyn asks through quirked lips.

I nod. "But it will be *way* outside our means. My uncle doesn't live in the real world. We couldn't come up with the capital needed in three lifetimes, much less one."

"Are you sure?" After giving me a moment to hear the confidence in his tone, Caidyn stretches his arms out in front of himself. He isn't suggesting for him to take Maddox's place. He's directing my focus to the mammoth residence behind him. To his family home.

"I-I couldn't ask them to do that. It's too much." I hate the stutter of my words. I'm not a complete imbecile. I just either cry or stutter. I went for the one that will be easier to hide once it's over.

"You don't have to ask them, Demi," Caidyn interjects. "I will."

His promise lightens the heaviness in my chest, but only by a smidge. "But they'll want to know what it's for, which means you'll have to break the promise you just made." I can't tell if my voice is crossed with anger or pleading. It could be both. "I don't care how people look at me, Caidyn, but I don't want Maddox subjected to the hatred I've dealt with my entire life."

"I won't break my word, Demi. What you told me will remain *solely* with me, but there are ways we could get the funds without telling them what it's for. I simply need to know if it is close to what we need."

I swallow to mollify my suddenly dry throat before saying, "I'll find out." When Caidyn leaps to his feet, eager to get started, I push him back onto his backside. "Alone. If your family is going to lose everything, I'd rather it be only materialistic things."

"Demi..." When his ruthless call of my name doesn't slow me

down, Caidyn tries another tactic. "Maddox will kill me if he finds out I let you visit your uncle by yourself."

I whip around to face him, smiling when he spots the key to his Jeep I pinched from his pocket when I shoved him back onto his backside. "Considering he'd need to be a free man to do that, I'm willing to take the risk."

When I turn back around, I smack headfirst into a steaming angry blonde with curls that would stretch for miles if they were ever ironed out. "Sloane."

Even though her taut shoulders and tapping foot reveals she over-heard the last part of my conversation with Caidyn, she returns my greeting when I throw my arms around her shoulders and hug her tight.

I'm not ashamed to admit it takes several long seconds for me to let her go, and even then, it isn't done without a protruding lower lip. "What are you doing here? I thought you had exams."

She arches a perfectly manicured brow. She looks so much more put together than she was months ago. Almost back to her full self. "I said I'd be here for you when the verdict was read."

"I thought you meant emotionally, not literally." I should have known better. Sloane never does things in halves. "Are you staying long?"

My silent prayers are answered when she replies, "For a couple of weeks. My professor thinks this will be a great learning curve for me, so he gave me a prolonged extension on some assignments."

I crank my neck to Caidyn, curious to see if he too heard Sloane's tone increase when she mentioned her professor. From his arched brow and quirked lips, I'd say he did.

"Anyway, enough about me." Sloane bumps me with her hip before snatching Caidyn's Jeep key out of my hand. "There is a wonderful thing these days called a telephone. You can use it to communicate with anyone." Her eyes narrow into thin slits. "Espe-cially men you shouldn't be associating with." She climbs the stairs, plants her backside next to Caidyn as if she belongs on the Walsh family porch even more than me, then holds her hand out palm side up. "Cough it up. If a bullshitter needs bullshitting, who better to make the call than another bullshitter?"

I shake my head. "I don't want you in the middle of this mess."

I freeze in place, frozen by a glare I didn't think Sloane could pull off. "It's a little late for that, don't you think?"

As she tugs down on the sleeves of her long-sleeve shirt, hiding the welts only she and I can see, I dig my cell phone out of my pocket. Is it cowardly of me to do? Probably, but you can't see what I can see. Not only is Sloane clawing her way out of the deep and dirty trench my uncle forced her in, so is our friendship. I can't give that up for anything—not even me.

6

MADDOX

I pull away from Owen with a hiss when his fingers probe the egg-shaped bruise covering a majority of my right eye. His facial expression exposes his sympathies, but he's still pissed. "You should have called me."

"And said what?" I'm asking a question, but I don't wait for him to answer me. "Some inmates showed their dislike about a new woman killer mowing their turf."

"It wasn't about your rap sheet, and you know it."

"Yeah, I do," I fire back, still agitated about the shakeup the guards organized this morning. They wanted an increase in pay, and for some stupid reason, they thought I could help them get one. The fuckers have no clue I'm in the Petrettis' debt as much as they are. "But I held my own. I don't see a second round occurring any time soon."

"If you truly believe that, then you're dumber than I realized." Ignoring my glare, Owen takes a seat across from me. I'm shackled to the table like a prisoner, and he's dressed like he doesn't pocket three hundred dollars an hour. "Is *this* why you refused Demi's request to visit this month?" During the 'this' part of his comment, he nudges his head to my bruised face.

As I lift my chin, my mood slips from pissed to sullen. It's only day thirty-three of a lifetime sentence, yet I'm already dying. I miss the silky softness of Demi's skin when she traces the bump in my midsection after I wake up in a sweat. The smell of her hair when it's tickling my chest. And her smile—my fucking god—I miss that even more than the scrumptious meals she arrived with every morning without fail during my bail incarceration.

"How did she take it?"

"You cutting her off?" My growl nearly gobbles up what Owen has to say next, "Not well, but you were right, just because you tell her something doesn't mean she'll listen." My heart beats in an unnatural rhythm when he confesses, "It took Caidyn holding her down so she couldn't follow me out to my car."

I blink several times in a row to clear the image of Demi crying in Caidyn's arms from my head before asking, "Did she mention why she called her uncle last month?" I could have asked Demi myself during her first visit three weeks ago, but we were surrounded by too many gangbangers to bring up their idol. It would have gotten me jumped weeks earlier.

Owen's Adam's apple bobs up and down before he shakes his head. "I suspect Caidyn knows, but he's keeping it under his hat for now." After tossing his suitcase onto the stainless-steel table wedged between us, he asks, "How did you know Demi had contact with her uncle?" He must see something on my face I didn't mean to express. "It was mentioned during your assault?"

I lift my chin for the second time. "Some of the guards recognized her." I shake my head to hide my smile. "I guess they figured she was more valuable to Col because she's related to him." I huff. "Little do they know."

Needing to drown my sorrows with a hundred push-ups, I move things along. "What are you here for, Owen? I thought you said you wouldn't be back until you had news on my appeal."

"I do have news about your appeal." My pulse spikes. Its surge doesn't linger for long. "Regretfully, it isn't good news. The new judge removed the no probation clause from your sentence, but the sentence itself remains unchanged." When my cuss reaches his ears, he speaks faster. "We still have other avenues to pursue. We're at the very low level of the court system right now. We can continue to appeal all the way to the highest court."

"And if that fails?"

Owen doesn't want to answer my question, and neither the fuck do I.

After an intense stare down, I lean back into my chair to contemplate. "Col could have made out Megan was dead. He didn't *need* a man to go down for her murder. He *wanted* one too. But why? What benefit does he get from having a man behind bars?"

Unaware I'm more thinking out loud than seeking answers, Owen jumps into the conversation. "Wallens Ridge has the highest number—"

"Of gang-affiliated inmates compared to any other prison in the country. Yep, I'm aware of that, but that can't be the reason I'm here." My chuckle is ill-timed, but it can't be helped. "If you want someone to strengthen ties with the prison underworld, you better get someone who likes you enough to follow your plans, or it could backfire in your face."

Owen sounds nothing like a stiff in a suit when he says, "If he wants a partnership, he ain't getting one from you."

"My point exactly."

After mimicking my position, Owen asks, "Then what's his purpose?"

I shrug, truly unsure. "Other than getting me away from his niece, I have no fucking clue."

When my eyes lock with Owen's, he reads me like the same blood is pumping through his veins. "She's safe. They haven't been in the same room as each other in months." He crosses his right ankle in front of his left before leaning forward. "Ezra is confident Col won't back out of your agreement. Demi is safe."

His comment should offer me more reassurance than it does. Unfortunately, I learned the hard way that Col isn't a man who can be trusted, and furthermore, our agreement only extended to Demi. My family's heads are still on the chopping board.

I flash Owen a warning glare to get the fuck out of my head when he says, "You should tell them. From what I've seen, your family won't hold anything against you."

Shame isn't why I'm keeping quiet. Respect is. My parents worked hard to get what they have. Everything they have was from years of hard work and determination. I don't want to see them give it all away for me. Col won't merely run them out of town if I don't jump on command, he will destroy them.

I can't let that happen.

After tapping my knuckles onto the table, I say, "Let Demi know how much I owe. We've got some funds tucked away." Owen doesn't look like he's a struggling intern. I just prefer to pay my dues than be in someone's favor.

He smiles a shit-eating grin. "Don't worry, my counseling rates are half that of my lawyer's fees."

I laugh at the wit in his tone before farewelling him with a lift of my chin. Since I have to be unshackled before I can leave, Owen exits the room a good thirty seconds before a guard advises I have another visitor.

"Who?"

The guard checks the paperwork in his hand before shrugging. "They didn't say."

Since I'm incapable of attaching Demi's name to a curse word, I grumble about her inability to listen before retaking my seat. This room is generally used for inmates to speak with their lawyers, but the guard wouldn't have nudged his head to the table if he wanted us to host our visit in the visiting area.

I drop my eyes to the watch circling my unshackled wrist, noting there's still an hour left for standard visiting hours when the door Owen walked through ten minutes ago pops back open. My visitor isn't who I was anticipating, and his smug grin boils my blood. It isn't Col. It is the man one spot down from him. Agent Arrow Moses.

While smirking at the shocked expression I didn't shut down

quick enough, Agent Moses signals for the guards to leave the room. When one puts up a fuss, Agent Moses is quick to remind him of his position in the Bureau. "And let's not forget the *other* acquaintances who are desperate to pay your family a visit."

The uneased guard's eyes flick to mine for the quickest second before he bows his head in shame and scampers out of the room. I don't know whether to be pissed about Agent Moses's pull or shocked when the guard's evacuation of the room is quickly followed by the security camera in the corner of the space switching off. He didn't just cut the feed to the security personnel at Wallens Ridge. He ended Col's live stream as well.

Col has to watch his minions because even he knows they don't fear him enough not to occasionally stray. I can't help but wonder if that is what Agent Moses is doing today. In a way, I'm hopeful. He'll find himself on Col's hit list remarkedly quick if he goes against him.

I smile at the thought.

It's wiped off my face when Agent Moses places a tablet down in front of me. It's playing a live recording of the visitor section of Wallens Ridge. Demi is seated behind a thick pane of glass, nervously fiddling with the hem of her shirt. Visitors to this prison have a strict dress code to adhere to, and Demi has followed it to the T. As I requested last week, she also came with a chaperon. Caidyn is sitting in the visitor holding area. He's mere feet away from her.

My brows furrow when Agent Moses switches screens on the tablet. The live surveillance this time around is from one of the many cameras mounted around the yards and eating hall.

He points to a man I'd guess to be mid-thirties with dark hair and a wonky grin. "He has something I need. I want you to get it for me."

I scoff instead of replying to the superiority in his tone with my fists.

Let me tell you, it is a fucking hard feat.

As arrogant as ever, Agent Moses balances his hip on the edge of the table before folding his arms in front of his chest. "I'm sorry, did that sound like I was asking you to do it." He leans in close like I'm deaf. "I wasn't. You either do as I ask, now, or I call in a tip that your girl is carrying contraband. You know how randy these guards are. It wouldn't take much to convince them to conduct a strip search."

My hotheadedness gets the best of me long before words form in my mouth. I pin Agent Moses to the wall separating us from the guards milling outside before throwing a precisely aimed fist into his ribs. It winds him enough to warn him I'm not playing, but it doesn't come close to knocking him out. I need him alert to ensure he gets my message loud and clear. "Demi is off-limits. I made sure *no one* could touch her before I agreed to come to this shit hole."

Agent Moses's words are as breathy as mine. His are just compliments to a possible cracked rib instead of red-hot anger. "Your deal is for a world far away from here."

I '*ha!*' out loud. "My agreement is for *all* corners of Col's realm, including the corrupt fuckers beneath him."

"*Beneath him*?" My reply seems to agitate him more than a fist to the ribs. "You think I'm below the likes of Col One-Foot-In-The-Grave Petretti?" He pushes me back with more gusto than I realized his weaselly frame had. "I'm more powerful than him. Have more drive. I could crush him like a bug."

I feed the ego beaming out of him like the Hulk breaking out of a suit. "Then why haven't you?"

Unfortunately, he's a little more clued-in than I give him credit for. He glares at me while the mask he generally wears slips back over his face. "Greatness takes time, Ox. Only fools rush in."

I'm about to tell him he's the biggest fool I've met, but a voice projecting out from the tablet left discarded on the table stops me. It isn't one I recognize, but the stunned reply of the person he's approaching is highly familiar. Demi is as put-off by the guard's accusation she's brought illegal substances into the jail as me.

Air traps in my throat when I spin the tablet around to face me. A guard I've never seen before is blocking a doorway opposite to the one Caidyn is manning. He's in the process of putting on a pair of latex gloves, his gleam way too familiar. It is the same glint Col's eyes had when he told Ezra he has no sexual interest in his niece, and she's often misunderstood. He even went as far as saying she was mentally challenged from a traumatic childhood. It's the gleam of a man willing to say anything to get what he wants. Nothing is below his needs.

Once the guard has his gloves in place, he steps into the room where Demi is the sole occupant. "Stop him," I demand Agent Moses, my voice a roar. I'd end the guard's campaign myself, most likely without words, but the visitors' section of the prison is near the front entrance. I'm in the east wing. I'd never get to Demi in time. "Stop him before I smash your fucking teeth in!"

Agent Moses doesn't even flinch when I grab him by the throat. Idiots aren't known for their smarts. He has no idea I could kill him in under a minute.

Well, so I thought.

"If you kill me, Demi will face an in-depth search by *all* former and current employees of Wallens Ridge State Penitentiary." I feel the screams of his lungs as they frantically hunt for air. "But if you do as asked, I'll ensure she remains untouched not just in here but outside of these walls as well."

The black hatred clogging my veins makes it hard for me to see sense through the madness. This can't be real. I can't be fucked by both the law and the people they're meant to take down at the same time. This isn't how life works. Justice is meant to be the balance between good and evil, right and wrong. It isn't supposed to fuck me over more than I've already been fucked.

I scream my annoyance into Agent Moses's face before loosening my grip on his throat. I hate that I'm giving in to him, that I'm acknowledging that he can play me like a fucking fiddle, but I don't have any other choice. Demi is being led out of a room by a gloved-up guard, and Caidyn is none the wiser about the impending danger she is facing. If I don't do as asked, I won't be the only one being fucked by both sides of the law.

After taking a step back with flaring nostrils and balled hands, I ask, "What do you want?"

Even with his lungs heaving, Agent Moses smiles. "A card. It's sewn into the waistband of his trousers." Shock must cross my face as he's quick in his attempts to relieve it. "It's what's on the card that's most important."

Having neither the time nor the care to seek further information, I point to the tablet playing live footage of Demi and a smirking guard. "Call him off first." When Agent Moses attempts to assert his authority, I speak louder, "Get her out, *then* I'll do whatever the fuck you want." I step closer to him with a scowl that leaves no doubt what I say next isn't a worthless threat. "But I'm not moving from this spot until you call him off."

He isn't happy, but he does as told. All cowards do. "Wait for further command," he instructs down the sleeve of his jacket, advising me he is wired up.

After a beat, he spins the tablet around to face me. It shows Demi sitting back on the chair where she was originally. I know it isn't dubbed footage. The fear on her face isn't something that can be doctored, much less the fact Caidyn is now in the room with her.

"Happy?"

He doesn't wait for me to answer. He moseys over to the chair I knocked over when I pinned him to the wall, then tips it upside down. Confusion twists in my stomach when he removes two items taped to the bottom of the chair. One product is a stopwatch. The other is an instrument I hoped to never see much less use during my time at Wallens Ridge—it's a shank.

Agent Moses sets the stopwatch for three minutes before he curls the frayed rope necklace around my neck, then conceals it with my plain white t-shirt. When he attempts to shove the shank into my hand, I shake my head.

He chuckles out a breathy laugh. "Do you really think he'll hand over a card he's gone to great lengths to hide?" He calls me a fool under his breath before he forces the shank into my hand. When I remain standing still, unsure what the fuck is going on, he nudges his head to the door. "You better hurry. Three minutes is already pushing it. You don't have time to waste."

It dawns on me what he's talking about when he nudges his head to the stopwatch dangling next to my heart. The timer is counting down. I'm on the clock.

With my jaw tight, I push back my anger for a more appropriate time before racing out the door of the meet-up room.

"Let him go," instructs the warden when one of the guards tries to stop my exit. He peers at me with remorse when I sprint by him, exposing he's being railroaded by Agent Moses as I am, but he doesn't attempt to slow me down.

I pass the guard's hall, a high-traffic area for employees coming and going, then stomp across the wide walkway down one side of C-Block. The narrow walkway is reserved for the guards. With recreation time coming to an end, it takes me dragging my eyes down the slow-moving line heading back to the hull three times before I spot the man Agent Moses pointed out. He's in the line across from mine. Although he appears to have no gang-affiliated tattoos on his body, I'm still cautious. He isn't being bumped into like several other new 'fish.' He has a four-inch barrier around him. That's unheard of around here.

I wait for the guard on the steel platform above us to switch his focus to a rowdy group coming in from the yard before switching lines. Much to the dismay of an Asian man with a series of face tats, I slot in behind the unnamed man.

Certain there's more to this world than constant violence, I give communication a shot. "You don't know me, but you can guarantee I wouldn't ask this if it weren't important." The man remains facing the front, but I know he heard me. Not only do the hairs on his nape stand to attention, but he also nods. "I need the card sewn into the waistband of your pants." Although the volume of my voice is on par with earlier, he acts as if he didn't hear me. "It's urgent."

"It always is," he murmurs back, his tone less than impressed.

I can't see the stopwatch's countdown on my chest, but I feel every second that ticks over. I'm running out of time, leaving me no choice but to grab the stranger's pants like Demi did mine anytime her impatience got the better of her.

As expected, the dark-haired man retaliates. "Back off," he warns before pushing me into the Asian inmate standing behind us. "I'm not someone you should mess with."

"And neither the fuck am I," I reply with a roar, my voice loud enough to prick the ears of several inmates. I wasn't lying when I told Owen I held my own this morning. I won't be jumped again any time soon, but slathering on an extra layer of attitude won't go astray. "Give me what I want or—"

"You'll steal my lunch money?" With a mocking grin, the unnamed man messes my hair. I know what he's doing. He's treating me like a kid since I'm a good twelve years his junior. It pisses me off to no end, and when it's followed by the alarm on the stopwatch sounding, it leaves me no choice but to use my fists.

Before he knows what hit him, I fist his shirt in a white-knuckled hold, yank him forward, then slam my fist into his nose. I would have preferred for him to go down after one punch, but it doesn't seem as if luck is on my side today—*or this year.* He retaliates to my punch by cracking his fist into my jaw, then he pushes me to the ground.

It's a bad move on his behalf.

I'm faster on the ground. More deadly. It only takes another three hits to his face to subdue him enough I can shift my focus to his pants. The crowd circles in on us, and I sense the heat of the guards' guns they're aiming at my head, but since the stopwatch's timer is the loudest of them all, I use the shank Agent Moses shoved into my hand to rip through the cotton material of the man's pants.

I already hate the person I'm becoming, but the disgust grows more rampant when I find the card Agent Moses wants. It isn't a business card as such. More an identification card for an undercover cop called Charles Tate. The photograph on the government official ID looks oddly similar to the man lying bloody on the floor as does the name tattooed across his chest.

Fuck!

I just dug my grave, and my burial site is only feet from Demi.

It dawns on me that Agent Moses has been planning this for some time when my sprint away from the beaten officer isn't shadowed by the guards who watched the spectacle unfold. They give me a clear passage like the warden ordered their counterparts only minutes ago.

I charge for the front entrance of the prison instead of the room I left Agent Moses in. My priorities are undeniable even to a man with a stone heart, so I know the direction I need to take.

My intuition is proven accurate when my race through the guards' hall has me spotting Agent Moses standing outside the entrance of the visitor waiting room. He's by the door the guard blocked while placing on latex gloves.

After shoving Charles's card into his chest, I sprint into the visitors' waiting room, praying like fuck Demi is still in there. My screaming lungs suck down their first full breath in over three minutes when I spot her and Caidyn on the other side of a thick pane of glass. Their eyes rocket to mine when I bang my fist onto the glass. Caidyn looks shocked, and Demi is straight-up devastated.

"Get her out of here." When Caidyn remains still, his shock at my bloody appearance too perverse for a nonchalant response, I scream. "Now, Caidyn! And don't bring her back here. She can never come back here!"

Caidyn clutches Demi's wrist, yanks her away from me, then spins her around in one quick motion. As he drags her toward the exit, she fights him with everything she has, but since she knows he isn't doing this to hurt her, her whacks are nowhere near as fierce as they'd be if it were me pulling her away.

I wait until they are in the clear in the parking lot before spinning around to investigate the ruckus behind me. It sounds as if someone is in the throes of battle, and I discover that is the case when my eyes land on the tablet in Agent Moses's hands. Even if I wanted to plead innocence for the brutal beating of an undercover officer, I couldn't. Agent Moses has footage of every sickening moment.

Fuck it!

7

DEMI

The further Caidyn's Jeep rolls away from Wallens Ridge State Penitentiary, the more my composure slips. Maddox was bloody and bruised. He had a swollen eye, a cracked lip, and an imprint of a boot on his cheek, and that's just the damage I took in before Caidyn pulled me away. Who knows how many more bruises, nicks, and cuts his body is harboring?

If his father hadn't taught him how to defend himself, he could have been seriously injured, or worse, killed. The thought makes me the most unhinged I've ever been, but since Caidyn is always one step ahead of the game, there isn't a single thing I can do about it.

"You put the child lock on?" Caidyn doesn't answer me. It's okay. I don't need his words to know his response. The faintest tug of his lips answers my question on his behalf. "I'm not a child."

"Then stop acting like one." He couldn't have shocked me more if he slapped me across the face. "How could rolling out of a car at seventy miles an hour help anyone?"

"I wasn't going to roll out." He strays his eyes from the road to give me a stern, sure-you-weren't look. "I wasn't. I was going to make you *think* I was about to roll out, so you'd stop as I've requested *numerous* times the past twenty minutes, then I would have hitchhiked back to Wallens Ridge."

When he has the audacity to smile, I whack him in the arm. I'm not angry at him, but he is the only person I can take my anger out on, so he has to suck it up.

Within a couple of hits, I'm out of breath and ready to discuss the real reason for my fury. "He was hurting, Caidyn. I could see it in his eyes." His silence speaks volumes. He's only ever quiet when he can't deny the truth. "He won't survive five years in there, let alone a lifetime. We need to get him out."

"We're working on it," Caidyn eventually replies, his tone solemn. "We just need to be patient."

Patience. That's the Walshs' solution for everything these days. They think everything works out with time. In the world my uncle rules, time is often a disadvantage. You don't have long, and what you do have is usually filled with memories you'd give anything to forget.

If Maddox is forced to stay in that realm for months on end, he will come out of it a shadow of the man he used to be. I can't let that happen. I love him way too much to see him suffer like that. I'd rather lose who I am than lose him.

With a heartbreaking sigh, I slump low in my seat, where I spend the remainder of our five-hour trip to Ravenshoe contemplating ways to make the impossible occur ten times faster.

I won't lie. It's a somber and intensifying time that grows gloomier when our arrival at the Walsh family home has us stumbling onto both a moving van and Owen's flashy sportscar.

The unnatural rhythm of my heart is heard in my tone when I ask, "What's going on? They couldn't have found a buyer this fast."

Caidyn's plan to sell the Walsh family home was approved during a second emergency family meeting the night Maddox was sentenced. Mr. and Mrs. Walsh were fast to accept his suggestion because they believed the money was going toward Maddox's attorney's fees. They have no clue their hard-earned assets will be handed to my swindling uncle.

Caidyn shakes his head. "I don't know." He flicks his wide eyes to mine. "But how about we go find out?"

Not waiting for me to answer, he throws open the door of his Jeep, then climbs down. His ride isn't one of those old-fashioned Jeeps with a soft-top roof. It's the size of an SUV and has all the fancy gadgets people want when eyeing their dream car on the lot.

I follow Caidyn's weave through the men removing anything of value from the front living room. We find Mrs. Walsh supervising their hunt. Although it's clear she's devastated about losing antiques she has been collecting for over two decades, her expression is also happy.

"We found a buyer," she says to Caidyn when we arrive at her side, doubling the teary glint in her eyes. "A *cash* buyer!"

I take a step back in shock, flabbergasted. "How? The agent said this price bracket would take weeks to sell, if not months."

Mrs. Walsh shrugs. "I don't know. It all happened so quickly. The buyer didn't even organize an inspection." The stunned expression on her face switches to dismay. "His offer was a little lower than we were hoping, but it's plenty for a good defense."

When she hands me the paperwork for an immediate sale, my heart falls from my ribcage. Not only did the buyer slice thirty percent off the asking price, meaning I'm short a little over one point four million dollars to reach the amount my uncle believes he is owed, but the company name at the bottom of the check is also familiar. It belongs to my cousin, Dimitri.

"You can't accept this offer." When I push the paperwork back into Mrs. Walsh's hand, her lips twitch in preparation to speak, but I steal the chance. "This deal isn't any good. It's not enough, and you can't sell your home to *him*."

The way I spit out 'him' has Caidyn paying very careful attention to the document clutched in his mother's hand. After a beat, he backs me up. "I agree. This amount isn't enough." He doesn't mention that he hates the idea of Dimitri being anywhere near his family home, but the growl of his words expresses it on his behalf. "You have to decline it."

"I can't," his mother argues. "It's a cash sale. There's no cooling-off period." When she steps toward her son, petrified she's made a mistake, her hand shoots out to caress his. "I thought this was what you wanted. That you'd be happy."

"It is what I want. It's just…" The willpower in Caidyn's eyes falters the longer he stares into his mother's tear-filled gaze. "You did good, Mom. This will help," he says after accepting the check she's holding out for him and shoving it my way. "We will get it straight to Owen."

Her smile exposes she's still cautious. She just doesn't have the willpower to fight anymore. It has been a rough couple of months for her family. She's drained, and the struggle is seen all over her face. "He's in the den with your father."

After thanking his mother with a hug, Caidyn guides me to the den at the back of the property. I wait until we're out of earshot before expressing my worries out loud. "It will take years to get together the money Dimitri shaved off the asking price."

"I know." The shortness of Caidyn's reply doesn't make it any less impacting. "It's been one shitstorm after another lately."

He drifts his eyes to the stairwell for the quickest second before pushing open the double doors that lead to the den. Even with Caidyn and I coming and going at all hours of the day and night the past two weeks, I've not seen hide nor hair of Justine. If Mrs. Walsh hadn't suggested that I put Max in the backyard last week when he got a little vocal about a heated conversation Landon was having with his father, I would have forgotten she was here.

The dean at her college granted her special leave, but that expires at the end of the month. I truly don't know if she has plans to return to her studies. She won't talk to anyone, much less me.

A ghost of a smile cracks on my lips when our entrance into the den has Max squashing his jowls against the French glass doors lining the back of the large space. He wasn't impressed when I said he couldn't come with us today. He will never admit it, but he's been missing Maddox. They have a unique connection that's founded more on respect than friendship.

"Don't get yourself into a fuss. A big ol' ham bone calmed him down mighty fast once you left. He only left it when he detected your presence."

Happy for Mr. Walsh to believe the angst on my face is because I missed Max, I thank him with a smile before moving to the outdoor patio to greet Max with a scratch of his chin.

"Max!" I shout when he darts past me. Usually, he knocks me over before covering my face with slobbery kisses. This is the first time I've been dissed for someone else.

"Shit," I mutter when he charges through the den at a mile a minute. I assume he's racing for Justine's room as he has tried many times before but am proven wrong when he bolts between a bunch of movers unaware he'd rip off their arms if they so much as touched him. "Max, wait!"

I follow him down the front stairs, across the manicured lawn, and partway down the street before it dawns on me that he isn't running away from me. He's charging headfirst for what he believes is a threat to my safety. Two suit-clad men barely make it into their dark SUV in one piece. Max chomps at their heels, growling and barking like he's possessed.

While Max follows their car down the street, I twist my torso in the direction they were facing before Max barreled around the corner. Their position makes no sense. All the show is in the front part of the Walsh residence. The big windows and flimsy window coverings make them prime targets for peeping toms, so why the hell would two camp out at the far end of their property?

I find an answer to the questions I'm asking when Max's loud barks force a woman now petrified of dogs to the window of her room. Justine's room is in the back far corner of the property. Her brothers forced her to have that room because it was the furthest from the front. If they were ever ambushed, Justine's bedroom would be the last one searched.

When Justine spots me on the sidewalk, I wave at her. If she waves back, I miss it. I'm too busy collecting my heart off the floor from Caidyn's sudden arrival. "A duo from your uncle's crew?"

It could be stupid for me to do, but I shake my head. "Their suits were too fancy for my uncle. He'll work you to the bone, but he only ever pays a dime for your time."

Caidyn breathes heavily out of his nose. My uncle throwing his weight around was an easy scapegoat. Now he has to be more inventive. "It could be the Feds making their presence known. They weren't happy when Justine refused to testify against Col." The Feds weren't the only ones mad at Justine. Excluding Maddox, all of Justine's brothers were pissed at her decision. They don't understand she saved more than her life when she refused to testify. Theirs were promptly scratched off my uncle's hit list as well. "To be safe, I'll let Saint and Landon know we're being watched." Caidyn bands his arm around my shoulders before spinning me fully around to face the house. "Come on. Owen wants to talk to us."

I can't help but smile when he drops his arm a second later. He isn't worried about how Maddox would feel about us getting cozy. Max gave him his marching orders this time around.

Things are tense between Owen and Mr. Walsh when we re-enter the den. So much so, I place Max back outside. Their anger isn't focused on me, but I don't want to take any chances.

I return from the lawned courtyard in just enough time to hear Caidyn say, "We already agreed to a second appeal."

Maddox's first appeal was turned down today. That verdict was the reason I was so desperate to see him. I wanted to make sure he doesn't give up. We still have many options up our sleeves.

Owen licks his suddenly dry lips. "I told Maddox the same thing this morning."

"But..." Caidyn and I say at the same time, weirdly synced.

The more we hang out, the more we finish each other's sentences.

Don't misread what I am saying. I look at Caidyn like a brother. There is no sexual attraction whatsoever—on either side. We're friends. That's it.

"But..." Owen follows along nicely. "I don't see any judge granting an appeal now."

My eyes bounce between his, stunned by what could have changed his opinion so quickly. He was all for a second appeal when he left here this morning with the promise of twenty thousand dollars in cash to kickstart Maddox's appeal process.

It takes a few seconds, but the truth finally homes in on me like a heat-sensing missile. "Maddox's bruises?" I should say more. I just can't.

Owen shifts on his feet to face me before nodding. "He was jumped by half a dozen inmates on the way to first break this morning." Untrusting of my legs, I plonk into the closest chair. Owen waits for me to nurse my head into my hands before continuing, "Maddox... *held his own.*" He looked as funny expressing that as he did saying it. "He came away relatively uninjured."

"If you class a swollen-shut eye as 'relatively uninjured,' I hate to see what you classify as near fatal," Caidyn jumps in before I can, his voice edgy.

Unwilling to leave him out on the plate, swinging alone, I ask, "Why would a fight hinder Maddox's appeal? He was defending himself. He didn't start it."

I simmer down the bitchiness in my tone when Owen interrupts, "That time."

"Maddox was in a second fight?"

The air sucks from my lungs when Owen dips his chin. "I got a call from the warden on my way here. The man he assaulted this afternoon wishes to press charges. With a second assault-related conviction tying our hands, we can't go any further with the appeal process."

"That isn't necessarily true," Sloane interjects from her post in the corner of the room. She is sitting behind Mr. Walsh's desk, hidden by stacks upon stacks of law books. "The right of an appeal is when a judge hands down a criminal sentence that does not meet the legal standards for the conviction." She stuffs a pencil into the messy knot in the back of her head before standing to her feet. "Maddox's sentence was far too harsh. The judge wanted to make an example out of him."

"I agree," Owen fires back, somewhat taken aback by both Sloane's unexpected debate and her undeniable beauty. "But we only have so many courts to push his appeal through. If we exhaust them due to impatience, we will have no avenues left."

"The basis of a client's current proceedings should have no ill effect on an appeal."

Owen steps closer to Sloane. "That may be what the rule books say, but you and I both know morally—"

"Law is different. It isn't a morality in the sense of the word."

"It creates a basic enforceable standard of behavior necessary for the community in treating all parties equally," Owen interrupts. "I've read the textbooks..." He leaves his question open for Sloane to answer.

She follows along nicely. "Sloane."

"Sloane," Owen says her name without the husky edge Saint used when he first laid eyes on her on the porch of his family home two weeks ago. "But the law only narrows its focus of ethics and morality. It doesn't completely ignore it."

Sloane pops a brow high into her hairline. "So you'd rather wait it out than risk a judge not doing his job?"

"Yes!" Owen throws his hands in the air, somewhat frustrated. "That is the recommendation from *his* lawyer."

"A lawyer I'd fire if he were my counsel."

Owen's lips tuck at one side. "Then it's lucky you're not my client, isn't it?"

Sparks are flying between Owen and Sloane. I just have a feeling not all of them center around Maddox. And I'm not the only one noticing. Saint hasn't advised his stalker watch from the corner of the room, but I notice the more Sloane and Owen bicker back and forth, the tighter his jaw becomes.

"Enough," Saint interrupts when Owen and Sloane's argument switches from morals and ethics to personal attacks on right and wrong.

Sloane immediately swallows her words, uneased by the fury radiating from Saint.

Owen isn't as quick to back down. Maddox hired him because he doesn't understand the meaning of the words. "Reading case file studies is nothing compared to real-life experience—"

"I said enough!" No one can deny Saint's roar this time around. It rattles my heart out of my chest as well as it causes Sloane's knees to curve inward. "Maddox's sentencing and today's incident are two completely different occurrences—"

"Precisely my point."

Saint keeps talking as if Sloane never interrupted him. "So they should be treated separately." He shifts on his feet to face Owen. "Continue with the second appeals process." When Owen attempts to interrupt him, he talks faster, "*If* the second appeal fails, we will regather and reform. Until then..." He gestures his hand to the door, giving him his marching orders. His facial expression exposes if Owen can't understand his silent hint, he will happily throw him out.

After gathering his suit jacket from the chair next to Sloane's desk, Owen twists his torso to face Mr. Walsh. "I will take counsel with my client. If he agrees with the suggestions brought forth here today, I will lodge the necessary paperwork." Not speaking another word, he exits the den.

When my troubled eyes shift to Sloane, she wrongly believes she needs to defend her motives. "Some appeals take months to be processed." As her watering eyes drift between three very familiar pairs, she mumbles, "Forcing him to endure a longer wait than necessary won't help him." She shifts her eyes to Saint's. "It won't help *any* of us."

We lose the chance to reply to her highly accurate comment when she regathers her composure by breathing out sharply. Then, after clapping her hands together two times, she gets back to work on tackling the mountain load of textbooks on Mr. Walsh's desk.

I'd thank her for the time and effort she's putting into studying cases similar to Maddox's with a hug, but since it appears as if not even Saint's signature move could get through to her right now, I mentally hug her before making a solemn trek up the stairwell to pack my belongings. I don't have many possessions, but what I do have is highly valuable to me—sentimentally more than monetarily.

My pace slows when I noticed the door to Justine's room is partially cracked open. It hasn't been that way in weeks.

Against my better judgment, I take a left at the stairwell instead of a right. "Justine..." I tap on her door with my knuckles before carefully pushing it open. "Are you in here?"

My question is stupid for me to ask. She hasn't left her room in weeks. This move will hurt her as much as it will Maddox when he finds out—*if* he finds out. Caidyn hasn't told him about our plans yet. We had intended to do it today. You know how badly that turned out, so I won't mention the fact Maddox demanded Caidyn to keep me away from Wallens Ridge indefinitely. My heart may not make it through the carnage unscathed. It's already in tatters.

"Hey," I breathe out slowly when I spot Justine in the corner of the room. The drapes are drawn, and the light is off, so with the sun beginning to set, her room is plunged into an eerie gray darkness. "Do you need anything?" When my question is answered with nothing but a sniffle, I step a little closer to her. "I could help you pack."

"Don't." My heart breaks all over again when her hand shoots out to stop me from touching her things. The number of scars on her hands exposes that she used them to protect herself. They look like they were shredded to pieces. The surgeons who put them back together did wonderful work, but there's no way her scars will fade to nothing within the next ten years. She will have them for life. "I will pack... just not yet. I need time." When she chokes, I choke. "It's all happening so fast."

"I know. It wasn't meant to be this way." I stop before I say something I'll regret, settle the croakiness in my voice, then try again. "If you change your mind, you know where to find me."

I race for her door so fast I trip over my feet like a clumsy newborn foal. The guilt hammering into me is horrendous, and it's only just beginning. Justine is irreparably scarred, her parents were conned to sell their family home under false pretenses, and their youngest son is serving life behind bars. Things couldn't possibly get any worse... until they do.

8

MADDOX

One month later...

$\mathcal{M}$y fifty-seventh push-up halts mid-push when a snarky voice booms into my windowless room, "Are you ready to negotiate yet?"

When the padded door of my cell creaks open, I end my workout regime. The light beaming into the almost black space is too bright for me to ignore. I need to shelter my eyes with my arm. I am also desperate to take in the one photograph of Demi the guards let me keep when they moved my belongings from my assigned cell to the hole.

The 'hole' is the padded cell prisoners are forced to visit when they break protocol. There's no time in the yard, no meal privileges, and absolutely no light outside of the two ten-minute allotments I'm granted to shovel down the slop delivered on a stainless-steel tray twice a day. I'm fucking starving, my vitamin levels are in the shitter, and I'm beginning to wonder how many times Demi and my family have been turned away from visiting me the past month. I told

Caidyn to keep Demi away. That doesn't mean she listened, though. My girl is as stubborn as she is beautiful.

After pulling down Demi's photograph from its hidey-hole, I run my thumb down her glossy black hair before shifting my focus to the person approaching me. Even with my hearing hardly having any use the past month, I recognize the voice of the man slotting his backside onto a chair behind a thick sheet of Perspex. The thought he needs a barrier between us makes me smile. If he were a real man, he would have confronted me without any gimmicks.

Agent Moses plants his feet at the width of his shoulders before leaning forward, so his elbows rest on his knees. "How long have you been down here?" He doesn't wait for me to answer him. "Twenty-eight days? Surely, you're missing the sun by now?" I keep my expression neutral, but he must read the hell-fucking-no expression on my face. "No? Then what about food you don't need a straw for?" When I don't even flinch, he hits me where he knows it will hurt. "Your family then?" That awards him the faintest twitch in my jaw, but he wants so much more. "Or perhaps the smell of her hair?"

Nothing can hold back the flicker of my eyelids when he pushes a photo of Demi through the slot my meals are served through. It's a recent shot. Unlike the image I have, her hair is styled in the pixie cut her uncle forced on her, and Max is protecting her front—like he always is.

I'm tempted to threaten Agent Moses as to what will happen to him if he gets close to Demi outside of these walls, but the pixilation of his surveillance image makes it unnecessary. Even to a novice, it's obvious his picture was snapped at a distance, assuring me he already knows the rules. I might have made a deal with the devil when I agreed to come to this hellhole, but I'm not stupid. I made Demi invincible before I handed her protection over to Max and my brothers. If you so much as bump into her in the street, you better watch your back. That's how fierce her protection is now. She is the safest she's ever been.

With my attitude at a pinnacle, I make use of the light by utilizing the bathroom facilities. It annoys Agent Moses more than my refusal to speak to him the last three times he's popped in to visit me. He almost rips his hair out of his head while raking his fingers through his messy locks. He's at the end of his tether, and the desperation is heard in his voice when he mutters, "Five minutes. Alone. With her." I'm unsure if his sentences are spaced because he has to work them through a tight jaw or if it's because he isn't good at negotiating on the spot.

I learn my answer when I spin around to face him. He is as surprised by his offer as me.

His shock doesn't mean his offer hasn't spiked my interests, though. I was already struggling knowing I couldn't touch Demi for years in a normal cell, but being locked in the dark for over twenty-three hours a day has made the knot in my stomach so much worse. Last month, I could settle my unease by looking at her beautiful face. This month, I'm left alone with my thoughts. That wouldn't be so bad if half of them weren't the instigators of nightmares. I've remembered the bad times far more than the good times the past couple of weeks, and they're haunting me even more than a lack of sunshine, fresh air, and food.

After snatching up Demi's picture to ensure Agent Moses can't leave with it, I compromise, "Twenty minutes."

He scoffs as if I'm being ridiculous before he blubbers out a string of words, "I can't do twenty minutes. Standard visitations don't last twenty minutes, so there's no way I could get you that long, alone. You need to be reasonable, Ox, or this experiment will be a woeful waste of time."

As I jackknife back, my brow arches. "Experiment?"

Agent Moses's Adam's apple bobs up and down as his eyes shoot to mine. It's rare for him to put his foot in his mouth, but there's no doubt that is what he just did.

"This is an experiment to you?" I approach the Perspex so fast he has no choice but to stumble backward. I cracked bulletproof glass with my fists to get to Demi, so you can be as sure as fuck a bit of plastic won't stop me. "This is my life! It isn't a fucking experiment."

The Perspex wobbles under the pressure of my fists a mere second before the hole is placed back into lockdown.

————————

I don't know if days or weeks pass before the door to my cell is reopened. The noisy grumbles of my tummy have me convinced they cut my meals back to one a day, but with my hunger hazing my mind enough for me to be on the brink of mental exhaustion, I could be mixing things up. I'm not in the right head space, and it's showcased in the worst way when I groggily mumble, "Ten-minute unsupervised visits once a month..." Agent Moses sighs in victory, unaware I hadn't finished my sentence, "... starting today."

"Today?" His shriek is so high, it pierces my ears.

I won't lie. It's an effort to bob my head. I'm as physically drained as I am emotionally, but I am confident it will only take seeing Demi in the flesh once to drag me out of the hole I'm in. She has a way of giving me strength by doing something as simple as smiling.

When Agent Moses spots the weak dip of my chin, he breathes out of his nose before waving his hand through the air. It dawns on me that our exchanges are being monitored when the Perspex slides away like an automatic door, and two guards enter my cell for the first time in weeks. They hoist me off the floor before dragging me out of the sweat-scented space.

Once I'm plopped onto a chair, Agent Moses shoves a cell phone into my face. "One call. Make it quick." He snatches back his phone before my hand gets close to it. "And only one visitor. No exceptions."

I'm too close to hell's gate to understand why he'd care who Demi arrives with. I'm barely lucid, and the fog in my head grows worse when I dial a number I know by heart only to be told the service has been disconnected.

How could that be? My family has had the same landline number for years.

"Try this number," Agent Moses suggests while thrusting a piece of official FBI paper my way. It exposes that Demi is under surveillance, but not because she's a suspect. They're afraid she could become a victim.

Through shuddering, frail hands, I punch in the cell number under Demi's name. The sweetest singsong voice I've ever heard sounds down the line a couple of rings later, "Hello."

You can hear the suspicion in Demi's voice. It raises my lips half an inch. "Hey—"

"Oh my God, Maddox." She instructs for someone to pull over before she sobs down the line. "We just left Wallens Ridge. They said you didn't want to see me. Please, don't shut me out. We're meant to be in this together. You and me, remember? Together forever."

I thought I'd be too dehydrated for her response to make me teary-eyed. It shows how much I know about my body. It could have lasted months in the hole if my heart hadn't convinced it otherwise.

"Can you come?" I want to say more. I just can't. I'm too choked up emotionally to form words, let alone the fact every word I speak is being scrutinized by Agent Moses, the warden, and two guards.

I hear Demi drag her hand across her cheeks before she replies, "Yes, of course. When?"

"Now?"

Her sob almost tears me in half. "Now?" she asks, certain she heard me wrong. She didn't, but I don't get the chance to explain. "We will be there in less than thirty minutes."

As gravel crunches under tires, Agent Moses hits me with a look, one that restates his terms in our agreement.

"Demi..."

Air catches in her throat like she's been dying to hear me say her name as I have been to hear her say mine. "Yeah."

"You need to come in alone." It dawns on me that she has me on speaker phone when the brutal swallow of a man uncomfortable with my terms sounds down the line. Since that is their only objection, it doesn't take me long to realize she must be traveling with Caidyn. "Tell Caidyn I will catch up with him on the next visitation day."

After a beat, Demi breathes out slowly, "Okay. I'll see you soon."

Just as Agent Moses snatches his phone out of my hand, she adds, "I love you."

"I love you back, baby. Don't ever forget that," I shout, hopeful she'll catch my first sentence before Agent Moses disconnects our call.

His lack of respect has me itching to smash his teeth in, but the knowledge Demi is only minutes away harnesses the desire. I haven't seen her in the flesh in weeks, and I'm not ashamed to admit it is killing me.

Twenty-two minutes later, Demi is guided into a room at the back of the west wing by the warden. The unease on her face at being deep in the underbelly of a prison system clears away for sheer, unadulterated panic when her eyes land on me standing across from her. I used the gap in the timeline in my favor. I shaved, scrubbed my teeth, and changed out of the soiled clothes I had worn the past six days straight, but you wouldn't know that when Demi's hand darts up to cover her fretful sob.

"It's okay," I promise her, hating that the first thing she feels upon seeing me is sorrow when all I'm feeling is euphoria. "I'm okay."

Tears are streaming down her face, and there's a mess under her nose, but I have no hesitation whatsoever in saying she is the most beautiful woman I've ever laid my eyes on. The pounds I lost the past couple of weeks she put on, her hair has grown almost an inch, and the glossy sheen in her eyes makes them the brightest they've ever been. She is truly stunning, and as predicted, her closeness gives the pain in my chest purpose.

I'm stuck here so she can be free.

That in itself is worth an eternity in hell.

I wait for the guards to leave us alone before gesturing for Demi to come to my half of the room. I would move for her, but I can't trust my legs. They're already wobbling under the strain of my weight. I don't think it would be wise to add walking into the mix.

Mercifully, the click of the lock latching into place sees Demi cross the room at the speed of lightning. She throws her arms around my neck so fiercely we topple onto the sofa I stood from when my body detected she was close. She kisses me, scrubs her cheeks across my freshly shaved chin, then cups my jaw in her hands, where she spends the next eight minutes gazing into my eyes. We don't speak. We don't need to. Everything we need to say to each other is relayed in our eyes. Our love. Our grit. Our fight. This tiny moment in time makes all the bad worthwhile.

"I love you," Demi whispers a short time later. "I love you. I love you. I love you. I love you," she says on repeat like she's making up for the times she couldn't say it the past six weeks. "And that love will get you out of here. I promise you that."

She repeats her promise when the guards return to tell us our time is up, then she says it again when I'm led out of the room in shackles. I'd be worried about the determination on her face if I didn't love it so much.

Although this isn't exactly how I envisioned our life, it is pretty damn close. Demi is strong, free, and so far out of her uncle's clutch that she can finally expand her wings. Her metamorphosis proves that even when you think your life is close to being over, you can still learn how to fly. I'll try to remember that the next time I'm cocooned by darkness.

As one of my father's favorite quotes says, "If we fail to adapt, we fail to move forward."

I can't afford to stay behind, so I have no choice but to adapt.

I'll do whatever is necessary to keep my relationship with Demi strong because it is our relationship that keeps me strong.

9

DEMI

*C*aidyn's eyes pop up to mine when I race across the dusty lot at the front of Wallens Ridge State Penitentiary. I'm fuming mad, hormonal, and oh-so-devastated. Maddox... *fuck*. I don't know how to explain what ripped through me when my eyes landed on him for the first time in weeks. Love was there—*it will always be there* —but there were so many other emotions attached to my response.

Regret.

Grief.

Fury unlike anything I've ever felt.

He was gaunt and pale, and his eyes were sunken as if pained by the sun's rays booming into the window where our meeting was held. He looked sick, so you can picture how hard it was for me to un-wrap myself from him when the guards said our time was up. I wanted to scream my frustration into their faces. I wanted to demand to see the warden, then I realized only one person is responsible for Maddox's pain, and for once, it isn't me.

"Keys."

Caidyn balks, steps back, then blubbers out, "Huh?"

"Keys, Caidyn! I'm driving." He doesn't get the chance to deny my request. I snatch the key for his Jeep out of his hand, climb into the driver's seat, then crank the ignition. He either dives into the passenger seat or hitchhikes home. Those are his only two options.

He goes for the former a mere second before I plant my foot onto the gas pedal. The swivels of his tires struggling to grip the asphalt do little to slow me down. I'm on the warpath, so it will take more than a threat of a wreck to slow me down.

Not even four hours of nonstop driving dampens my annoyance.

It's as blistering as the spit that seethes from my mouth when I find my uncle in his office at the back of his compound. "You are a lying piece of shit!"

Caidyn is denied access into my uncle's private space by two goons weaponed up with machine guns, but I'm given a clear path. I find out why when Ezra stops me from beating my uncle to death after only three pounds of my fists to his chest.

It isn't what he says that alerts me to the unknown term in Maddox's contract, it's what he says to one of my uncle's men when he attempts to retaliate to my foot smacking into my uncle's nose. "If you so much as ruffle a hair on her head, you'll be dead."

Ezra doesn't issue threats he doesn't plan to execute. If he tells you you're a dead man, be sure to enjoy your last breaths.

The fact he keeps his word won't have me going easy on him, though. I'm so angry, when he releases me from his grip, I shove him with enough force, he lands onto the chair opposite my uncle with a bang.

"You said he would be taken care of! That he wouldn't suffer!" I thrust my hand at the door like the three men's faces I mentally sketched onto my hit list five hours ago are standing behind it. "They're starving him. He was so gaunt, I hardly recognized him."

Caidyn is as shocked by my confession as Ezra. He pushes past the guards, preferring to risk a bullet wound than to leave me up at the plate, swinging the bat for his brother alone. After absorbing the truth from my eyes, he shifts on his feet to face Ezra. "You promised."

With his eyes bouncing between Caidyn and me, Ezra tries to weasel his way out of a fucked-up situation with four little words. "I've kept my word."

If my anger hadn't made my mouth bone-dry, I would spit at his feet. That's how much he disgusts me. "You are full of shit. You aren't a good guy. You're like every other man here. Evil and corrupt."

When the heat of my uncle's sly smirk burns the side of my face, I crank my neck to him so fast, my muscles groan in protest. The Petretti genes are undeniable when I discover my kick caused blood to trickle from his nose. It's nowhere near enough to endanger his life, but it feels so good knowing I hurt him, I can't help but replicate his smug grin.

It slips from my face when I remember what my visit is really about. Maddox is drowning, and my uncle owns the only life jacket in sight.

"Transfer Maddox's debt to me."

"He cannot negotiate with you. It is against the terms of his agreement with Ox."

I shove my hand into Ezra's face, shutting him up before redirecting my focus to my uncle. He is the most cunning fox I've ever met, so there's no way in hell he'd fully give up his rights to me. He would have hidden something from Maddox during their negotiations so he can use it against him at a later date. It's how he operates.

"If I can't transfer his debt to me, it is only fair I'm given a chance to pay my share. I can't do that if you don't tell me what you left off the table."

"We covered all sides. You can't work for him," Ezra interrupts for the second time, his tone confident.

It's unfortunate for both of us that I know my uncle better than I let on. "You crave control as much as you do fear. You'd never give it all away."

"He did," Ezra continues, grating my last nerve. "Ox's debt can't be transferred to you, and your uncle can't accept any *favors* from you to reduce the liability of his debt."

The way he says 'favors' has vomit racing up my throat.

After checking an official-looking contract he snatched out of his briefcase, Ezra quotes, "You cannot be put into the trade, strip, run drugs, or be your uncle's personal assistant. Even Petretti's Restaurant is scratched off the list of potential ways for you to contribute to Ox's debt. We covered all bases—"

"Except one," I murmur when the truth finally dawns. For the first time in my life, my uncle smiles like he's proud of me when I add, "You failed to mention my time as a fight recruiter."

The gurgle of Ezra's stomach reveals I hit the nail on the head, much less my uncle's deep timbre. "In the past six months alone, millions of dollars in profits went unearned for the sake of maintaining *one* man's reputation." He holds his index finger in the air to emphasize his point. "I believe it's time for us to get back into the game."

I don't believe there will ever be a time I won't shiver when he includes me in his comments by using the word 'us.' We're not a team, but I am happy to pretend we are if it will help Maddox.

"Five thousand per signed fighter." My uncle scoffs as if I am being ridiculous. It does little to douse my campaign. "If you want the cream of the crop, I will find them."

"Even with this term not being stated in your agreement with Ox, you can't seriously be considering this," Ezra says to my uncle when his amused expression switches to musing. "You agreed to keep her out of this life."

After wiping away the blood pooling on his top lip, my uncle *tsks* him. "I agreed for her not to follow her mother's footsteps." He smiles in a way that makes my skin crawl. "The only fighter Monica ever faced was her husband."

I fold my arms in front of my chest, hiding the shake of my hands. I know what he is doing. He's trying to sully the memories I have of my father. It won't work. The only time I remember my father shoving my mother was when she was hurting me, and it wasn't done lightly. It took him months to forgive himself, and even then, it was only a half-pledged apology.

My thoughts shift from the past to the present when my uncle counterbids, "Three thousand per contract."

Months ago, I would have agreed without a second thought.

Today, I shake my head. I need to get Maddox out of his predicament as soon as possible. Three thousand per fighter won't cut it.

"Four thousand."

My jaw falls to the floor when my uncle displays his annoyance about my sudden backbone by throwing in a lowball offer. "One thousand."

"You just said three thousand. How can you knock it down to one?"

Ezra is pissed at me, and Caidyn is lost as to what the fuck is happening, but they both move in to protect me when my uncle stands. He finds their protectiveness amusing. It frustrates me to no end.

"What was your father's favorite saying?" He waits a beat before filling in, "Beggars can't be choosers." He drags his eyes down my body in a long, prolonged gawk. "You, my dear, are a beggar."

After grabbing his hat from a coat stand in the corner of his office, he heads for the door. He knows I'm desperate, and so does everyone else when I say, "Okay. Fifteen hundred per fighter and a promise that you will ensure Maddox is fed and protected for every day of his incarceration."

He stops partway out the door before spinning around to face me. Think of the most vindictive person you've ever met. You wouldn't even be close to how callously my uncle looks at me while saying, "I don't make promises. Your father learned that the hard way. But I will give you my word. One thousand dollars per contract and *he* will have everything he needs." The way he sneers 'he' exposes he is talking about Maddox. He hasn't spoken his name since we handed him our souls because we'd rather live without a soul than each other.

Upon spotting my agreeing nod, my uncle dips his chin, then exits his office with Ezra hot on his tail. His departure returns the oxygen his aura always pinches from the air.

I've barely sucked in a full breath when Caidyn mutters, "What did you sign on for?"

"You don't want to know," I breathe out slowly. *And neither the hell do I.*

10

DEMI

Three excruciatingly long months...

I breathe out the nerves twisting my stomach before pulling open a door with a KC's gym logo in the middle of it. The sweat, blood, and tears that pumps into my nostrils as I scan the over-flowing gym should ease my unsettled stomach. It's the smell of determination only true fighters have, but I'm beyond acting naïve.

I saw the statistics in black and white. I know the odds these men face after being handed my business card. I just don't have any other choice. The sale of the Walsh family home combined with the two hundred thousand dollars Maddox stashed away didn't come close to repaying Maddox's debt with my uncle, and with Maddox's second appeal denied even quicker than his first, I needed funds, and I needed them fast.

Over the past three months, Maddox's health has bounced back to what it was before he was incarcerated, but my prognosis only extends to his outer shell. I have no clue what is going on in that head of his. Our once-a-month meetings are still held in a room at the back of Wallens Ridge, but since I'm wary our visits are monitored, I've lost the ability to openly communicate with him.

It's hurting our relationship more than our contacts being non-physical.

I hate keeping secrets from him, but even more than that, I hate the fact I'm suspicious he's doing the same to me. Tension is mounting the longer we ignore the massive elephant in the room, and I'm petrified it is getting to the point of snapping.

After swallowing to relieve my suddenly dry throat, I get back to work. Maddox's terms make it clear my uncle can't punish me if I don't fulfill his impossible demands every month, but it doesn't make my job any easier to do. The statistics aren't as bad as they were when I had no clue what these men would face, but the guilt remains the same.

Regretfully, the bruises I see on Maddox's face and hands each visit has me desperate enough not to be picky. Not every man I recruit is winning material. I just have to remind myself that it is for the greater good. Since I can't exchange my life for Maddox's, I have to push strangers into the firing line.

I hate that it has come to this, but rarely is life fair.

I free my face of controversy before approaching a man I've been eyeing the past couple of weeks. His left hook is kryptonite, but he needs to water down his theatrics if he wants to make it out of my uncle's ring in one piece.

"I think that's everything." I join together the official-looking contract my uncle had drafted to authentic his ruse on the hood of Samuel's car before storing it into my soft-leather briefcase. "In good faith, the first three fight payments will be deposited into your bank account by tomorrow afternoon." I don't mention the fact his first deposit could be his *only* deposit. "Details for your first match will be sent to this number later this week." I hand him a one-in-a-million cell phone—an iPhone 10. "As per your contract, it is unadvisable to bring family or friends to your match. This is an invitation-only event, and tickets sold out months ago."

Samuel smiles like he's proud to be included in such an exclusive event.

It doubles my guilt.

"Do you have any questions?" *Or a legally drafted will?*

I shut down my snarky inner monologue when Samuel shakes his head. "Nope. You've pretty much covered everything."

"Great. Then I guess I'll see you around."

He stops me from walking away by grabbing my wrist. His hold isn't firm, but I'm not in the right mindset to recognize it as friendly. I yank out of his hold like he's a convicted rapist before poking my finger into his chest. "Don't ever touch me without permission."

Samuel holds his hands out in front of himself, acting innocent. "All right, sista. You don't need to tell me twice." He does an edgy shuffle that shrinks his size to that of a child. "I just wanted to ask if you'd be at the fight?"

Dark tresses of the locks I'm endeavoring to grow back fall into my eyes when I shake my head. I already feel horrible sending these men to their possible deaths. I don't need to witness the travesty firsthand.

Upon spotting my response, Samuel delves his tongue out to wet his top lip before saying, "Well, I guess I better do this now then." His voice is somewhat sheepish as if he's attempting to pull the wool over my eyes instead of the other way around. It dawns on me that I'm not far off the mark when he asks, "Did you want to grab a bite to eat sometime?"

"Oh... umm... I have a boyfriend," I stammer out, truly shocked. Since I now understand what I'm recruiting these men for, I took flirting off my drafting credentials. It isn't possible to schmooze a man you're sentencing to misery. Guilt makes me half a woman, so I won't mention what remorse does when I fail to see them at their gym the week following their first fight.

Samuel's natural arrogance is showcased in the worst light when he replies, "Yeah, but he's in lockup, so our hookup wouldn't technically count." He hits me with a frisky wink to ensure I can't misunderstand what he classes as a 'hookup.' "*Nothing* counts when your man is out of town."

"Perhaps not to you, but it does to me." While rolling my eyes, I twist on my feet and walk away from him. "Don't be late to your fight. If you're late, I'll dock your pay."

The guilt that's been bombarding me the past forty minutes clears away when Samuel fires back, "I'll let you keep it all for one round of naked Twister."

His comment makes it seem as if my nights at the cabin with Maddox were years ago. I truly can't remember the last time I smiled without it being forced. I smile every time I meet Maddox in the secret room at the back of Wallens Ridge, but it isn't a genuine smile. I'm too busy worrying about the horrid things he's experienced the previous weeks to be truly happy, so I plant a fake smile onto my face and make out that everything is fine.

I plaster the same smile onto my face when my uncle's Audi pulls into the curb at the front of KC's gym, and the back-passenger door pops open.

After shimmying away my nerves, I slip into the back seat like not the slightest bit of fear is encroaching me. My uncle feeds off fear, so I act as if I don't know pain. "He signed on with the agreement that the first three fight payments would be deposited into his account by tomorrow afternoon."

When I hand my uncle Samuel's contract, my smile becomes authentic. His hands are so frail and old. They expose I'm not the only Petretti burning the candle at both ends the past couple of months.

"Why three payments? That exceeds the offers you made the other men you've recruited the past two and a half months."

This question didn't come from my uncle. It came from Ezra, who is sitting in the front passenger seat next to Mario. Ever since I confronted my uncle in his office twelve weeks ago, it's rare to do business with him without Ezra tagging along. He seems to have more say in my family's businesses than I do, and he doesn't have a drop of Petretti blood in his veins.

I swish my tongue around my mouth to loosen up my words. "A fight promoter from Vegas was scheduled to come and see him this weekend. If I didn't make my offer enticing, Samuel would have turned it down."

"That wasn't what I saw." I angle my torso to my uncle, my interrupter. "He seemed willing to fight for free... *under certain conditions*."

"Conditions I wasn't willing to abide by." My last two words come out with a quiver when my uncle lifts his hand to my face. Mercifully, my stammer is barely noticeable over Ezra's warning growl for him to back off. Compliments to both Maddox and Ezra, my uncle's hands haven't made it to within an inch of my face the past several months. The knowledge would be more freeing if Maddox hadn't spent the last five and a half months of that time behind bars.

I settle my unrequired nerves before finalizing my sentence. "Samuel's command of the canvas is undeniable. I am confident he will last several months on the circuit, so if you're worried you won't get your money's worth, don't be. He will be a good earner." I hate myself for my last sentence. I truly, deeply hate myself.

After flicking my hair off my face like that was his intention all along, my uncle says, "Very well. I will organize payment this afternoon." He nods his head at Ezra, giving him the go-ahead. "Until then, I need another three fighters. Pickings are slim since the Walsh brothers stopped training."

I act as if there isn't an ounce of disdain to his voice. "I have another three appointments this afternoon. I will reach my quota this month."

"Good." He dismisses me from his car with a wave of his hand. I almost make it out without controversy, but five little words freeze both my heart and my feet. "Are you forgetting something, Andy?"

As horrid memories fill my head, I stray my eyes to the stream of traffic rolling past my uncle's idling Audi. There's no Prince Charming on a fat-wheeled motorbike I can beckon to save me. I'm alone, defenseless, and so very tired of the sick, neurotic games I'm continually forced to endure. My life has never been full of rainbows and sunshine, but I can't remember a single time where it was this draining.

When I lean over my uncle's side of the cab with knocking knees and tear-filled eyes, a soft-leather briefcase is shoved into my face.

I exhale in relief, doubling the mocking grin on my uncle's face.

He loves how quickly he can make me fold.

I hate it.

It's another item on the long list of things I hate about myself lately.

My short haircut, my roller-coaster moods, and my ability to lie without blinking are the top three items on my I-loathe-Demi list.

I've barely stumbled into the alleyway that sides KC's gym when a second, more confronting encounter steals the air from my lungs. "I had wondered where you were getting the money from." When I twist to face Sloane, she shakes her head, sending spirals of curls into her face. "I told Saint there was no way you'd have the money to fund an Ivy League lawyer's trip to the Bahamas. Lo and behold, I was right."

"It isn't what you think."

Sloane is ridiculously smart, but you wouldn't know it when she splays her hands across her cocked hip and says, "It isn't?" When I sheepishly shake my head, she growls at me. "Out of all the people in the world, I would have never accused you of being daft. He..." she thrusts her hand in the direction my uncle's Audi went, "... is a monster who will have no qualms throwing you in the deep end when the shit hits the fan, and believe me, it will hit the fan, and then you'll join Maddox at Wallens Ridge on dual life sentences."

Even against the caution of my stomach, I fight back. It's a known Petretti trait when our backs are against the wall. "I'm recruiting fighters, not killing them."

"It's the same thing!" Sloane's shouted words bellow down the almost empty alleyway. "Previously, you had an excuse... you were completely in the dark. You can't say that this time around."

She's right. I hate that she is, but there's no denying the truth. "I need the money."

"If the leftover *debt...*" she air quotes her last word like she understands more about my family than she has let on, "... is anything close to the amount Saint and I have calculated." She's too gripped by annoyance to register my shock that she included Saint and herself in the one sentence. She usually refers to him as 'he who shall not be mentioned.' This is the first time she's used his name in months. "You have to recruit another seven hundred fighters to break even. *Seven. Hundred,* Demi. That's more than dual consecutive sentences. You may be the first woman in Florida to be executed."

Her reply hits me for a six, but it won't stop me from saying, "Not all of them will die. For all we know, none of them will. Dimitri put a stop to the death matches. This could be a standard circuit recruitment drive."

"Could be?" Sloane rolls her eyes before stuffing her hands under her arms. "Could be isn't a defense, Demi!"

When she spins on her heels, too angered to look at me, I take off after her. "Where are you going?"

Her brutal speed chops up her words. "To get my head examined because between you and your boyfriend's brother, I'm certain more than one screw came loose." When she suddenly stops walking, I crash into her back. "I understand what love makes you do. I get that it's crazy and unhinged and probably something I will *never* experience, but being in love doesn't give you the excuse to forget who you are. Maddox is serving a life sentence that is growing in length because he'd rather follow the commands of a Nazi than not hold you in his arms for a month." Shock must cross my features as she's quick to relieve it. "How do you think you've been getting those special one-on-one visits every month, Demi?" She continues talking, stealing my chance to answer. "Maximum security prisons don't accommodate personal requests. Inmates are there to learn a lesson, not cozy up with their childhood crush. Maddox is getting those favors because he's earning them... *unlawfully.* If you don't believe me, ask him the next time you see him. I bet he doesn't even attempt to deny it... *if* he knows what the truth is anymore."

I shake my head. "Maddox isn't like that. He wouldn't—"

"Become a shell of himself for you?" Sloane strays her disappointed yet still hopeful some good is hidden inside me eyes down my body. "There is such a thing as loving someone too much. You and Maddox are living proof of that."

Too disappointed to continue with our conversation, she steps onto the curb, then hails the next available cab. I let her leave, too shocked to move, let alone speak. I did wonder what had changed between my first private visit with Maddox compared to our last three. We went from a room built by massive panes of glass to an intimate space perfect for two, but since I got to touch him, smell him, and hug him, I stupidly told myself my uncle was being generous since he lowballed me three months ago.

Was it wrong of me to do? At the time, I didn't think so. Now I feel like a fool—even more so when my stomp down the alleyway has me stumbling into a pothole I missed earlier. It painfully distorts my ankle and has me whimpering in pain.

"I'm fine. Please, just go," I say to a dark-haired man when he bobs down to help me up.

If this is Karma biting my ass, I don't want my punishment thrust onto another unsuspecting victim.

The stranger flashes me a flirty grin. "It's okay, I'm a police officer."

He shows me his badge like it will immediately disarm me.

It's a pity for him I wasn't born last week.

"I just need to walk it off..." My words shift to a pained groan when I attempt to place pressure on my ankle. It hurts—a lot!

"Lean on me. My car is right there. I'll drop you off at the ER, then be on my way. You'll never hear from me again." Officer Daniel Packwood holds his hands out in front of himself to ensure he means no harm before he slides them to the holster on his hip. "I'll even let you hold my gun during our ride, that way, if I become too endearing for you, you can tell me to back off with more than words."

Normal, non-neurotic women would be charmed by his witty personality and good looks. All I see is a snake in the process of shedding its skin. His ring finger has a thick indent right where a wedding ring should be, yet there isn't a ring to be seen, so I won't mention the packed lunchbox on the dashboard of his car. Only two women go to such efforts—a man's mother or his wife. Considering the fact his sandwich is cut in half instead of quarters, I'd say his lunch was lovingly packed by his wife.

Since my argument with Sloane is still at the forefront of my mind, I get snappy. "How does your wife find your witty intelligence?" I hit him with a stern, evil-pronged glance before finalizing my question. "Endearing or nauseating?"

When his lips tuck in the corner, announcing he's aware he has been busted, I nudge my head to his left hand. "Not only do you have a ring indent, but the obvious lack of tanning on your finger shows you only took off your *wedding* ring mere seconds before approaching me."

He's an ass, but I can give credit when credit is due. He doesn't try to fight his way out of a wet paper bag. He accepts my rejection like a knock to the chin.

After pulling his wedding ring out of his pocket, he slides it back onto his finger. "Those are some mighty impressive investigative skills. Have you ever considered joining the force, Miss..."

I leave his invitation for an official greeting hanging. "Good afternoon, Officer Packwood."

Ignoring the pain darting up my leg, I hobble back to Caidyn's Jeep parked half a block down before slipping behind the steering wheel. Officer Daniel watches me the entire time, his eyes only shifting from my ass so he can mentally jot down the tags on Caidyn's Jeep. It won't do him any good. Not only is Caidyn's Jeep not registered in either of our names, but it is addressed at a business location that no longer exists since Caidyn torched his up-and-coming multi-million-dollar business to even the score between Maddox and my uncle.

My uncle was so embarrassed when Maddox knocked him out, he

demanded immediate retaliation. Maddox seemingly had nothing to give. Caidyn had everything, and he sacrificed it all for his baby brother.

Perhaps I'm more like the Walshs than first perceived.

The thought makes me smile.

I've wanted to be a part of their dynamic for years. I just wish it could have occurred without murder, mayhem, and an uncle I'd rather kill than obey. Alas, my father was right, beggars can't be choosers, and I've been a beggar longer than I've been a woman.

11

MADDOX

Three weeks later...

"What do you want me to say, Arrow? That I personally promise he won't do it again?" I stand from the desk in the room our monthly meetings are held in with a puffed chest and balled fists. "He got the message. He won't talk to anyone from the Feds again." I work my jaw side to side before correcting myself. "Sorry, he won't talk to anyone *but* you."

Agent Moses walks around the desk I haven't been shackled to for over four months. "He's said that before—"

"Before *I* got to him. Before *I* advised him otherwise." I bang my chest with my fist during my last 'I' to emphasize my point. "He won't make the same mistake twice."

I never understood Agent Moses's wish to command the cells at Wallens Ridge until I discovered how far the roots of this network spread. Prison systems are an entirely new underworld. They are full of violence, corruption, and wheeling and dealing. The only difference between prison-run operations like Wallens Ridge and the ones outside of these walls is that I'm aware every man I cross is a murderer, rapist, or thief. There are no cloaks to hide behind, no corporations. They are criminals, and they're not ashamed to admit it.

I've been incarcerated for a little over six months now. In that time, I've seen millions of dollars traded between mafia sanctions, overheard the organization of two dozen hits, and have personally seen pounds upon pounds of drugs walked through the front entrance. And what has the warden done about it?

Not a single fucking thing.

"I handle over three thousand dangerous criminals day in and day out. I don't have time for your concerns, boy." That's what he said to me when I tried to explain the undercover police officer's beatdown was staged, and how I was set up to become Agent Moses's bitch. "But if you unearth a way to increase my share of the pie, my door is always open."

When I found out Agent Moses wasn't working directly off Col's orders, I could have manned up and told him to fuck off. I could have shown him exactly how damaging my right hook is, but when I recovered from his first exploit, my roommate got me thinking otherwise.

I don't need to use my fists to get my point across. How I defended myself against a gang of thugs already had the prisoners cautious about getting on my wrong side, then the beatdown I gave the undercover cop and the weeks I survived in the hole saw them award me their unwanted respect, so all I needed to do was capitalize on that.

Words. That's pretty much all I've used the past couple of months. The occasional fist has been thrown, but that's only when new fish enter the pond, and they're unsure of the rules.

Am I'm worried I'll become addicted to the power associated with such a high-up role in the underworld? No. Why? Because Demi keeps me grounded. If it weren't for her, I would serve my sentence in silence. Neither the warden nor guards would know my name, but since that isn't the case, I do what needs to be done to ensure she's never a stranger to me.

The perks will never be the equivalent of a free man, but they're better than a kick in the teeth. I get to hold Demi in my arms for a minimum of ten minutes once a month, am served first each meal-time, and my newly assigned cell is close to the yard, meaning I see the sun set every single day.

Even hundreds of miles away, Demi sees the same stars I do.

That awards me an immense amount of calmness in an extremely volatile world.

After taking a second to revel in the rarity, I get back to my conversation with Agent Moses. "Henley advised the shipment would continue as arranged with you last week. Your cut will be twenty percent."

When his eyes gleam, I know I have him.

He's a sucker when it comes to profits.

His greed will be his downfall. To begin with, mafia figures will accept it as part of his package, but eventually, his inability to see through the dollar signs forever flashing in his eyes will wear their patience thin.

It has mine, and he doesn't make a dime from me.

After propping his hip onto the desk, Agent Moses folds his arms in front of his chest. "Location?"

I slant my head to the side and arch a brow, silently mocking him.

He acts as if we can communicate without words. I can assure you we're not that close. "By the docks. That's right. It slipped my mind for a second."

While pushing in my chair, I keep my eye roll on the down-low. He thinks he's 'cute' when he acts daft. In reality, it makes the urge to punch him in the face ten times worse.

"Tell the guards to bring Demi in."

My eagerness to see Demi for the first time this month is all over my face. Things have been a little rocky for us, but I'm confident they'll settle once she realizes this is our life now. I'm stuck here. There's no possibility of me getting out without making another deal with her uncle. Since I can't do that and guarantee her safety, this is the only option we have. It isn't close to the life I had planned for us to have, but it's better than not having her in my life at all.

I'm just hoping like fuck she's accepting of the new terms because without her in my life, everything I've done the past year will be worth diddlysquat.

My already tense jaw doubles when Agent Moses replies, "Your meetup is being held in the holding room near reception today."

"What's behind the change-up?" Shock highlights my tone. Today is my fifth private one-on-one meeting with Demi, and this is the first time the location has changed.

The knot in my stomach tightens when Agent Moses answers, "Demi tore a ligament in her ankle three weeks ago. She's fine, but I didn't have time to waste waiting for her to hobble down here."

"Yet you have plenty of time to watch every fucking move I make."

After *tsking* him, I'm out the door before a single pathetic denial can leave his mouth. The distance between the entrance and our meet-up room would only be about three football field lengths. If Demi can't walk that far, her ankle must be pretty fucked up.

Furthermore, I'm super curious to find out how she got injured. She's untouchable, so if this was anything more than an accident, there will be hell to pay, and I won't even need to leave my cell to instigate it.

12

DEMI

*W*hen Maddox bursts through the door of a meeting room at the front of Wallens Ridge, sweating and out of breath, I push out in a hurry. "It's just a sprain. I fell into a pothole. It doesn't hurt." *Anymore.*

Even with communication not being a strong point for us right now, I'm confident Maddox is still tapped into my inner-workings. After crossing the room at the speed of a bullet, he scoops me into his arms like he heard my unvoiced comment before he walks us to a desk in the middle of the blank-looking space.

The room we generally meet in once a month isn't what you think when you hear 'an intimate setting for two.' There's no bed, mini-fridge, or television. It's basic and bland, its sole limelight reserved for the man fussing over me like I snapped my leg in two three weeks ago instead of partially tearing a ligament.

"Did you get it checked by a doctor?" Maddox places me onto the desk I imagine prisoners are usually shackled to before he drags a chair in close to inspect my injury. "That's badly swollen for a three-week-old sprain."

His eyes float up to mine when I mutter, "Kind of like your knuckles?" The bruises on his knuckles aren't as noticeable as his first couple of months of incarceration, but there's no doubt they're fresh.

After remembering how well we used to communicate, I attempt to spark a conversation we should have had months ago. "How are you getting us this private time every month, Maddox?"

Anger steamrolls into me when he snaps out, "It doesn't matter," like my concerns aren't important.

"It does matter, Maddox. *You* matter." I'm a bitch for using his words against him, but I can't keep denying the obvious. Sloane was right. There's no doubt he's getting perks, but I know as well as anyone that *nothing* is given in this industry without a stipulation attached to it.

Not even love.

My voice comes out brisker than intended when I say, "If the things *he* is making you do are illegal, you will never get out of here. You know what Owen said. One more wrong move will see you stuck here for life."

Reddish-blond hair is tussled in the woosh of Maddox's head shake. My sneered 'he' must have clued him in as to whom I was speaking. "It isn't your uncle. I haven't seen him since we finalized our agreement."

"Then who is it?" When his eyes subtly sling to the two-way mirror on our right—the same mirror he gawks at numerous times during our ten-minute visitation slots—I follow the direction of his gaze. "Are they in there?"

When I attempt to hobble toward the secret room hidden behind a mirror, Maddox seizes my wrist in a firm grip, then plonks my backside back onto the desk. His rough-handedness doesn't annoy me as much as it did when Samuel grabbed me in the same manner, but what he says next most certainly does. "It doesn't matter who they are. They're giving me what I need."

I stare at him like I don't recognize him. The Maddox I knew a year ago wouldn't have cared if you offered him ten million dollars. If it were illegal, he wouldn't do it.

Boy, how times have changed.

"What you *need*, Maddox? You have a roof over your head, a bed to sleep in, and food in your stomach. What else could you possibly need?"

"You, Demi." He tugs on his hair, leaving it standing on its ends before he strays his eyes to mine. They're full of pain and torment. "If I don't do what they want, I can't see you, touch you, or smell you. That will kill me more than any of this." He throws his hand at the door he walked through only moments ago. "I'm in here for life. I'm not getting out. You need to understand that."

"No. Because that isn't true." Ignoring the tears welling in my eyes, I secure his hand in mine. "You're not stuck here. We still have options. Many of them."

I feel like I've been stabbed in the chest with a dirty knife when he mutters, "We're out of options. My last appeal was denied this morning. I'm here for life."

I shake my head, too shocked for a better denial. Owen said that the verdict for Maddox's final appeal was months away. That things are slower this time of the year.

When I see the truth in Maddox's eyes, I say matter-of-factly, "Then we will look at other options, take the matter elsewhere."

"There's nowhere else to take it—"

"There are *always* options, Maddox. You're just not looking hard enough." When I'm spiraling, I generally speak words I don't mean. Today isn't any different. "Take your terms off the table with my uncle. Let me share the burden of your debt."

"No!" It's rare to see Maddox angry, but there's no denying it today. His cheeks are as red as his bloody knuckles, and don't get me started on the tightness of his jaw. "I will *not* have you indebted to him. I'd rather—"

"Rot in jail?"

He waits a beat before jerking up his chin. "It could be worse."

"How, Maddox? You're being puppeteered for ten minutes a month. That isn't living."

With both our moods frayed, he takes my comment way harsher

than intended. "Do you have any idea of the hell I went to for those ten minutes, Demi? The hell I'm still going through."

While throwing his fingers through his hair that's overdue to be trimmed, he paces the room and rambles to himself. I've never seen him so unhinged. He's hurting—badly—and the knowledge immediately alters my campaign.

Air hisses through my teeth when I hobble to Maddox's side of the room. The pain spasming up my leg is intense, but it has nothing on the hurt stabbing my chest.

When I reach Maddox, I fist his plain white t-shirt, halting his strides before I endeavor to use words to clear the angst from his face. "I'm sorry. I shouldn't have said what I did."

I'm anticipating for him to immediately accept my apology. It is what the Walshs do, so you can picture my shock when he replies, "I may not be living the life we envisioned, Demi, but there's no reason you can't."

"What?" I pause, needing a minute to work what he said through my head. When it gives me nothing but more confusion, I endeavor to clarify it. "We agreed to do this *together*... as a unit. We come as a package deal. You can't have one without the other. Are you saying you feel differently now?"

His voice is barely a whisper when he replies, "I don't feel any different. I just think we need to re-evaluate things to make sure this is what we *both* want."

"This is what I want, Maddox. *You* are who I want."

Nothing but sheer panic is seen in his eyes when he asks, "Are you sure about that? Because that's not the vibe I've been getting from you lately."

Before I can assure him our argument is more about a bad week than the strength of our relationship, a guard enters the room announcing our time is up.

Maddox requests a minute before he cups my quivering jaw in his hands. Part of me wants to pull away, to demand the chance to give my side of the story, but I can't. No matter how angry I am, I could never deny him the opportunity to say goodbye. We're not given a specified amount of time, and I'd never forgive myself if my stubbornness stole me one last moment with him.

My heart cracks when Maddox gently presses his lips to mine. It isn't the kiss of a man in the throes of passion. It's resolute and final. Like it's the commencement of the end for us.

"No," I murmur over his lips, my voice on the verge of sobbing. "This isn't the end for us. What I said to you was wrong. We're doing whatever needs to be done to stay together." When the guard tugs him toward the corridor, annoyed his numerous requests for us to disband were ignored, I follow them. "I'm not giving you up, Maddox. We will make it through this. *Together.*"

Tears splash down my cheeks when I wordlessly beg for him to hold on, not to let the darkness of this life swallow him whole. He is stronger than this. If anyone can make it through this in one piece, it will be him.

Just before he is tugged out of eyesight, I mouth, "*I love you.*"

The shattered pieces of my heart float back toward my chest when he replies, "I love you back. Always." The hesitation in his tone exposes he's torn about his response, but I'd rather a cautious response than the one I was anticipating—*it's just one of those days.*

Within seconds of Maddox being hauled out of the room, my arm is snagged by a massive guard with a ginormous chip on his shoulder. Instead of showing me the way out, he marches me to the door like he's angrier about my confrontation with Maddox than me.

He probably is. If the guards are behind my one-on-one visits with Maddox, they wouldn't be happy about the prospect of losing their only bargaining chip. You can't manipulate a man who has nothing to lose. That's why my uncle can be so rigid with his negotiations. He can't even lose his soul since he didn't have one to begin with.

Caidyn's eyes shift between my tear-stained face and the guard's grip on my arm three times before he stands to his feet. "I take it you weren't raised with a father figure present?" he says after hitting the guard with a vicious glare I didn't know he had in him. "Because no *man* I know would touch a woman like that."

With an amused grunt, the guard shoves me into Caidyn's chest. His aggression has me worried what the female half of Wallens Ridge encounter day in and day out. Maddox can protect himself. I don't see the female equivalent of Wallens Ridge being able to say the same thing.

"It's fine," I assure Caidyn when the guard's mocking grin doubles the tick of his jaw. He's as worked up as Maddox was, making me wonder if tonight's moon will be full. "I'm fine. Let it go."

Caidyn is usually the one dragging my unwilling ass into the parking lot.

Today, I'm dragging him out.

We make it twenty-five miles away from Wallens Ridge when the hurt in my chest is too painful to ignore. "Did you know Maddox's final appeal was denied this morning?"

Caidyn swings his eyes from the road to me before jerking up his chin. "Owen called while you were in with Maddox. It doesn't mean anything. We still have options. I'm doing a ton of cash jobs right now, and you've... got... your... thing."

His last four words are spaced by annoyed breaths. He knows I'm recruiting fighters for my uncle, but he has no clue how deep down the rabbit warren I've burrowed. His confusion is understandable. I'm not even one hundred percent sure what my uncle does with the men I recruit. Living with your head in the sand is sometimes easier than facing a truth head-on. It's less painful. More tolerable.

Mistaking the disgusted expression crossing my face as worry, Caidyn squeezes my hand. "We'll get there, Demi... *eventually*." His last word is a whisper.

"If I increase my contracts to five a week, that will shave..." I pause to do a quick mental calculation.

Caidyn beats me to it. "Two years off the clock." He sounds as disheartened as me. I learn why when he says, "It's encouraging, but I don't see it being feasible. You're already running low on candidates. Almost every boxing gym in Florida has been weaned of fighters."

"Then, I'll expand my horizon. Go further out. We have options."

Options. That seems to be my solution for everything these days, which is odd considering it literally means a thing that is or may be chosen.

Nothing happening is via my choice. I wouldn't have picked any of this. But regretfully, we have to live the life we were handed. There's no second choice and no better option.

Sighing, I request Caidyn to pull over at an all-night pharmacy coming up on an exit ramp.

He signals to turn before asking, "Do you need to pee?"

I shake my head. "My ankle is killing me. I need to fill one of my pain medication prescriptions."

I hate how easy it is for me to lie these days. The pain I'm experiencing isn't anywhere near my feet. I just can't tell Caidyn I want to numb the hurt in my chest with a medication the ER doctor demanded I only take when completely necessary.

My ankle may not believe it's vital, but my heart most certainly does.

I wait for Caidyn to pull into a spot in front of the pharmacy before asking, "Did you want anything?"

When he shakes his head, I peel out of the Jeep. It isn't overly hot today, but I'm sweating like a woman in the middle of a change of life. I guess, in a way, that's true, and just like menopause, this change isn't my choice either.

After filling my prescription and paying for a bottle of water, I head to the washroom to calm the redness on my cheeks with some water. I've barely splashed my cheeks when a text message pops up on the screen of my cell phone. I sigh in gratitude when I spot who it's from. Sloane and I have hardly spoken since our argument in the alleyway three weeks ago. I don't even know where she's staying. I'm assuming at her parents' place, but since I wrongly believe all the world's problems are on my shoulders, I haven't sought a better answer.

It makes me a terrible person who is unworthy of the promising verse in her message.

Sloane: *They muddy the water to make it seem deep —Friedrich Nietzsche*

I understand what she's saying and appreciate she is still trying to give me hope even while angry at me, but it makes the heaviness on my chest crippling.

Murky waters don't just make the water appear deep. They also hide what's beneath.

That's what I'm worried about the most. The hideous underbelly both Maddox and I are ignoring because we forever use love as an excuse. I'm sending hundreds of men to their deaths so I can free one man from incarceration. How I ever thought this would be okay is beyond me, but I can't stop now. Maddox is barely holding on. If I give up, he will soon follow.

I can't let that happen. We're a team. We play on the same field. I just need to find the strength to keep going—a strength I stumble upon when I accidentally take two painkillers instead of the recommended one. The buzz it gives me doesn't make me immune to the carnage. It merely weakens the weight on my shoulders by a smidge, freeing me to continue fighting as I have the past seven and a half months.

I've walked into the dark. Now I need to find the light on the other side.

13

DEMI

Six weeks later...

I spit minty bubbles into the cracked sink of my childhood home before rinsing my toothbrush and placing it into the holder at the side. While staring at my reflection, I act as if I can't hear my painkiller prescription beckoning me to it.

I only take a minor dose when absolutely necessary.

Regretfully, today is one of those days.

I recruited a father this morning—a single dad of two. He approached me with a story you hear far too often around these parts. His wife had died when his youngest was six months old, and the factory he was working at closed down not long after that. He needed money, and he was desperate enough to admit that to a stranger.

I gave him everything I had on me. Notes, coins, even the coupons I had clipped out of a newspaper earlier this month, but it wasn't close to what he needed.

Some of the fighters at his gym bragged about the contracts I had offered them. It frustrated him to no end because he wasn't being cocky when he said he was a far better fighter than the men I had signed in front of him. I tried to explain that the fighting circuit I recruited for was different than a standard fight ring and in no form whatsoever was it suitable for a single parent, but nothing I said made any difference. If I didn't give him a contract, he would soon approach my uncle. That would have seen his entire family placed onto my uncle's radar, so once again, I had no choice. The decision was taken out of my hands. I had to sign him.

I've felt sick to my stomach all day, and I don't see the painful twists ending with a minor dose of oxycodone, so I swallow down two tablets instead. It gives me an instant buzz. Even the dreariness of my family home doesn't seem as bad.

I've lived here a couple of months now, yet it still feels foreign. The carpet smells musty, every room has water damage of some kind, and a lack of floor space hasn't hidden the fact I have hardly any furniture. Mr. and Mrs. Walsh helped me as much as they could, but with them selling their antiques to fund Maddox's 'legal fees,' they didn't have much left for themselves.

They're living in a rental house a similar size to my family home. That's why I moved out—much to their dismay. They went from an eight-bedroom mansion to a three-bedroom home with only one bathroom. We were practically living on top of each other, and Max wasn't making the tight confines any less noticeable. He scratched at the door every night, begging to come in, but since the den I was using as a bedroom didn't have a door, I couldn't let him in. Justine had heard the story of the time he broke the bathroom door in her family cabin, and she was petrified he'd do the same to her bedroom door.

I held off for as long as I could, but eventually, the tight confines became too much to bear. I had to move out. Of course, the entire Walsh family tried to talk me out of it, but despite their multiple confirmations that I wasn't intruding, I could see the weariness in their eyes. Landon has yet to forgive me for Maddox's incarceration, Justine is still a recluse, and one night I heard Mrs. Walsh express concerns to her husband about my 'constant need to work out.' She has no clue my multiple trips to the gym are to help her son, and in all honesty, I want to keep it that way. The fewer people aware of my murderous ways, the better.

One of the good things about moving out on my own is that there is less chance of anyone finding out my secrets. I can come and go as I please. My only watch dog without fur is the same man who knows almost all my deepest darkest secrets—Caidyn. He's asleep on my couch at the moment. I did offer him to camp in my parents' room during his almost nightly sleepovers, but he declined my offer with a shiver, acting as if their corpses were in their bed.

I freeze partway into my bedroom when a disturbing notion enters my thoughts. I always talk about my mother as if she is dead, where, in reality, I have no clue if that is true. No matter how often I begged my uncle in the months following my father's death for an update on my mother, he never succumbed to my tears.

Within a year, I stopped asking about her. It hurt more wondering if she was alive than it did pretending she was dead, so I did the latter. I feel guilty about it, but those first couple of months when I was shipped from foster home to foster home were really tough for me. There's only one time that comes close to competing with it—the past couple of months.

You can only surround yourself with darkness for so long before you eventually forget the colors of a rainbow. Maddox is learning that the hard way, and if the bundles of cash Saint is entering my room with is anything to go by, he isn't far off discovering the same thing.

"Saint, where did you get this money?"

He answers me by lifting his head high enough the 69ers cap he's wearing unshadows his right eye. It's bruised in an obvious manner. Ungloved fists mark the same way.

"Please tell me you're not fighting for my uncle?" Sloane will never speak to me again if she finds out. Things were super awkward between us last week when she drove with me to visit Maddox. I doubt she would have come with me if Caidyn hadn't begged her.

With the Walshs' reputation in the crapper, thanks to Maddox's incarceration for murder and Caidyn being investigated for a failed arson insurance claim, jobs in the local area soon dwindled to nothing, leaving a majority of the Walshs scrambling for work in other states. It's been a ghost town around here lately, and the gaping vacancy in my chest is the most obvious.

I tried my best to fake happiness during my one-on-one visit with Maddox, but he saw through it in under a second. I broke down when he reiterated his comment about how I could have a life without him and that he wouldn't hate me for putting myself first. He truly has no clue those very short minutes we have each month are the *only* things keeping me going. They're the equivalent of a person counting down to a long-awaited vacation. I circle them on the calendar tacked next to my bed and shed a tear for every day I cross off. I truly don't know how I would cope if I didn't have them to look forward to. It would be one dreary day after another.

That isn't a life I want to live.

I'd rather die than face that day in and day out.

Mistaking my horrified expression as disappointment, Saint shakes his head. "I'm working the circuit independently. This one is separate from the Petretti route."

I shouldn't sigh in relief, but I do. Even though I'd rather he not fight at all, it would be so much worse if he were doing it under my uncle.

"Will that help?"

I drop my eyes to the bundle of cash he nudged his head at during his question. There must be at least twelve thousand sitting on the end of my bed. "Yeah, it could... if I had any plans to accept it."

"Why wouldn't you accept it?"

I raise my eyes to his, which are glaring at me like I'm gum stuck under his school desk. "Because Maddox will never forgive me if he finds out I took your money, not to mention how you earned it."

My back molars smash together when Saint replies, "Then don't tell him." An expression crosses his face. It shows he's been struggling as badly as me the past couple of months. "What's one more item on the laundry list of things you and Caidyn are keeping from him? It will take you recruiting twenty fighters to get that much money. I earned it in one weekend."

"Saint..." I should say more. I just can't. I'm too shocked. He would have needed to fight at least four times to earn this much money in a weekend. That's a recipe for disaster, and it will get him killed.

When I say that to him, he scoffs. "I have to do something. I trusted the law. It failed."

Although he doesn't mention Sloane in his comment, I have a feeling this centers around their relationship as well as Maddox's numerous failed appeals. "So you thought spitting in its face would make things better?" When he attempts to answer me, I talk faster. My question was rhetorical because I knew his response would be filled with lies. It's what most men do when they can't express themselves without admitting their feelings. "I get it, okay? I understand. What I'm doing isn't lawful either, but it is expected of me. I am a Petretti. I am meant to be evil. You are not, Saint. No one in your family is."

"Yet we're all rotting in hell." I'm glad to see his hotheadedness hasn't changed when he storms out of my room like he has a rocket strapped to his back. "And that's why I'm going to continue fighting, so you either give the money to your uncle on my behalf, or I'll visit him every Monday after fight nights. The decision is yours."

I curse him to hell before flopping onto my bed with a groan. It doesn't matter whether it is a Walsh family member doing it or my tirade of an uncle, manipulation hurts in every form. I thought Saint knew that. His parents raised him right. I just hope Maddox will remember their teachings when he learns about all the secrets I'm keeping from him, and don't get me started on Sloane, or I'll never get any sleep.

14

DEMI

*T*hree weeks later, I breathe out a heavy sigh while padding into the bathroom to fetch a glass of water. Tonight is Saint's fourth fight this week. I'm exhausted for him. Black rims are circling my eyes, and my footing is sluggish and slow. I'd give anything for an early night, but since I can't fight for Saint, I attend every match to emotionally support him instead.

After placing two oxycodone tablets onto my tongue, I swallow them with a mouthful of water. While waiting for them to perk me up as once only Maddox could, I stare at my reflection. The disheveled appearance peering back at me announces my prescription is the only thing keeping my eyelids open the past few weeks. They remind me that the sun always rises no matter how stormy the day. I've just got to keep moving, one foot in front of the other.

With that in mind, I snatch up my coat, then jog to the front door of my family home. With the hour late and Caidyn's visits sporadic since Saint started popping over more often, I race out of my empty house and into the driveway without incident.

Saint greets me with a smile when I slip into the driver's seat of his flashy car, but no number of pearly white teeth can hide the disdain crossing his face. He isn't happy Max always rides shotgun, but since he doesn't want to lose an arm, he keeps his grumbles to himself

When I latch my belt into place, Max gives my cheek a big sloppy kiss. I thank him for his love by scratching under his chin before locking my eyes with Saint's in the rearview mirror. They're a lot harsher than they were this time last year, but I know a good man is still hiding in him somewhere. It's just an extra grumpy version now.

"How far out is this comp?" I ask while reversing out of the driveway. Just like my search for new recruits, Saint broadened his horizons the past couple of weeks as well. It was the only suggestion I had to keep him off my uncle's radar, although I don't see it lasting long.

I now travel as inland as Gainesville and as south as Miami to seek new fighters. I want to say my guilt has lessened since I'm no longer recruiting in my hometown anymore, but that would be a lie. It remains heavy on my chest morning, noon, and night.

Saint waits for me to crunch through the gears before replying, "It's a four-hour round trip."

"Four hours?" I clarify loudly.

When Saint jerks up his chin, I pull into the curb at the front of my home.

"Did you forget something?" He rolls his eyes when I nod my head. "Then get a wiggle on. We're already pressed for time."

After nodding for the second time, I jog up the cracked concrete driveway before galloping across the stained carpets in the living room. When I enter the bathroom located across from my room, I stand frozen for a couple of seconds, stumped. I'm certain I left my painkillers on the vanity sink. My toothbrush is where I left it along with the product I use to style my now bob haircut, but my medication is nowhere to be seen.

I call myself an idiot under my breath when my re-entrance to my room has me stumbling onto the canister on my bed. "I could have sworn you were in the bathroom," I tell it, confused enough to talk to an object as if it can respond.

Once I have the unresponsive canister in my hand, I retrace the steps I took.

Saint eyes me with suspicion when I slide back into his car. "You went back to get your prescription?"

Even unsure as to why his voice is laced with suspicion, I jerk up my chin. "I'll be due for another dose before we get back."

"So..." Asking personal questions seems to be one of Saint's favorite pastimes of late.

Although I don't appreciate the interrogation in his tone, I reply, "If I don't take them regularly, my injury will flare back up."

"That isn't the way painkillers work, especially when it comes to an ankle injury."

I click my belt into place with more aggression than needed before recommencing our trip. "Who says? I don't recall seeing sports therapy on your list of studies when you were at school."

I steal his chance to reply by cranking up the volume on his radio. I've had enough arguments the past couple of months to last me a lifetime. I'm not interested in another one, especially if it's with someone who doesn't have a clue how I operate.

The oxycodone isn't for my ankle.

It's for my heart.

With Saint's annoyance as obvious as mine, we complete the two-hour trip in silence. It isn't all bad. I listen to some songs I haven't heard in months, and Saint gets in a little nap. It could only be better if Maddox were snoring in the back seat instead of his brother.

"Come on, Max," I say after unclicking his doggy seat belt. He joins me ringside every match. I feel safe with Saint, but it's nice having a fanged backup for when he's on the canvas. My family name already makes people hesitant in approaching me, so you can imagine how rarely it occurs when Max is at my side.

My steps falter when we break through the crowd circling the ring. I'm not shocked about the number of people out of their seats, clapping and cheering, but I am stunned by the man causing the ruckus. Samuel, the fighter I signed two months ago, is in the middle of the canvas, brutally punishing his opponent with the left swung hook I had him sign on the dotted line for.

"Who organized this tournament?" I ask Saint, shouting to project my voice over the loud crowd.

Saint stops partway down the bleachers before cranking his ear my way, wordlessly advising he missed what I said.

When I repeat my question, he shrugs. "I was given this contact last month. It's a solid lead."

While shaking my head, I attempt to push him back out of the warehouse. "We need to go."

His footing is too solid. No matter how hard I shove him, he barely budges an inch. "It's a twenty-thousand-dollar fight, Demi. We need that money."

"You won't have *anything* if you stay here, Saint! He will take it all away." Conscious he is as stubborn as a mule, I switch my shouted words for pleading ones. "Please trust me on this. I wouldn't say it for no reason. I want Maddox free as much as you do, but we need to leave, now!"

"Okay. All right. Calm down." Anyone would swear he hates my tears as much as Maddox. I usually loathe them as well. Tonight, they give me no shame whatsoever. If it gets Saint out of here before his ankle is snared in one of my uncle's vicious traps, I'll wear them with pride. "We'll go."

We make it halfway to his car when Max announces we have company. He growls at a shadow under the awning of the warehouse before he bares his teeth. He's only ever responded to one man as viciously as he is now. It was the night Col punished Justine instead of me.

"Run!" I don't give Saint the chance to dig in his heels this time around. I push him with everything I have, kick-starting his feet before I yank on Max's leash to ensure he follows us.

Saint, Max, and I barrel into Saint's car at the same time. The tension in the air is so high, Max doesn't protest to Saint helming his car. He's too busy staring at the shadow of death floating toward us, aware of the real danger facing us.

The dust Saint's tires kick up when he plants his foot onto the gas pedal should hinder the image of my uncle stepping out of the shadows, but the smug grin on my uncle's face is impossible to miss. It exposes he doesn't just want one Walsh brother under his command. He wants as many as he can get, and Saint was a hair's breadth away from falling for his ruse.

The knowledge has me reaching for my prescription canister hours earlier than required. Confident a one-off double dose won't become a problem, I tap four pills into my shaky hand.

I need something to take the edge off.

Something to calm me down.

This won't become an issue.

I'm surviving, and survivors do whatever it takes to stay alive.

The following Friday, I crunch my teeth through three oxycodone tablets before pulling open the single glass door at KC's gym. It takes straying my blurry eyes across the entire gym before I spot Samuel in the far back corner.

Although I am grateful he's alive, I'm also mad. He killed a man last week, so how can he smile and joke today as if another man's blood isn't on his hands? He's prancing around like a tomcat, lapping up the attention of the women who book classes here merely for the eye candy.

My frustration about Samuel's lack of remorse is heard in my tone when I storm to his side of the gym to demand the phone I gave him when I signed him on to be one of my uncle's fighters. "*The* phone, Samuel. The one that advises you the location and time of your fights."

"Oh." He rakes his teeth over his lower lip. "I thought perhaps you wanted *my* phone so you could give me your number."

I chewed on my painkillers with the hope they'd reach my system quicker. I'm conscious now that my theory may not be accurate. If oxycodone were tracing through my veins, Samuel would be more tolerable, wouldn't he?

After rummaging through his bag next to the boxing mat he was prancing around on, Samuel hands me his phone. "Here you go."

Since he's too busy showboating to his friends my supposed desperation to give him my number, he misses me logging into the iPhone settings to forward his messages to my number. It's an old trick I learned from my uncle during my first recruitment drive. All the iPhones in his arsenal are set up with the same Apple ID to ensure a fighter can't use the excuse that they never got a message if they fail to arrive for fight night. My uncle has proof of every message both sent and received.

When I hand Samuel back his phone, minus my number, he clutches his chest like he's heartbroken. "Don't do it, Demi. My heart may shatter."

"Good, then perhaps it might make room for compassion." After hitting him with a stern glare, I twist on my feet and walk away.

Samuel is on my heels two seconds later. "Come on, Demi, you can't be mad at me for gloating. You signed me because you knew I'd be a moneymaker, but now you're mad because I'm proud of my victories."

"Being proud about an accomplishment and showboating about murdering someone are two *very* different things," I snap out before I can stop myself.

He takes a step back, shocked. "What the fuck are you on? I haven't murdered anyone."

I want to deny his claims. I want to call him a liar, but behind his cocky exterior is a man who prides himself on honesty. He has the same kind, honest eyes Maddox does. They're just ten times more brazen.

When he grabs my arm like he's endeavoring to check it for track marks, I yank my wrist out of his firm yet worried hold. "It's fine. Pretend I didn't say anything."

I race out the door before he can stop me, then, only seven short hours later, I arrive at the location on a message he received an hour after I left him dumbfounded at KC's.

Death matches will never be entertaining for me. I'm merely here to authenticate the honesty I saw in Samuel's eyes.

After lowering a cap over my hair, I slip out of Caidyn's Jeep before entering an industrial warehouse on the outskirts of Erkinsvale. Many of the areas surrounding Ravenshoe were founded by hardworking factory and textile workers. Although the towns have greatly benefited from new infrastructure and a truckload of money, the outer areas remain relatively untouched. There are hundreds of vacant warehouses dotted along the coastline. They make the perfect locations to hold death matches.

Because I've arrived late, I enter the dingy and dark space without having my name crossed off an exclusive list.

That's the first sign Samuel wasn't lying.

It wouldn't matter if there were only seconds remaining for an event. If you didn't pay to be a part of it, my uncle wouldn't let you enjoy a single second of it.

My knees knock when the crowd's boos overtake the sound of two men going to war on a leather canvas. In this industry, booing is worse than frantic calls for death. The crowd only ever boos when they believe they're not getting their money's worth. To them, that generally means someone's life was spared.

I discover I'm on the money when the hissing crowd parts enough that I spot the ring. Samuel stands to one side. He's being held back by the referee. He has hardly broken into a sweat, but his opponent is on the mat, wheezing and out of breath next to the white gym towel his 'owner' tossed into the ring to save his hide.

"This isn't a death match," I murmur to no one, genuinely shocked.

I freeze like a statue when a rough, Italian voice behind me murmurs, "You could have learned that last week if you weren't so distrusting."

After cursing myself for not bringing Max with me, I spin around to face my uncle. The panic surging through my veins gets a moment of reprieve when I spot who is standing behind him. Ezra is either my uncle's shadow or a thorn in his backside. I really hope it's the latter.

"Can you blame me for being suspicious? Twenty thousand is an excessive offer for a single fight."

"Very true," my uncle agrees while stepping closer. "But as you can hear, the men are growing restless. Too many trainers are throwing in the towel before the fights have truly begun. I want to exert some new blood into the industry. The Walsh name could do that."

"The Walsh name already *did* that and look how it turned out for him."

Only months ago, my comment would have had me tasting my own blood.

Today, I live to tell the tale.

I discover why when my uncle says, "Convince Saint to fight for me, and I'll half the remaining debt on his brother's ledger."

If it were anyone but him offering to reduce Maddox's debt by fifty percent, I'd jump at the chance. Since it isn't, I give him the only answer he will ever get from me when it comes to anyone in the Walsh family. "No."

He acts as if I never spoke. "And on top of that, I'll pay him ten thousand dollars per fight. His brother will be out within two years. Not even you could convince him to turn down an offer that enticing."

"Wanna bet?" I respond against my better judgment. I could blame painkillers for hazing my mind, but in all honesty, that's a cop-out.

I'm finally growing a backbone.

It's just years too late.

My back molars smash together when my uncle leans in close to whisper in my ear, "You should never risk more than you can afford to lose. I thought you'd know that better than anyone."

Stealing my chance to reply, he heads to the ring like the king is about to address the court, and just as quickly, I put as much distance between us as possible. I came here for answers. I got them. No good will come from adding more mess into the equation. That is one thing I am certain about.

The rest is up for negotiation.

15

DEMI

One and a half months later...

*A*fter straying his eyes from Harlow Murphy, Maddox's ex-girlfriend to me, Caidyn asks, "You good?"

I lift my chin before clipping my seat belt into its latch. "I'm fine. Thank you."

Shocked by my blasé reply, Caidyn peers at me with worried, uneased eyes.

I laugh. "Don't look at me like that. She's Maddox's friend. Nothing more." That could have been articulated a little less bitchy, but it is what it is. "Furthermore, I doubt anything she could say will have him smiling as largely as we did."

We've just finished an hour-long impromptu visit with Maddox. It wasn't held in the secret room where my monthly ones with him take place. It was in a standard, rectangular-shaped area with corded phones and assigned cubicles, but the message we came to give him wasn't dampened by the location.

His baby sister *finally* left her room.

We didn't mention the fact it was to go on a date with a man Maddox would rather pummel than welcome into the family.

Brax Anderson has been good to Justine. He forced her out of her room, took her to a concert, and encouraged her to renew the studies she indefinitely postponed many moons ago. She is finally getting her life back on track, and it has me hopeful the rest of her family will soon follow.

"All right. If you're sure…"

I sock Caidyn in the arm for leaving his question open before nudging my head to the exit of the lot. "I'm sure. Maddox and I are solid." Ignoring the quickest flare of doubt blistering through Caidyn's unique eyes, I add a request to my command. "But can we stop by a drug store on the way home? I need to fill a prescription."

Caidyn swipes his tongue across his lips before asking, "A prescription for…"

"For my ankle, dummy." I knock my knee against his, silently egging him about getting senile in his old age. He did turn twenty-six last week.

My playfulness doesn't weaken the snip of interrogation in Caidyn's voice in the slightest "Why do you need a prescription for your ankle?"

"Because I had a partial tear—"

"Almost *four* months ago, Demi."

I don't appreciate his father-like tone, but I take it in stride. I missed having a fatherly figure during my teenage years, so I won't give this up for anything. "Yeah, but my pain threshold remains the same."

"In your heart. Your ankle is fine."

When I read between the lines of his snappy tone, I reply matter-of-factly, "I only take the recommended dose."

"From what I've heard and witnessed, like clockwork, every four hours," Caidyn fights back. "You've not missed a single dose the past three months."

"Ouch!" I push out with a grunt when he kicks me in the ankle responsible for our argument. "That hurt!"

He slants his head and cocks a brow. "Well, at least now you have an excuse for the pills you'll pop today."

When I sock him in the arm, he veers onto the wrong side of the road.

"You're being extremely rude."

"Yeah, I am," he agrees without pause for thought. "But I'd rather be honest than have Maddox chew my ass out for another thirty minutes like he did back there." He thrusts his hand to Wallens Ridge State Penitentiary disappearing on the horizon.

"What are you talking about? You guys were discussing Justine, w-weren't you?" My stutter can't be helped. I've never seen Caidyn so mad. If he holds the steering wheel any tighter, I'm afraid he might snap it.

I discover the reason for his anger when he barks out, "Justine barely got a look in... because when it comes to you, no one else matters to Maddox."

Now I feel extremely guilty and nervous. I'm not anxious I am the axis of Maddox's world. I know my importance in his life. He's never made me doubt that. I'm fretful about Caidyn steering his Jeep past the drug store we generally stop at every trip. I took my last lot of pills four hours ago. I'm due for another dose.

Painkillers are the last thing on my mind when Caidyn asks, "Did you see the way Maddox looked at you, Demi? How he couldn't take his eyes off you."

"He always does that."

"Not like that. Not how he did today. He was staring at you because he didn't know who you were. He couldn't see you under the cloak of sedation. You're becoming a zombie, and your addiction to painkillers is the cause of that."

I stuff my hands under my arms. "You're over exaggerating. Maddox was looking at me with love. Perhaps you'll understand that more once you fall in love."

My hands shoot out to brace the dashboard when he slams on his brakes. While grumbling that he never gets the chance to woo anyone because he's always babysitting me, he yanks his car off the freeway. I'm not scared about his aggression. We had a similar argument after I told him about my uncle's offer to lower Maddox's debt. Saint wanted to accept it. It took Caidyn backing me up to get him to see how that would be a huge mistake. It was a massively heated debate that saw the three of us exchanging words we didn't mean.

Things haven't been the same since.

I can see today's argument following a similar path when Caidyn swings his eyes to mine and says, "If I'm exaggerating, you won't have any issues giving me your prescription." When I balk, he adds, "You sprained your ankle *months* ago. Your claim that it still hurts is no longer valid."

When he does a two-handed clap, wordlessly demanding my prescription, I act as if my heart isn't racing a million miles an hour. "Fine. Take it. I don't need it."

Caidyn snatches the prescription out of my hand, scrunches it into a ball, then tosses it out of the window. I'm not ashamed to admit it only takes half a mile before I commence contemplating ways to find a ball of paper on the side of the freeway, but I am ashamed to admit if those efforts fail, I'm reasonably sure I am not above taking much more drastic measures.

I've reached a point I'm not even sure Maddox could fix me now.

16

DEMI

*B*utterflies take flight in my stomach when I peer down at the final oxycodone stamped pill in the bottom of my canister. I had a private stash Caidyn didn't know about. It only had a dozen pills in there, but it was better than the none Caidyn thought I had.

I've only taken them when absolutely necessary the past couple of days—before my meeting with my uncle, when Saint took a beating so severe he was forced to pull out of his last two fights this week, and today, because it's the first time I'm going to see Maddox after he supposedly ripped Caidyn a new asshole for my overfriendly demeanor.

It's scary contemplating the fact that Maddox and I have been apart more than we've been together the first year of our relationship, and it appears as if that will get worse long before it gets better. Owen is lost on where we can go from here. Maddox is out of appeals, and despite me scouring every boxing gym within four hundred miles of Hopeton, I've barely made an indent to the one million dollars remaining on Maddox's debt.

Feeling too edgy to ignore, I swallow my final tablet without water before spinning to face my bedroom. Nerves aren't something I handle well anymore. They make me so anxious, I have to give myself a mental pep talk every day just to leave my room.

My steps into the living room are super sluggish, although they have nothing on the groan Caidyn releases when he attempts to stand from the couch he's been crashing on the past couple of days.

"Are you okay, Caidyn? You sound like I need to take you out to the woods."

I shift my frown into a smile when Caidyn gets my sick sense of humor. "Don't tempt me. With how tired I am, I might take you up on your offer."

While dragging his bloodshot eyes down the dress I wore on my double date with Sloane, Saint, and Maddox last year, he attempts to stand from the couch. I say attempt as the usually simple task sees him almost falling over the coffee table.

He isn't drunk.

He's sick.

The number of used tissues dotted around the sofa exposes this, much less the fact he left the dinner I cooked for him last night untouched.

"You're burning up," I announce after a quick check of his temperature. He's so hot, I need to check my hand for scorch marks. "When was the last time you took Tylenol?" I cock my hip when his lips tug at one side. "You won't be laughing about me sounding like your mother when I call her to tell her you're sick."

That swipes the smile off his face.

After licking his bone-dry lips, he mutters, "An hour ago."

"Only an hour ago and you're still this hot! You must have a fever." I make a beeline to the medicine cabinet in the only bathroom in the residence. Once I have a bottle of ibuprofen in one hand and cough syrup in the other, I fill a glass with water, then re-enter the living room. "I would have offered you one of my painkillers if I had any left, they would have knocked your fever on its ass, but since you were adamant I had to give them up, you'll have to stick with the good old cough syrup and ibuprofen ass-kicking."

The heaviness of Caidyn's eyelids does little to deter his stubbornness. "I can't take that brand of cough syrup. If I do, I can't drive."

"And?" I ask, missing the point.

He drags his hand down my body like his eyes did only moments ago.

It doubles the annoyance on my face. "You know I can drive, right? I have been capable since I was sixteen."

"Maddox would—"

"Kill you if you make me sick? Yeah, he probably will." I shove the almost empty bottle of cough syrup into him before saying, "That's why you're going to stay here."

"Demi..." Caidyn grumbles like he could stop a tornado with an angry tone.

In case you're wondering, he can't. I'm not exactly a tornado, but since I'd rather my confrontation with Maddox occur without an audience, I'm willing to pretend as if I am.

"Fine! I'll pretend I need a bodyguard even with me living in a big-ass protective bubble the past eleven months." I spin around to face Caidyn before gesturing my head to Max, who is eyeing Caidyn like he's breakfast. "I'll take Max with me instead of your germy self." When Caidyn pulls a face, I add, "Or he could stay here with you if you want? I'm sure he'll listen to you... *eventually*."

We're thrust into an intense standoff for the next two minutes. Caidyn is as stubborn as hell, but unlike the rest of his brothers, he has no issues backing down when he knows he isn't going to win.

"Fine..." he grunts out a couple of seconds later. "But you're not taking your father's truck. I don't care what Saint says, that thing is a death trap." He tosses a set of keys my way. "Take my Jeep. I filled it up last night."

He only collects half the air kisses I blow his way because he rolls over with a groan, covers his head with a blanket then commences coughing up half a lung. The duration of his coughing fit announces how poorly he is. It has me wishing I could stay and take care of him, but the reminder of how Maddox perceived things the last time we saw each other has me heading for the door before I truly consider it.

After buckling Max into his doggy seat belt, I jog around the hood of Caidyn's Jeep before slipping behind the steering wheel. Since I'm in Caidyn's car almost as much as him the past couple of months, my phone automatically syncs with the Bluetooth in his radio.

While pulling my seat belt across, I request Siri to dial a number I only added to my phone two weeks ago.

Justine answers several rings later. "Hello."

"Hey... umm... it's Demi." Don't ask me why I'm blubbering on like an idiot. I'm in the dark as much as you.

Worry overtakes the confusion in Justine's tone. "Is Maddox okay?"

Even though she can't see me, I nod. "Yes. I haven't seen him yet. I'm just leaving." I wait for her relieved sigh to give me the same level of comfort it gave her before adding, "I was calling about Caidyn. He's unwell. I would call your mom, but Caidyn mentioned she was going on a business trip this week."

Air whooshes down the line before Justine confirms, "Yes, she won't be back until Friday..." She pauses, then exhales sharply, finally clueing on to the reason for my call. "Do you want me to keep an eye on Caidyn? I could be there in around an hour."

"No," I reply a little too sharply. She's only just returned to her studies, so the last thing I want to do is encourage her to come back to a place full of bad memories. "Maddox told me how you always made him chicken noodle soup when he got the sniffles. I was wondering if you could do the same for Caidyn? I could swing by and pick it up this afternoon after I've visited Maddox." Her school is a couple of hours south of Wallens Ridge. I drive straight past the turn-off but will need to track inland by about thirty miles. It will be worth it if it benefits both Caidyn and Justine.

Some of the butterflies in my stomach stop flapping their wings when Justine replies, "Ah... sure. I'd have to go to the store first."

"Is that okay?" I ask, wary that venturing out isn't something she's comfortable doing right now but willing to push her since I believe it's for the greater good.

"Umm..." She pauses long enough for my spiking hope to careen toward the negative. "I guess that would be okay."

I smile like a loon, so very grateful my intuition was wrong this time around. "Great! Text me your details, and I'll come by after I've visited Maddox."

I tap on the steering wheel like it was announced Maddox would walk free from prison today when Justine replies with a second 'okay' before she ends our call with a faint goodbye. I understand today will be hard for her, but I'm so very pleased she's taking steps in the right direction.

It gives me hope that I'll be able to do the same.

"Today is going to be a good day, Max. I can feel it."

When he barks in agreement, I wind down the windows, then crank up the radio, confident a bit of car karaoke will make our four-hour trip fly by.

Three hours and fifty-seven minutes later, I pull into the dusty lot at the front of Wallens Ridge. It's almost midday, meaning it is far too hot for Max to stay in the car during my visit with Maddox. Our meetups may only be ten minutes long, but the darkness of Caidyn's Jeep means I could fry an egg on the hood in around eight minutes even with all the windows down. That's too close for comfort for my liking.

After snatching up Max's lead from the back seat, a bottle of water, and the water bowl I never travel without, I unbuckle Max from his seat belt. Once I have his leash clipped onto his collar, I walk him to the far back corner of the lot. A large selection of trees hide Wallens Ridge's ghastly exterior from the motorists on the freeway, and the steel fence required to keep prisoners at bay should be sturdy enough to contain a beasty dog for a couple of minutes.

Once I have Max's water bowl filled and his leash wrapped around a fence post concreted into the ground, I squat down to his level. "I cross my heart and hope to die if you be a good boy, I will buy you the fattest burger you've ever seen." I hold my hand out palm side up. "Deal."

The sweaty mess on the back of my neck is forgotten when he places his paw into my hand so we can shake on it.

"I love you, Maxxy," I whisper into his ear while squeezing his ginormous head. "I'll be back soon."

He watches me cross the parking lot before he finds the perfect patch of grass to rest his spit-foamed lips on. He isn't happy about being left behind, and neither am I, but I'm certain if push comes to shove, he'd pick a greasy burger over protecting me any day of the week. He loves their heart-attack qualities as much as Maddox.

After a final check of Max, who appears to be the size of an ant from this distance, I enter the foyer of Wallens Ridge State Penitentiary. I've barely dotted the 'i' in Petretti in the visitor log when I'm accosted by the warden. He usually makes his presence known to me at each visit, but this is the first time he's personally escorted me down the noisy corridors.

Our trek is done in silence, which doubles the alarm ringing in my ears when he requests that I take a left at the end of the corridor. I usually go right.

As my knees knock, I raise my purse to my chest before inconspicuously hunting for Caidyn's keys. A key isn't mace, but when braced between a sturdy pair of knuckles, it can be as lethal as a shank.

I grip Caidyn's Jeep's key so tightly it pinches my skin when I'm guided into a windowless room in the belly of a maximum-security prison. There's no natural lighting, no guards, and no two-way mirror, so there's no way in hell I'm staying here, but before I can make a break for it, the door I walked through is closed and locked with only me on the inside.

17

DEMI

*I*t dawns on me that I have the situation all wrong when a highly familiar voice says, "I got us twenty minutes this time." My knees tap for an entirely new reason when Maddox huskily adds, "Twenty *non-scrutinized* minutes."

After stuffing Caidyn's keys back into my purse, I spin around to face Maddox. The dams in my eyes almost spill over when he says ever so casually, "Hey."

I should have known he wouldn't be mad at me for acting a little skittish the past couple of months. Holding grudges isn't a Walsh trait. They forgive even when they shouldn't.

"Hey." Although I only say one word, there's no denying the amount of emotion it was delivered with. I was really worried he was disappointed in me. Really *really* worried.

When Maddox spots the wetness in my eyes, he flops his head to the side in a manner way too adorable for a man who's been able to grow a beard since he was fourteen. "Dem—"

I push off my feet before all my name leaves his mouth. My crash into his body is brutal, but since it's quickly chased with chuckles, gropes, and a million teeny tiny kisses, the pain soon subsides.

"This isn't why I brought you here," Maddox murmurs against my mouth while groping my breast with his big hand. "I wanted some- where private where we could talk, but I can't control myself around you."

He isn't the only one lost. When he tweaks my nipple through my bra, I yank on the elastic waistband of his pants like we're not in the underbelly of a maximum-security prison. "I need you." My words are equally breathy and desperate. "In me. Now."

When his dick springs free from his pants, I moan like I'm possessed. I love the heaviness of his cock in my hand and how my hands seem too dainty to handle so much girth and length. His cock is perfect, almost as picture-perfect as his outrageously handsome face.

When I squeeze his dick, encouraging more gooey goodness to pool on the tip, Maddox stumbles us backward until his backside finds the only piece of furniture in the room. A hard stainless steel chair.

His butt cheeks have barely graced the gleaming material for half a second when I hoist my dress up my thighs, slip my panties to the side, line up the head of his cock, then drive home.

"Fuck, Demi, fuck!" Maddox curses at the same time I throw my head back and moan. The pain of taking a man his size hurts, but it's a good pain women crave time and time again. "You feel so good, baby. Hot. Tight." He finalizes his compliment with a healthy groan.

After giving me a couple of seconds to adjust to his girth, Maddox grips my nape and hip so he can control the speed of our exchange. With his eyes bouncing between my face and overstuffed pussy, he slams his fat cock in and out of me over and over again.

There's nothing gentle about our fuck.

Nothing sweet.

We grunt like wild animals, the uncontrolled thrusts of our hips rough and without restraint. It's a blistering couple of minutes that grows even more blinding when the rim of his cock finds the sweet spot inside of me.

It usually takes a couple of perfectly crafted strokes to have me succumbing to the tingling sensation overwhelming me, but today, it only takes one, and when it's combined with Maddox finding his release, it's ten times more intense.

We're fully clothed, in a windowless room of a prison that's home to some of the world's most notorious criminals, yet we're shuddering through a set of blistering orgasms like we have the world at our feet. It's crazy but undoubtedly beautiful at the same time. Even more so when Maddox grunts out breathlessly, "Jesus Christ, I almost did a Flint."

I shouldn't laugh. It's terrible for me to do, but it can't be helped. I feel so incredibly happy right now, the woes of the past eleven months have disappeared. It's once again my childhood crush and me —exactly how it is meant to be.

The giggles springing tears to my eyes louden when Maddox arches a brow while saying, "You never, I repeat, *never* laugh about a man's sexual capabilities when his dick is still inside you." He hits me with a frisky wink to ensure I know there's not an ounce of malice to his tone. "Because if you do, he might come up with a way to keep you enslaved to him for eternity until he gets it right."

"I wish you could," I murmur before I can stop myself. "But you don't need to get it right. That was perfect."

"It was two minutes... if that. I'm so fucking ashamed of myself." Air whizzes out of his nose as he rakes his fingers through his damp-at-the-ends hair. "My brothers will never let me live it down when they find out I'm a minute man. They'll start calling me two strokes. Just you wait and see."

Confident he's playing, I slap his chest. That was most certainly the quickest sex we've had, but its speed didn't make it any less enjoyable. My womb is still cramping in the aftermaths of a fantastic orgasm. It's also been nearly a year since we've been sexually promiscuous, so a quick trigger is understandable.

Before I can tell Maddox that, a hiss whizzing through his parted lips notches my heart rate up a couple of beats. "Are you hurt?"

He stops me from shredding his shirt off him by curling his hands over mine. After smiling in a way I'll never forget, he playfully nibbles on the edge of my palms then locks his eyes with mine. "Promise me you won't get mad."

"At you? Sure. But if you're injured for anything more than exhausted muscles, all bets are off."

Maddox grins. He loves my protectiveness because he has no clue about the time I attempted to beat my uncle to death. We're still keeping secrets from each other. It hurts more than Maddox raising me off his lap so he can slide his semi-erect penis out of me and back into his pants.

When my panties slip back into place, the cotton material absorbs most of the gunk spilled at the end of our escapade, but forever a gentleman, Maddox tugs off his shirt to get what my panties miss.

I realize it isn't just his chivalry being showcased when he bobs down in front of me to clean his cum from my thighs, so are a very extensive set of tattoos. On his back, torso, and stomach. He even has a handful of new designs on his arms.

"Is that…" I swallow, then try again, too choked up with emotions not to need a quick breather. "Is that Max?"

Maddox nods before he twists his forearm so I can see how the tattoo artist included Max's sloppy jowls in the picture. "Max took around an hour, but this one was over several sessions."

My hand shoots up to cover my mouth when he shows me the large tattoo covering a majority of his left shoulder. It's a photograph I have of my dad and me. It was taken the week before he killed himself. The tattoo artist captured him so perfectly, even the gentle giant glint his eyes forever held can be seen.

"I miss you, Daddy," I whisper to heaven while wiping crazily at my face to ensure it's dry.

I love Maddox's thoughtfulness and how he didn't exclude my father during his epic declaration of love, but I'm still confused. How can a prison inmate get such high-quality tattoos? I've heard of back-yard jobs, but that isn't what Maddox's are. They're art.

"Were these all done the past month?"

After peering up at me, Maddox shakes his head. "The ones on my back were a couple of months back. But the arms, chest, and the one on my right hip were within the last two months." He clears away the mess between my legs before standing to his feet. "Henley has mad skills, and he keeps his equipment hygienically sterile. I wouldn't have let him near me with a needle if he wasn't legit."

"It's obvious he knows what he's doing." I trace my fingers over one of his tattoos I've never traced before, smiling when I take in the amount of detail Henley put into each piece. "I'm just curious how he has access to his equipment here."

Maddox's sigh is soundless but robust enough to ruffle the sprouts of hair now hanging past my ears. With my haircut being twelve months ago, it now sits in a bob just below my ears.

"Because we fooled around for a minute or two, I don't have the time to go into all the details..." He doesn't give me the chance to issue a plea or declare it was longer than a minute. He just continues talking, "But you deserve to know what's going on. It was wrong of me to keep it from you."

A squeak pops from my mouth when he plants his backside on the chair we had sex on, then pulls me until I'm sitting on his lap. I listen intently when he tells me how the favors he does for Agent Moses and the warden award him certain privileges—better meals, a better cell, and better one-on-one time.

He holds me a little firmer during his last confession.

"Almost every favor exchanged is of a non-monetary amount." He drags his finger down my nose, halving the tension bristling between us in an instant before starting again, "Naturally, I tried to have our arrangement changed from monthly to weekly." He works his jaw side to side to lessen the anger in his voice when he says, "Agent Moses couldn't get the warden to budge on his terms, ours is the first of its kind, then I realize it was kind of selfish of me to expect you to drive ten hours every week just to see me for ten minutes—"

"Totally worth it."

He grins. "But this month, I managed to get them pushed out to twenty minutes."

"Does that mean you'll get fewer tattoo sessions now?"

He mutters something about me being cute when I'm jealous

before he shakes his head. "Henley is also a lifer." I want to correct him that he isn't stuck here for life, but he continues talking, foiling my ruse. "He'd go nuts without his equipment. Agent Moses knows that, so he uses it to his advantage."

Curious, I ask, "What is Henley giving Agent Moses in exchange for his gear?"

Maddox licks his lips before breathing out slowly. "Information that could get him into a lot of trouble." I nuzzle into his hand when he drags his thumb across my kiss-swollen lips. "The ripple effect shouldn't get anywhere near you, but I need you to be careful, okay?"

"Always," I reply without hesitation. "And you too. If Henley is spilling secrets while you're around, you could be implicated with him."

He smiles like there's no possibility he'd be dragged into Henley's mess before he eventually jerks up his chin. Then, not even a second later, he hands the invisible confession baton to me. "Is there anything you want to share?"

I was afraid this would happen, but alas, I'm a sucker for being honest when being awarded honesty. "There are a couple of things I've been meaning to tell you." Before a single concern I see in his eyes can be expressed, I pull the band-aid off in one fell swoop. "I moved back into my family home, Saint has been fighting in an underground fight circuit the past four months, and I've been recruiting fighters for my uncle's circuit a little longer than that."

"Demi..." The disappointment in Maddox's tone hurts more than how hard he's gripping me. "My agreement specifically states that you *cannot* work for your uncle in any form of the word."

"I'm not working for him." When he attempts to interrupt me, I talk faster. "I am technically a private contractor."

"That's the same fucking thing." Needing to pace out his annoyance, he stands to his feet, places me onto the chair, then commences pacing back and forth. "He will use this against you. He will find a way to turn it on its head, and then you'll once again be indebted to him."

"That won't happen. I've made sure of it."

I take a step back when he shouts, "How did you make sure of it, Demi? Did you just take his word for it? Or better yet, did you ask him to pinkie promise that he won't hurt you again."

I'm stunned by how swiftly our conversation went from sexually intense to dangerously volatile, but it won't stop me from telling him how much of a dick he is being. "You're being an ass—"

His glare cuts me off more than his shouted words. "And you're acting like an idiot! I came to this fucking hellhole so you could be free, and what do you do the instant your wings can *finally* expand? You run straight back to him."

"For you!" I fire back, my voice as loud as his. "The sale of your parents' house with the two hundred thousand you put away wasn't close to the amount he requested to get you out of here. We needed more!"

I realize my error when Maddox chokes out, "What? My parents sold their home?" When he reads the truth in my eyes, he asks, "Why, Demi? Why would you let them do that?"

Mindful my hole has already been dug, I set to work on taking down those closest to me. It is another horrible Petretti trait. "It was Caidyn's idea."

I didn't realize a heart could be broken by a growl until now. "You dragged him into this after I specifically asked you not to?"

"No," I deny with a shake of my head. "You asked me to keep him out of this *months* after he got involved. He has been a part of it since you were sentenced."

Maddox stares me dead set in the eyes. "Then why didn't you tell me back then that I was too late?"

I try to answer him. My lips twitch, but not a word spills from my mouth.

My silence maims him more than anything I could have said. "Because you chose to lie."

I drag my hand under my nose before lifting my chin. "Yes, but not because I wanted to hurt you. I was trying to stop you from being hurt."

"By lying to me." The disgusted mask I was anticipating earlier slips over his face before my very eyes. "Shows how well you know me, doesn't it?" When I step closer to him, he cuts me off by slicing his hand through the air. "Don't, Demi... I just... *fuck!*"

His nostrils flare as he sucks in some big breaths. It isn't like him not to show restraint when he's angry, but siding with criminals wasn't on his dossier only months ago either. He's worked up, and for once, he's finally taking it out on the person deserving of his wrath.

Once he has the redness on his face settled, he locks his eyes with mine. The pain in them cuts through me like a knife. "Where are they living?"

I don't want to answer him, but I must. "In Hopeton."

"Hopeton," he mutters to himself. "Of course they are."

His laugh doesn't belong to a sane man. It's unhinged and brimming with danger that becomes undeniable when I interrupt his request for the guards to bring Caidyn to our secret room. "Caidyn isn't here. He's at home because he is unwell."

When he rakes his fingers through his hair, I grab his wrist, afraid his anger will pluck his head bald. My heart falls from my ribcage when he pulls away from me like my touch scorched his skin.

"I need a minute to wrap my head around this. I can't do that with you right there," he mutters under his breath when he spots the tears burning my eyes. "It's just..." This is the first time I'm grateful for our lack of communicating skills. If he had finished his sentence, I'm reasonably sure he would have ended our relationship.

"Okay. I'll go."

I snatch up my purse from the floor before making a beeline for the door. A sob escapes my lips when Maddox seizes my wrist before I make it halfway out. He doesn't beg me to stay or tell me he loves me. He places a single kiss on the top of my head because even while angry, he can't risk leaving what could be our last goodbye unsaid.

"Goodbye," I mumble on a sob before I race for the exit.

I'm so eager for fresh air, I push past the guards who usually guide my walk, then sprint down the corridors. I make it to the front entrance in a record-breaking twenty seconds, and I dash across the dusty lot even faster than that.

My speed is so brutal, the movements of my feet are too fast for me to keep up with. I stumble in my stilettos, re-jarring the ankle I hurt when I fell in a pothole. I doubt it's sprained, but it hurts enough not even Caidyn could give me hell for requesting some form of pain relief.

"Come on, Max," I say to him when I reach the fence line, shocked he has his back facing me. My knees are cut up from the gravel, and tears are streaming down my face. He should be on high alert.

At the same time I discover the reason for Max's ignorance, the lady he's staring at in the yard of Wallens Ridge spots his watch. Dark strands of hair fall into her face when she adjusts her line of sight to make sure she isn't mistaking what she is seeing.

"Max?" she murmurs loud enough for me to hear before she pushes off her feet to head toward the fence line.

Panicked that I'm about to lose everything I've ever loved sees me snatching up Max's lead and dragging him toward Caidyn's Jeep.

"Come on, Max, *please*. It's time to go," I beg when he pulls me in the opposite direction I want him to go. "Don't you want that big burger I promised you? You won't find that here. She can't give you that." I know I'm reflecting my anguish onto the unknown lady, but beggars can't be choosers. "Please, Max."

When he fails to listen to my pleas, I lift my drenched eyes to the lady cautiously approaching us. "Please stop. He's all I have. Please don't take him away from me." I'm blubbering like an idiot. It can't be helped. I am truly heartbroken. First, I was rejected by Maddox, and now Max wants to leave me too.

The unchecked tears streaming down my face stop the mousy-haired lady in her tracks. She bounces her eyes between Max and me for several seconds before she eventually notches up her chin. "Promise me you'll take good care of him." The wind whipping between us chops up her words, but there's no doubting what she said. It was as confident as my reply.

"I promise," I pledge without pause for thought. "I'll never let him out of my sight."

She takes a couple of seconds to contemplate the authenticity of my pledge before she eventually spins on her heels and heads back toward the main yard area.

It takes another five minutes for me to convince Max to come home with me, and even then, he leaps in the back seat instead of the passenger seat, proving not even he can't stand the sight of me right now.

18

MADDOX

*T*he warden's eyes lift to mine when I storm into his office. He remarks about how he thought he'd have to order the guards to drag me out of my first private one-on-one meeting with Demi, but I'm too blinded with anger to take a bite out of the bait he's dangling in front of me.

Not only did my parents sell their home, the very thing they worked tirelessly for the past thirty years, but Demi's uncle also has his claws back into her. That doesn't just break the agreement I made with Col. It wholly fucking up ends it.

I came here to save Demi.

I refuse to stay if my sacrifice was for nothing.

The warden's mouth itches when I snatch up his phone from the desk, but not a word spills from his lips. He isn't stupid. I may not pocket a dime for the numerous favors I do for him and Agent Moses, but I make them a fortune. He better remember that when I signal for him to get the fuck out of his office so I can hold my conversation with Ezra in private.

He leaves, albeit hesitantly, then, two seconds later, Ezra answers my call.

"Wallens Ridge now!" When he attempts to fire an objection, my bad mood gets the better of me. "I wasn't asking, Ezra. You either come to Wallens Ridge now, or I'll start singing like a fucking canary."

A deep sigh rustles down the line. "If you do that, I can't guarantee your family won't suffer the consequences of your actions."

"Suffer how, Ezra? Watching their youngest son become an inmate at a maximum-security prison? Selling their family home? Or how about moving to fucking Hopeton? How much worse could it get for them?"

My anger is sideswiped when he mutters, "How does death rate on your scale?" Now that he has my attention, he speaks more calmly. "I know this isn't something you want to hear right now, Ox, but I need you to be patient. Times are changing. This will all be over soon."

"It won't be over until Col is dead."

My emotions don't know which way to swing when he replies, "That's precisely my point." He lowers his voice to a whisper. "Dimitri is growing impatient. I have a feeling he's going to act sooner rather than later."

Months ago, his comment would have given me hope. Today, it fills me with anger. "Dimitri is in another country. He's all but given up on overtaking his father's reign."

I hear Ezra scrub at the five o'clock his jaw holds no matter the time of the day. "Have you not seen Dimitri yet?"

He can't see me, but I shake my head, too stunned to talk. He's speaking as if Dimitri is stateside. Agent Moses assured me only last month that he isn't.

I grip the phone like it's Agent Moses's neck when it dawns on me what's happening. That lying fucking snake hung me out to dry —again.

I can't wait to return the favor.

Ezra takes my growl as a response to his question. "I thought Dimitri would have stopped by months ago. There have been numerous developments the past six months."

"Developments I don't give a flying fuck about unless they affect Demi. Her uncle reneging on our deal affects her!"

His shallow snarl warns me he's getting close to losing his cool. However, the temperament of his voice remains the same. "Things aren't exactly as you are seeing them, but if you can give me a couple of hours, I'm sure I can give you a clearer picture of proceedings."

I'm about to tell him he has an hour, but his next sentence shuts down my anger by immediately replacing it with worry. "While I do that, why don't you work out who is allowing Demi to dose herself up with oxycodone, because this time, I can guarantee you it isn't her uncle."

19

DEMI

$\mathcal{W}$ith my mood dangerously teetering off a very steep cliff and my ankle throbbing from my fall, I hit the 'decline call' button on the console of Caidyn's Jeep, silencing a third call from the warden's office at Wallens Ridge in the past ten minutes before steering Caidyn's Jeep down the off-ramp he refused to take six weeks ago. I've had enough heartache for today. One more thing will see all my marbles spilled. Considering I only have a handful left, I'd rather save Warden Mattue's pompous rant for another time.

Max lifts his head when I pull into a disabled parking bay at the front of a twenty-four-hour pharmacy to investigate where we are, but he doesn't follow me out when I peel out of the driver's seat and hobble to the front door. He's too depressed to function, and I plan to join him at Depressionville once I have the goods needed to fix both the gaping hole in the middle of my chest and my stupid ankle.

"I'll be back in a minute, Max," I mumble, mindful of the pledge I made only moments ago. I'm not supposed to leave him out of my sight, but if I were honest, I don't see this being the first promise I break this afternoon.

Almost robotic-like, I pull open the door of the pharmacy and walk inside. I'm greeted by a smiling staff member two lengthy strides later. "Hello, how can I help you?"

Not having the time nor the patience to ask politely, I snap out, "Is it possible to have a prescription filled without having the paperwork with me?"

The man I'd guess to be in his mid-thirties cocks a brow. "That depends. Was your original prescription filled here?" When I lift my head, he smiles. "And is your physician local?"

His smile tapers when I shake my head. "He's from Hopeton."

"Hopeton?" he confirms, his brow raising more in suspicion than eagerness to help. "In Florida?" When I dip my chin, the demeanor on his face changes in an instant. He's no longer flirty and helpful. He looks pissed and scared. "What medication are you after?"

I swallow the brick in my throat before replying, "Oxycodone."

"Right." He tries to shut down the disdain on his face, but there's no denying it. "*If* you have a prescription, it will come up in the system." He walks around the counter, stopping once he reaches an outdated computer. "What is the name of the patient?"

"Demi." I spell it out for him in case he is as deaf as he is rude. "Petretti. P-E-T—"

My words snag halfway up my throat when his eyes snap to mine. "Petretti?"

I don't need to nod. The fear forming in his eyes tells me he's familiar with my last name. It's the same petrified glint Donny had when my uncle arrived at his pizzeria in the middle of the night to 'negotiate.' It's the look of a man with a ton to lose but with no ability to alter the outcome.

After slamming shut the keyboard his fingers were busily tapping on only seconds ago, he walks back around to my side of the counter. "We don't stock oxycodone here."

When he grabs my arm to walk me to the door, I yank myself out of his hold. It sends pain rocketing up my leg, but I refuse to be roughly handled by a stranger. "I have a prescription—"

"That will not be served here."

He all but shoves me out the door before he latches the lock into place, then spins the open sign to closed. He stops dragging his eyes over the empty parking lot when I slam my fist on the glass in annoyance. I'm in pain, and I have a current prescription for painkillers, so how can he deny my business?

My anger switches to regret when he begs, "Please don't tell him you came here. We are a legitimate business. I swear to you. We can't afford to go under a second time."

"I'm not—"

"Please," he begs again, too scared to give me the chance to speak.

Nodding, I take a step back. The fear pulsating out of him weakens when it dawns on him that I'm retreating. He's so clutched by panic, he has no clue I'm not the enemy. His disbelief doubles the clamminess slicking my skin and has me acting so erratically, I dive into Caidyn's Jeep without taking into consideration my throbbing ankle. The only good that comes from it is Max's attention when he hears the whimper I couldn't hold in. He jumps into the front passenger seat before he licks one side of my face. His reminder that he still loves me coats my cheek with slobber, giving me the perfect cover for the handful of salty blobs I wish weren't splashing down my face.

"I'll take you to visit her one day, Max. I just need to get my head screwed on straight first."

Proof he can understand me is undeniable when he does a second lick up my cheek. He then rests his slobbery jowls on my thigh, where they would remain if it weren't for the quickest tap of knuckles on the steel next to my head.

The police officer who tried to woo me months ago has his hip propped on the driver's side door of Caidyn's Jeep. His arms are folded in front of his chest, and he's smirking smugly. "You do know I could fine you for leaving an animal in the car unattended. It's at least eighty today. Most likely one hundred in there."

Guilt is the main emotion highlighted in my reply, even with me trying to weasel myself out of the stupid situation I find myself in. "It isn't like I had any other choice. He refused to leave the car, and I had to get..." My words trail off when I realize I don't have to explain myself to him. He cheats on his wife, who lovingly packs his lunch every morning. He couldn't possibly understand the hell I've been through today. "If you want to fine me, fine me. I don't care. *Especially not after the day I've had.*"

It dawns on me that I said my last sentence out loud when he asks, "What happened today?"

"Nothing. I just..." Realizing I need to give him something to get him off my back, I blubber out. "I fell and twisted my ankle."

"Again?" he says with a chuckle. "Or is that your go-to excuse to cover your addiction to painkillers?" I shouldn't be able to hear his mocking rile over Max's growl warning he's overstayed his welcome. Unfortunately, I hear both his snarky comment and his even more venomous second jab. "How long have you been taking oxycodone? From your jittery response and the desperation in your eyes, I'm going to say since you sprained your ankle in the alleyway bordering KC's gym."

With my mood in a ditch, I get bitchy. "Not that I need to explain myself to you, but I didn't just *sprain* my ankle. I tore a ligament. It was very painful."

He nods before twisting his lips. "I'm sure it was... when it happened."

Over people continuously lecturing me, I dump my purse onto the seat Max's bottom hasn't touched for the past two minutes, then commence guiding the driver's side window into its slot, hopeful it will give Officer Packwood the hint that our conversation is over.

"Careful," Officer Packwood cautions while watching the window glide into place. "I wouldn't want your hand getting pinched by the glass. With both your hand and foot out of commission, how will you manage the remainder of your four-hour commute?"

After hitting him with an evil glare, I shove my key into the ignition column, then shift the gearstick into reverse. I'm about to plant my foot onto the gas pedal when Officer Packwood presses something onto the window separating us, distracting me. It's a business card for a family doctor in Hopeton.

"He won't ask any questions," he assures me, his tone as smug as the gleam in his eyes. "He'd rather his patients get what they need than be in pain."

I stare at the card like my first thought wasn't to roll down the window and snatch it out of his hand. I don't want him thinking I'm desperate, even though I am.

After a beat, I give in. I roll down the window even quicker than I begged it to climb.

"Nuh-uh." Officer Packwood yanks the card out of my reach before I can secure it in my hand. "He won't ask any questions, but you need to be upfront about some things."

"Such as?" I ask, too anxious to act anything but. Today couldn't end fast enough. I'm at my absolute limit at pretending I'm okay. I am drowning, and this card could very well be my only life jacket.

"Such as..." Officer Packwood follows along nicely, "... your health insurance information. He'll need to run it through the system. If it's fake like the tags on this Jeep, you will leave his practice empty-handed. Do you understand?" He waits for me to nod before he hands me the card. "Tell his receptionist I sent you. That will get you straight in."

"Thank you." The gratitude in my reply hides my shock that the tags on Caidyn's Jeep are stolen. He's always been the more level-headed one of the Walsh brothers. Assisting in the management of an underground fight circuit isn't legal, but I thought that would be as far as his criminal proficiencies would extend. I guess I'm not the only one pushing boundaries. One of my daddy's favorite quotes was, "You'll never know your limits unless you push yourself to them."

I've been pushed and pushed and pushed for years, so it's only fair I start to push back. Fingers crossed I come out of the carnage with fewer scars than my insides are now holding. They've been nicked so badly the past twelve months I don't believe even Maddox could fix them now.

Two hours later, the burn of the card Officer Packwood handed me becomes too much to bear. I yank it out of my pocket like it's the solution to everything before punching in the number handwritten on the back into the dashboard of Caidyn's Jeep.

A friendly female voice answers a couple of rings later, "Dr. Terry's office, this is Nicky. How can I help you?"

"Oh... hi. My name is Demi." I stop my introduction to give myself a quick pep talk. Only once I'm convinced I sound like the adult I am, do I commence talking again. "I recently fell, reinflaming an old injury. An officer who assisted me at the scene gave me this number. He thought you'd be able to help."

Her pause is only short, but it doubles the knot in my stomach. "Certainly. Can I ask which officer recommended our practice?"

"Officer Packwood," I answer. "Daniel Packwood."

"Wonderful. Let me see what appointments we have available. Is the matter urgent?"

To her, perhaps not.

To me, very much so.

"Yes, I am in a lot of pain."

"Okay." Fingers tapping over a keyboard sound down the line before she murmurs, "How does tomorrow morning at eleven o'clock sound?"

With it being a little after three in the afternoon, I should be pleased Dr. Terry has managed to squeeze me in within twenty-four-hours, but I'm not. My ankle is throbbing, and don't get me started on my heart.

"Is there anything available this afternoon?"

I picture the receptionist shaking her head when a woosh sounds down the line. "The cancellation you're filling was only called through minutes ago. If you had been ten minutes earlier, your appointment wouldn't have been filled until next month."

"Then I guess I'll see you tomorrow at eleven." I try to keep the desperation out of my tone. I miserably fail.

"Wonderful." Keyboard tapping continues as she says, "Let me grab your details so I can place you into our system. It will mean less paperwork when you arrive tomorrow morning."

Over the next two minutes, I give the receptionist everything she needs—my full name, cell phone number, residential address, and any health insurance details. Her politeness has me feeling so good about my appointment tomorrow that after disconnecting our call, I tackle the mammoth number of unanswered text messages on my cell phone.

I scroll past the numerous missed calls from the warden's office at Wallens Ridge, only stopping once I reach a message from Justine advising that Caidyn's chicken noodle soup is ready for collection.

With how deranged I feel, I should say that I've caught what Caidyn has, so I can't stop by. Instead, I punch in the address she attached to her message, then pull off the interstate.

I don't want to disappoint another member of the Walsh family.

An hour later, Justine greets me at the front of her dorm. She has a thermos in her hand and a welcoming smile. Although almost every inch of her skin is covered with a long-sleeve shirt, a scarf, and a pair of body-hugging leggings, her grin alone gains her the attention of numerous sophomores around her. She has dozens of scars, but her beauty is so skin deep, I doubt the number of admiring glances she's getting would dwindle if she were wearing a skimpy dress more appropriate for this time of the year.

I can't say the same thing about me.

I feel horrid, so I can only imagine how horrendous I look.

After accepting the thermos from Justine, I nudge my head to her dorm. "Would you mind if I use the bathroom? I've been driving for hours."

"Oh, yeah, sorry. I should have offered. Come in." She pulls open the double glass door before waving her hand toward the front door of her first-floor apartment. "The bathroom is the second door on the left once you pass the kitchen."

When she attempts to follow me inside, fragments of my conversation with Officer Packwood filter through my head. "Could you please keep an eye on Max for me? He's latched in with his doggy belt, but I doubt it will keep him contained if someone walks by with a greasy bag of takeout." I inwardly curse myself for my stupidity when panic crosses Justine's features. "He's harmless. I just..."

Having no excuse for my stupidity, I smile through a grimace before entering her apartment. It's nice and cozy, but it exposes the Walshs are still penny-pinching for Maddox's sake.

A reason for my topsy turvy moods is unearthed when I lower my panties over the toilet bowl. A byproduct of Maddox's climax isn't the only thing slicking the cotton material. Blood is evident as well. I've been waiting for my period to arrive for the past three weeks. I knew I wasn't pregnant—you need to be sexually active for there to be a chance of conception—so I brushed its disappearance off as a stressful couple of weeks.

Embarrassed I've been caught out for the third time today, I stuff a wad of toilet paper into my panties before moving toward the vanity sink. When my rummage through the medicine cabinet about the cracked sink fails to come up with the goods I'm seeking, I bob down to the cabinets below the sink.

"Come on, you've got to be here somewhere," I murmur to myself when my hunt for womanly products comes up empty-handed.

When I stand back onto my feet, not only do cramps manifest but so do the products I was seeking. They're stacked on the dresser in Justine's room like she took advantage of her trip to the store to restock on more than ingredients for chicken noodle soup.

Excluding Sloane, I never had a female influence growing up. Since Sloane was from a well-to-do family, we never openly discussed dithering cycles, bloating, cramping, or any of those other horrible side effects of being a woman.

I don't see that changing today either, so instead of asking Justine if I can borrow a tampon, I check to see if the coast is clear before sneaking into her room. Her bathroom is a two-way design, meaning you can enter and exit via two different sides.

My brisk strides slacken when I spot a canister next to a pack of tampons. I try to ignore the pharmaceutical-labeled cylinder. I tell myself time and time again to borrow a tampon then leave with some dignity left intact, but before the first suggestion can filter through my head, I snatch up the canister and drag my eyes across the label.

"Oxycodone," I murmur to myself, my voice a cross of panic and excitement. The solution for the pain in my heart, stomach, and ankle is directly in front of me, but my name isn't on the label, so would it be wrong of me to act as if they're mine?

After a tense day, I say whatever the devil on my shoulder wants to hear. My ankle is throbbing, and the canister is full even with the prescription being filled over a month ago. I'm sure Justine wouldn't mind if I borrowed a tablet or two. I'll only borrow enough to tie me over until my appointment with Dr. Terry tomorrow, then I'll follow his advice on pain management to the T. I swear.

My plan to only take enough tablets to get me through until tomorrow falls wayward when Justine calls my name. "Max is getting restless." She sounds way too close for me to believe she's still outside babysitting Max and way too scared. If the shadow under the door is any indication of her closeness, she's seconds from walking in on me creeping around in her room.

Panicked, I stuff her prescription into the pocket in my dress before exiting via the door in front of me. In the haste of my bad decision, I enter the hallway via her bedroom instead of the bathroom.

"I couldn't remember which door led to the hallway," I blubber out nervously, feeling immensely guilty. Her canister of oxycodone is burning a hole in my pocket even worse than Dr. Terry's card did, but since I'd have to admit I have a problem to return it to its rightful owner, I act as if I can't feel its scalds.

Justine eyes me with suspicion before she hooks her thumb to the door she's standing next to. "It's that one." She licks her parched lips before asking, "Did you go to the bathroom? I don't recall hearing the toilet flush."

"Yeah... I... ah... went." I push past her before making a beeline for the door. "But I better get back on the road. It's almost dark."

"It's not even four," she murmurs while following me outside. When I snatch up the thermos I dumped on her entryway table, she seizes my wrist in a gentle hold. "Is everything okay, Demi? You look very upset."

You have no idea how hard it is to talk when all you want to do is cry. I'm so ashamed of the person I've become, but that shame is also the reason I can't tell her what's really wrong. "I'm fine. I am just... *tired.*"

Justine doesn't utter another syllable, I don't give her a chance. I'm in the driver's seat of Caidyn's Jeep in under a second, then racing down the street two seconds after that.

The guilt associated with my brisk departure should have me waiting a couple of blocks before I pull her prescription out of my pocket, but unfortunately, I'm spiraling too quickly to realize how far down the rabbit warren I've fallen. I rip off the lid of her prescription and toss down a handful of the pills before I can make sense of anything.

They calm me in an instant, meaning I'm left blindsided when my arrival home has me stumbling onto an emergency Walsh brother meeting. They hold them here instead of their family home, so Justine and their mother are left in the dark about the sordid things the male half of their family have been doing the past twelve months.

"Sorry."

My attempt to tiptoe to my room is thwarted when Caidyn says, "This meeting concerns you, Demi, so you may as well join us."

My heart constricts when Maddox's voice sounds out of Caidyn's cell phone a nanosecond later, "Is she there?" Frustration is echoing in his tone, but he sounds worried as well.

"She's here," Landon answers on Caidyn's behalf, his reply clipped and stern.

Things have been tense with us for a year, but it irritates me more than usual today. I hate what happened to Justine, and I begged for Maddox not to take my uncle's offer to do a seven-year stint to free me from his clutch, but neither of those things were my choice, and if I could change the outcome of them now, I would in a heartbeat.

I guess to Landon, the perfect solution would have been for me to walk off the cliff with my father. That would have solved all his problems long before they became an issue.

With that snippet of information souring my mood even more, I say, "I can't deal with this right now. I'm not in the right head space."

My eyes snap to Landon when he interrupts, "Because you're high on prescription painkillers?"

"No," I blatantly deny. "I haven't filled a prescription in days."

It feels like the world caves in on me when Maddox asks, "Is that why you took Justine's prescription, Demi? Because you ran out of pills?"

I want to lie. I want to say his brothers have exaggerated everything and that Justine's canister slipped into my pocket by accident, but I can't fire another lie from my mouth. The shame on their faces already has me on the backfoot, not to mention when Landon rips my purse out of my hand to shamefully call me out as the liar I am.

Justine's pill canister is the first thing to topple to the floor. It's closely followed by my cell phone that shows I didn't just ignore Warden Mattue's calls the past hour, Justine's went unanswered as well.

I lift my watering eyes to Caidyn when he says, "Demi, Justine called us because she's worried about you."

"I'm fine."

Maddox's sigh shatters my heart beyond repair.

"I am. I'm just..."

I got nothing.

Not a single thing.

I thought the day my dad died would remain the worst day in my life. Now I'm not so sure. The man I love is beyond disappointed in me, his sister most likely thinks I'm an addict like Officer Packwood does, and his brothers are looking at me in disgust.

Today has broken me. It has shattered me beyond repair. I

honestly don't feel like I can come back from this, and it has me saying the last thing I thought I'd ever say, "It's just one of those..."

I can't force the remaining word out of my mouth. I'm in a world of hurt, and I am extremely ashamed of the woman I've become the past year, but if I don't have Maddox, I will have *nothing*. It makes me selfish, but that's okay. My dad always said you're allowed to be selfish when it comes to love. I've always wondered if that was why he killed himself. He wanted to be selfish just once, and what better way to do that than to fully erase his pain?

"Demi..." Maddox murmurs like he can sense my tears from hundreds of miles away. "Talk to me, baby. Tell me what's going on. If we don't start communicating, all the good we've done will unravel."

"It hurts," I stammer out before I can stop myself, the pain in my chest too perverse to ignore for a second longer.

"Where?" Maddox asks, his voice softening with understanding.

I accept Caidyn's cell phone he's holding out for me before replying, "I fell in the parking lot. It re-flared my old ankle injury."

Nothing but empathy resonates in Maddox's tone when he asks, "Is that why you took Justine's prescription? Because your ankle hurts?"

I nod my head at the same time I whisper, "No..." I exhale before confessing something I shouldn't. "They were for my heart."

Maddox's sigh is silent this time around, but I'm still aware of its existence.

"I hadn't planned to take them all. I just..." Out of excuses, I give straight-up honesty a whirl. "I wanted to numb the pain in my chest." When I plonk onto the couch, the mess in my nose almost spills out. "It's easier to swallow tablets than admit I'm struggling."

As I swipe the back of my hand across my top lip to ensure the contents in my nose remain put, Caidyn ushers Saint and Landon outside. Landon isn't pleased with his request for their meeting to reconvene at another time, but Saint is more than happy to miss the shit-fest most people call a deep and meaningful conversation.

Once I'm confident Maddox is the sole recipient of my confession,

I blubber out, "I'll try harder. I-I'm not addicted to popping pain medication. I'm just having a bad—"

"Year?" Maddox interrupts.

"Something like that," I reply with a half snivel, half giggle. It's the worst time for me to smile, but you didn't hear the jest in Maddox's tone. He could be deflecting his anguish with humor again, but since it halves the tension bristling between us, I have more appreciation of his unusual traits.

I hear him scrub at his cropped beard before a chair rolling across floorboards projects down the line. It has me curious as to where he is. The only part of Wallens Ridge that has polished floorboards is the reception area. "It's okay to admit you're struggling. The past year has been unprecedented. We're all struggling to keep our heads above water. Even Caidyn."

When I raise my eyes, Caidyn dips his chin in agreement. The flu he's battling has added to the puffiness of his eyes, but dark rims have been circling them for almost a year now. He looks as exhausted as I feel.

My eyes return to the screen of Caidyn's phone when Maddox pledges, "I'll make this right, Demi. I will do whatever it takes to fix this. Us. *You*. And we will do it together."

None of the burden for my fuck-ups belong on his shoulders, but in all honesty, I'm too tired for another argument. Today has been one bad thing after another. I'm drained, hormonal, and reasonably sure a week of sleep won't fix the bags under my eyes, so instead of pulling up my big girl panties and taking responsibility for my mistakes, I take the coward's way out.

"Okay," I murmur a couple of seconds later. "But can we commence that tomorrow? I'm too tired to think straight. Those two minutes really wore me out."

Maddox's chuckle is only half its strength, but it's still a nice thing to hear. "All right. Give me back to Caidyn for a few, then I'll come tuck you in."

I'm aware he means in the spiritual sense, but my heart still skips a beat at the thought of him walking through the front door to physically undertake his pledge. The increase it caused my pulse is heard in my reply, "Okay. I love you."

The weight on my shoulders feels nowhere near as intense when he mutters without pause for thought, "I love you back, Demi. Always."

20

MADDOX

I'm not going to lie. The rattle of my hands is felt up my arm when Demi hands Caidyn his phone. The woman I've been crushing on since second grade came close to saying words that would have completely ended me. They expose how much she's struggling and how badly I fucked up today when I requested a moment to think.

There's no quiet in Wallens Ridge. Not a single moment of peace. The grind never ends, and the crunching of the cogs became more apparent when my desperation to hold Demi for longer than ten minutes saw me doing shit I swore I'd never do.

Over the past two months, I've been feared more than I have been respected. My presence instills panic instead of calm. I've become the very essence of the man I swore to save Demi from, all the while endeavoring to keep her at my side, fighting a battle we will never win.

How can I pledge to protect her from a monster, only to become a monster myself?

I can't, and that's why this needs to end. I'm just praying like fuck I can still see the light at the end of the tunnel, or nothing I've done the past twelve months will be worth anything. I'll once again be forced to watch proceedings unfold via the sidelines.

I hear Caidyn's Adam's apple bob up and down when I ask, "How much money is left from the sale of our parents' house?" When nothing but silence resonates down the line, I coerce him into a conversation. "I don't give a fuck about what you did or did not suggest for them to do, Caidyn, we will have that discussion at a more appropriate time. I just need to know how much money is in the kitty?"

It feels like I'm punched in the gut when he replies, "None."

"None? How the fuck can there be none left? The house was valued in the millions."

"Believing it would benefit you quicker, Mom took a cash offer that—"

"Dramatically lowered the asking price," I interrupt, annoyed but also understanding of my mom's frame of mind at the time. She never thought she'd have to pay bail for one of her children, much less fund legal expenses exceeding one hundred thousand dollars.

I can't see Caidyn, but I imagine him dipping his chin when a rustle sounds down the line. "I didn't know Demi wanted all the funds together before paying off her uncle, so I cashed the check and deposited it into Col's account." On the assumption Demi aired all his dirty laundry today, he adds, "We have a few thousand put away from Saint's fights, and about twenty thousand left of the original two hundred thousand you put away."

"Only twenty thousand?" I ask, my tone as high as my brow. Demi is frugal with money. She penny-pinches more than our parents did when they were saving to purchase the block of land their family home was built on, so I'm not only shocked she burned through so much cash in a short period of time, I'm worried. You can get anything with the right amount of money. Drugs. Guns. Oxycodone. You can even make an entire family disappear, hence the reason I'm crunching numbers. "Owen agreed to work on a flat fee."

"Yes, he did," Caidyn agrees. "That wasn't where the money went. It was put toward an expense none of us were planning but wanted to occur more than anything." I wait, knowing there's more, and am proven right when he says a couple of seconds later, "Demi paid the remainder of Justine's college tuition."

Although I am not surprised by his comment, Demi is as generous as she is beautiful, something doesn't add up. "Justine had a scholarship."

"Had being the operative word," Caidyn replies. "She took too much time off. They granted her leave for as long as they could, but eventually, the funding got redirected to more appropriate candidates." He licks his lips before adding, "Demi is aware her generosity could set back your release by a year or two, but she's also hopeful it could shorten your time behind bars. Justine switched her studies from architecture to criminal defense. You know how stubborn she is when she sets her mind to something. She'll have you out by Christmas... *once she's graduated.*"

I'm confused and grateful at the same time, but since curiosity is always my strongest emotion, I go with that first. "Demi is paying for my release?"

I was unaware you could hear brows pulling together until now. "Yes," Caidyn answers, his tone as high as I am picturing his dark brows. "Did she not tell you that?"

I shake my head, truly stunned. With my mind hazed by all the information Demi bombarded it with hours ago, I haven't had the chance to sit down and contemplate what Demi was paying her uncle for. I knew it wouldn't have been for anything good, but I had no clue it centered around my incarceration.

Too curious to discount, I ask, "How much did he request?"

My heart rate spikes as fast as my hope when he answers, "A little over three million. We've sliced it down to one point one the past twelve months."

"One point one," I murmur to myself. Months ago, that would have seemed like an unachievable figure, but after seeing the numbers Agent Moses has flashed around the past couple of months, it seems like barely a drop of water in the ocean. It isn't an amount I can get overnight, but it could be possible within a couple of months. I just have no clue if Demi's mental well-being can wait that long.

I guess there's only one way to find out.

"I need you to find out *exactly* the terms Demi agreed to. If there's a timeframe, who it will affect if it goes through, or if there will be an aftermath of any kind." Caidyn stops jotting down everything I'm saying when I whisper, "And I need you to do it quietly. If people inside these walls find out I may have a way out, they'll try and stop it from happening."

I'm not being presumptuous when I say I'm an extremely valuable asset in the prison system underworld. My dependency on Demi sees me doing anything Agent Moses and Warden Mattue have suggested the past nine months, and they've greatly benefited from my addiction. I've made them a fortune, so I have no doubt saying the overturning of my conviction would greatly impact their operation. It's hard to run a criminal entity from a prison when the face of your empire is no longer a convict.

My thoughts shift from one sly snake to another when a tap hits the door of the warden's office. Warden Mattue wouldn't be game to interrupt me, he knows as well as I do that he isn't running the show around here, but Agent Moses has no qualms shaking the fist of justice when he feels he's been done wrong. Me not being at his beck and call the past seven hours is about as controversial as things get for him lately.

"Time to wrap things up, Ox. I thought you'd know better than anyone that you earn benefits here. They're not a given."

I work my jaw side to side before jerking up my chin. "Caidyn, I need to go. Can you put Demi on the phone real quick?"

He doesn't seek clarity for the quick change in our conversation. Agent Moses kept his voice loud enough to ensure not only I know he's endeavoring to stamp his authority, but so do half the inmates at Wallens Ridge as well.

A reminder of the change-up in Demi's living conditions smack back into me when her groggy voice sounds down the line only three boot stomps later. In our old family home, Caidyn would have needed to sprint a mini-marathon to get to my room from the living room.

"Hey." Just like earlier today, Demi's one word speaks volumes. It exposes her struggles, but it also shows there's still a warrior hidden deep inside her, biding its time. "I know we agreed to save this for tomorrow, but I want to say how sorry I am about today. I don't know what I was thinking. It's all so..."

"Confusing?" I fill in when words elude her.

"Yeah," she breathes out heavily. "And painful. I miss you so much, it physically hurts." Just as panic makes itself known with my gut, she lessens its constrictive hold. "But that doesn't mean I should have done what I did. It won't happen again. I promise you that."

Conscious she never makes a promise she can't keep, I ask, "Say that again?"

I hear her cheek incline into a smile before she repeats, "I promise."

A brief moment of silence teems between us. It isn't uncomfortable. It's more heart-fixing than anything. This is the peace I was looking for when I stupidly thought I couldn't do it with Demi in the room with me. It returns my perspective and reminds me that good things do come to those who wait.

When a cough sounds across the room a couple of seconds later, I put steps in place to make sure no length of time will stop good from prospering. "Do you remember the place we visited your birthday weekend between the ice rink and the café?"

I picture Demi's smile when her voice comes out super husky. "Of course. I'll never forget that day."

The curving of my lips is heard in my reply, "Do you still have the gift I bought you that day? Not the ones I picked, the one you did?" She remains quiet, but I take her hearty swallow as confirmation she knows where I'm going with this. "Can you keep it close by for me?"

"Maddox..."

"Please. I need to know you're safe, and there's no better comfort you can offer me than knowing you're protecting yourself." I'm about to commence tiptoeing through a minefield, but before I can do that,

I need to make sure none of the bomb shards could reach Demi if I take a step in the wrong direction.

The actuality in my tone halves Demi's frantic breaths. "Okay. I can do that for you…" My smile snags halfway when she tacks on, "On one condition." She waits a beat before murmuring, "Go easy on Caidyn. You can't throw a non-swimmer into the deep end and expect him not to occasionally choke on some pool water. He's doing the best he can."

"We all are," we say at the same time before Agent Moses's impatience gets the better of him. He doesn't disconnect our call by snatching the receiver out of my hand. He shreds the cable with a knife—an extremely familiar-looking pocketknife.

A tiring day could have me mistaken, but I'm reasonably sure his knife is the one Demi stuffed down her bra before we traveled to what should have been my second death match. If that's the case, that means he's been in my house, or worse, in Demi's room.

My blood boils over when I lock my eyes with Agent Moses's. He doesn't even try to hide the confirmation on his face. He wants me to know how close he's been to Demi because he knows she's the only person capable of bending my spine.

It's a pity for him, my spine snapped hours ago. "You fucking son of a bitch."

In quicker than he can blink, I pin him to the wall of the warden's office by his throat before jabbing my fist into his face. I get in three solid whacks before my campaign is ended by the brutal zap of a taser. It brings me to my knees in an instant, but no amount of electric charge can slacken my smile when Agent Moses bobs down to my level. I may have only got in four hits, but his face will carry the marks of my beating for days to come.

As will the scorches his next set of words burns my heart with, "Trace the location of the last call received from this phone." He nudges his head to Warden Mattue's now ruined landline before he scoots closer to me. "It's time to level up, but I can't do that if you refuse to fall into line." He sighs like he's disappointed it's come to this. In case you're wondering, he's a woeful liar. "So perhaps I should remind you exactly how much is at stake here?"

He steals my chance to reply by signaling for the guard to taser me for a second time. The prongs' close proximity to my heart and the high voltage of the zap have me on the verge of coronary failure, but no amount of wattage has me missing Agent Moses's next set of demands. "Call India. I've waited long enough. It's time to get this show on the road."

21

DEMI

I stare at Caidyn's cell phone for over twenty minutes, willing it to ring. Lengthy telephone conversations weren't a privilege Maddox had before today, and if the duration of his call this afternoon is anything to go by, I don't see them becoming a regular occurrence. In all honesty, I'm more than okay with that. Ten minutes of one-on-one time cost him valor, dignity, and respect, so I'd hate to consider what he had to give for a seventy-three-minute call.

After another ten minutes of rueful staring, I dump Caidyn's cell phone onto my bed before slotting my body next to it. I'm only planning to rest my weary eyes for a couple of seconds but soon realize my downtime is closer to an hour or two. Perhaps even three when I spot how much drool is on my pillow.

As guilt makes itself known with my stomach, I stand to stretch my spine. The painkillers I gobbled down like they can't kill me should have me feeling on cloud nine, but for some reason, they don't. I'm too edgy to feel calm, too restless. It truly seems as if today's events were the start of the storm, and the real battle is still to come.

With that in mind, the pledge I made to Maddox during our call pops into my head. I shoved his understanding through the grinder today, so the least I can do is follow through with his request before crawling back into bed for another couple of hours.

"Come on," I say to Max while motioning my head to the closed door of my room. Caidyn is a stickler for privacy. He will never be a guy who pees with the bathroom door open. "We may as well kill two birds with one stone."

Too embarrassed to face Caidyn just yet, I take a detour to the kitchen via the two-way bathroom attached to my parents' bedroom. The depressive cloud above Max's head thins when I grab two microwavable cheeseburgers from the freezer and pop them into the microwave. "I know this isn't the big greasy burger I promised you, but any burger is better than no burger, right?"

I smile when he barks in agreement.

It's my first genuine smile this afternoon.

While the microwave does its thing, I sneak back into my parents' room. Creeping around in my own house feels stupid, but I'd rather sneak than face the onslaught I did when I returned home, especially since I'm weaponing up like Armageddon is about to commence. I can't guarantee I won't be tempted to shoot the sneer off Landon's face if he glared at me again, so this is the safer, less dangerous option.

"Don't look at me like that, Max," I mutter under my breath when the removal of the gun Maddox purchased me on my birthday last year from the safe in my parents' room has his eyelids drooping. "I don't like this any more than you do, but I promised."

Before he can increase my guilt, the microwave dings, stealing his devotion.

What did I tell you? He will always choose a greasy burger over me.

After telling Max I'll be a minute, I race back into my room to store my gun somewhere safe. My options are limited. My room has three basic necessities—a bed, a dresser, and a hanging rack that's more empty than full.

"The bed it is," I murmur to myself before stuffing my gun under my pillow. I'll find a better spot for it later when my stomach isn't announcing it's at the point of starvation.

My strides out of my bedroom halve in length when I spot an amber-colored canister sitting next to a bottle of perfume on my dresser. It isn't the empty canister I hid in the trash bin this morning so Caidyn wouldn't find it. It is the one I stole from Justine's apartment.

A clot forms in my arteries when I fail to locate Caidyn's cell phone. It's been removed from my bed.

Clearly, I'm not the only one sneaking around, although it does seem as if I am the only one being tested.

Determined to show I have a better grasp on things than perceived, I dump Justine's script of oxycodone into the bin next to my dresser before marching out of my room with my head held high. I understand that I'm deserving of Caidyn's mistrust, but it doesn't make the sting any less brutal. Second only to Maddox, I thought Caidyn knew me better than anyone. Evidently, that's no longer the case.

Some of the despair wreaking havoc with my stomach clears away when I enter the kitchen. Max's drool is extending from the bottom of his jowls to the tiled floor. He's so eager to eat, he doesn't wait for me to plate up his dish. He devours his dinner with one big swallow the instant I remove it from its packaging.

"You're meant to chew *then* swallow."

I roll my eyes when he slants his adorably fat head to the side and arches a doggy brow. He isn't confused by my comment. He's begging for some of my untouched burger.

Smiling, I take a seat at the dinette my father always sat at when he pretended he couldn't cook before ripping my burger in half. "Promise me you will chew it this time around."

He looks seconds from pinching both halves of the burger from my plate when something outside steals his attention. He leaps to his feet, the hairs on his back as sharp as his uneasy growl.

"It's probably just Caidyn," I assure him before moving toward the kitchen window.

Just as I'm about to peer outside, Max scares the living daylights out of me by spinning around and barking in the direction opposite to the way I am facing.

Now his attention is devoted to the living room.

"Caidyn..." I murmur, uneased by the viciousness of Max's growl. "Is that you?"

Mindful a burger is barely an appetizer for a dog as big as Max, I curl my hand around his collar before allowing him to guide me into the living room. I don't want him taking out his annoyance about our dinner being interrupted on Caidyn's backside.

"Caidyn," I repeat when our entry into the living room has us walking into a dead-quiet space. "You're scaring me."

My neck cranks back so fast I feel something pop when a deep, gravelly voice says, "That's the point, isn't it?"

There's a man in my kitchen. A balaclava is covering his face, and he's holding a butcher knife in his gloved-up hand.

I am ashamed to admit it takes a couple of seconds for my survivor instincts to kick in, and even then, they're slow off the mark. Instead of releasing Max to do what he's been trained to do, I attempt to drag him away from the masked intruder. He is brave, but I don't want to test his heroism against a man wielding a knife.

The decision is taken out of my hands when the man sneers a vicious grin before he pushes off his feet to chase us down. Max is so frantic to get to him, he slips out of his collar before he leaps through the air, fangs first. My panic that he's about to be injured subsides when his teeth shredding through the man's forearm sees his knife falling to the floor with a clatter.

After scooping up the blade to ensure the masked intruder can't regain control of the situation, I snatch my cell phone off the coffee table where Caidyn must have placed it before sprinting into my room. My bare feet struggle to gain traction on the slippery wooden material. I more skid into my room than enter it with a smooth sprint.

My hands shake a million miles an hour when I dump the knife onto my dresser before latching into place the locks my father fixed on my door when I was thirteen. At the time, I didn't understand why

I needed so much protection. Now, I'm so very grateful for his some-what obsessive traits.

Once the third deadlock is bolted, I log into my phone then attempt to dial 911. I say attempt because before I can hit the second 'one,' an orange canister on the dresser next to the discarded knife gains my attention. It's Justine's prescription—the canister I threw into the bin. It's back sitting on my dresser like I never disposed of it —like it was returned to its unrightful place by someone who shouldn't be in my room.

Oh, shit!

Before I can push the last digit on my phone, a baseball bat is swung through the air. I call out when its connection with the back of my head causes a horrifying crack to boom through my room. The pain is so intense, my phone slips from my grasp and crashes to the ground when I raise my hands to my head to protect my skull from a second hit.

When nothing but ringing sounds through my ears for the next several seconds, in desperation, I stretch out for the knife. My unseen attacker foils my endeavor to protect myself by swinging a bat through the air for a second time. This time, it cracks into my dresser instead of my head. His swing is so powerful, it cracks the varnished top and shatters my trinkets. It also assures me I'll never reach the knife without broken limbs, so instead, I work on undoing the dead-bolts I just locked.

The second latch springs free a mere second before my torso is flattened to the warped wood by a man I'd guess to be six foot three or four. He breathes heavily into my neck while jabbing the pointy end of a knife into my right ribcage.

"Is this what you fantasized about?" he questions in a heavy accent before he licks the bead of sweat careening down my nape. "Or should I be rougher?"

Before a single syllable can escape my mouth, he flings me across the room. I crash into the hanging rack with a thud, hurling both my minimalist wardrobe and my backside to the floor. I'm tempted to act fatally wounded, but the movement of black boots in my peripheral vision declares that I can't. He doesn't want me down for the count. He wants to hear me sob.

There's no chance of that happening.

After weaponing up with a bent coat hanger, I stand on a shaky pair of knees. The man wearing a similar balaclava to the one Max is wrestling grins when he takes in my aggressive stance.

"Much better," he murmurs on a moan before he charges me.

I slice the rigid end of the coat hanger across his midsection before raising it to his face. The sharp end of the coat hanger shreds a hole into his balaclava when it gouges his cheek. I see the inch-long gash dribble three droplets of blood before a backhanded slap hazes my vision. His hit is so brutal, I begin to wonder if he struck me with his fist or the bat. It dazes me so much I have to aim my swings in the direction his excited breaths are coming from. If I didn't, I'd be swinging wildly.

I get in two solid whacks before he retaliates to my jab of his ribs with more than fists. He slices me with his knife. Air hisses between my clenched teeth when he skims the sharp blade across my hand before he backs up his slash with a deeper cut to my forearm.

With one of my arms out of action, it doesn't take my attacker long to get the advantage. He beats into me like my body is a boxing bag before he sends me sailing onto my bed with an uppercut punch to my chin. I try to regain my footing, but within a second of me landing on my bed with the lifelessness of a ragdoll, he squashes me into the mattress with his large frame, then compresses my jugular with his knife.

I can't breathe under the pressure of his weight.

I can't scream for the fear he will slit my throat.

I'm motionless and in shock, which seems to agitate my attacker more.

"Fight me!" the deranged maniac screams in my face before he rips apart my thighs, trying to make me balk.

When his roar doesn't revive my fighter instincts, he bites a chunk of my skin high on my thigh. I kick out, the pain both extreme and heartbreaking. The digging of my feet into his shoulders pushes him off me enough I can secure a full breath, but the relief it gives my screaming lungs is short-lived. All the air I sucked in is forced back out when the hand he isn't using to hold his knife to my throat shreds my panties from my body.

"No!" I scream in fear when his rough removal of the cotton material is quickly chased by his hand fumbling with the opening of my vagina.

I thought he was here to kill me.

I didn't factor rape into the equation.

When my survival instincts activate for the second time, I bite him on the shoulder, momentarily stopping his fingernails from jabbing through the folds of my pussy. It pisses him off, but I don't care. I'd rather die than be touched by any man who isn't Maddox.

I taste more of my blood than the rapist's when he hits me for the second time.

This time, he uses his fist.

It stuns me so much, he works his belt through the loops of his trousers without protest before he lowers his zipper. When he pulls his erection out of his pants, I slant my head to the side, confident I'm about to be sick. The change in position pulls my brows together. A fluorescent pink object is peeking out from beneath my pillow like a beacon of hope in a very dark and demented world.

My chin wobbles when it dawns on me what it is. It's my ticket out of this mess. A torch capable of guiding me out of the dark, but only if I'm willing to take the life of another to save my own.

That's a bitter pill to swallow when you're grappling for self-confidence.

Although I'm barely with it, both physically and mentally, it doesn't even take a second to recall that what happens to me doesn't solely affect me anymore. This will hurt Maddox as much as it will me, so for that reason, and that reason alone, I slide my hand under my pillow, flick off the safety of my gun, then direct the barrel so it sits under my attacker's ribs.

"Stop!" I beg through a sob, giving him a final chance to redeem himself.

When he ignores my screams and his penis probes me enough that I feel violated, I pull back the trigger, ending both the stranger's life and mine with one bullet.

22
___

MADDOX

When the light in the hole slowly flickers on, I scamper for the slot in the door. My sense of time is warped, but if the number of meals that have been delivered to me are anything to go by, I've been locked in the dark the past three days. There have been no daily visits by Agent Moses. No ransom demands. Just meals through a slot and endless silence.

The latter is killing me more than anything.

How can I protect Demi when I'm in the dark as to what is happening? Agent Moses would be a fool to hurt her, she is the only bargaining chip he has, but his comment about leveling up has me worried. Col is a constant blocker to Agent Moses's wish to dominate the underworld, but you can't take down the king without his subjects being placed into the firing zone alongside him.

"Where is Agent Moses?" I repeat for the umptieth time today. "I want to see Agent Moses—"

My demand is cut off by a familiar yet apprehensive tone. "Arrow is currently indisposed."

"Indisposed where?" I query while peering through the slot, curious as to why Warden Mattue's usually dreary pitch is piqued with apprehension. He doesn't run the show around here. From what

I've gathered the past year, Agent Moses took over the reins not long before I was sentenced, but this is the first time I've seen him so cautious. His arrogance is normally as haughty as Agent Moses's.

After returning my stare, Warden Mattue mutters, "That doesn't matter right now. We have more pressing matters to attend to." He gestures to the guard standing next to the slot to open the door before he adds in a warning tone, "No tomfoolery, Ox. If you make a fool out of me, you'll spend the remainder of your sentence in the hole."

It dawns on me that it's super early when the guard pulls open the door. The sun has barely risen, meaning it's glaring through the head-high windows in the basement of Wallens Ridge.

The warden shoves a freshly laundered jumpsuit into my chest before nudging his head to a set of shower cubicles. "Go get cleaned up."

Although I have a ton of questions rolling through my head, I shuffle toward the bathroom. Yes, I said shuffle. My legs are so cramped, they're as anesthetized as my heart the past three days. Something feels off. I'm just hoping like fuck it has nothing to do with Demi or my family. The last time there was this much edginess in the air, my sister was sentenced to be mauled by a dog.

After a record-breaking shower, I scrub my teeth with a toothbrush a guard left on the last vanity sink in a line of many, then shove it into the pocket of my jumpsuit like the bristles aren't wet. It's useless as it is now, but you'll be amazed at how dangerous it could become when a man's nerves are bordering on insanity. Mine are there now, dangerously teetering over a very steep cliff.

Once I'm shackled, I am shoved into an elevator four guards are manning with machine guns strapped to their chests. During our short ride, Warden Mattue states his terms. "No discussions about the prison operation whatsoever, and neither Agent Moses nor I are to be mentioned. If you abide by those two stipulations, Ox, I will increase the meal roster in the hole from one meal a day to three."

So my calculations were correct. I've been in the hole for three days.

Feeling edgy, I give Warden Mattue's seemingly impenetrable

composure a little push. You can't learn someone's limits without occasionally pushing their boundaries. "And if I don't agree with your terms? What happens then?"

Bile scorches the back of my throat when the warden replies, "Demi will join you here via consecutive life sentences." I assume he's referencing Demi's recent confession that she's recruiting fighters for her uncle's tournament again but am proven wrong when he mutters, "You can't blow a man's brains out during a drug-fueled bender and not pay for the consequences of your actions."

"What the fuck did I miss?" I mumble to anyone listening, too stunned by the honesty in Warden Mattue's eyes to seek confirmation with my fists.

He straightens the collar on my jumpsuit like I'm not seconds from going on a rampage before gesturing for me to enter his office before him. "We don't have time to go over matters now, but once we have this settled, I'll tell you everything I know." He guides me to his desk, pushes me into the chair opposite his, then weaves his fingers through my damp hair to straighten out the kinks.

"Get the fuck off me."

Anyone would swear he was polishing me up to meet royalty.

It dawns on me that that is the case when he suggests, "Keep the focus on him. There's no better way to defuse a Petretti than to stroke their ego. You can talk shop, tattoos, drugs, or the girl who's got his head in such a tailspin, he put thirty million dollars on the line to protect her, but whatever you do, do *not* mention his daughter."

The last part of his comment announces my visitor is Dimitri, but the first three-quarters of it confuse the hell out of me. Dimitri only ever protects himself. The way he left Demi high and dry after pledging to protect her is sure-fire proof of this, much less what he let happen to Justine. He could have stopped his father. He's the only person capable of getting through to him, yet he left Justine to face his wrath alone. That's all the proof I need that Dimitri doesn't have a heart in his chest. He'd need one of them to care about anyone but himself.

Before I can unravel a smidge of my confusion, Warden Mattue pulls a folded piece of paper out of the breast pocket of his jacket. "Memorize this."

My eyes only scan the first three lines of the document before they snap to the warden. "Is this true?" The document states a Russian sanction is attempting a resurge in Ravenshoe. Several contenders are stated in the brief, including one highly familiar name to anyone who grew up in the Ravenshoe/Hopeton region. Katie Byrne. She was abducted from Ravenshoe years ago, and despite several key witnesses coming forward to assist police with their investigation, she hasn't been seen since. "Or is Agent Moses attempting to start a mafia turf war?"

My back molars smash together when the warden's eyes rocket to mine. He couldn't lie his way out of a speeding ticket even if his life depended on it.

"I'm not doing it." I toss the document onto his desk before slouching low in my chair. "When Dimitri finds out you've lied to him, you and *every* member of your family will be struck from the records."

I don't give a shit about Warden Mattue. As far as I am concerned, he can rot in hell. I'm more concerned as to why he wants me to deliver his lie. That not only places me in Dimitri's firing line but my family as well—including Demi.

"They're not lies." When I arch a brow, wordlessly calling out his deceit, he talks faster. "It's legitimate information he's been seeking for years."

His tone is honest, but I've been burned far too many times to believe anything without solid proof. Furthermore, why would he give up the opportunity to get into Dimitri's good books? Rocco has stated time and time again that being owed a favor by Dimitri is priceless. Surely, that's more beneficial to him than being Agent Moses's lackey.

Too curious to ignore, I ask, "If this intel is true, why aren't you giving it to Dimitri yourself?"

I scoff when I read his reply from his facial expression. He stupidly believes Dimitri trusts me. That's as ludicrous as me saying he could be a good man if he found the right woman. He's too corrupt to turn good now. Too greedy.

It's showcased without a doubt when he says, "This could change everything for you, Ox. Better privileges. More leniency." He doesn't gain my interest until he adds, "Conjugal visits." He stares me straight in the eyes while promising, "The world will be your oyster... *once* you veer Dimitri's focus in the direction we need it to go."

"We?" I already know who he's referencing, but I want him to spell it out for me, so there's no misconception on who's helming this operation. It isn't Warden Mattue.

Warden Mattue's pupils widen as his throat works hard to swallow, but before he can sing like a canary, gravel crunching under tires trickles through a partially cracked open window on our right. He cranks his head to the window so quick, my neck muscles feel his neck's strain. "Shit. He's early." After licking and spitting my hair into place like it won't be cited as the cause of his death on his death certificate, he reiterates, "Remember, no—"

"Mention of Agent Moses, you, or the botch-shop operation you're running here. I heard you the first time."

After taking a moment to gauge my true response—that my heart made me his bitch long before morals did—he snatches the handwritten piece of paper from my hand before spinning to face a mirror in the far corner of his office. He's not only sprucing himself up for his visitor, but he's also assuring himself that he has what it takes to be the business partner of an underworld associate.

Once he has his wild brows contained with some spit, he murmurs, "We have a good thing going here, Ox. Let's not ruin it by getting ahead of ourselves." He straightens his jacket, breathes out the nerves he wishes weren't fluttering in his stomach, then commences heading to the door. Before he breaks into the corridor, he issues one final warning. "Just to be sure we're on the same team, these walls have ears. It'll do you best to remember that."

My hands ball into fists when he nudges his head to the spot his landline phone once sat. Now Agent Moses's ill-timed arrival when I was talking to Caidyn three days ago makes sense. He heard every word I spoke, which means he knows I was seeking ways to shorten my stay.

That makes this way worse than first perceived. Agent Moses gets reckless when something stands between him and the profits he wrongly believes he's entitled to. He schemes up wildly eccentric ideas, then implements them before anyone can talk him out of it.

If that occurred this time around, Demi could face something much more severe than a false murder wrap. She could be in danger —grave danger—and I'm shackled to a desk in a warden's office three hundred miles away.

Fuck.

Fuck.

Fuck!

I halt cursing myself to hell when the door to the warden's office pops open a couple of minutes later. You can't curse yourself to hell when the devil is standing in front of you.

The anguish wreaking havoc with my stomach is heard in my voice when I hit Dimitri with so much attitude, he'll never smell a rat. "If I knew it was you, I would have gotten dressed up for the occasion." I lick my bone-dry lips before folding my arms in front of my thrusting chest. "What the fuck are you doing here, Dimitri?"

His lips tug at one side. "I thought we were friends. Isn't this what friends do? Visit the other while they're locked up."

I would give anything to show him what I really think of him, but since that could fuck me over more ways than Sunday, I glare at him instead of spitting at his feet like I really want to.

"We ain't friends," I mutter when it takes him a minute to get the point.

With a grin that exposes I responded how he was hoping, Dimitri flattens his palms on the warden's desk, then stares me straight in the eyes. Something has altered in them since the last time I saw them, but since they're still full of hurt, I'm reasonably sure their change-up isn't compliments of finding his daughter.

"That's right. We're not. You just used my contacts to line your pockets with money, and then you wonder why we're not friends."

I stare at him, too shocked to speak.

I run drugs for him to repay a debt. I didn't do it to become rich.

Unless he's talking about the understudy program at STEM Academy.

If that's the case, he is correct. I did use his contacts to fatten up my bank balance because back then, I thought every dollar I siphoned from the Italian Cartel would weaken their stronghold on Hopeton. Up until a couple of months ago, I had no idea it would have taken more than three lifetimes of fights to drain one of Col's bank accounts. I knew he had money; I just had no clue how much until I calculated the funds I helped Agent Moses amass the past eight months. The number of digits in his bank account would have you convinced greed makes the world go around.

Mistaking the annoyance on my face as agreement to his comment, Dimitri sneers, "Sit down, Maddox, and for once in your fucking life, listen. If you had done that from the get-go, you wouldn't be here."

He doesn't need to say Justine's name to know who he's referencing. The quickest flare that darted through his eyes told me everything I need to know, although it has nothing on the wistful glint his eyes get when his thoughts drift away from our confrontation for the quickest second.

"He was right. You're so fucking gone," I mutter out with a chuckle before I can stop myself. You can trust me when I say I know a man under the spell of a woman. I've been gone since the second grade.

Dimitri tries to regain control of our conversation. "I'm gone? *Ha!*" He tsks me with a shake of his head. "I'm not the one in cahoots with the man who marked up my sister with a mangy mutt." Red hot fury burns through my veins, but before I can disperse in an unhealthy manner, Dimitri switches some of my anger to confusion. "What did he tell you, Ox? That I ordered for her to be punished?"

He has no clue Justine was punished because of Demi and me. He still thinks it's all on his shoulders. In a way, I believe the same. He put Justine in his father's line of sight, so he should have protected her as he pledged to Demi only months earlier.

As should I.

My negative thoughts are pushed to the back of my mind when Dimitri asks, "What's he got on her? If my father has a noose around Demi's throat, I can help."

It takes everything I have not to laugh. He saved Demi once, but in the process, he threw my baby sister into the deep end without a life jacket. I can't forget that. Her screams that night will never leave me. They will haunt me until the day I die.

As will the flare that darts through Dimitri's eyes when I say, "Like you did Justine?"

"She's alive, isn't she?"

"And crying every week on the phone," I spit out as memories of the last time I talked to Justine filter through my head. Although we talk once a week, she still hasn't come to visit me yet. She is practically a ghost. "You fucked her over good, D. I don't know if she'll ever come back from this."

The cuffs circling my wrists and ankles become super heavy when he hits me right where it hurts. "So you're gonna let him do the same to Demi?"

He doesn't need to say his father's name for me to know who he's referencing. The way he spat out 'him' is indicating enough. He hates his father as much as I do, and it has me curious if his disdain is the reason for his visit.

I lose the chance to investigate my theories further when Dimitri's short fuse gets the better of him. "You kept my daughter's existence a secret. You didn't do that for no reason, Ox. I'm here to find out why, and I ain't leaving until I do."

He takes a seat in the warden's chair before he hooks his boots onto his desk. His aggressive stance is impressive, but the quickest flash of red beaming out of the warden's cracked closet ensures my stance won't budge. If I want to protect Demi, I need to keep my mouth shut. It fucking sucks. I'd give anything to rat Agent Moses and Warden Mattue to the man they're endeavoring to overrule, but disappointment seems to be the story of my life lately.

Not even a minute later, it becomes apparent that Dimitri is pressed for time. His boots haven't graced the warden's desk for even thirty seconds before he returns them to the floor—unfortunately minus a mess. Warden Mattue is as anal about cleanliness as he is about having first dibs of the new female inmates.

I stop picturing the pleading looks I get from female inmates every induction day when Dimitri gives a well-used trait a whirl. He threatens me. "With Megan Shroud being alive and well, your debt has not been fulfilled." He waits for our eyes to lock and hold before adding, "Since you're an inmate in a maximum-security prison, I have no choice but to transfer that debt back to its original owner."

"You wouldn't fucking dare."

He stares me dead set in the eyes so I can't miss the truth in his statement when he says, "Try me, Maddox. I've got a heap of anger and no one to take it out on."

"My debt is with your father," I seethe through clenched teeth.

Even aware his threat stems more around Justine's safety than Demi's doesn't weaken the clench of my jaw. I'm fucking ropeable, and it's taking everything I have not to blow this entire fucking operation to smithereens, even more so when Dimitri shakes his head, denying my claims. "Not according to you. I punished your sister, that means her debt falls on me." He takes a moment to remove the command from his tone before adding, "I am willing to negotiate—"

"With what? I gave your father everything I have! I have nothing left to give!"

I'm not lying. My family home. My sister's sanity. My fucking soul. Col has it all. There's only one thing he doesn't have, and I'm not willing to give her up for anything, even when it would be better for her if I did.

Dimitri balances his elbows onto the warden's desk before leaning close to me like he is aware our every word is being overheard. "Give me information."

"I don't know anything."

He continues talking as if I never spoke. "And in good faith, I'll repay the favor. Special perks, hours outside these walls..." My brows arch when he drags his eyes over a smattering of tattoos peeking out of my jumpsuit. "I could even organize some additional conjugal visits."

When he stares me down, his aggressive stance falters, and the glint in his eyes I couldn't recognize earlier is exposed. It's a protectiveness he'd give anything to keep hidden. A gleam a father's eyes get when they're looking out for their children. It reveals what Rocco said all those months ago was true, except Dimitri doesn't just see his daughter when he looks at Demi, he sees the ghost of his sister as well.

Demi and Ophelia have the same pained look in their eyes because the same monster haunts their dreams. Their anguish is one and the same, and Dimitri was the first man to realize that.

How could I not have seen this sooner? In a warped, twisted way, everything now makes sense. Dimitri left Justine to face his father's wrath alone because to him, she was just another woman to bed. He can't off-hand Demi's safety in the same manner. Not only does she have his blood, any hurt she'd endure, Dimitri would imagine it happening in the past to his sister and in the future to his daughter.

That alone will keep Demi protected better than I ever could, and the knowledge has me speaking words I never thought I would. "Can you get Demi out?"

My question stumps Dimitri for all of two seconds. "Out of what, exactly?" When he reads my reply from my face, his whole demeanor shifts, proving my theory is right. He has a heart hidden in him somewhere. It has just never had the chance to shine. "If she's out, she can't come here anymore, Ox. When you are out, you're out. You can never get back in. Are you willing to face that?"

A montage of my last twelve months at Wallens Ridge plays through my head like a movie. When it dawns on me there's been more bad times than good of late, I reluctantly lift my chin. Dimitri isn't the answer to my problems, but neither are the men who want to keep me locked up for life. In here, I can't protect Demi. The shitty attempt I've made the past twelve months leaves no doubt to this.

Air whizzes out of Dimitri's nose when I bob my chin for the second time. "All right... but I'm going to need to know *everything*."

As snippets of information on the sheet of paper Warden Mattue demanded I memorize pop back into my head, I ask, "Have you got a pen and a piece of paper? You're gonna need it."

23

DEMI

I jolt awake, startled and confused. I'm in the living room of my childhood family home. My entire body is throbbing in agony, I'm bleeding from multiple knife wounds, and my head is so woozy, I have no idea what time it is or how long I've been here. Hours or days could have passed since I killed the man who tried to rape me. I'm truly unsure.

I thought the police would have swarmed my room within minutes of my gun firing. Instead, I had to crawl out from beneath the man who rendered me unconscious with a brutal head collision in the second leading to his death. I think I was knocked out for a couple of hours. It's hard to tell time when you're barely lucid. The dark sky didn't help either. It was as black as the veins weaved around my heart, lifeless and cold.

When I first freed myself from the man who felt much heavier than he did hours earlier, I crawled toward the front door to call for help. A change-up only occurred when I reached the living room. Max was whimpering in the far corner of the bloodstained space. He wasn't putting any weight on his back leg, and his face was nicked up and scratched, but I was confident none of the blood soaking the floor was from him. He maimed our first intruder as effectively as I did the second one.

My home was the scene of a massacre, and it's in the town my uncle rules more than he nurtures. I'm not ashamed to admit I was scared to seek help. If I got one of the rare, good police officers in Hopeton, they'd take one look at my surname and lock me up for life. If I got one of the men on my uncle's payroll, I'd be indebted to my uncle even more than I already am. It was a lose-lose situation for me, so instead of finalizing my shaky crawl to the door, I joined Max in the corner of the room, where I've drifted in and out of consciousness for God knows how long.

I've used the bathroom a handful of times, and I think at some stage last night, I poured some kibble into Max's bowl for him, but a majority of the time has been spent in the living room, staring at the door, confident Caidyn will eventually show up. I could have called him for help if the man lying lifeless in my room hadn't smashed my phone. It's sitting in pieces on the floor in my room with Justine's cracked canister of pills.

I'd probably have a better grasp of reality if I took some of the oxycodone sprayed across my bedroom floor, but since I promised Maddox I wouldn't take pills to numb my pain, I'm facing my demons head-on instead of in a drugged haze. Is it stupid for me to do? Probably, but tell me one time I've been rational the past sixteen months?

"Hey, Max," I breathe out slowly when a furry head rests on the top of my thigh.

One of my eyes is so swollen, I can't see out of it, and the other isn't much better, but I know I'm safe because Max is with me. He's limping, and his ego is as bruised as my face, but he gave up a greasy burger to protect me. When we get out of here, he's going to be spoiled rotten.

"What have you got there?" I stammer out when I feel something cool brush against my leg. I identify the object he dragged into the room with my hands more than my sight. "Is it juice?"

My cheeks ache when he barks in response to my question.

He's so damn clever, I can't help but smile.

The pain stretching from the roots of my hair to the tips of my toes eases when I uncap the bottle of juice and pour a generous portion into my hand. Max laps up the sticky goodness rolling down my palm before he nudges the bottle with his head, encouraging me to take a sip.

I realize how weak I am when it takes a mammoth effort to lift the bottle to my mouth. I can only hold it in one hand since my right one was cut by the masked intruder.

"That's enough for now," I say to Max when he announces his annoyance about the minuscule sip I take with a growl. My throat feels as dry as a desert, and I'm as thirsty as hell, but with how weak I feel, I don't think I could make it to the bathroom if the need arises, so I need to keep my intake of fluids to a bare minimum. "I'll have some more later."

I scratch Max behind the ear when he flops his head back onto my thigh with a whimper. If he could talk, I'm sure he'd express concerns that we're never going to get out of here.

I feel the same way.

Over the next forty or so minutes, I teeter between lucidness and incoherence. There's peace on both sides of the coin. When I'm lucid, I remember why I fought so hard to live, the promises I made, and who they were made to. When I'm incoherent, my thoughts drift to the weeks I spent at the cabin with Maddox after his first death match, then the two months where I felt truly free from my uncle's reign. It's a heart-mending time that sees my hope rising instead of dithering when the sound of car doors closing breaks through the ringing in my ears.

As shadows dance across the faded drapes hanging in the front window, Max backs away from the front door. He never removes his eyes from the entryway, not even when the warped wood splinters under the force of someone's boot.

I slant my head to the side to protect my eyes from the blinding sun rays beaming in through the door just as Max's backside braces against my knees. He's in the prime position to pounce. He's just waiting to assess whether this intruder is a villain or a hero.

We're left a little unsure when the vision clears enough to spot who's cautiously entering the living room. Dimitri isn't as evil as his father, but the apple didn't fall far from the tree.

Even with Max growling and barking like he's about to rip Dimitri's face off, Dimitri bobs down to my level. He's a good four feet away from me. Max won't let him any closer. "Is there anyone in the house with you?"

I shake my head, grimacing through the pain it causes. "H-He's dead." His eyes follow the direction mine take when I drag them to the room a petite female is pacing toward. Well, I assume from her height and size that she's a female. My vision is too blurry to confirm without hesitation. "T-There was another man. I don't know where he w-went. Max took care of him."

"Okay." He looks like he wants to say more but is too shocked to speak. He isn't the only one. Even with my eyesight poor, I can see the remorse in his eyes. He won't ever say it, but he's suspicious my assault was orchestrated by his father.

When a flurry of red re-enters the room, Dimitri stands to his feet. "Stay with her while I clear the area. If this blood is from a second perp, he wouldn't have gotten far."

"He may have if the man in the bedroom's rigor mortis is anything to go by. He's been dead a couple of days," replies a highly distinctive female voice.

"Days?" Dimitri verifies, his tone a cross between a mass murder craving a bloodbath and a man bogged down with grief.

I can't see the woman he's conversing with, but I picture her jerking up her chin when a curse word seethes from Dimitri's mouth a couple of seconds later.

I abandon my pain for a minute when she asks, "Should I call in the authorities?"

"No," Dimitri and I shout at the same time.

Dimitri drags his eyes over my battered face and body before he cranks his neck back to the slim silhouette. "I'll take care of it." He tosses what I think is a set of keys her way. "Take her back to your grandparents' ranch. I'll organize for a doctor to come and see her there."

With the command in his tone leaving no room for a rebuttal, a female with piercing green eyes and plump lips squats down to my level a few seconds later. "Can you walk?"

I halfheartedly nod. "Umm... I-I think so."

The kind stranger would be at least two inches shorter than me, and she has a slim build, but you wouldn't know it for how strong she is. Within a couple of seconds, she has me on my feet and walking toward the front door.

Just before we break through the threshold, she cranks her neck back to the living room. "Dimi..."

Although she leaves her question unspoken, Dimitri has no trouble reading the worry in her tone. "I'll be right behind you, Roxanne. You couldn't get rid of me that easily."

After taking a moment to breathe out the nerves I hear twisting in her stomach, Roxanne assists me into a car similar to one I've seen Rocco get around in previously—a Mercedes Benz G Class.

I lay across the cool leather material before calling Max to my side.

"Come on, Max," Roxanne chimes in, stealing his devotion from a detached garage at a neighboring house. He isn't growling and going crazy. He's sniffing around like he's dying to use the bathroom as badly as me.

Before he can lift his leg, Roxanne bribes him into the car with leftover food from a fast-food chain I've never heard of. After accepting half a chicken Caesar wrap without the gobbles mealtimes are usually filled with, Max jumps into the passenger seat, leaps over the middle console, then dumps the now drool-covered wrap next to my head.

"Thanks f-for the offer, Max, but I-I'm not hungry."

Since neither of us are in the right frame of mind to tackle food right now, the unwrapped sub teeters between us for the next hour. I'm not sure where we're going, and in all honesty, I don't care. I'd let Roxanne drive us to Mexico if it continues to eradicate the smell of death that's been hovering around me the last few days. I didn't realize how bad it was until I sucked down the dirty air of Hopeton like I was standing in the middle of Switzerland.

After inhaling another big breath of freedom, I float into my fourth bout of unconsciousness today, only waking when someone jabs their fingers into the bump covering a majority of my right eye.

"Sorry," murmurs a female paramedic with long dark hair. I want to say her eyes are as caring as her words, but I can't. My vision is too blurry for me to see her facial features. "I need to make sure there are no obvious breaks beneath the swelling."

She assesses my eye for a couple of seconds before she asks me to sit so she can shift her focus to the back of my skull. Dizziness bombards me when I swing my legs off a bed in a residence I've never been in before, but it has nothing on the unease I feel when my dreary eyes lock in on a man-size shadow blocking the only door out of the modest-size room.

The situation worsens when I blink to clear my vision. Max's toothy growl will ensure Officer Daniel Packwood keeps an amicable distance, but I don't like being eyeballed by a man who tries to use his public service position to woo women into an adulterous relationship, much less one who thinks I'm addicted to painkillers.

"It's okay," advises the paramedic when she feels my skyrocketing pulse firsthand.

She's in the process of taking my vitals, so she knows how erratic my heartrate became from spotting Officer Packwood. Adulterers and a rapist aren't on par with one another, but the knowledge doesn't lessen my discomfort. Furthermore, not in a million years did I think Dimitri would bring the authorities into this. There are more Ravenshoe PD officers on the Petrettis' payroll than not, but this still isn't unkosher. My family usually handles instances like this in-house.

I drift my eyes back to the medic when she explains, "Officer Packwood is here to take a statement about your assault." After giving me a second to hear the honesty in her tone but not enough time to register why she appears familiar, she twists her torso to Officer Packwood before gesturing for him to enter. "Keep this quick. She's still very groggy."

My already dangerous heart rate spikes even more when Officer Packwood asks, "From an opioid overdose?"

"N-no," I answer before the medic can, aware of what he is insinuating even with my head and eyesight being as hazy as hell. "I haven't taken *any* p-pain medication in days."

The slurring of my words would have you believing otherwise, but everything I'm saying is true. I promised Maddox I wouldn't have another slip-up. No matter how hard the circumstances become, I plan to keep my promise.

"Then why was there an empty canister of oxycodone at the scene?" Too scared to come closer, Officer Packwood pulls out an office chair tucked under a desk butted against the doorframe his shoulder was braced on, then straddles it backward. Once he has himself comfortable, he hands the medic a printed-out photograph to hand to me. It shows Justine's canister of oxycodone on the floor of my childhood bedroom. It's empty as he stated.

I thrust the photograph over Max's head before replying, "My attacker knocked it off the dresser during his assault."

He halfheartedly shrugs. "Then why were no pills found sprinkled across the floor?"

Shocked, I sheepishly pull the photograph back to my side of Max's protective barrier to peruse the evidence for the second time. I didn't give it the attention it deserved the first time around. I was too busy denying Officer Packwood's second underhanded claim that I'm addicted to painkillers to look at all corners of the blown-up image.

Regretfully, a more in-depth perusal doesn't alter the facts. It is as Officer Packwood stated. Not a single orange pill can be seen. Shards of the canister are sprayed across the carpet, and the knife my attacker knocked off the dresser before I could reach it, but not a single tablet of oxycodone can be found.

"P-Perhaps the second perp took them with him?"

Officer Packwood raises a dark brow. "Why would he do that, Demi?"

"I don't know," I reply, truly unsure. "Perhaps you should ask him once y-you arrest him." That's my polite way to say he should concentrate his efforts on the men who did this to me instead of the victim. This is my impolite way. "Why are you here interrogating me? *Two* men assaulted me. Only one was gunned down for his stupidity."

Don't let the confidence in my voice fool you. I feel sick to my stomach knowing I ended another man's life, but I'm not going to let someone like Officer Packwood make me feel bad about what I did.

I did what needed to be done.

There's no shame in that.

Officer Packwood doesn't look happy about my response, but I don't care. I owe him nothing. "My job requires me to interview victims of sexual crimes."

"Sexual crimes?" I double-check, certain I heard him wrong. When he nods, proving otherwise, I blubber out, "I wasn't... T-They didn't..."

When words elude me, Officer Packwood fills them in. "You have trauma that indicates your 'assault' was of a sexual nature." While air quoting 'assault,' he acts as if he can't see the rapid shake of my head. "Bruising to your inner thighs. Grab marks on your face, neck, wrists, and breasts." He briefly licks his lips before continuing, "Traces of semen and blood were also documented during a preliminary examination of the crime scene—"

"He didn't rape me," I interrupt, my voice higher than intended but thankfully free of the annoying stutter I seem to have developed overnight. "He didn't get the chance."

"So he tried?" This question didn't come from Officer Packwood. It came from the medic watching our exchange from the side.

After pulling down on the long-sleeve shirt someone must have slipped over my head after carrying me out of the back of Roxanne's car, I lift my chin. It quivers when I advise, "To begin with, I didn't realize that was his intention. I thought he was there to kill me." My last two words are barely mumbles. "When I realized what he was doing, I-I... ah..."

"Protected yourself?" the female medic fills in, stealing the words from my mouth.

I nod again.

"I can't put down self-defense," Officer Packwood pushes out with a huff. "Victims reach out for help. They call 9-1-1. You did neither of those things. You just sat there with a dead man in your house for three days."

"Because I was scared what would happen to me, that I-I'd be treated the way you're treating me now." When I stand to my feet, Max copies my movements. His nerves are already on edge. One misconstrued signal will see Officer Packwood attacked as vehemently as the first assailant in my kitchen. Although I'm tempted to use Max to wipe the arrogance from his face, I can't. Instead, I demand a lawyer.

"That isn't necessary."

Despite the command in his tone demanding otherwise, I stand my ground. "I'm not s-speaking to you without a lawyer present."

"That's your cue to leave," the paramedic says to Officer Packwood. "My patient has rights, not to mention the fact she is clearly suffering from a grade-three concussion and many other injuries I've yet to put a name on. Now is *not* the time to interrogate her."

Not waiting for him to answer her, she marches Officer Packwood to the door, pushes him over the threshold, then she slams the door into his face. I'd give her an encouraging pat on the back for a job well done if I could get my woozy head to cooperate with the screams of my lungs. They're heaving in desperation, as windless and empty as the gaping cavity in my chest where my heart once stood.

I'm on the verge of hyperventilating, and the medic seems well-versed on this level of stress. "Nice calm breaths for me, Demi. In via your nose, out via your mouth." She keeps me upright by circling her hands around my elbows. Her hold isn't rough, but I'm no longer worried about falling. "Slow your breathing down a little. I know you think you're not getting enough air, but I assure you, you are. In and out. Nice and steady."

After studying the soothing movements of her lips for another oxygen-quenching three breaths, I raise my eyes to hers. My brows pull together more in confusion than panic I'm about to suffocate to death when the familiarity of her eyes smack into me. I've seen them before. I'm certain of it.

"Y-you're—"

"A nurse yesterday. A medic today," she fills in with a smile. "Who knows what I'll be tomorrow?"

I suck in another prolonged breath before replying, "From what Maddox t-told me, a career pickpocketer wouldn't be an overstretch."

Agent Machini, the only surviving female member of agent Brahn's Florida division, throws her head back and laughs. "I would have preferred for him to gloat about my motorbike racing skills, but I guess beggars can't be choosers."

I don't get the chance to bask in the warmth her comment instigates. I'm too busy reeling about the reason for her undercover assignment smacking into me to let an old saying force sentimental tears into my eyes. "I can't go with you. I-I refuse to leave Maddox to face this craziness alone."

She doesn't try to deny my claims she's here to reinstate Agent Brahn's earlier ruse. "It's time, Demi. If we don't move now, if we don't use this assault to our advantage, we will lose the opportunity. You and Maddox will be stuck here for eternity."

"That isn't true. There a-are options. We just need to look harder."

I almost choke on my assurance when she spits out, "Officer Packwood was so short with you because the man you killed was a police officer."

"What?" I ask, equally shocked and terrified.

The air I've only just replenished my lungs with sucks back out when she shows me an identification card for a twenty-year veteran police officer at Ravenshoe PD. Although his face was concealed during a majority of his assault, I absorb it in great detail while endeavoring to push him off me after I came to the first time. The unique birthmark under his left eye is an obvious identifying mark.

I rake my fingers through my hair, certain this couldn't possibly get any worse. When it gets out that I killed a police officer, I'll be burned at the stake, and don't get me started on what Maddox will face, or I'll be tempted to end it all right now. My wish to live could hurt Maddox more than it would have if I had let the rapist kill me.

He's been hurt enough.

He can't face more controversy.

He's barely holding on as it is.

But that doesn't mean I can accept Agent Machini's offer. I couldn't hurt Maddox like that. I love him too much to deceive him this way. It would kill him.

When I say that to Agent Machini, she asks, "More than losing one of his siblings? Or worse, all of them?" My eyes bounce between hers, shocked and confused. She attempts to relieve it by saying, "Caidyn was found in a neighbor's garage. He required resuscitation. It's touch-and-go. They don't know if he will make it through the night."

I grant one final whimper to break through my lips before I emotionally shut down, the weight on my chest too immense to ignore. I thought Caidyn abandoned me, that he left me to face my demons alone because he was disappointed and angry at me. I didn't even look for him when I came to. I just left him to die when all he's ever done is look after me.

If that doesn't prove I should have let my attacker kill me, I don't know what will convince you. My family's business took the life of my father, mother, and sister. Justine will never fully recover from her injuries, Sloane still has night terrors about her kidnapping, Maddox looks set to spend the rest of his life behind bars, and now Caidyn is fighting for his life.

This needs to stop.

I just have no clue how to end it without breaking the promises I made to Maddox.

My eyes float up from the floor when Agent Machini says, "Maddox wants this too, Demi. He's tired. He can't keep fighting as he has the past twelve months."

I want to call her a liar, but the undeniable truth in her tone is proven without prejudice when she commences playing a surveillance image recording on her phone. It shows Maddox in the Warden's office at Wallens Ridge, speaking with Dimitri.

My hand shoots up to clamp my mouth when Maddox asks Dimitri, "Can you get Demi out?"

Dimitri warns him that my removal from the family will be permanent, that once I'm out, I'll never be able to get back in, but instead of shaking his head to announce he couldn't handle that, he does the opposite. He nods.

After giving me a minute to absorb the facts, Agent Machini says, "They're killing him, Demi. They're breaking him down piece by piece. First with you, then Justine, and now Caidyn. They won't stop until they've removed every last bit of good from him and manipulate him to replicate the very man he *never* wanted to become, and they're using you to do it." She stares me dead set in the eyes when she asks, "How can you claim to love him only to sit by and watch him be hurt over and over again?"

"I do love him."

"Then stop this from happening. Get him out of here before there's nothing left to save."

Salty blobs come close to rolling down my face when I blurt out in frustration, "I've tried! Nothing works—"

"This *will* work, Demi. I promise you it will. You've just got to be brave enough to try something new."

Confident it couldn't be anywhere near as easy as she's implying, I ask, "How will Maddox believing I'm dead help him?"

My heart cracks when she replies, "Because we've reached the stage where we can only salvage scraps from the wreckage. There are no survivors. Can you not see that? They've got Maddox walking on eggshells now. Imagine how bad it will be when they put you away for murder."

"I *d-defended* myself," I correct, shocked about her forgetfulness. "I didn't murder anyone."

"That isn't what is on the report being filed at the DA's office as we speak. You had an excessive amount of oxycodone in your system when you shot and killed a police officer—"

"Who tried to rape me."

"Then you attempt to conceal his murder by having your mobster family dispose of the body."

"I-I didn't ask Dimitri to do that."

Agent Machini shrugs like our conversation isn't half as serious as it is. "Do you think the courts will care about that minor detail? You were witnessed by a decorated officer being forcefully removed from a pharmaceutical chain two hours before you made an appointment with a doctor who's being investigated for multiple malpractice suits—"

"Officer Packwood gave me Dr. Terry's number."

Her skills in ignorance are top-notch. She continues talking as if I never interrupted her for the second time without a single hiccup. "Then you didn't call for help after you 'defended' yourself against a police officer you believed was a rapist."

"I didn't 'believe' anything. He tried t-to rape me." Confident I still have the truth on my side, I say, "They were wearing balaclavas. They did this to me." I wave my hand over my bruised face and hacked hand.

"Allegedly," Agent Machini replies, her tone as low as my mood. "With no bodies and no witnesses, it will be your word against the forensic officers who worked alongside Officer Tarrant and Gailter every single day, and let's not forget the DA who turns a blind eye for the right amount of money." Her eyes bounce between mine. They're kind as suspected earlier, but I can't say they are nice. They're gutting me too much to ever compliment them. "I'm not trying to scare you, Demi. I simply want you to know what you are walking toward."

Air whizzes out of my nose when I huff out my frustration. "Why would they do this? W-What benefit would they get from arresting me?"

I answer my question before Agent Machini can.

Maddox. They want me arrested so they can continue to puppeteer Maddox.

Since we only met in passing over a year ago, Agent Machini doesn't know me well enough to notice when I'm giving in. She continues chipping away at my seemingly hard exterior. "They want to use your incarceration so they can manipulate Maddox more than they already are, and no matter how hard he fights, he won't be able to escape their clutches because he'd rather walk through hell a thousand times than see you knock on its door once." As she steps closer to me, the angst on her face is replaced with understanding. "I get that you're worried about hurting him, Demi, but if you truly looked at him, you'd know he's already hurting. They are killing him. They're just doing it in an extremely slow and painful manner."

Tears flood my eyes when my head replays the video she showed me earlier. Maddox's cheeks aren't as gaunt as they were his first month of incarceration, but there's no denying he's lost as much weight the past three days as I have. His eyes are sunken, and I can barely see a speckle of blue in them. He is hurting—badly—and once again, I'm responsible for his pain.

"Prove how much you love him, Demi. Protect him as fiercely as he has you." Agent Machini silently commands my eyes to hers. When she gets them, she pledges, "If you do that, I promise never to stop fighting for him. I will work tirelessly on his case until the truth is exposed, and he is free. You have my word."

Her promise should mean nothing to me. I've been issued them a dozen times before, and very rarely have they been upheld. But she has honest eyes like Maddox and empathy by the bucketloads. Then there's the fact that every word she spoke was the God's honest truth. The man I love is dying before my very eyes, but instead of doing whatever I can to fix the tumor leeching him of his soul, I'm encouraging its sucks.

I'm killing Maddox.

I'm destroying the man I love because I put my own selfish needs before his.

So I need to be the one who breaks promises to stop it from continuing.

After wiping my hands over my cheeks to dry them, I ask, "Can we tell him about o-our plans?"

I shouldn't have bothered fixing my face. A new flood of tears threatens to bombard my cheeks when Agent Machini shakes her head. "We need his grief to be real, Demi. If it isn't, we will hurt him for no reason."

I understand what she's saying, but that doesn't mean I have to like it.

"Can I at least say goodbye?" The last time we spoke, we didn't get to say a proper goodbye. I don't want that to be his last memory of me.

The absolute despair in my stomach gets a moment of reprieve when she lifts her chin after only a couple of seconds of deliberation. "Give me your word you'll fully support me with this, and I'll guarantee your final hours together will be explosive."

Although I'm certain there's more to her comment than she's letting on, I lift my chin. When you're drowning, you don't get picky with life jackets. Even if it isn't ideal, you take the first one thrown. I'm drowning. I just refuse to continue pulling Maddox under the murky waters with me.

24
_____

MADDOX

"*I* followed the script." When Warden Mattue's jaw twitches in preparation to deny my claim, I scream, "I followed the fucking script to the wire! I told him every lie written on that fucking sheet of paper." I point to the crumbled piece of paper the warden ripped out of my hand a nanosecond before he raced out of his office like his ass was on fire. "I did as you asked."

"There was no mention of Demi on any part of the dossier."

I work my jaw side to side while shifting on my feet to face Agent Moses, the interrupter. He rocked up at the hole hours after Dimitri left, acting as if he didn't have a front-row seat to our earlier festivities. His act would have been more convincing if I didn't hear his ramblings during my guided walk back to the hole. He was pissed he had lost a bargaining chip in his endeavor to rule the underworld. I was relieved.

"I know... but Warden Mattue gave me free rein. His terms, which I'm reasonably sure you're aware of since you've got nothing better to do than listen in on our conversations, was that I was not to mention you, him, or the operation you're running out of Wallens Ridge at any time." I hold my hands out palm side up, all pompous like. "I did *exactly* as asked."

"You're a fool, Ox—"

"Why? Because I found a way to stop you using Demi to manipulate me?" I don't give him the chance to answer. I step right up close to him until our chests compete for space. "I'm not playing your games anymore, Arrow. To get to me, you'll need Demi. You can't get to her without going through Dimitri, and we both know you won't do that because you're too much of a coward."

Like a fool with no wish to live, he laughs in my face. "You saved yourself by handing the safety of your girlfriend to the man who almost killed her, yet you call me a coward?"

I'm about to scoff at his claims, but the blown-up surveillance photographs he shoves into my chest freeze both my words and my heart. The first image is of the canister I saw on the vanity sink in the cabin. It's behind Demi's three positive pregnancy tests. The second zooms in to reveal Demi's name printed on the label, and the third shows the pills inside. They're not the size nor shape of a vitamin tablet. They look remarkably similar to the images my google search popped up when I put misoprostol into the search bar alongside Dr. Franklin's name.

"You didn't save Demi, Ox. You pushed her straight into the firing zone." The knocks keep coming when he removes a final Bureau-certified surveillance image from the breast pocket of his suit jacket. It shows Rocco placing down a pharmacy stamped bag onto the front porch of the cabin. Since the sun is bright and the paper bag is thin, you can see flecks of an orange canister inside. "He may be a 'nice guy'..." Agent Moses air quotes his last two words, "... but at the end of the day, all paid goons do as they're told."

Warden Mattue feels the disrespect in his tone harder than me. I haven't pocketed a dime of the millions of dollars I've earned him the past ten months. The warden can't claim the same. His hands are so fucking dirty, if the truth ever comes out, he will be a prisoner instead of overseeing them.

My head slants to the side when Agent Moses mutters, "But there's a way we can fix this." He twists to face Warden Mattue before jerking up his chin, giving him the go-ahead to speak. It advises who is the head of their operation. Once again, it isn't Warden Mattue.

After clearing his throat of nerves, Warden Mattue says, "Dimitri's team called in a favor. They're requesting your attendance at a ranch in Erkinsvale."

"What for?" The highness of my tone unearths my unease. Something feels off, but since it's been one shit storm after another lately, I can pinpoint exactly who my focus should be on.

Before the warden can answer me, Agent Moses slices his hand through the air, cutting him off. "We haven't been given all the details yet, but we believe it may be in gratitude for the information you gave him this morning." Even if I couldn't hear the deceit in Agent Moses's tone, I'd still know he is lying. If Warden Mattue's jaw could hang any lower, it would touch the ground, but it's all forgotten when Agent Moses adds, "Sources say Demi is in attendance."

"She's there now, at the ranch?"

I don't watch Agent Moses's response. I keep my eyes locked on the warden. He couldn't fight his way out of a wet paper bag, and his lying credentials are as poor as his fighting skills.

When he bobs his chin, I continue with my interrogation. I don't trust Agent Moses, but there's a niggle in my gut cautioning me to slow down and access all the facts. "When is the meet-up?"

I choke on my spit when Agent Moses answers, "Now."

"Not even my lead foot could get us to Erkinsvale in two hours. We'd never make it on time."

It dawns on me how desperate Agent Moses is for this meeting to go ahead when he mutters, "That's why I brought in the big guns." Just as his sentence ends, the distinct noise of a helicopter circling above grows loud enough to be heard in the underbelly of Wallens Ridge. "If this is a matter of national security, we can't take any chances."

"Dimitri would *never* invite the Feds for a cup of coffee... unless it was laced with arsenic."

Agent Moses's smile is as slick as his dark hair. I discover the reason for his pompous attitude when he switches his suit jacket, vest, and tie for a buttoned-up shirt with a Ravenshoe PD badge pinned to the front. When he adds a dark blue blazer to the mix, he looks like an everyday beat cop. Even the change-up in his gun adds to his ruse.

"Now we have nothing to worry about, do we?"

I lift my chin, incapable of lying with words. There's more at play here than a chance for him to get his hooks back into Demi. I'm simply lost as to what it could be. Agent Moses is a snake, but he rarely sheds his skin. He's gotten better with the game the longer he has been playing it. He's learned from Col's mistakes, but I still don't think he's smart enough to rule the roost just yet, so I doubt today is a takeover bid.

Perhaps he's looking for a way into Dimitri's crew? Today's meet-up presents the perfect opportunity for him to get into Dimitri's good books. I've just got to hope like fuck I get Demi off both their radars before the shoot-out begins.

I drift my eyes from the lights of Erkinsvale to Agent Moses when he attempts to hand me a sandwich from the vending machine in the visiting area at Wallens Ridge. I haven't eaten in hours, but my stomach is too twisted up in knots to even consider it. That fucked-up, end-of-the-road feeling I experienced when Agent Moses disguised himself as a police officer hasn't quit the past two hours. I could blame it on the fact this is my first time in a helicopter or that I'm surrounded by FBI agents pretending to be a part of the corrupt Ravenshoe PD team, but I'm done playing stupid. I've had my head in the sand the past twelve months. It's time to take a new approach, and today is as good a day as any.

"When we land, a fleet of Ravenshoe's finest will take your team the rest of the way," says a man with thick biceps and a butt-chin face to Agent Moses, his grin indicating finest means corrupt. "If the opportunity arrives, you will be introduced as the newest recruit of the SVU branched off Ravenshoe PD."

"Why SVU?" I ask, too curious to discount. I watch enough crime shows to know what that acronym stands for. It is a specialized division within Ravenshoe PD that typically investigates crimes of a sexual nature.

Rape and prostitution are part and parcel of the Italian Cartel, so they'd never bring in a specialized unit to investigate either of those things unless it was for someone outside of its realm.

My inner monologue trails off when a disturbing thought smacks into me. The warden mentioned something about Demi blowing some guy's brains out, and now she's at a ranch surrounded by law enforcement officers dedicated to victims of rape and sexual abuse.

She couldn't have been raped, surely.

I would have known if she was hurt like that.

I would have felt something.

Like the sick, twisted feeling my stomach has been facing the past few days.

"How long?" My voice is barely audible. Not only are we landing, so the rotors are extra noisy, but I also can't open my mouth for the fear I might vomit. That's how much my stomach is swirling. "How long ago was Demi attacked?"

Realizing his ruse is up, Agent Moses sits on the very edge of his seat. He isn't assuring his words are only for my ears. He's reminding me he's weaponed up and ready to fire if I so much as move an inch in any direction he hasn't approved. "With the body being disposed of before the forensic team could arrive, we are of the belief the assault occurred approximately three days before Demi was located."

His reply sends my head into a tailspin. *Three days? Three whole motherfucking days Demi was left to fend for herself. Where were my brothers? Max? Where was the protection Ezra promised when he assured me things weren't as bad as perceived?*

I silently warn Agent Moses to get the fuck out of my head when he answers some of the questions bombarding it. "At Caidyn's request, Landon and Saint gave Demi some much-needed space to get her head straight after her almost overdose on oxycodone—"

"She didn't almost overdose. She has a prescription for a bunged ankle."

My jaw muscle tenses when he has the audacity to laugh. I'd ram it back down his throat with my fists if my hands weren't shackled to my seat. "Whatever you want to call it, Ox, Caidyn's request for downtime left Demi 'vulnerable for an attack.'" He must have something with air quoting today as 'vulnerable for an attack' is his fifth foray this afternoon.

The touch of a smile gracing his lips fades to a sneer when I mutter, "An attack you organized." Don't misconstrue. I'm not asking a question, I am stating a fact.

A *pfft* noise vibrates his lips. "Why would I do such a thing, Ox? I'm not a monster."

Not a single man around him attempts to back up his claim because they know as well as I do, he'll do anything to stay at the top of the pack. He'd even go as far as leaving his team open to infiltration if it helped him get one step ahead. I thought the rumors circulating throughout Wallens Ridge about him being a traitor to his country were exaggerated. I should have known better.

"Tobias was onto you, so you orchestrated his demise. Now you're trying to do the same thing to me. But unlike Tobias, you need me, so instead of coming after me, you're going after the only person capable of making me fall into line."

"You have quite the imagination." He tilts in even closer. Not close enough that I can reach him, but close enough for me to smell the celebration drink he had earlier today. He truly thinks he's won this battle. I'm not yet ready to announce defeat. "For curiosity's sake, if I were the villain in this story, would I leave Caidyn alive, or would I kill him to ensure you knew I wasn't playing? He didn't visit the range like you and Demi did every week, so I doubt he would have had the means to protect himself from two home invaders."

I balk, both physically and emotionally stunned. "Caidyn better be—"

"Alive? He is... *barely*." I clench my fists when he expresses his last word with a snicker. "But from what I've heard, it's touch-and-go. He may not make it through the night." I almost crack my jaw from how hard I hold it when he squeezes my shoulder. "I'll be sure to keep him in my thoughts. We're all one big family around here."

Once the pilot gives him the go-ahead, he unlatches his seat belt, then clambers out of the helicopter like he didn't shred the last of my composure. I've never felt more unhinged in my life, but instead of letting my hotheadedness get the better of me, I give it my best shot to act cool, calm, and collected. Leaping into the deep end won't help anyone. It won't help Caidyn, and it won't help me. And it most certainly won't help Demi.

"Come on," says a soft female voice at my side when the occupants in the twelve-seater helicopter is shrunk to two—the pilot and me. "Let's get you unshackled and prepared for transport."

The helplessness shutting down my emotions gets a small moment of reprieve when the agent outside of the helicopter tilts her head enough, she shows her face. I'm not one of those men who remember every face they've seen, but it would be pretty foolish of me to forget the face of the woman who pickpocketed me on what I thought would be my darkest day.

"Sorry," I stutter out when my scoot across the seat sees my knees scraping past Agent Machini's chest.

Our contact is only brief but long enough to inflame her cheeks with redness. "That's okay. It's just one of those days, right?"

As she hunts for a key to switch my shackles to regular cuffs, she stares straight into my eyes. Her eyes are as dark as Agent Tobias's once were, and they speak just as many words. She knows I tried my best to protect Demi, but she also believes the time has come for me to admit I can no longer give her the protection she needs. I either concede or watch the light slowly fade in her eyes as it has the last twelve months and risk every member of my family being hurt in the process.

Once she has my shackles unlatched from a deadbolt in the floor of the helicopter, she assists me out of my seat. The tight confines leave barely an ounce of air between us, so it means I have no trouble hearing her when she whispers, "The men who attacked Demi were police officers." I scarcely register the shock of her first confession when she hits me with another one. "They're going to claim it wasn't self-defense. I saw the paperwork they forwarded to the DA before they left Wallens Ridge. They're requesting Demi be charged with first-degree murder."

"They?" I keep my voice as quiet as a whisper, but there's no denying the anguish behind it. Agent Moses's wish to attend this meeting now makes sense. He can't arrest Demi if Dimitri hides her before he gets the chance.

Agent Machini bobs down to jab a key into the shackles circling my ankles before she inconspicuously nudges her head in the direction Agent Moses is standing. "They."

He is with two gentlemen I haven't seen before. One is little with sandy gray hair, and the other is around my age. They don't look rogue, but I stopped judging people by their appearance many months ago. Some of the most down-to-earth people I've met the past couple of years are covered head to toe in tattoos. Why do you think I've added so many to my collection the past six months?

After ensuring we don't have any additional eyes on us, I drop mine to Agent Machini. "What benefit would they get from locking Demi away?"

I read the truth from her eyes long before her lips part in preparation to speak.

Me.

I did whatever they wanted for ten minutes alone with Demi once a month, so imagine how far I'd go to ensure she doesn't go through the hell I went through my first couple of months at Wallens Ridge.

As she leans across my body to dump the shackles from my ankles into a bag behind my left leg, Agent Machini whispers, "It is time to call it, Maddox. You're tired, your family is tired, and Demi is very *very* tired."

"You've spoken with her?"

The faintest smile touches her lips before she bobs her chin. "Briefly. She is very stubborn." I can't help but smile. Demi is as stubborn as she is beautiful. "But I'm confident if permission to put herself first for a change came from the right person, she'd realize following Agent Brahn's original plan is best for all involved... including you, Maddox." After adjusting the cuffs on my sleeves to hide the welt on my wrists, she adds, "He will never find her. I promise you that." If her eyes didn't unconsciously float over my shoulder during her comment, I would have taken her statement as solely meaning Col. I know better now, but just in case, she backs up her silent pledge with words. "We're not all like Agent Moses, Maddox. There are far more good agents than there are b-bad."

She stammers over her last word, her stutter compliments of Agent Moses's sudden appearance at her side. "Is everything okay? You're taking a long time to organize the perp for transport, Ms. Machini."

Agent Machini wets her lips, rolls her shoulders, then twists her torso to face Agent Moses front on. The sun is already blinding since it's hanging low, but its rays become more intense when she breaks out her biggest smile to date. "Arrow," she purrs his name in a husky tone before playfully bumping him with her hip. "You know how I am with cuffs. Always nervous when they're being placed on but grinning ear to ear when it's time to remove them."

The huskiness of her words already announces she meant her comment in a sexual manner, but if it didn't, Agent Moses's uncomfortable shuffle would soon set you on the straight and narrow. He only needs to grab his crotch, and he'd have the nervous virgin shuffle down pat.

After ensuring he doesn't have the eye of the other three dozen agents surrounding him, Agent Moses leans in close to Agent Machini's side. "Should we grab a drink after this? You seemed to enjoy it the last time we did."

If the Bureau doesn't work out for Agent Machini, she should consider acting. She knows how to dick-tease a guy into doing anything she wants. "Sure. *If* you have time for me? You've been so busy the past twelve months, I often forget we're meant to be on the same team."

When Agent Moses grabs the fingers she's tiptoeing across his chest to suck them into his mouth like a soft-cock, Agent Machini's eyes snap to mine. It isn't Agent Moses's actions she wants me paying attention to, but the words he speaks. "Don't worry, I can see my calendar gaining a ton of new openings by tomorrow afternoon. We could have happy hour every morning, noon, and night."

If he arrests Demi, he won't need to travel three hundred miles to undertake any threats he tosses my way. He'll merely need to walk a couple of hundred feet.

Agent Machini makes sure the disdained mask she's wearing disappears before she plucks her hand out of Agent Moses's mouth. "Then I guess we better get a wiggle on. The faster this is over, the faster we can..."

When she leaves her question open for Agent Moses to answer how he sees fit, he does the prepubescent crotch grab I was seeking earlier before shouting, "Let's move out!"

In quicker than I can snap my fingers, the officers and undercover agents surrounding us pile into a line of five patrol cars, and I'm guided into an SUV at the back of the pack. My spot is wedged between two armed police officers and directly across from Agent Machini.

Agent Moses prefers to ride up front. It makes him feel superior.

After taking in the tension bristling between Agent Machini and me, Agent Moses strays his eyes to me. "We good?"

It didn't matter if we were about to exchange words with a drug lord who tried to undercut his profits or demand money from a rich 'fish' he organized to be sentenced to Wallens Ridge so he could fleece him of his inheritance, he asks the same question every single time, and I answer the exact same way, "We're good."

Except today, I tack on another six words I'd give anything to change but am finally able to admit they need to be said. "It's just one of those days."

25

DEMI

I raise my eyes from my balled hands to Roxanne when she places down a mug of coffee in front of me. She's been the perfect hostess the past three hours. She stacked the fireplace with wood, wrongly believing my shivers are because I'm cold, offered refreshments to the police officers Dimitri brought here for an unconventional trial, and she even steered my conversation with Dimitri back on mutual territory when his short temper got the better of him.

I never told Dimitri about his father's inappropriateness when I was a teen because I thought he wouldn't care. His reaction to my re-enactment of the event that occurred three days ago exposes that I was wrong. I stopped counting the number of times he promised to find the second assailant and gut him where he stood when I reached thirteen. He even offered to keep him alive so I could finish what Max started.

In a sick, twisted, and very Dimitri way, his offer was kind, but I couldn't accept it. I'd owe him more than I already do, which would prolong the Walshs' suffering I immediately ended when I accepted the life jacket Agent Machini tossed my way two hours ago.

Even hours later, I can admit everything she said made sense. If you have no chips to bet with, you have nothing to lose. When you have too many, you risk them spilling over and losing the occasional one through the cracks.

That's what happened to Caidyn. No matter how much I wish it were different, he's fighting for his life because of me. This vicious cycle won't end until I wedge a plank of wood into the cogs, and to do that, I have to give up Maddox.

That hurts more than the throbbing of my brain. I'm in so much pain, I truly have no idea how I am functioning. I'm merely putting all my faith in Agent Machini's plan. If it fails, I honestly don't know where we will go next, but I do know we can't keep living like this. Sloane was right. There's such a thing as loving someone too much.

Maddox and I are living proof of this.

My thoughts shift back to the present when Roxanne asks, "Are you sure you don't want anything to eat? I can whip up a batch of mean pancakes. Ask Dimi, he ate them and survived."

I smile in gratitude for her offer before shaking my head. My stomach is way too messed up to consider eating, and don't get me started on my heart.

Roxanne gently touches my arm before muttering, "If you change your mind, my kitchen is open twenty-four-seven." Her tone dips toward the end of her sentence. She hasn't clicked that she's speaking to a once-enamored sous-chef. She is as startled by a fleet of police cruisers kicking up dust on her driveway as I was when they commenced arriving here over three hours ago.

When she sprints for Dimitri, Max leaps to his feet. He barks and growls at the procession of cars like he's aware our biggest enemy three days ago were members of Ravenshoe PD. With my head too achy to stand and my heart in lockdown, I remain seated instead of greeting my guest with the respect he deserves. The only good that comes from my disrespect is my low-hanging head grants me the ability to see Max return to the non-aggressive stance he's had the past few hours. He feels no threat at all because he knows I'm not in any danger.

After scratching behind Max's pointy ears, I swing my eyes in the direction he's peering. My heart leaps in my chest when the fleet of police cruisers stops at the front of Roxanne's grandparents' estate, and the back door of the final car pops open to expose Maddox.

When he races across the room without a single shackle clanging between his feet, I try to stay strong. I try to remember what he said in the second grade about not letting the bullies win, but within seconds, my cheeks are flooded with more tears than Maddox's hands can keep up with.

I'm not solely sobbing about how cautious he's being with my battered face, but also because his face is gaunter in person than it was on the video Agent Machini played. His eyes are rimmed with dark circles, and his skin is clammy. His punishment has only just begun, but it's already taking a toll on him both physically and mentally.

"What the fuck did they do to you?" he murmurs under his breath, stealing the words from my mouth.

"I-I'm okay." My voice is weaker than I'm hoping, but it does what I need it to do. It halves the anguish on his face. "Have there been any updates on Caidyn?"

He shakes his head at my last question before he drifts his eyes between mine. "But he will be okay, I promise you that. I just need to get you safe first." His last sentence is barely a whisper, meaning only I hear it. It also proves Agent Machini was right. It wouldn't matter how badly injured he or a member of his family were, he'd walk over lava to get to me.

Desperate not to hurt him more than necessary, I cup his cheeks like he is mine before whispering the words he desperately needs to hear. "It's just one of t—"

My SOS is interrupted by the roar of my cousin, "Take Roxanne to her room!" Dimitri is standing beside Maddox and me, so more than my ears ring from his shouted words. My bones jump out of their skin as well.

When the tablet in Dimitri's hand dings, he thrusts it into Smith's chest before he races outside. Rocco screams Roxanne's nickname at the same time Dimitri pole drives Officer Daniel Packwood to the ground. He throws his fists in his face like I wanted to when he returned to take my official statement after a prolonged breather, then he lowers them to his body.

I'm blocked from seeing what happens next when Maddox steps into my line of sight. "Let's go. Me and you. Let's leave now."

"W-What?" I stammer out, confident I must have suffered a brain injury during my assault. He couldn't have said what I thought he did, surely.

I realize there's nothing wrong with my hearing when Maddox nudges his head to an overstuffed gym bag at our left. Rocco has a favorite brand. He uses the same one for every delivery, which means the extra padding in this one exposes it's brimming with Benjamin Franklins.

"We'll go to Mexico. My family loves it there. I'm sure they'll join us as soon as it's safe for them to do so."

"Madd—"

"Please, Demi. I thought I could live without you, but I'm no longer convinced. I can't give you up. You're the reason I breathe. I exist through you."

"Maddox..." I should say more. I just can't. The love projecting through his eyes has rendered me speechless. It's so powerful, so strong. It has me convinced we're invincible.

"O-Okay." With how cloudy my head is, I should take more than a second to deliberate. Regretfully, love makes you foolish. "Why not."

"Yes," Maddox double-checks, his smile one I'll never forget.

I briskly nod. It rattles my brain against my skull, but no amount of dizziness can hinder the crispness of my reply, "Yes."

After kissing me ever so gently, Maddox snatches up the gym bag full of cash under a side table, curls his hand around mine, then hightails it to the back entrance. Max follows us through the first two rooms before he overtakes the reins.

Since everyone's focus is on Dimitri killing a man with his bare hands in front of dozens of his colleagues, we make it to Rocco's Buick undetected.

"Put on your belt," Maddox demands after tossing the gym bag into the back seat Max's large frame is hogging.

While I do as requested, he does the same for Max. He weaves the seat belt through Max's studded collar before knotting it to a bolt usually reserved to secure baby seats.

Once he's confident Max is safely buckled in, he slips behind the steering wheel before he peels off the steering wheel's column cover. My brows furrow when the connection of two wires brings Rocco's car to life.

"H-How do you know how to hotwire a car?" I have a stern talk with my brain to get with the program. I thought my stutter was because I was scared. Maddox's presence reveals that isn't the case. I always feel the safest when I am with him.

Maddox throws the gearstick into first and slowly guides Rocco's car toward a back, more tree-lined exit before he swings his eyes to me. "It isn't as you're thinking." His smile would have you convinced we're not in the process of undertaking numerous felonies. "When our parents went out of town, they took their car keys with them. Saint googled, Caidyn kept watch, and I zapped myself with wires to ensure our infamous Walsh parties had the beverages necessary for a horny bunch of teens."

It's ridiculous for me to feel jealous. He's gone to the end of the earth for me, he can't prove his loyalty any more than that, but I'd be lying if I said the faintest scorn wasn't being felt.

"God, I've missed this," Maddox says a couple of miles later. He gauges Max's response in the rearview mirror before he slips his hand onto my thigh. My unwarranted jealousy is pushed aside when he sighs in relief to Max only protesting with the faintest whimper. He's finally learned Maddox isn't the enemy. "At one stage, I was beginning to wonder if we'd ever do this again."

"M-me too," I agree before rolling my eyes. The pain it rockets through my head is so intense, it almost has me bending in two.

"Are you okay?" Maddox asks, his pace slowing.

I nod even though I feel seconds from barfing. "I'm fine." I point to the intersection coming up. "Take a right at the end. My u-uncle has a private airstrip not too far from here. He doesn't own the aircrafts, so the pilots negotiate with anyone for the r-right number of greenbacks."

"Dem—"

"I'm fine. I am." I breathe out slowly before adding, "Get me out of here, then we can worry about my head in private." When he continues peering at me, I beg, "Please, Maddox. If you're c-caught, this will be so much worse."

When I choke on my words, he accepts the begs of a desperate woman. "Okay. Just promise me you're okay."

"I am. I promise you."

He takes a moment to gauge the authenticity of my reply before he signals to turn right. I can see in his eyes that he doesn't believe me, but he also knows now is not the time to bicker about my stubbornness.

Over the next ten minutes, I guide him through the backstreets of Erkinsvale. Ravenshoe, Hopeton, and Erkinsvale are wedged together like a triangle. Erkinsvale and Hopeton are the fatter, lower half, and Ravenshoe is the tip. My uncle controls Hopeton and a majority of Erkinsvale, and if he has it his way, Ravenshoe will soon follow.

"A concealed entrance is half a mile down..."

When flashing lights pop over the horizon, my words are replaced with a growl of an upset Doberman. Max is as uneased now as he was when a fleet of police cruisers kicked up dust at the front of Roxanne's grandparents' estate. He can sense danger is close, and he's warning me the only way he can.

"Go back!"

Maddox locks up the Buick's brakes before he skids its tires across the asphalt. Once he has us facing the direction opposite to the way we were just traveling, he flattens his foot onto the gas pedal.

We make it a few hundred feet before a sliver of silver stretched across the road catches my eyes.

"Spikes!"

Maddox tries to go around them, but they pop out the Buick's back driver's side tires, sending us careening toward a dense layer of trees. In a terrifying two seconds, Maddox grabs my seat belt, tugs on it so harshly it traps me to my seat, then slams his fist into the airbag compartment in the dashboard. It activates my airbag a mere nanosecond before we collide into a massive tree trunk. My seat belt holds my body in place, but there's no stopping the brutal whiplash of my brain. It impacts with my skull so fiercely, I black out long before the shrill of police sirens trickle into my ears.

26

MADDOX

*T*hrough a groan, I raise my hand to my left shoulder, squinting when the sharpness of a stick scratches the tips of my fingers. The branch isn't pierced through my skin. It just grazed me enough to produce little nicks all over my body.

Come to think of it, the shimmery debris scattered across my torso and stomach resemble shards of glass more than chips of wood.

Wooziness bombards me when I sit up to seek answers as to why I'm lying on muddy ground in the middle of the woods. The sky is darkening, and stars are beginning to peek through the clouds. It's a beautifully peaceful view, but it won't give me answers to the questions my weary head is seeking.

The dizziness overwhelming me doubles when I crank my neck in the direction a dog is barking. Max is standing next to a horrifying wreckage of twisted metal and glass. He's barking in the direction flashing lights are coming from.

His warning that danger is imminent kickstarts both my heart and feet. I race toward the crumbled Buick that driver's side windshield has a circular hole in it like the driver was ejected when it collided with the tree.

That's what happens when a man worries more about his girlfriend's dog safety than his own.

As the meaning behind my inner monologue smacks into me, I freeze before darting my eyes to the passenger seat of the totaled Buick. My heart leaves my chest when I spot a petite raven-haired woman in the front passenger seat. Her head is flopped to one side, and blood is pouring out of a split down her forehead.

The world crumbles in on me when I take in what she's wearing. She has on the same outfit Demi was wearing when I suggested we run to Mexico, and even from a distance, the low neckline of her dress can't hide the scar running down the middle of her chest.

My attention is forced to the Buick's hood when smoke commences pluming out of the engine. There's enough smoldering fog to announce the fire under the hood isn't a little blaze. The Buick is seconds from exploding, and the love of my life is trapped in the wreckage.

"Demi!" I scream while pushing off my feet with a roar.

I charge for her, unconcerned about the number of sticks that jab into my shoeless foot during my charge. It appears as if I lost one during my sail through the air. It's dumped halfway between the wreckage and the sloshy ground where I woke.

I sprint past it during my efforts to reach Demi. My speed is relentless but horrifyingly too late. Just as I reach the tree trunk I crashed into, the Buick explodes. The power of the explosion sends both Max and me sailing backward. Max lands in the ditch we sailed over when the spikes took out the Buick's back tire. I crash into a tree. My body's collision with the tree trunk winds me, and it shatters my heart into a million pieces, but I don't give up. I bounce back onto my feet before sprinting toward the fiery blaze.

The skin on my hands melts on the Buick's hood when I leap over the inferno so I can reach Demi's door without needing to race around the massive trunk we collided with. The flames are intense. I feel like I'm on fire, but I fight through the pain to reach her, to pull her to safety. I give it my all, except it isn't enough. The flames are too high, and I'm pulled away from the wreckage by two first responders acting as if Max won't gnaw their nuts off for touching me.

As my Wallens Ridge jumpsuit soaks up the remnants of an earlier shower, a crew of two fire trucks and three police cruisers do everything they can to save Demi. They peel back the roof of the Buick like it's a can of tuna before they cover the blackened wreckage with white foam.

The blazing inferno is extinguished in a remarkably quick thirty seconds, but no number of genie wishes can hide the truth.

Demi is dead, and the accident that claimed her life was my fault.

27

DEMI

"Keep walking."

Acting ignorant of the ruckus behind us, a male agent with blond hair and thick biceps continues guiding me through the dense bushland surrounding the crash site. I can hear Maddox's screams from here, feel his pain. He truly believes the charred remains in the passenger seat of the Buick are me.

His confusion is understandable. Even I didn't know Agent Machini's plan until she ordered the man walking with me now to unbuckle an unconscious Maddox from his seat and place him two hundred feet in front of the crash scene.

I was barely lucid when a second agent smashed out the Buick's front window to replicate the outcome of someone being ejected from a vehicle on impact. Proof of this was displayed in the worst light when I let out a shocked giggle about them dumping one of Maddox's running shoes partway between our wreckage and him to authenticate their ruse. It was sadistic of me, and it has me worried I'm more like my uncle than perceived, but I was so dazed and confused, I couldn't hold it back.

I was also grateful Maddox was alert enough after our accident that they had to subdue him with a sedative. He was alive. It was only his heart Agent Machini was determined to destroy.

"H-How did she know we w-were going to run?" I ask when the complexity of the situation dawns on me. This wasn't an on-the-whim ruse. It was a thoughtfully hatched plan.

The blond agent's lips tuck at one side. "Macy has a way of reading people. She knows what they're thinking long before the words have left their mouths." He drops his eyes to mine. They're full of cockiness, but there's also a gleam to them that makes me feel safe. "After speaking with you both, she knew the instant you saw each other again, those hooks would sink back in."

"S-She spoke with Maddox?"

He gestures his hand to a rusted car parked halfway up the dirt road we're walking before notching up his chin.

I wet my lips with the hope it will ease out my words before asking, "What did h-he say?"

The agent assists me into the passenger seat of the car he pointed at, jogs around the hood, slips into the driver's seat, then hands me a cap. Once I have it covering my throbbing skull, he mutters, "It's just one of those days."

The knowledge that Maddox agreed with Agent Machini's plans won't remove the frantic screams he released while endeavoring to free me from the wreckage from my head, but it does give me enough peace to answer the pleas of my thumping brain.

I pass out before the 'd' of my name leaves the unnamed agent's mouth.

"Hey there, baby girl, welcome back."

With my vision too blurry to take in the person's features in front of me, I leave it up to my intuition. "Caidyn?"

"Close," the stranger whispers. "But I'm ten times better look-ing…" I realize who he is when he laughs "… have at least a dozen more tattoos, and let's not get me started on my cock."

"All right, Rocco. E-Enough showboating. Can you help me up?"

"I'd rather you stay down—"

"And I'd r-rather you not talk about your cock, but w-we can't always have what we want, can we?"

With a chuckle, he helps me into a half-seated position. I don't know why the change-up unclogs my ears, but I go from not hearing Agent Machini's heated conversation with a male voice I don't recognize to hearing every single word.

"She's badly concussed. We can't move her now."

"If we don't move now, we will lose the opportunity. Is that what you want, Macy? Do you want her stuck here for eternity?"

"No, of course not," Agent Machini answers. "But I don't want to compromise her health for her safety."

"You're a trained trauma nurse—"

"Who is advising you that moving her now could end disastrously."

I shift my eyes to Rocco when their conversation either hits a stalemate or they take it to another location. My eyesight is still too poor to see the concern in his eyes, but I can feel it. "What's t-that about?"

I hear Rocco scrub his hands together while he replies, "They're worried about how much you're sleeping." I whack him in the arm when he adds with a breathy laugh. "I told them to buy you a couple of pregnancy tests."

He's just like Maddox. He tries to suffocate every bad situation with humor.

"Has a-anyone heard from Maddox?"

After a brief cough to clear his throat of nerves, Rocco replies, "Yeah. He's okay. He did spend the night in the hospital, though."

I cut him off by leaping to my feet. My brisk movements almost send me toppling onto my ass. I've never felt more dizzy in my life.

Rocco guides me back to bed before saying, "He isn't hurt... physically." I sigh when he mutters, "Those Petrettis are hard to get over. Even an ox needs a moment to gather itself."

Maddox told me about Rocco's multiple slip-ups about Ophelia. It's clear even years later that it still affects him. I can only hope Maddox's grief doesn't last as long. It was never my intention to hurt him this badly. I just wanted him to be free of the burden of my protection.

I stop cradling my throbbing head in my hands when someone knocks on the bedroom door. After telling me he'll see me around—that's as formal as it gets for Rocco—he heads for the door to let our interrupter in. I'm not sure if he and Agent Machini have met before, but they don't give off the vibe of strangers when they bypass each other in the doorway of my room.

"It's time, Demi," Agent Machini says after handing me a pair of shoes.

Despite the begs of my achy head, I slip my feet into a pair ballet flats before standing on a wobbly pair of knees.

After watching me sway like a leaf in a fall wind, Agent Machini asks, "Are you still dizzy?"

"Only a little," I lie, confident most of my pain centers around my heart. "I'll be okay." *I have no choice but to be.*

She waits a beat before bobbing her head. "Okay. This way."

After spinning on her heels, she guides my walk outside. To say I'm shocked she veers me through Roxanne's grandparents' ranch is an understatement. I assumed we were in a safe house. I had no clue I was hiding in plain sight.

With Dimitri's head seemingly in lockdown mode, he only throws the quickest glance my way when I'm loaded into the back SUV in a fleet of five and driven away. I'm interested to learn what he thinks of Agent Machini's plan, but I'm not in the right frame of mind to ask questions just yet. I only walked a few feet, yet I feel seconds from collapse. My nape is drenched with sweat, my stomach is swirling, and I have no doubt the thump of my skull is more a migraine than a standard headache.

Who knew heartache was so physically exhausting?

"Are you sure you're okay, Demi?" Agent Machini asks from her station across from me a couple of miles later. For the past thirty minutes, she's been fiddling with an iPad, proving there's no rest for the wicked.

When I nod, she places down her device before balancing her backside on the edge of her seat. "I know this is hard, and you're probably pissed as hell at me about the operation I ran last night, but it will get better." She nudges her head to the report she's in the process of filing. "There's stuff in there that will see this *all* coming to an end very soon. The real people responsible will be brought to justice, and the innocent will be freed. I just need you to give me a little bit of time. Miracles don't happen in a day."

"Okay."

I hate giving in. Even when we're wrong, it's rare for a Petretti to admit they are, but I'm just too tired to continue fighting. I am physically and mentally exhausted. I want to close my eyes, fall asleep, and forget this world exists, and I'm allowed to do that forty minutes later while thirty thousand feet in the air.

"Demi..." Agent Machini's shouts from her seat across from mine before she unbuckles her seat belt and darts across the aisle of the private jet.

I'm shuddering out of control, choking on my tongue, and experiencing the most splintering headache I've ever experienced, yet I feel at peace like the best is still to come.

I finally feel free.

"Take this aircraft down!" Agent Machini screams toward the cockpit while removing me from my chair and laying me flat on the ground. The blinding light she flashes into my eyes doubles the pain in my head, so there's no way I can follow her command for me to stick out my tongue. "Come on, Demi. Open your eyes for me and poke out your tongue. You're stronger than this."

I try to follow her command, mindful of the despair in her voice, but I'm in too much pain to do anything but shut down.

I want the pain to end.

It hurts too much.

Several extremely painful seconds later, Agent Machini mutters,

"The patient's Glasgow score is a five if that. I believe she's suffering from an acute subdural hematoma."

It dawns on me that she's talking to someone outside of the plane when a mature male voice crackles into my ears a couple of seconds later. Everyone seated around us wouldn't have been over the age of thirty-five. This man sounds in his sixties, if not a little older. "If that is the case, you'll need to perform an emergency posterior fossa craniectomy."

"No—"

"You can do this, Macy," the stranger assures, his tone confident. "You've performed it before, and I will guide you like I did back then."

"I was in a hospital then, and I had the right equipment. I-I can't perform it here."

"You can," assures a third voice. This one sounds similar to the one who guided me out of the bushland last night, just primed with apprehension. "Tell me what you need and what needs to be done to save her. Without her, you may never find Kendall."

Just before I surrender to the pain overwhelming every inch of me, Agent Machini replies, "Find me a corkscrew or a wine opener. Something that can burrow through bones."

Her clipped request would scare me if my slip into the black void didn't award me the image of my dad standing across from me with the biggest smile on his face. He holds Kaylee in one hand while stretching out the other in offering to me.

When I slip my hand into his, fully void of the pain that's been crippling me the past twelve hours, he whispers, "Welcome home, baby. There's nothing to be scared of here."

28

MADDOX

I died fifteen days ago. My heart stopped beating, it no longer pumps, but somehow, my feet still move when my brain commands me to walk. I eat, sleep, and pee like an everyday person. Only I know I'm dead because only I can feel the hollowness inside of me.

Under different circumstances, a life inmate would have relished the freedom I've had the past fifteen days. I was cuffed to my bed, but the door of my hospital room could have been a revolving door of visitors if I didn't turn them all away.

I love my parents and siblings, but a man without a soul can't do idle chit-chat.

I'm also sick of pretending I am fine when I'm anything but. Grief doesn't go away. It comes in like waves. Sometimes it's a calm, nurturing flow. Other times it represents a tsunami.

Today is the latter.

The burns on my hands have healed, so my time at Ravenshoe Private Hospital is over. I'm being transported back to Wallens Ridge, and none other than the warden himself is helming my transport van. He felt like a fool when he was informed by Ravenshoe PD that one of his inmates was detained hundreds of miles from his prison. I can only imagine how beetroot red his face was when Agent Moses was assigned to investigate how an inmate escaped a maximum-security prison unnoticed.

Agent Moses's eagerness to get in Dimitri's good books placed his entire operation on the line. Production came to a screaming halt, and the seven-figure digits in his bank account dwindled to a pittance when he learned the guards couldn't be bribed with 'what ifs.' They wanted money, and who better to get that from than the man who has profited from them for months on end.

I want to say Agent Moses's downfall made my grief less noticeable, but unfortunately, that would be a lie. I feel Demi's loss every day because in my heart, I know she's gone for real this time. My belief doesn't stem from the fact I saw her demise. It comes from deep within me, from a part of my soul only she could activate. The flame extinguished. There isn't even a wick left to relight if the opportunity arose.

The woman I love is gone, and I plan to become just as invisible.

I'll serve my sentence in silence. I will bide my time, then, when the timing is right, I'll join her on the other side. I can't do that now because there are matters I need to attend to, but soon, I'll be as free as Demi. Finally unshackled from this miserable existence.

"Let's go," Agent Moses says with a clap of his hands.

He tugs on the shackles curled around my wrists and ankles, assisting me from my hospital bed before nudging his head in the direction he wants me to walk. I don't miss the heated glances of the nurses and admin staff when I shuffle past. When they look at me, they don't see the man Demi did. They see a monster, a murderer, and a man without a heart, and since their assumptions are spot-on, I haven't bothered to correct them.

I am the lowest of the low. There are only four men beneath me. Col, Agent Moses, Dimitri, and Rocco. I plan to trim my list down to one as soon as I can.

When I'm guided out through the delivery entrance at the back of the hospital, my eyes shift to the right from the quickest flurry of red capturing my attention. Justine is standing at the end of the guarded alleyway, peering my way. When she was young, her hair matched the vivacity of her personality. Now, it gains her the attention neither of us want her to have. She'd hate for her admirers to gawk long enough they'll see the scars of her assault no number of layers can hide, whereas I'm afraid they'll see her scars as proof of the fierce woman hiding beneath them.

I want her to find her prince charming and achieve her happily ever after. I just want it to be far *far* away from here.

"If you want your bank account returned to what it once was, keep your eyes front and center, Arrow," I warn Agent Moses when his hooded gaze slings to my baby sister, who's eyeballing my transfer like she's an up-and-coming journalist instead of a defense attorney. "You don't need to bribe me to get the goods. You merely need to shut the fuck up and listen."

He doesn't appreciate my tone, but like the whiny bitch he is, he takes it up the ass like he was born to follow instead of lead. After slotting into the seat next to me in the transport van, he signals for the driver to go. His eyes don't drift back to peruse Justine for the second time. It's unfortunate. The toothbrush I stuffed into my pocket two weeks ago is still in its rightful place, except it no longer has smooth edges. They're sharp and edgy—as is the razor blade I fixed to one end.

As my thumb authenticates the sharpness of the blade on my shank, I sling my eyes to Agent Moses. "Did you do as I asked?"

After lifting his chin, he discloses, "It wasn't easy convincing him, but when I said it was you, he accepted your next available appointment." As his lips curve into a smug grin, he twists the top half of his body to face me. "That's proof it was smart of you to realize what we had was a good thing. If you scratch my back, Ox, I'll *always* scratch yours." When air involuntarily whizzes from my nose, he tries to make out he isn't the scum on the bottom of a seedy one-star motel shower floor. "I really wish things had turned out differently. Demi didn't deserve to go down the way she did." Forever a cockhead, he showcases a side of his personality he should have kept hidden. It makes the shank in my pocket super heavy. "I guess that's what you get for trying to play both sides. When you try to pit good against evil, it doesn't matter which way the chips fall, you'll always be on the losing team."

He shrugs like he didn't place Demi's death on my shoulders before he hooks his boots onto the seat in front of him. After scooting down in his seat, he drops his chin onto his chest. He's out cold not even ten seconds later.

I could take him out now with one nick of the big ugly vein pulsating in his neck, but as I said earlier, there's a time and a place for everything. Now is not the time nor the place to sentence Agent Moses for his crimes—unfortunately.

Approximately five hours later, I enter the secret room Demi and I had our last meeting in without shackles or the shadows of burly, money-hungry guards. The chair Demi and I fucked on sits in the middle of the windowless room, and the scent of her sweat-slicked hair is still lingering in the air. It should make me hesitant about what I'm about to do. Instead, it fills me with so much remorse, I don't wait for the guards to latch the locks into place before I show my guest the shank I prepared specifically for him.

Rocco doesn't flinch when his eyes drop to the toothbrush/razor combination in my hand. He has the audacity to smile. "What's the matter, Ox? Having a bad day?"

"More like a bad year," I reply, my voice unrecognizable. "And it all started with you."

I don't give him the chance to recant my accurate statement. I nudge my head to the documents I requested Agent Moses leave in plain sight, so he's so bogged down with evidence, even if he wanted to speak, he couldn't.

After taking in the surveillance images of him at a well-known pharmacy chain, collecting the misoprostol prescription that killed my unborn baby with Demi, Rocco raises his eyes to mine. "I bought your girl pregnancy tests. I didn't knock her up." Like a fool who has no clue I'm barren of a soul, he raps his knuckle against my chest. "You would have known if I had been in with her aft—"

Before all his scorn can leave his mouth, I pin him to the padded wall of the cell before I squash his jugular with my shank. "She lost our baby because of *you*. She almost fucking died because she took the *tablets you* supplied her. *You're* the reason she bled out."

"What the fuck are you on about? I didn't give Demi any tablets. I told India..." His words trail off as his brows pull together in confusion. After a couple of silent seconds, he mutters, "India offered to buy the tests for me. She said she was going to the pharmacy." His chest heaves as well as mine does when it dawns me on where I've heard the name India before and who said it. "She wouldn't have... he'd fucking kill her if she..."

His pupils widen to the size of saucers as his stomach gurgles. Barely a second later, he pushes me off him like grief hasn't doubled my weight. When I object to his aggression with a perfectly structured left swung hit, he shouts into my face. "Dimitri is in India's house now! He's there with his fucking daughter."

"Fien?" I ask, my one word a cross between pleased and mortified. I'm pleased Dimitri has finally found her, but I'm worried Fien is the only surviving female member of the Petretti entity. If Dimitri doesn't pull his finger out of his ass, her life will replicate Demi's. That isn't a life you'd wish on anyone. I would have given anything to free Demi from it.

When I say that to Rocco, he murmurs, "She won't have a fucking life to live if you don't back the fuck up. If India could harm an unborn baby, she's most likely fucked in the head enough to fiddle with one while she's still in her mother's womb. She could be the woman Dimitri's been searching for the past four days."

Despite the vengeance that's grown inside of me like a weed the past fifteen days demanding I do otherwise, I step back until my elbows brace on the wall opposite Rocco. The pieces of the puzzle hazing my head are slowly slotting together, and the picture exposes as much as I want Rocco to be the villain of my story, the evidence no longer points at him.

Rocco looks desperate to flee, but when a side of him he rarely shows outranks his wish for carnage, he looks me dead set in the eyes and asks, "If I find out it was India who hurt your unborn baby, what do you want me to do?"

A man not in the throes of grief would contemplate his question for longer than a second.

I don't.

"Kill her."

His lips pull high at one side. "It'll be my pleasure."

Agent Moses's perplexed gaze bounces between Rocco and me when I pull open the weighted door his ear is pressed against, wordlessly commencing Rocco's campaign to bring India before the courts. He came prepared to hide Rocco's murder. He relinquished the guards from their watch and has a body bag and transportation at the ready.

"What happened, Ox? We discussed this," he queries after watching Rocco sprint down the isolated corridor while shouting Smith's name on repeat. "You were going to take care of business, then share his contacts with me." By contacts, he means the drug manufacturers I met while running coke from town to town for Dimitri. "If that's no longer our agreement, you'll need to come up with a new—"

"Who's India?" I interrupt, my tone nothing close to pleasant. I'm sick and tired of being played like a fool, and for once, the man orchestrating the prolonged intermission of my life is standing in front of me, alone and without protection. Not even a weasel of a man like Warden Mattue can be bribed to bring guns inside Wallen Ridges's walls.

Agent Moses stammers out a faint, "Who?" before he realizes his gig is up. I'm onto him. "She's only ever said nice things about you." His tongue delves out to wet his lips, hopeful it will hide his smile. "She never had a mule turn down an offer of an untouched girl before, then you let Dr. Franklin live when you should have killed him. It had her wondering if you were one of us."

"Is that why she placed misoprostol into a canister labeled as a pregnancy vitamin? Because she thought Demi would stop me from becoming one of you?"

With a half-smirk, he shakes his head. "No. India doesn't work like that. She'll woo you into being her lackey before she'll show her claws."

I hate the truth in his tone, but there's no denying it. "Then why did she hurt Demi?"

"She hates competition," he states matter-of-factly. Confusion must cross my features as he's quick with his endeavors to relieve it. "Your son or daughter would have been the prince or princess of the Italian Cartel. India wants that title reserved for her children."

"She isn't Italian," I shout, stating the obvious.

"No, she isn't," Agent Moses agrees while his eyes flicker like he's recalling a fond memory. "But her daughter is, and if she has it her way, her son will be Russian. To her, this is the perfect solution. Why rule one entity when you can have them all?" He laughs at the shocked mask that slips over my face. "Don't look so stunned, Ox. In your wildest dreams, you couldn't imagine half the things India is capable of."

After gathering up the documents Rocco dumped when I pinned him to the wall, he spins around to face me. "In a way, you should be grateful about how fucked in the head she is. If she hadn't encouraged Col to smear the blood of his niece on his cock, Demi's grave would have been dug years earlier." He rubs his thumb over his lip before asking, "Did I tell you about the time India gave Col a hand job while whispering in his ear how she's fantasized about seeing a woman's beauty destroyed by a viciously-trained attack dog?" He doesn't wait for me to answer him. It's for the best. I doubt I could talk through the anger enveloping me. "When Col couldn't get to Demi to fulfill her sick fantasy, he settled for Justine."

The nonchalant way he refers to my baby sister's attack causes black hate to clog my senses.

I can't see through the darkness engulfing me.

There's no light at the other end.

It's black, dark, and lonely, and it snaps my last nerve.

"Saved from a brutal mauling only to be burned alive." Agent Moses *ha's!* out loud. "I don't know about you, but the smell of her charred skin won't leave my nostrils for years to come. And your sister's screams..." I'm engulfed with rage when he finishes his sentence with a growl. "I'm hard now just thinking about them."

With the roar of a wounded animal, I lose everything about me that I use to be. I slam my fist into Agent Moses's spleen. Since it's the same hand still clenching my shive, blood drains from his face both metaphorically and figuratively only seconds later.

"She was a fucking human being. An angel. A woman too good for the life she was born in," I scream into his face.

While staring in the eyes of a monster, ensuring there's no way he can miss the hate I have for him in my blackened gaze, I stab him another three times.

As his knees buckle out from beneath him, the pain too much to keep him standing, he fists my jumpsuit in a white-knuckled hold, bringing us closer, before issuing one final plea for mercy. "O-Ox... t-think about this."

"I have," I reply, my voice unwavering and confident. "I've thought about this *many* times the past twelve months."

It feels like he hits me in the jugular with his fist when he stammers out, "Y-Your family—"

"Will be safer once you're dead."

When the twisting of the shank only forces a handful of tears to slide down his cheeks, I withdraw it, then jab it back in over and over and over again, only stopping when there's no doubt the light in his eyes will never return.

His shallow, pain-filled breaths fan my cheek when I whisper in his ear, "I was sentenced to life behind bars for a murder I didn't commit, so it's only fair I do the crime that fits the time."

A wheezy breath escapes Agent Moses's mouth when I leave nothing to chance. I've heard stories of men surviving bullet wounds to the head, have seen prisoners back in the yard only a week after multiple stab wounds to their stomachs, but I've yet to hear a single account of a man surviving a fatal stab wound to the heart. He'll be dead before the medics arrive, and I'll be one step closer to seeing Demi again.

As I slowly come out of the rage Ezra used with the hope it would pull the wool over the judge's eyes during my trial, Agent Moses slumps to the floor. I should feel guilt while looking at a man who's been bludgeoned to death, but I don't.

What I said earlier was true. Up until today, I wasn't a murderer.

I killed to protect Demi.

I claimed the life of another man to save my own.

Just like soldiers on the battlefield killing the enemy, it isn't wrong if it has a purpose.

Revenge isn't a purpose, but when it's the only thing keeping you going, take from it what you may. Furthermore, it only took counting the beats in Agent Moses's neck when he spotted Justine today to know who he'd focus his attention on if I stopped jumping on cue. Justine has been through enough. I couldn't put her in more danger.

After discarding the bloody shank next to Agent Moses's slumped form, I spin on my heels and exit the room. I make it halfway down the corridor that leads to the main hub of the prison when my name is spoken by a husky and familiar female voice.

I spin around to face my greeter so fast, the hope filling my head is pushed aside for dizziness. I wouldn't forget Demi's voice in a million years. My veins are just too thick with adrenaline to recognize the distinct differences between the two female voices.

Fortunately, the boost of testosterone keeping me upright doesn't affect my eyesight. The woman standing in front of me has hair as dark as Demi's once was, and her eyes are a similar color, but Demi had the face of an angel, and Agent Machini's position has aged her more than her years on this earth.

"You're too late," I mumble, my words barely legible through the guilt of not accepting her offer to get Demi out on my behalf. If I had done that, Demi would still be here. "Demi is dead. I killed her."

Agent Machini scarcely shakes her head before she takes a staggering step back. It dawns on me how much of Agent Moses's blood is on my hands when she breathlessly asks, "What did you do,

Maddox?" Before I can answer her, she cranks her neck to the room I just left. "No!" she pushes out with a sob.

When she glances back my way, she looks more concerned for me than Agent Moses. I understand why. He's dead. He can't hurt her. She can't issue the same guarantee for me. To her, I'm a cold-blooded murderer. She has no clue I only gained that title mere seconds ago.

The heaves of Agent Machini's chest match mine when I issue her the faintest grin before I continue with my travels. I was caught red-handed—*literally*—and although I'll never feel guilty about killing Agent Moses, only a monster would be content walking around with the blood of a dead man on his hands and not feel sick.

I'm not one of them.

I'm just a man who wanted to do a little good for his community.

29
_____

AGENT MACY MACHINI

I stand frozen in the underbelly of Wallens Ridge State Penitentiary, shocked and confused. I came here to throw a life raft to a man drowning in grief. I'll leave unsure if he is a victim or a perpetrator.

Maddox Walsh isn't a bad man. His childhood crush saw him thrust into a world he knew nothing about, then he was propositioned by a man he would have instantly trusted because his parents raised him to respect the law.

He doesn't belong here, but now his grief has left him with no other option but to remain here—grief I forced him to endure. That places Agent Moses's murder on my shoulders as much as it does Maddox's. I didn't inflict a single stab wound to Agent Moses's body, but I knew about his corruption and the torment he was putting Maddox through, but instead of speaking out against a bully who had his division too scared to speak, I trusted that justice would eventually prevail.

As I look at Agent Moses's lifeless form slumped in a non-surveillance, soundproof room, I begin to wonder if it finally did. He's everything that is wrong with the system. From the police officers falsifying witness statements to the judges who accept payments for unfair sentencing and the housing of inmates, Agent Moses had his hand in every piece of the pie. And now, stupidly, his years with the Bureau will see him honored as a hero instead the immorally corrupt man he was.

Unless...

Before I can talk myself out of it and needing to move quickly before I lose the chance to implement my ruse, I pace into the room that smells a strange mix of blood and floral perfume. I close the door behind me before forcefully ripping at my blouse. Once the cotton material is hanging limply off my chest, I grab Agent Moses's hand and drag his nails across my inner thigh, then I make him painfully squeeze my breasts.

With the simpler tasks ticked off my list, I move toward the harder, more painful items. It takes three attempts to slam the only object in the room onto my hand hard enough to shatter bones, then I headbutt the wall like I'm unaware of the damage a knock to the head can cause.

Demi flatlined in the jet because of a whack to the head. She died three times during a ten-minute operation, and when we finally landed, no amount of chest compressions could bring her back.

Demi Petretti no longer exists.

The recollection of the horrifying day means only the slightest whimper escapes my mouth when I slice the shank that ended Agent Moses's life across my forearm and thigh before removing my panties and placing them in Agent Moses's pocket.

After taking a moment to ensure I have my story straight, I rip open the door I closed only minutes ago and commence screaming for help. My cries bounce down the isolated corridor before they're gobbled up by boots thumping on polished concrete floors.

When two guards reach me at the entrance of the surveillance-free room, I collapse into guard number one's arms while the other moves toward Agent Moses to check him for a pulse.

"H-He tried to r-rape me," I stutter on purpose, hopeful it will authenticate my ruse. "I-I-I had to protect myself. He left me no choice." When guard two shakes his head at guard one, announcing he feels no pulse, I release the tears I saved when I slice the recently wiped clean of fingerprints shank through my arm and thigh. "No. He can't be dead. I just wanted to stop him from hurting me. I-I didn't mean to k-kill him."

As I rant and rave that I only meant to protect myself, I'm carted out of the prison and placed into an awaiting ambulance. When the medic suggests a sedative to calm me down, I lower my sobs before pulling my knees to my chest, where they stay until Agent Grayson Rogers enters my hospital room five hours later.

I don't know whether to be stoked about my top-shelf performance or displeased. It isn't every day an impromptu script gets you placed into the psych ward of a hospital. I guess I didn't really need to act when it came to portraying Agent Moses as the man he really was. I found it harder pretending I liked him during Maddox's transport than I did faking his assault.

"Are you sure this is the story you want to run with, Macy?" Grayson asks, his tone void of the usual cheekiness it has.

I confidently nod. "It isn't a story. I defended myself from an attacker."

"By stabbing him fourteen times in the stomach before inflicting a final wound to his chest."

I wish I had counted Agent Moses's stab wounds before jumping the gun, but I honestly don't think it would have changed my mind. Maddox reacted the way he did because of me, so it's only fair I take some of the blame.

"You know how much adrenaline you get hit with when survivor instincts kick in, Grayson. It was all a blur. One minute, he was holding my face to the wall while tugging at my panties, the next minute, I was standing over his bloody body."

A shiver rolls down my spine. There's too much similarity to my reply for me not to respond. There's just one difference. In my dreams, Agent Moses ends up dead. In my nightmares, I let my rapist roam free—*until today.*

My eyes float up to Grayson when he says, "The DA said you're refusing a physical examination."

I lift my chin. "He didn't get to the point of p-penetration..." I stop before I say too much.

Unfortunately, Grayson is more clued on than his handsome face indicates. "Today?"

My chin wobbles before I faintly nod. I've kept this secret for over twelve months. It's time to let it go.

When my woozy head has me mistaking Grayson's sigh as disappointment, I blubber like a narc. "I reported it the day after it happened. I took it directly to the head of our department. But instead of prosecuting my rapist, he gave him a big fat promotion."

Grayson doesn't lecture me about Bureau protocol like his father did or scold me for not going directly to him. He just holds me in his arms like my mascara-stained tears won't ruin his shirt.

I'm not sure how long we stay huddled in our little bubble. It isn't long enough for me to feel uncomfortable, but it is long enough for Grayson to make a verdict on his ruling. With Agent Moses dead, he is now the interim supervisor of our division.

After rubbing his thumb under my eyes to clear away the last bit of moisture on my cheeks, he says, "I'll recommend for the Bureau to suspend you *with* pay for six months."

Money isn't something I have to worry about, but my badge, that piece of gleaming metal that convinces me I contribute to this world in a positive manner, that means the world to me, so I'm so very grateful it wasn't immediately stripped from me.

"Before you can come back, you'll be required to undergo a psych exam. *If* you pass that, we will slowly ease you back into fieldwork."

I interweave my fingers to stop me from reacting with violence for the second time today before saying with a pout, "You don't have to say it like that. I'm not mentally unstable."

"It's a pity," Grayson murmurs with a grin. "The loopy ones have always been my favorite." He laughs when I sock him in the stomach before he offers me a ride home.

"I'm good, but thank you."

Blond hair flops into his face when he slants his head to the side. "Do you have somewhere else you need to be?"

I take a moment to acknowledge the unexpected jealousy in his tone before replying, "Yeah. She doesn't have anyone right now, and I have six months of vacation time." When Grayson groans, I smile. "I'm joking. I'll use it wisely. Neither you nor the Bureau can get rid of me that easy."

When I rub my hand down his arm in an unprofessional manner, it sees me pulling away like his arm set my hand on fire. It did, but that isn't the point. I took the blame for Agent Moses's murder because he sexually assaulted me on the clock.

I should *not* be objectifying anyone.

The knot in my stomach gets a moment of reprieve when Grayson calls my nickname. "Mace."

I freeze partway out my hospital room door before twisting my torso to face him.

He smiles at the unease on my face before he mutters, "For what it's worth, I would have done the same." I assume he's referencing me killing the man who attempted to rape me for the second time but am proven wrong when he adds, "I'm not sure I would have gotten away with stuffing my briefs into his pocket, but I would have given it a shot if it was the only way I could shift the focus to me."

Protocol is the last thing on my mind when I race back to his side of the room. I throw my arms around his neck and hug him tight before whispering in his ear, "Thank you."

Grayson holds me as firmly as he did only minutes ago. His hug takes care of any guilt I was wrongly experiencing. I didn't kill Agent Moses. I merely supported a man who had been wronged by him over and over again.

That's justice.

I did my job.

"Go do what needs to be done so you can get back to where you're meant to be," Grayson murmurs a couple of seconds later.

I command my eyes to dry like the Sahara before I inch back so I can see his face. Words won't express what I'm feeling right now, so I have to leave the impossible task to my eyes. It's no easy feat. I'm not known for showing emotions, and it's clear Grayson isn't either when he musses my hair like he does Brandon's when he can't find the right words to say.

Our heart-mending scene is still spreading warmth across my chest when I walk into the hospital room of what I believe will be a long-term patient many *many* hours later.

Demi's crystal blue eyes pop up to mine before she cocks a brow. She studies my face for several long seconds before she breathes out in a slow yet precise manner, "Macy, right?"

I grin a proud smile. "Yep! That's me."

A giggle rumbles up my chest when the pride on my face jumps onto Demi's. She looks so much closer to her age now that the strains of her life have been removed from her memories.

With back-to-back head injuries—first the baseball, then the whiplash her brain endured during her single motor vehicle crash—Demi suffered a traumatic brain injury. Blood was practically swarming her brain, slowly killing it. It took a mammoth effort to save her, but the combined exertions of both Dr. Nesser and me on the phone achieved the impossible.

Demi was placed into an induced coma for ten days, but that was more a precaution to ensure her swollen brain couldn't inflict any more damage. When she came too, her recovery was quite remarkable. She spoke with only the slightest slur, could remember basic points such as counting to ten, telling the time, and her body was receptive to things such as the difference between hot and cold.

It was a miracle no one expected, but the phenomenon didn't linger for long.

Demi couldn't remember her name or where she was born. To begin with, Dr. Nesser believed she was suffering from the standard amnesia most patients face after a TBI. It was only when she failed to remember things about her past did Dr. Nesser dig a little deeper into her condition.

Typically, patients with amnesia know who they are, but they have trouble learning new information or forming new memories.

That isn't the case with Demi.

As displayed just now, she remembers who I am, even with us only meeting a handful of times since she woke from the induced coma. She remembers to brush her teeth morning and night, plays memory games with a competitive edge, and gobbles down a romance book every single day. Her brain function is perfectly normal, it just seems as if the area vital for memory processing was damaged in a unique, often unheard-of way.

It could have been post-traumatic amnesia, but since Demi's memory loss extends well past childhood, Dr. Nesser was skeptical. There are techniques he could use to enhance memory and psychological support for Demi, but Demi's case isn't just unique because of her TBI. The circumstances of her injuries are also one of a kind. Who wants to 'brain train' a patient with horrible, second-hand stories of abuse, neglect, and possible sexual assault?

Demi has the scars of an abused woman. Her file at the Bureau is almost as thick as her uncle's, but instead of it being filled with crimes she had undertaken in her short life, they were brimming reports from when she was the victim.

That saw Dr. Nesser diagnosing Demi's condition as more a psychological amnesia than a medical phenomenon. Have you ever been hurt so deeply you have no choice but to bury the pain? Children raised in traumatic households often use this technique in adulthood. They blame a lack of memories on poor memory function, where in reality, they don't want to remember what they went through.

Demi's abuse wasn't a one-off incident. She was hit from all sides multiple times. I'm shocked she survived. Unfortunately, I can't say the same thing about other members of her family. Most particularly, Kaylee.

A little over two weeks ago, the body of a toddler was found in the wall of a home hundreds of miles from Hopeton. The child was identified as being approximately three years old. She was so badly malnourished, forensic investigators initially struggled to identify the cause of her death.

Even with no ligature marks or bruising noted to her neck, it was eventually ruled that she died of asphyxiation. Her injuries were all internal, and the manner as to how she got them made even the hardest criminal investigators' eyes water.

When evidence emerged that Col Petretti was known to the family, the coroner included his DNA in preliminary tests. It was discovered only days ago that the child in the wall was Kaylee, except she wasn't just Demi's sister as believed, she was also her cousin.

Kaylee, along with a handful of other children, were conceived by Monica Lewis at a baby-making farm the Shroud's hosted in their barn. From what we've unearthed, Monica and Demi's father, Sean, met three months prior to Monica falling pregnant with Demi. Although their relationship moved at the speed of lightning, all appeared well on the home front—until Col intervened.

He forced Sean to pick. The life of his wife or his three-week-old baby daughter.

The aforementioned should indicate who he picked, but I'll spell it out for you just in case it doesn't.

He chose Demi.

His decision to save his child from a madman didn't hinder his endeavor to free Monica from Col's clutch, though. Just like Maddox did for Demi, Sean went to hell and back for Monica. He changed who he was to free her, and it appeared to work. Within months, Monica was returned to him. But unbeknownst to Col, she was carrying a stowaway. Kaylee was a byproduct of a brother willing to do anything to hurt one of his siblings, but in the end, she ultimately ended Col's reign.

This will never be doctored in any report you'll ever see, but the coroner determined that the bullet that ended Col's life only yesterday wasn't fired from any of the guns seized during a joint Ravenshoe PD/FBI sting. It came from an outside source. An outside source, I'm reasonably sure ended his father's reign to ensure he couldn't kill his granddaughter in the same manner he did his own child.

Ending a child's life is already heinous, but when it's done in the manner Col ended Kaylee's life, there's no room for clemency. He deserved to die.

The same can be said for Demi, but not in the physical sense. Her TBI presents the perfect opportunity for her to start her life afresh. Imagine how free she'll feel if Dr. Nesser only reprograms her brain with the good parts of her life? It's the ideal solution for her memory loss, and the reason for my impromptu across-country trip to visit a life inmate.

With Demi's father deceased, and the whereabouts of her mother unknown, Maddox was the only good part of Demi's life the past umpteenth years. We were hoping he was the key to unlocking Demi's memories less painfully, but regrettably, instead of stumbling onto Prince Charming yesterday, I found a villain instead.

It isn't as bad as it sounds. A quote I saw in a reader's group one day said, "A hero would sacrifice you to save the world, but a villain would sacrifice the world to save you."

In a way, that's exactly the man Demi needs at her side. Maddox tried to save her with fairness. When that didn't work, his moral compass pulled him in another direction.

That's proof everything happens for a reason.

Impatience forced me into the underbelly of Wallens Ridge, but it was morality that saw me taking the blame for Maddox's unexpected yet understandable lapse in judgment, and I'd do it all again tomorrow if forced.

My thoughts shift back to the task at hand when Demi asks, "Did you find him?"

I dump my coat onto the end of her bed before moving closer. "Find who?"

A ghost of a smile creeps my lips higher when Demi hits me with a stern sideways glare. For a woman with no memories, she has confidence by the bucketloads. It has me curious to see how she will flourish without the disdains of her past sullying her future.

"No," I reply with a brief shake of my head. "He wasn't who I thought he was."

"Oh," Demi replies, undeniably disappointed. I told her I was going to track down a man I thought she might know. She clearly remembers our conversation.

The distress on her face shifts to curious when I mumble, "But I did find someone I think you might like to meet. He's a little bossy and probably hairier than you're used to, but from what I've heard, he's a fantastic companion."

I wait until Demi is at the point of bursting with eagerness before I gesture for the only security officer brave enough to wrangle my new friend into submission to enter Demi's room.

It takes Max half a second to slip out of his collar when he spots Demi across the room. He leaps onto her bed before covering her face with sloppy kisses. His affection for his owner doubles the size of my heart as does Demi's joyous laughter. It's a tear-producing scene that assures me I've made the right decision.

I can't change Demi's past, but I can hide it from her to ensure she has a happy future.

Four years later...

30

MADDOX

Four years later...

*C*orrectional Officer Brooks's deep rumble booms through my ears when he opens the visitor door at Harbortown Correctional Facility. "Keep it short, Ox. Your all-hours-of-the-day-and-night visitors are worse than the ones who used to sneak into my room during my fraternity days."

The sun beaming into the windows of the medium-security prison bounces off his white teeth when he grins about the memories popping into his head. Everyone in this place thinks he's a surly bastard, but I see the man hiding beneath his hard exterior. He's the giant teddy bear Demi accused me of being. He's hard when he needs to be and soft when he doesn't.

"Craps later?" I ask like my mood isn't close to dropping off a cliff from my fifth memory of Demi this morning. It's understandable I'm teetering on the edge instead of sailing over it. This one was a good memory. I can't say the same about the ones that wake me in the middle of the night.

They say grief gets easier the longer it is. I say they're full of shit. You might act like you're doing fine, but in reality, you never catch a break. It's always there taking up space in your head you wish you could use for something good.

It hasn't stopped me from doing my part for my community the past four years, though. I just contribute from behind bars. I commenced an outreach program at Wallens Ridge that took in the new 'fish' in the pond and guided them away from dealings that would have seen them return time and time again. The success rate is high, and I can see it climbing when it's implemented across states.

I didn't lie to Justine last year when I said Harbortown is like a country club. I don't share a cell, the food could be restaurant quality if I hadn't been spoiled by Demi's culinary skills, and the prisoners aren't shackled a majority of their day. We're like RSPCA-approved chickens on a farm. Free, yet somehow still contained.

Brooks lifts his chin before he slaps his hand against mine to seal our agreement. He lost two packs of cigarettes and a carton of Coca-Cola last week. To the inmates here, that's the equivalent of an ounce of coke and the choice of a female inmate for ten minutes in Wallens Ridge. He won't be able to show his face around here if he loses again this week.

My swagger into the visitor hub slows when I spot who's come to visit me. Yes, I said swagger. I'm no longer the gun-banging, shank-wielding gangster I was forced to be at Wallens Ridge, but notoriety is an invaluable asset. I'd be a fool to give it up.

"Agent Machini, to what do I owe the pleasure?"

She waits for me to spin around the chair opposite the stainless desk she's seated behind and straddle it before she hits me with her trademark one-sided grin. It's the smile she always does when she wants to remind me how she went to bat for me.

Agent Moses's death wasn't broadcasted across the globe. Excluding a teeny tiny little obituary in the classifieds of *Ravenshoe News*, his death wasn't mentioned in the newspaper. I thought I was imagining things, that I had dreamed about killing him instead of actually doing it, then I found an article hidden amongst the headlines of political corruption and a billionaire getting married. An unnamed agent had been placed on a paid suspension pending an investigation by the Bureau's Internal Affairs Department. Her suspension was the same day I killed Agent Moses.

The story was buried so deeply, it took eight weeks for Smith to attach a name to the case file. I wasn't shocked when he came back with Agent Macy Machini, but I was stunned to learn the lengths she went to protect me. It made it obvious I wasn't the only one feeling guilty about what happened to Demi.

I rub the burn scars on my palm with my thumb when Agent Machini replies, "Can't I visit my favorite prisoner just to say hello?"

"They have this thing called a telephone. You should look it up sometime."

She laughs before telling me the real reason for her visit. "I'm in town working on a case."

"Dimitri's?"

My contact with Dimitri has been sporadic for the past four years. The first thing he did after murdering his father in the middle of a joint FBI/Ravenshoe PD operation was offer to get me out. I declined.

Why you ask?

For one, I don't want to owe Dimitri for a single thing. He isn't as bad as his father, but he doesn't deny who he is. He'd destroy the world for his family. He just didn't come to that conclusion until it was too late for Demi. And two, I'm not innocent anymore. I killed Agent Moses. I stabbed him to death, so I deserved to do the time for my crime.

Do I believe four years is a long enough sentence for murder? If it were for anyone but Agent Moses, I would say no. Since he was the victim, and my actions were clearly in self-defense, my feet are beginning to itch. The desire to scratch them isn't enough to have me reaching out to Dimitri for help just yet, but if the offer came from any other source, I'd consider it. My chances of finding India will dramatically improve once I'm outside of these walls.

My lips twist when Agent Machini confesses, "Not exactly. I'm more aiding Dimitri than searching for ways to convict him... *for now."*

The smile she delivers her last two words with lifts my lips. I'm not shocked by her statement. Tobias trained his team to use the gray in every situation to their advantage. They don't break the rules, they merely bend them to suit their needs.

I've done the same the past four years. Dimitri's visits are nonexistent, but I hear from Rocco every couple of months. He keeps me up to date on the only person responsible for the oxygen in my lungs. India Dvořáks.

The evidence Agent Moses let slip before I murdered him already had India on my shit list, but her top placement was undeniable when Rocco explained exactly how far her crimes extended during a one-on-one visit a month after Agent Moses's death.

There's evil, then there are people like Col and India.

They deserve their own category of fucked-up.

Col paid for his crimes. India has yet to be brought to Justice. Dimitri's team is working on it, and if Agent Machini's confession is anything to go by, they've sourced help from avenues outside the norm.

"I'm going to show you a selection of photos," Agent Machini says, drawing my focus back to her. After digging a confidential-stamped manila folder out of her briefcase, she places down a set of surveillance images on the desk between us. "Take your time perusing them—"

"It isn't like I have anywhere else I need to be."

She rolls her eyes about my interruption before waving her hand over the blown-up photographs. The first three are obvious drug-manufacturing hideouts, but the last two pique my interest. They're of young women bordering legal age with grubby faces. They're all wearing plain cotton nighties.

When I gather those images into my hand, Agent Machini's brow involuntarily arches. That's a telltale sign I headed in the direction she was hoping. If you haven't caught on yet, we've played this game a handful of times the past four years. It isn't a you-scratch-my-back-

I'll-scratch-yours arrangement, it's just two people who mutually respect one another enough to value their opinion.

"How long ago were these pictures taken?"

Agent Machini checks a yellow-lined notepad at her side. "Approximately a month ago." She breathes noisily out of her nose before adding, "They packed up and moved camp two hours after they were captured."

"So India knows you're onto her?"

It kills her to do, but she halfheartedly shrugs. "Possibly."

I dump the photographs back onto the desk before slouching low in my chair. "How do you think that's occurring?" The answer to my question pops into my head before her lips part a millimeter. "Agent Moses wasn't the only agent India was working with." I take a moment to deliberate before giving her my findings. "It makes sense. She didn't get out of New York without help. She had a bullet wound and Henry Gottle tracking her down. She would have needed someone high up to move her through his city without being seen."

Agent Machini nods, agreeing with me. "I forwarded my findings to the head of my department. They—"

"Want more concrete evidence?"

Her nod isn't as liberating this time around, and it's quickly chased by a squeal-free growl. "This case is frustrating me to no end. Like how can men not see how evil she is? Yes, she has tits and ass and a stupidly pretty face, but her insides are so rotten, how can they pay them an ounce of attention?"

"Damaged people attract damaged people. They forgive her fuck-ups because it's the only way they can forgive themselves."

I'm not talking out of my ass. I'm speaking from experience. It's why Justine fell under another mafia prince's spell so quickly when she flew to the other side of the country to take up an internship at the number one defense firm in the country. Nikolai, a Russian mafia prince, is as broken as Justine, but my mom assures me that when they're together, you have no clue any parts of them are missing.

It was the same for Demi and me, and it was the reason I always put her first. When I was with her, she was whole because it took pieces of me to fix her.

I'd give anything to have the chance to slot the final piece back into place.

My thoughts shift from the negative when Agent Machini exhales a big breath. "Sorry, that was very unprofessional of me. I just wish we could see people's insides as easily as we see their outsides. It would make everyone's life a whole heap easier." After scooping the photographs off the table, she stuffs them into her bag, then stands to her feet. "Are you good? Do you need anything? Ibuprofen, cigarettes, Coca-Cola? I don't see you having much use for them, but I can't help but ask."

Although I'm confused by the last half of her offer, I shake my head. "I'm good, thanks."

"All right. Bye." My confusion catapults to a new high when she leans over the desk to hug me goodbye. She isn't usually the affectionate type. Most of the time, I don't even get a wave out of her. "Keep in touch."

I watch her stalk through the reception area of Harbortown before spinning on my feet to face Brooks.

"Everything good?" he asks after taking in the expression on my face.

"I think so."

He jerks up his chin before requesting me to raise my arms to be frisked. Since prisoners aren't shackled to tables during visitation, we have to be searched after each visit. Brooks loves when my mom comes to visit because he gets to sample her dishes before I do.

My eyes shoot down to the pocket in my jumpsuit when Brooks says, "Ox, you know the rules. No pornographic material of any kind." He recants his statement when he unfolds a printed image that's the same size as the ones Agent Machini showed me only seconds ago. "I guess this is okay. They're dressed. *Kinda.*"

The reason for his confusion smacks into me when I take in the photograph. It's one of the underaged women with grubby faces, except it's zoomed out. There are several identifiable landmarks in the background, leaving me no doubt where this image was taken.

As Brooks shoves the photograph back into my pocket, I stray my eyes in the direction Agent Machini walked. I gasp in a sharp breath when I spot her standing just inside the glass exit doors. She smiles at my stunned expression, throws me a quick wave, then disappears into the parking lot like a bat out of hell.

I move just as fast, except I don't head for the exit. I race for the payphones lining one wall of the recreation room. Four years haven't moved the goal posts. I just won't be the man kicking the ball, but that doesn't matter. A win is a win no matter what position you play.

I've only punched in the first three digits of Rocco's cell phone when Brooks calls my name. When I peer at him, he nudges his head to the visitor hub. "You've got another one. Despite what his Instagram followers will tell you, he isn't as pretty as your first visitor."

Curious, I place the phone receiver back onto its dock, then head back to Brooks. The reason behind a lack of rebuttal is unearthed when my eyes lock on the man standing in the middle of the visitor hub. Saint announces his sexiness to the world. Caidyn lets it speak for itself.

"What the fuck are you doing here, Caidyn? It isn't the first Friday of the month."

Everyone around here calls the first Friday of the month 'family day' because without fail, at four o'clock every first Friday of the month, Harbortown Correctional Facility is swarmed by members of the Walsh brethren. Even Sloane occasionally joins in the festivities.

After returning my greeting, which replicates the man hug I gave him the first time I saw him after his prolonged hospital stay, Caidyn pulls me back to arm's length. "Macy didn't tell you?"

My face twitches as I struggle to conceal the dishonesty in my reply. "Tell me what? It was just a standard visit. What's going on?" I don't want my family to know of my plans. They've been through enough. I don't need to give them more grief.

I double back when I realize how contradictory my inner monologue is to my plans. I don't want to hurt my family, but I'm planning to hurt them in a way they'll never forget.

I'm not ashamed to admit that is fucked-up, but I'm at a loss as to how I can make things different. I don't exist without Demi, she was my world, so how can I be expected to live without her?

I shelf my deliberation for a more appropriate time when Caidyn says, "Your verdict was overturned. You're getting out." He glances back at the reception area like he's aware Agent Machini was there only moments ago before he mutters, "Macy arrested Megan yesterday afternoon. When the judge was presented with undeniable DNA evidence she was who Macy said she was, she overturned your conviction on the spot. You're a free man."

The shock thickening my veins is heard in my reply. "I can leave? I can walk out those doors?" I thrust my hand to the front doors of Harbortown to emphasize my point. It makes the rattle of my hands more obvious, but I don't give a shit. I thought I'd eventually have to beg at Dimitri's heel to get out of this place. I never thought it would occur because my 'victim' was found alive. From what Rocco has shared with me over the past four years, Megan's revival will be as shocking to him as it's to me. He didn't kill her. He just made it impossible for her to show up unannounced—*supposedly.*

"Umm..." Caidyn seeks Brooks's assistance to answer my question.

He comes through with the goods. "I'd suggest waiting for the official paperwork to come through. I don't want to taser your ass, but I will if I have to." He squeezes my shoulder to ensure I know there's no malice in his tone before suggesting for me to go pack.

I do precisely that *after* updating my team about my game plan.

I'll never be a part of the Italian Cartel, but teamwork is a powerful advantage when you share a common goal.

31
___

DEMI

"Come on, Max. We only have a mile to go." My words are chopped up by big breaths. I can't remember the first time I ran through these woods, but it soon became a favorite thing for Max and me to do after I was discharged from the hospital three and a half years ago.

Dr. Nesser is great, and he has a wicked sense of humor, but I'd be a liar if I said I wasn't glad to see the back end of him. I was just shy of my twenty-fourth birthday when I was discharged. Dr. Nesser is sixty-three.

Enough said.

"If you hadn't stolen *all* the bacon from the skillet, you wouldn't be so sluggish."

I laugh between breaths when Max barks out a reply. I can't understand a word he says, but I guarantee he's cursing me. He does that a lot lately.

The older he gets, the grumpier he gets.

When I reach the top of the range, I wipe away the sweat streaming down my face with a rag before taking in the landscape. Montana is truly breathtaking no matter what season you are in. The air is fresh, the people are kind, and their bluish-green lakes fascinate me. I can stare at them for hours, mesmerized at how their coloring alters depending on the day's moodiness. If it's overcast and miserable, they appear greener. If it's a cloudless day, they're almost the color of the sky.

If memories of my childhood weren't sloppy black pits of nothing, I'd confidently declare I've said something similar before, but since they're nothing but goop, I yank my water bottle out of my backpack, then squeeze a generous portion of water down my throat.

Once I'm rehydrated, I bob down to Max's level. He eyes me excitedly when I dig my hand into my backpack to pull out the collapsible water bowl I'm never without. Don't let his heaving lungs fool you. He isn't eager for a drink. He's hoping the snack he saw me sneak into my backpack before our run falls out.

He's so quick off the mark, half the time, I don't even realize I've dropped something before he's gobbled it up. I doubt it even hits the floor.

"One snack, then you have to drink some water. It's important for our bodies." *I think.*

I don't get the chance to wallow in self-pity about my inner monologue. I'm too busy ensuring two female hikers that they don't need to take a wide berth around Max to have a pity party for one.

Max is harmless, but I understand people's hesitations. He has that look about him, that protective gleam I'm positive my daddy had even with my memories never returning, but he wouldn't harm a fly.

Except perhaps Benjamin.

Serves him right, though. He is as quick out of the gates as Max, but his drug of choice is glazed donuts. Max still hasn't forgiven him for the time he ate the last glazed donut. It doesn't matter if we buy a box of fifty or three, everyone this side of the country knows Max dibbed the last donut many years ago.

Ben didn't believe my claims.

He learned otherwise when Max gnawed his backside to express his annoyance.

Ben steers clear of the donut cabinet now.

While laughing at the memory of the time Ben got stitches in his right cheek, I toss Max a second stick of jerky before packing away his empty dog bowl. We do this run a minimum of two times a week, but the scenery never gets old, and neither does the smell.

After sucking in a big breath that will see me through a hectic week, I toss my backpack onto my back, then commence our jog down the mountainside. It's warm today, so I don't need to watch my footing like I do in the winter. I'm like a newborn foal in snowy conditions. I'm on my ass more than my feet.

With Max helming our race down the track, we make it to the parking lot with a new personal best on my stopwatch. It's amazing the hoops people jump through when they're scared. I don't need to remind them to stick to one side. Max's presence almost sees them leaping right off the track.

"Home to shower? Or breakfast first?" I ask Max while latching my belt into place. "Well, it is technically a second breakfast for you, Mr. Piggy. It's my first since you stole *all* the bacon." I scratch behind his pointy ears when he flops his fat head on my thigh with a sniffle. "I'm not angry at you, Maxxy. I could never be mad at you."

I shake my head to rid it of the confusion that forever bombards it when I say something that seems familiar. I've undertaken all the programs Dr. Nesser suggested to regain my memories. Nothing worked. It truly does appear as if I buried them deep inside my head because they hurt too much to remember. It seems like the cowardly way to go about things, but I can't be too hard on myself. I don't know what I went through, so who's to say I don't have good reasons to bury the truth?

"I'm okay," I assure Max when he pulls me from my thoughts by dragging his tongue up my cheek. "I was just thinking we should probably pick up some bacon on the way home. Ben will get super grumpy if he's denied an artery-clogging staple."

A giant grin stretches across my face when Max expresses his opinion with a toothy snarl. He doesn't care what Ben wants. He tolerates him for my sake, not because he likes him.

It's that way with all the male members in my life.

32

MADDOX

$\mathcal{T}$he air outside of Harbortown Correctional Facility is the same air inside its walls, but when I walk past the barb-wire-topped fences, I suck it down like it's infused with Demi's perfume.

I'm a free man.

My criminal record has been expunged.

For now.

When my eyes pop back open, the first person they land on is Justine. I haven't seen her in over a year, but I have no hesitation in saying the past twelve-plus months have been good to her. She looks healthy, mentally stable, and happy. Three things I wasn't sure she'd ever experienced again.

"*Ahren*," Nikolai, Justine's boyfriend, rumbles out in a stern tone when the locking of our eyes sees Justine racing across the dusty lot.

From what Rocco has told me, *ahren* means angel in Russian. It's been Nikolai's name for Justine since the day she knocked him on his ass with her purity and witty comebacks.

When Justine gets to within a couple of feet of me, I dump my duffle bag of clothes onto the ground. It kicks up as much dust on my feet as Justine does when she throws herself into my arms.

Her excitement is contagious. I spin her around and around until Landon accuses Justine of being a hog. When I place Justine back onto her feet, Landon pats me on the back before he pulls me in for a man hug. Things are still a little awkward for us, but since a prison setting wasn't the ideal place for a heart-to-heart, we've not had the chance to hash things out.

After making a mental note to have that talk soon, I greet Caidyn with a hug before playfully rapping my knuckles onto Saint's chin. My greeting with my parents is the most gut-wrenching part. My dad doesn't say a word. That's as foreign as Saint not doing his signature move more than once a week.

Well, if he still does it.

I'm a little unsure of his relationship status at the moment. Sloane is around, but I don't know if that's for my benefit or Saint's.

Once the reunion is done and dusted, Justine commences official greetings with the men I don't know. "Maddox, this is—"

"Nikolai," I interrupt, moving her along.

If things are as Rocco explained the past two days, Nikolai doesn't have time to pussyfoot around, and I've never been one to delay the inevitable—*unless it's in the bedroom.*

I band my arms around Nikolai's back and pull him into my chest to ensure my next set of words are only for his ears. "Dimitri sends caution. The flock is about to fly."

I begin to wonder how soon when the distinct noise of a police siren shrills through my ears. An unmarked dark sedan is gliding down the dirt road Brooks suggested my family use to keep the media out of our reunion. Supposedly, my release is front-page news.

"Stand down," Justine demands when she recognizes the occupants of the car a nanosecond before me. "They're practically family."

Nikolai mumbles something to Justine, but I miss what he says. I'm too busy greeting Ryan and Brax with handshakes to pay his jealousy any attention. Ryan has been a regular at Harbortown the past couple of months. The work he put in with Agent Machini is one of the reasons I'm out. And Brax, although I'm still pissed as fuck he got down and dirty in the hot tub with my baby sister, it was his friendship with Justine that saw her leave her room for the first time in months. That gives him a little leeway. For what it misses, I'm sure Nikolai will take up the slack. He looks set to murder Brax where he stands, especially when Justine almost greets him with a kiss on the cheek.

"I love you," Justine announces to Nikolai loud enough for the world to hear. "I've never spoken those words to another man before. And I never will again unless he is you. Please remember that."

Confident she's tamed the beast as only their soulmates can, Landon overtakes Justine's greeting on the family's behalf. "What are you guys doing here? I thought the authorities wanted to keep Maddox's release on the down-low?"

I call him an idiot under my breath. He just ousted Ryan in front of a known criminal.

Either unaware who Nikolai is or stupidly not worried, Ryan replies, "They do. I'm not here officially. Although this case was handed to the Feds years ago, I've kept an eye on it. I've been waiting for this day as long as you guys." He shifts his eyes to Justine. "Savannah wanted to be here, but Rylee has chickenpox, so she didn't want to risk... *you know.*"

I feel like I missed the punchline of a joke when Nikolai's eyes snap from Justine's midsection to Landon. A local law enforcement officer is no longer on Nikolai's hit list. My eldest brother might not fair too well, though.

Nikolai stops glaring at Landon like he's imagining his insides hanging out his stomach when Justine extends an invitation to a party I know nothing about. "Did you guys want to join us? We're having celebratory drinks at my parents' house." She curls her arm around my torso before resting her head on my shoulder. I figure she's cozying up to announce who the celebration centers around but am proven wrong when she adds, "It's a few miles from here, but you're more than welcome." She's putting herself in the danger zone, so I won't blow my top at the reminder my family now lives in Hopeton—the very bane of my existence. She has no cause for fret. No matter how much she pisses me off, I'd never put her in danger.

"If you wish to join us, Gavril can travel with you," Nikolai offers while waving his hand at a guy who is tall, Russian, and has a massive scar down one side of his face.

"I really should head off," Ryan mutters. "I start night shift next week."

"Since he's my ride, I guess I better head out too." Like a man unaware how far some men will go to protect their women, Brax leans into Justine's side and whispers. "It was good seeing you again, JJ. You look good." He stops, smiles, then adds, "Please don't tell Clara I said that. I may not survive."

When Justine nods, assuring him his secret is safe with her, Brax shifts on his feet to face Nikolai. He doesn't say anything. He just sizes him up like I did when I found out who was sniffing around the fresh meat in Las Vegas.

This is wrong of me to admit, but I think we've established by now I don't think there's any depth a man shouldn't sink to protect the woman he loves, so I was pleased when rumors circulated that Nikolai had killed the man who attempted to assault Justine in her home. He did what he needed to do to make her feel safe. I can't judge him for that. If anything, it makes me respect him more.

After a thirty-second stare down, Brax ends their standoff with an offer, "If you ever want to finish that piece, I know a guy who could help you out." He drops his eyes to a snakeskin tattoo dangling off an unmarked crest on Nikolai's lower right arm.

Nikolai considers his offer for a couple of seconds before replying, "Maybe one day."

When Justine smiles as if Nikolai scratched Brax's name off his hit list, I recall the work Henley did on my shoulder. Demi's face is on a part of my body I can't see without a mirror, but I don't need to look at it to recall every perfect detail. They're stored in my mind, where they'll remain until the day I die.

When Justine and Nikolai start making out like teens at the prom, I head for the first car in a fleet of many.

I'm not jealous of their affection.

I'm merely letting them relish the calm before the storm.

Nikolai braces his hip onto the kitchen counter before folding his tattooed arms in front of his chest. He isn't trying to intimidate me. He doesn't need to use tactics like aggressive stances to command a room. His reputation alone gains him the attention of every person in his realm, but mercifully, this time around, we're without an audience.

"Why did you remain in jail after Col was killed?"

I could tell him the truth, but honesty seems to be a lacking trait of mine lately. "My debt was with Dimitri."

"And that's been paid in full now?"

I twist my lips before shaking my head. "Not exactly. It was more transferred to another assignment."

It dawns on me that Nikolai is more clued on to Dimitri's crews' inner-workings than realized when he asks, "The Dvořáks?"

When I bob my head, Nikolai looks set to kill. I find out why when he spits out, "I took care of the Dvořáks more than once... *personally.* They're also not Russian as you're insinuating." He drops his arms before he takes a step closer to me. He hasn't reached for his knife yet, but the murderous gleam in his eyes assures me his hands are twitching to slash the gleaming metal across my jugular. "Justine is with child. *My* child." There's no denying the pride in his last two words. "So I don't care who I have to take down to protect her. My *ahren* comes before anyone."

Although shocked at his admission Justine is pregnant, the similarities between their story and Demi's and mine is too similar to ignore. Agent Moses stated seconds before his death that India killed my unborn child because her wish to rule the world with as many cartel monarchs as possible makes her extremely jealous of any future princes or princesses. That means it isn't just Justine's life precariously hanging on the wire, so is her unborn baby's.

"You took care of the Dvořáks sipping tea in their Czechia palace, but you missed the most vital player of their crew." I dig the surveillance image Agent Machini gave me three days ago and thrust it into Nikolai's chest. He doesn't like being manhandled, but since he'd take bullets to the chest for my sister, he sucks up my aggression like his hand isn't itching to slip behind his back to retrieve his knife. "From what I've heard, you know what a monster looks like." I point out India standing in the very far corner of the photo. "Here's a scarce female version you rarely hear about."

Nikolai laughs. "This is who Dimitri is cowering from? A housemaid who's pissed her husband couldn't keep his dick in his pants?"

His response makes it obvious he's heard of India before, but he's downplaying his knowledge. For what reason, I don't know, but I don't have the time nor the patience to find out.

"You won't be laughing when she organizes for your baby to be cut out of Justine's stomach with no anesthetic on a dirty mattress in a room an addict would screw his nose up at." He pins me to the kitchen cabinet with one hand on my chest, and the other pierces the tip of his knife into my neck, but I continue talking as if we're having a friendly chat. "And that's if Justine's pregnancy makes it that far. India has a way of making men do anything she wants. Abortion pills. Birthing a child from every nation. She can even convince them that watching a woman be mauled by a dog would be a fun time." I take a moment to get my emotions in check before muttering, "She was right fucking there, Nikolai, smiling while my sister was screaming."

"Right there... *with you*," Nikolai breathes out heavily, his voice as still as death.

I'd take a step back in shock if I could. "No. I was there at Dimitri's request—"

"To watch my *ahren* be mauled by a dog like she was a fucking animal!"

His accusation makes me want to vomit. "I was there to *stop* her attack! My life for hers. Dimitri said Col wouldn't accept anything less." I'm not ashamed about the wetness that fills my eyes when I mutter, "But he didn't want my life. He wanted hers."

The way I articulate my last word must clue Nikolai onto the fact I'm not talking about Justine. He lessens the pressure on his blade for a couple of seconds before he wholly removes it from my throat.

Once he has his knife housed back into the back pocket of his jeans, he asks, "Who was she?"

It takes me working Demi's name through my head three times before it squeaks through my dry lips, and even then, I stumble over her last name. "Demi P-Petretti."

As he takes a step back, Nikolai nods like everything suddenly makes sense. "Where is Demi now?"

The quiver of my chin answers him on my behalf.

"Is *she* the last name on your list?" He nudges his head to the photograph he released to pin me to the kitchen cabinets during the 'she' part of his comment.

An ill-timed chuckle rolls up my chest. I should have realized you can't hide murderous intentions from a mafia prince. He would have sniffed them out the instant I was released from Harbortown.

After taking a quick breather to pull myself together, I jerk up my chin. "Dimitri took care of Col." The arching of Nikolai's dark brow doubles when I add, "I took care of the agent who put Demi and Justine on her radar." I stray my eyes to the photograph on the ground during the 'her' part of my reply. "That leaves only one name on my hit list. India Dvořák's."

I float my eyes back up to Nikolai when he asks, "And then what? Once she's taken care of, where do you go from there?" I barely breathe out half a sigh when he shakes his head. "You don't walk to death. You make death come to you, and you fucking smile while doing it."

"Demi wouldn't want that. She didn't want me to be a part of this world."

"But she'd want this?" He backhands me in the chest while a *pfft* vibrates his lips. "When your woman has been done wrong, you don't take down a handful of names and call it a day. You destroy the entire fucking world, so not a single soul on this hellhole doubts what she means to you." He takes a moment to complete by saying, "I will give you resources and men, anything you need to find her, but I need your word that when you've done what needs to be done, you will come back here and start a new list." I shake my head, but he acts as if he doesn't see it. "It wasn't a suggestion, Maddox. There were more than two people in that room watching Justine's attack, which means there are more people left for you to punish." My smirk takes on a new meaning when he mutters, "I also promised Justine she wouldn't be hurt again." He bounces his eyes between mine. "*This* would hurt her, and I'll kill a thousand men before I let one break my promise to her."

When he holds out his hand for us to shake on our agreement, I weigh up my options. I get what he's saying, and in all honesty, when my grief really hits me, I do feel like I could take down the world, but I struggle imagining a life without Demi in it, especially here, in the Ravenshoe/Hopeton area. Her family stamped their legacy here, but because she was a part of it, not all their legacy leaves a bad taste in your mouth.

Nikolai's inflated chest collapses when I slap my hand against his before briefly shaking it. I'm not above a little white lie if it greatly benefits me, and I'd be lying if I said I wasn't excited about becoming an uncle, so I'll agree to his terms now, then reflect on them deeper when I'm alone.

"I'll make some calls. Get you what you need. While I do that, you need to speak with my second-in-charge, Trey." He scribbles a cell phone number onto a notepad on the refrigerator before preparing to leave.

Before he can leave, I draw his focus back with a secret that isn't mine to share. "Dimitri isn't as bad as he seems. He's... *softened* the past couple of years." He scoffs like it isn't the first time he's heard those words the past twenty-four hours. "He didn't mean for Justine to get hurt. Technically, her punishment falls on my shoulders, so if you are looking for someone to blame, you're looking at him."

The firmness of Nikolai's jaw would have you convinced I'm seconds away from having my throat slit, so you can imagine my surprise when he says, "If you keep your word, we'll be even."

"If I don't?" I ask, forever curious.

Nikolai smirks a grin that exposes his killer insides before he drags his thumb from one ear to the next. Certain I've got the message, he pushes through the swinging door of the kitchen, conjuring up memories of the many times I searched for Demi through the swing of the door at Petretti's.

Today, the memory doesn't hurt me like it usually does.

It actually makes me smile.

33

MADDOX

"Thanks for agreeing to meet with me on such short notice."

Agent Machini's eyes pop up from the milky beverage she's drinking, hissing when she spots the bruises smattering my face. There aren't many people I trust anymore, but she gained both my respect and trust when she kept quiet on what really happened to Agent Moses.

While running her index finger across a bruise on my cheek, she whispers, "You're not fighting again, are you? You only got out of jail a couple of days ago. Don't push your luck."

It's the fight of my life not to laugh at the fret in her tone. If she thinks a bruise from a three-day-old wrestle between Saint, Landon, and I can replicate the injuries fighters gained from Col's underground fight circuit, Agent Brahn clearly kept her chained to her desk.

A black eye was child's play on that route.

After slotting my backside on the empty bar stool next to hers, I signal for the bartender. "What are you drinking? Can I get you another?"

I slant my head to the side and arch a brow when she mumbles out nervously, "It's milk... plain old ordinary *milk*."

The shame in her eyes clears away when I say with a chuckle, "Whatever floats your boat."

Her giggle is unexpected when I order two glasses of milk from a big burly bartender, but it's nice to hear. I didn't copy her order to douse the tension radiating out of her. I've got so many tidbits of information coming at me at once, the last thing I should do is muddle my head with alcohol.

The photograph Agent Machini snuck into my jumpsuit five days ago kickstarted my campaign to track down India, but within a couple of hours, Rocco, Smith, and I hit a stalemate. Since India has men on both sides of the law assisting her, she's clever at hiding her tracks. That isn't surprising considering how long she's been doing this. She's had a lot of time to practice—almost as long as I've had to grieve.

After tipping the bartender for our generous schooners of milk, I twist my torso to face Agent Machini. "Have you been waiting long? Traffic is worse than I remembered."

"All right, Maddox, enough with the small talk. What do you want? Why do you want it? And for how long do you want it?"

I'm glad to see neither her suspension nor taking the wrap for murder altered her feistiness. She's still a firecracker.

"I need your help tracking down India."

As she sips on her fresh serving of milk, she slings her eyes across the bar. Once she's confident we're not being eyeballed by anyone with the same characteristics she exudes, she mumbles, "I gave you everything I could."

"I need more, Macy. What you gave me wasn't enough."

I was hoping to butter her up by using her real name, but it seems to have the opposite effect. She slams down her glass, spilling milk, before snatching her briefcase from the sticky countertop and slipping off her bar stool.

I stop her brisk exit by grabbing her arm. My non-firm hold isn't what keeps her feet grounded. It's the words I speak, "India was behind Demi's miscarriage. She is the reason we lost our baby."

When she locks her eyes with mine, I give her everything Rocco gave me four years ago. How he let slip who the tests were for in India's presence. Her offer to buy the tests since she was going to the pharmacy for supplies anyway, and how she asked him to meet her there, so he'd be seen in the pharmacy's parking lot on their surveillance cameras.

I tell her everything.

"And the girls in the pictures, they're not whores for sale. They are incubators."

"What?" Agent Machini chokes on her one word, certain she heard me wrong.

She didn't.

"Agent Moses..." I pause when her face whitens from the mentioning of his name. "Arrow said before his... *death* that India killed our unborn child because she didn't want any cartel heirs competing with her future children."

Agent Machini's brows pull together. "That doesn't make any sense. Subpoenaed records expose that India can't have children..." Her words trail off as her throat works hard to swallow. "That's why she needs surrogates."

I hit her with a look as if to say, *Bingo!* "Arrow hinted that she didn't want to section herself to one nationality. She's going for them all."

She rakes her teeth over her bottom lip before asking, "Is that why she took Fien? To commence world domination?"

"Not exactly." Since Dimitri's story isn't mine to share, I steer our conversation in the direction I need it to go. "But I believe the talk about a Russian sanction reforming footholds in Ravenshoe is because of India." She doesn't deny my claims, assuring me Dimitri's sources are on the money. A mafia war is about to start because India never moves onto a new target without first imploding the one she sucked dry of resources. "If India has gotten what she needs from her current john, what nationality will she move onto next?"

When Agent Machini halfheartedly shrugs, I glare at her. She isn't the daft wallflower she's portraying. She pinned a sexual assault on a dead man, then flew home to Montana the following afternoon. She has balls—big ones.

During a deep exhale, she soundlessly squeals her annoyance that she's succumbing to peer pressure before she murmurs, "If what you're saying is true, and India is picking suitors by demographics, she still has half the world to explore." I almost call her a killjoy but the removal of a confidential file from her briefcase stops me. "But... it's obvious she has a type."

She lays out a set of photographs across the countertop. It's a timeline of the men India has dated, starting with her husband, Achim Novak, and ending with a man whose nationality isn't easily depicted. He could be American for all I know.

I tap my index finger on the last image. "Who is this?"

"Maxsim. Son of Alexis Vasiliev."

I'm sure I've heard that name before, but it's slipping my mind. Confusion is understandable. My mafia days ended over four years ago. "Nationality?"

I push out a curse word when Agent Machini answers, "Russian."

"And let me guess... currently living it up in Florida?"

She gives me the same look I gave her earlier before adding words into the mix, "Don't fret. If India's timeline remains on course, he'll be buried under a pile of dirt by the end of the month."

After reading between the lines, I ask, "All these men are dead?"

Agent Machini barely nods before she switches it to a shake. "All except these two." She points out two men at the very start of her timeline. "Achim Novak and Trey Corbyn." She plucks the two men's photographs out of her lineup, then hands them to me. "India is legally married to Achim. We haven't worked out Trey's association yet." While she checks handwritten notes on a yellow-lined notepad, I work my throat through a brutal swallow. I've heard of Trey before, from both Nikolai and Rocco, but the knowledge is too basic to be shared. "Achim resides in Czechia, but he hasn't been sighted by Interpol in over a year."

"Interpol was after him?" I ask, shocked. Smith didn't disclose that yesterday. I guess he didn't have the chance. Achim's crimes were pages long. We would have been there for weeks if we scoured through every dot point.

Agent Machini's chin barely lifts an inch before she continues as if I didn't interrupt her, "Trey is a British citizen, but he resides in Las Vegas full time now. Has for around four years."

While nodding my head, I wet my lips. "Right around the time India's family's compound was ambushed for the first time."

I realize I said my last comment out loud when Agent Machini clarifies it, "Ambushed? The Bureau thought it was a takeover bid orchestrated by India."

"We initially thought the same thing." I inwardly curse my second slip-up. I was meant to say 'I.' It's better for all involved if both sides of the law think I'm working independently. "But nothing of value was taken, and the ruins remained untouched for years." *Until recently.*

While smirking about how justice is served in many ways, I remove Achim's headshot from Agent Machini's hands and place it back onto the timeline, leaving only Trey's remaining. "Assuming Achim's disappearance is sinister, we're left with only one man from India's past still breathing oxygen. He lives in Vegas, which is run by the Russian Cartel. That should mean something, shouldn't it?"

"Perhaps..." She peers up at the ceiling for what feels like minutes but is barely seconds before asking slowly, "You're going to Vegas, aren't you?" She groans like I asked her to marry me during a first date when I nod. "Maddox, as your friend, I would advise you against this."

"Oh, so now we're friends? How convenient." I bump her with my shoulder to ensure she knows there's no hatred in my tone. When a ghost of a grin pops onto her face, I add, "If you don't recommend this, what do you recommend?" I don't allow her to answer. "I sit on my hands for another five years while waiting for the Bureau to pull their finger out of their ass."

"We're doing everything we can." Even if we hadn't met previously, I still would have heard the deceit in her tone. It was as obvious as the sun in the sky. "Well, *I* am."

"But your hands are tied with bureaucratic tape." When she nods, agreeing with me, I mutter, "Mine aren't."

"Maddox..." I don't give her the chance to spill the concern I see in her eyes. I dump a bunch of bills on the counter to pay our tab, hit her with a wink to show my thanks for her support the past four years, then spin on my heels and walk away.

I'm not surprised when a familiar ringtone plays through the speakers of Caidyn's Jeep not even half a mile later. Smith doesn't just have eyes all over Dimitri's residence. He has all of Hopeton covered as well.

"Anything?" Rocco asks when the click of our call connecting advises him I've answered.

He can't see me, but I shrug anyway. "I'm going to head to Vegas for a couple of days. There's an old contact there that may give us an insight into India's mindset."

"She's a fucking psycho. What more do you need to know?"

Rocco laughs about Smith's interruption before asking, "Want me to come with?"

"No," I steer my car toward the only exit and entry point of Hopeton before adding to my reply, "The intel Dimitri received about a Russian invasion is valid. India's current john is of Russian heritage."

Rocco curses while Smith asks for further details. I give him everything I have that doesn't include Trey Corbyn. I'm not being sneaky. I am merely ensuring I don't squash the toes of the man who breathed air back into my sister's lungs. Nikolai's attention didn't merely return Justine to the woman she once was, he helped her leap over her previous standing. Saint and Landon want to believe she's a better woman now because she's matured. I know that isn't the case. There's good and bad in all of us, you've just got to find a person who'll cherish both sides of the coin. Justine and Nikolai do that for each other.

There's more sentiment in my tone than I care to admit when I promise, "I'll keep you updated as I go. I expect you to do the same."

I wait for Rocco to hum out his agreement before ending our call, then I flatten my foot to the floor. Hopeton isn't as seedy as it once was, but it still has a long way to go before it doesn't make my skin crawl when I'm in it.

I make it home in just enough time to see Nikolai on his knees in front of Justine. It's surreal seeing someone the world has enamored as this massive, untouchable being at the feet of my baby sister, pleading for her hand in marriage.

It shows the true power of love.

Strength is pointless when the faintest grin can buckle your legs out from beneath you.

I had that type of love with Demi, and I will have it again.

It just won't be in this lifetime.

After watching Justine grant Nikolai's every wish with an overexcited bob of her chin, I head to my room to pack a bag for a couple of nights away. My intuition could be completely askew. It's been a bit funky since I left prison, but part of me wonders if that's because I'm not accustomed to being in these surroundings without Demi. I was obsessed with her since the second grade—*I still fucking am*—and that's why I need to listen to my gut.

Even if my intuition is leading me astray, staying here will make me insane, so I'm merely picking the lesser of two evils.

34

MADDOX

*W*hen I walk down the gangway of McCarran
International Airport the following day, a husky laugh
leaves my lips. I should have realized a woman with enough gall to
plead guilty to a murder she didn't commit wouldn't hesitate to bend
the rules.

Agent Machini won't follow any guy out of a bar in Hopeton like a
barfly eager for a one-night stand, but she has no hesitation standing
at the end of the gangway in a pair of snug jeans and a midriff top.

If I didn't know she was an agent, I would have pinned her as a
dancer. I'm not going to say an erotic dancer. Just because I can't see
her gun doesn't mean she isn't carrying. I don't want to get shot.

"Don't look at me like that, Maddox," Agent Machini says with
narrowed eyes before she snatches my gym bag out of my hand like
she's eager to search it for contraband. "I'm not the only one under-
going a makeover today." Before I can ask her what the fuck she's on
about, she squashes her finger against my lips. "India has a type. A
very distinct type, and after some research, I think you could very
much be her type..." She drags her eyes down my body. "With the
right number of accessories."

She pinches my chance to seek clarification on her plan by

darting through the thousands of commuters arriving in Vegas with me. Her pace is so fast, I have to double the length of my strides to catch up to her.

The thuds of my heart match the thumps my feet took when our taxi pulls in front of a tattoo parlor on the outskirts of the strip a couple of minutes later. I have an extensive collection of tattoos, but I've not added to my collection since Demi's death. In all honesty, I lost interest in a lot of things I once loved. Tattoos included.

Worry she's about to mess up my mindset even more than my body art flies out the window when Agent Machini explains, "Tails usually works on the set of Hollywood blockbusters, but he agreed to meet us here today to help with your disguise."

"Tails? As in a tail on a dog?"

She looks like she wants to sock me in the arm, but instead, she answers, "Tails, as in the operating system that preserves privacy and anonymity." She hands the cab driver a bundle of bills before slipping onto the footpath. Once I follow suit, she adds, "He's under the impression you are part of the Bureau. If possible, I'd like to keep it that way."

Although she doesn't directly say she's once again gone out on a limb for me, the pleading in her eyes most certainly does.

"Let me guess... the head honchos want more evidence?"

I faced the same issue when I commenced proceedings to have Warden Mattue taken down. He wasn't as bad as Agent Moses, nothing he did specifically affected Demi, but he didn't deserve his position. For a change, I went about things the right way. I gave the investigators enough evidence to place 'inmate' in front of Warden Mattue's title, but somehow, he wasn't found negligent in his position.

I had planned to push the matter further, but Rocco took the decision out of my hands. He trialed Warden Mattue in the court he fucked over, and when he was sentenced to death for his crimes, Rocco took care of his execution as well.

It kills her to do, but Agent Machini lifts her chin. "We don't have anything solid on India. It's all hearsay or out of our jurisdiction. Then when we stumble onto a witness, they're either too scared to talk or end up dead." She locks her eyes with mine. "I don't see that being the case with you. If we work together, we can do this. We can bring India to justice."

It's clear her idea of justice and mine are two starkly contradicting notions, but I'm not sure I should admit that to a federal agent, so instead, I hit her with a wink that could mean many things before gesturing for her to lead the way.

<hr>

Three hours later, I'm the same Maddox on the inside, but my shell has been reconfigured. Tails's artistry skills are as out of this world as Henley's, but they're not permanent. He used the same process when actors and actresses require tattoos. The transfers will wash off in two weeks, perhaps a couple of days if I really scrub them.

"What do you think?" I ask Agent Machini while doing a twirl to show her my new ink.

A grin tugs my lips when she mutters, "Say that again... with the right accent this time around?"

Every stencil Tails placed on my body represents England in some way—Big Ben, the Tower Bridge everyone often confuses for London Bridge, and even their infamous black cabs and red buses got a placement on my arms. I'm tatted up like my hair coloring is compliments to a UK heritage.

I won't lie. At first, I wasn't convinced with Agent Machini's plan. It was only after she explained the information she had unearthed about Trey Corbyn the past twelve hours did I realize she could be on the money.

India's plan to birth children of all mafia ethnicities started when she was betrothed to Achim Novak. Since he was obsessed with a housemaid he'd known since childhood, India shifted her focus on another equally powerful man—Trey Corbyn.

When Achim heard about her overzealous affection of a rival, he hatched an evilly cunning plan that not only saw Trey's family stripped of their mafia lineage, but it also commenced India's fixation to rule from all corners of the globe.

If rumors are true, India's surrogates have most of the top nations in the world covered. There's only one country she's yet to tick off her list—the United Kingdom. When the Corbyn's reign fell, the Russians moved in. Excluding the true monarch, there hasn't been a home-born ruler in over six years—*until today.*

Noel Corbyn has a nice ring to it, doesn't it? The youngest brother of Trey and Cole, Corbyn was left to fend for himself after his family's downfall since he was birthed to a whore instead of the queen of the Corbyn entity.

When you truly stop and think about it, Agent Machini's plan is quite brilliant.

I stop grinning at her brilliance when soft fingers trace the tattoo covering a majority of my left shoulder. "The resemblance is uncanny," Agent Machini whispers while taking in the tattoo of Demi with her father. "The tattoo artist did a wonderful job." She waits for me to tug on a shirt, then spin around to face her before asking, "Do you miss her?"

"Every single goddamn day," I reply without fault, my tone the most honest it's been the past five years. "She's always on my mind, day and night. I'll never forget her."

After bracing her hip on the bed I was lying on the past couple of hours, she asks, "Is she the reason you served time?"

I take a moment to consider her question before sheepishly shaking my head. "Demi wasn't to blame for anything her uncle did."

"Some could say the same for you, Maddox. You did at the time what you thought was right. None of us should feel sorry about that." I don't know why, but I'm reasonably sure her comment includes some skeletons of her past as well, but before I can call her out on it, she asks, "If you could go back and change one thing, what would you change?"

I almost say I wouldn't be a prick to Demi when she mashed her head into my crotch, but then I realize my dithering moods were the least of our problems back then. I can't even place the blame on Col's shoulders.

Agent Machini looks shocked when I say, "I would make sure Agent Moses's claims that I would help my community were legitimate."

"You wouldn't change the family Demi was born in?"

I shake my head. "Demi was who she was because of what she had been through. I would have given anything to stop her from being hurt, but I wouldn't have changed her for the world. She was perfect the way she was."

She stares at me for a few seconds, stunned in silence.

Just as she regains the ability to talk, her cell phone silences her for the second time. After peering down at the screen, she lifts her eyes to mine. "I should take this. It could be important."

When I jerk up my chin, giving her the go-ahead, the friendly Macy Machini mask she's been wearing the past four hours is replaced with Agent Machini, an all-round hard-ass yet still a fierce federal agent.

I discover why when she murmurs, "Grandma is good. She's doing a lot better than the doctors let on." She swivels on the spot, a telltale sign she feels guilty about lying. "I don't think I'll need to stay as long as first perceived. I should be back in a couple of days." Her sigh is both pained and worrying when she asks, "When?" I pay more attention to her conversation when she shifts on her feet to face me. "How many casualties?" The widening of her pupils tells me her caller's number is high. "No, no, I'll tell him... I'm sure. We've developed a weird bond the past four years." I'm confident she's talking about me, and I am given a chance to seek clarification when she breathes heavily down the line, "I love you too. Always. Bye."

She doesn't sugarcoat her news, nor does she roll it in glitter to make it appear not as dreary as it is. She merely hits me with straight-up honesty. "It's your sister. She's missing."

35

MADDOX

"Jesus fucking Christ! How do they have no clue where they went? There's only one way in and out of an elevator... via the front fucking door."

I've never seen Agent Machini worked up enough to swear once, much less twice, but from the bits of her conversation I caught on the fly, her dual slip-up is understandable.

During the raid that saw Justine and Nikolai disappear without a trace, Dimitri was arrested by the Feds. If Rocco's chuckles trickling through my ears right now are any indication of how his escape went down, the Feds aren't just scratching their heads, they're scrambling for an excuse to pacify the massive media contingency following this story.

The mafia entities in this country are royalty in their own right. They're hounded by the paparazzi like movie stars, pursued by people purely for their money, and play by their own set of rules.

It's the latter I'm hoping to work in my favor.

Rocco has assured me time and time again that there are rules not even Dimitri can break—rules that see enemies join forces to ensure they're upheld.

Justine is pregnant with the next Russian heir, which means she is protected by the rules Nikolai and Dimitri have been governed by their entire life. I need to remember that every time I peer at my watch to check the time. Nikolai and Justine have been gone for almost seventy-eight hours, yet no one has any idea where they are.

"I'll reach out once I know more," Rocco says down the line before he disconnects our call.

I begin to wonder how many eyes he has on me when his abrupt ending of our call is quickly chased by Agent Machini returning to my side of the room. We've been camped out at the Popov compound for three days now under the guise we arrived in Vegas for a quickie wedding. Five years of lockup supposedly made me restless, but since Macy was raised as a good Catholic girl, she wanted us to seal the deal the old-fashioned way before taking up the traditional route.

Don't worry, you weren't the only one skeptical about our story. Trey eyed my new ink as much as he did Macy when we were ushered into Nikolai's office by five armed goons three days ago. He's certain we're playing tricks, but since Nikolai gave me full access to his crew, Trey has no choice but to follow his command.

"Did they know anything?" Since the information Rocco shared wasn't more than Agent Machini already knows and hoping to side-step an interrogation as to how I have a high-up member of the Italian Cartel's cell phone number on speed dial, I shake my head. "Great..."

She flops onto the sofa next to me before lowering her eyes to the paperwork spread across the coffee table. The rooms in Nikolai's mansion are bigger than a hotel. With the maids doubling as cooks, we haven't needed to leave our room the past three days. It hasn't been all bad. It's given me plenty of time to run several theories through my weary brain.

"What are you working on?"

I sling my eyes to Agent Machini. "A timeline of Trey's life."

She glares at me like I am insane. "Maddox..." She stops, swallows, then tries again. "I understand your eagerness to see India brought to justice." *I want her dead, but since I can't say that, I don't interrupt her.* "But right now, you need to focus on the present instead of the past. Your future needs you. Your past doesn't."

"I know that," I lie. "I'm not tweaking Trey's timeline for India. I'm doing it for Justine. You're assuming that these cases aren't related, but what if they are." When my simple approach doesn't ease the groove between her brows, I hit her with the hard facts instead. "Justine is pregnant with the next heir of the Russian Mafia."

"Shit."

Yes, that's all she says.

Shit.

Then a few big breaths later, she adds, "If India already has a Russian on the hook—"

"She needs to get rid of the competition," I fill in. "But I have a feeling this isn't solely about future monarchs. It's personal for India." When confusion crosses her features, I try to settle it. "Nikolai raided the Dvořáks... *twice.* The first time was f—"

"Four years ago," Agent Machini breathes out heavily, advising me she isn't as far off the mark as I thought.

I jerk up my chin. "And the last one was as recent as nine months ago." I place down a photograph of a grubby-faced blonde with big blue eyes before covering it with one from an auction that was held in Czechia weeks after the original photograph was captured. Although she looks completely different once she's scrubbed clean, there's no denying the blondes in the photographs are one and the same. The features of a face don't alter with makeup. "The rumors we heard aren't rumors. Achim was obsessed with his housekeeper. So much so, when he sold her to prove to his wife he wasn't, he went to great lengths to get her back."

I give Agent Machini a couple of minutes to take in images Smith swiped from an agent's hard drive earlier before I gather them up and dump them into the fireplace that makes the disgusting Vegas heat even more intolerable.

"Maddox! That is vital evidence—"

"Vital evidence your agency has sat on for months." She doubles back, but she doesn't dispute my claims. "During their marriage,

Achim and India killed dozens of women, sold hundreds of them, and have destroyed the lives of *thousands* of families, but not once has the Bureau arrested them. They didn't even bring them in for questioning."

"Because the crimes were not conducted on US soil."

"That isn't true," I fire back. "My unborn baby was killed here."

"Maddox..." She pauses, truly unsure what to say next.

It's for the best. If she had continued talking, our conversation might have been overheard by Nero, a high-ranked servant in Nikolai's crew. "Am I interrupting something?" he asks, his tone crammed with suspicion.

"No," I reply before Agent Machini can. She's a terrible liar. I'm not much better, but I've been known to play a trick or two the past five years. "What do you need?"

"Justine was spotted by a courier during a run. She's being brought here now. Trey wanted me to let you know."

"Is she injured?" This question didn't come from me. It came from Agent Machini. I'm too relieved to speak.

Nero shakes his head, answering her, but his eyes remain locked on me. I'm not surprised. There isn't a single female in this place who is respected—except Justine. I can't guarantee that will continue if she's left to govern this realm without Nikolai. Before India took hold of the Dvořáks' reign, a female leader was unheard of.

"Where are they taking her?"

Nero nudges his head to the left. "To the private quarters. First stairwell past the foyer. You can't miss it. It's the big elaborate bastard."

I jerk up my chin in thanks before skirting past him. When Agent Machini attempts to fall in step behind me, Nero blocks her path. "This is family business, and you ain't family."

"I'm going to be," she argues, desperate not to miss out on any action.

"Going and am aren't close to the same thing, sweetheart." After spinning on his heels and joining me in the hallway, Nero searches for a key on a massive keychain. Once he finds the one he's after, he locks his eyes with mine. "Do you want to say goodbye first, or are you happy to leave things as they are?"

Since it would be mighty suspicious for me to leave my fiancé locked in a room without so much as a cheek peck, I re-enter the room, curl my arms around Agent Machini's stiff torso, then plant my lips on the top of her head. Our exchange is as innocent as fuck, but since it's the first time I've had my lips on any female not named Demi in over five years, it's as awkward as fuck as well.

"I'll be back soon," I murmur like I can't feel her slipping something into my pocket.

She waves before adding words to our ruse. "Love you."

Mercifully, Nero's grumble about Catholic girls being the neediest means I don't have to break a promise I made to myself four years ago. I only spoke those words to one girl who doesn't share my DNA. I don't plan to say them to anyone else.

"But my God, their tight little cunts are too tempting to give up."

After moaning in a way a grown man shouldn't when in the company of another, Nero gestures his hand in the direction he wants me to walk. When the image of Trey carrying an angry blonde outside steals his attention for a second, I slip my hand into the pocket of my jeans, smiling when my fingertip rolls over a smooth bead-like apparatus. Agent Machini is locked away like a prisoner, but once I stuff the listening device she hid in my pocket into my ear, she'll be a part of the action as much as me—*if* I stuff it in there.

Her remorse during our heated talk was authentic, but she didn't deny my accusation that the Bureau is sitting on their hands regarding anything Cartel-related. Does that mean she thinks they're as liable for Justine's disappearance as I believe? Or is she here for an entirely different set of reasons?

Hopeful it's the former, I stuff the listening device into my ear.

Two minutes after that, I enter Justine's room on Nero's heel. Justine's blood-tinged hair fans across a pillow when a man with a fat head and sleeves of tattoos places her on a dingy sofa sitting in the middle of the room. It doesn't match the elegance of Nikolai's home.

It's shabby and outdated, and if I'm not mistaken, the couch our mother begged my father to throw out when they moved in together.

After shrugging off my confusion, I kneel in front of Justine to check the dilation of her eyes. Her skin is blistering red like she's spent the last couple of days in the sun, her lips are parched, and she has a massive bump on the back of her head. "Was she like this when you found her?" When Nero shrugs, truly unsure, I boss him around like I'm higher-ranked than him. "Get her some water... and a bucket." I tack on my last command when I recall how upset my stomach was in the hours following me being freed from the hole. I brought up more water than I kept down those first few days. "Do you have an in-house doctor?" I ask after recalling the one Ezra arrived with to check the wound Demi got from her uncle running his blade up her chest.

Nero nods before he switches it to a head shake. "We did. Dok was killed during the takeover bid."

His assumption Nikolai's disappearance centers around a takeover bid is what Dimitri's crew is running off as well. They haven't connected the dots the same way I have just yet. I see that changing when I update Rocco on my findings. Justine is marked and nicked all over, but a bruise on her stomach can be seen through the thin material of her shirt, assuring me her midsection was the focus of her attacker's assault.

This is India's doing.

I'm certain of it.

"I'll be back in a minute," Nero announces before he heads for the door.

When the goon follows him out, the room's silence becomes obvious, assuring Agent Machini it's the perfect time to talk. She isn't overly loud, but her voice is undeniably girlie. "Is Justine okay?"

Her comment swipes the last bit of hesitation from my stomach. If she were rogue like Agent Moses, she would have asked about Nikolai long before requesting an update on my sister.

Although she can't see me, I nod. "She's all right. Barely coherent, though. Her skin is blistering red, and her hair is a mattered mess."

"Is there anything in her pockets that could give us a clue to where she's been?"

I run my eyes over her clothes before shaking my head. "She's wearing a skirt and..." My reply trails off when it dawns on me it's the same clothes I saw her in days ago. "She hasn't changed her clothes. She's wearing the same items she had on when she dropped me off at the airport."

Before she can reply, the door to Justine's room creeps open, and Trey enters. He gives me the same riling look he did days ago before asking, "Has she said anything?"

I shake my head.

He drifts his eyes over Justine's sun-hardened body and face before asking, "Where's the blood coming from?"

Carefully, I angle Justine's head to the side before pulling back a section of her hair to expose the bump I mentioned earlier. While Trey bobs down to better assess her wound, I snatch up a bottle of water Nero left on the table next to the couch.

I almost have the lid undone when Trey says, "Don't give her any water. You could fuck her over more. Nero is organizing a doctor to come check on her. She'll be here in a few..." He stops talking when an unexpected giggle parts Justine's bone-dry lips. "Does she generally laugh in her sleep?"

"I wish." I pause when it dawns on me how out of the loop I am in all aspects of my family's lives. Old Justine never laughed, but since I've been so focused on tracking India down, I can't confidently say that is the case now. "I haven't heard her giggle since she got them." My stomach gurgles when I move my head to an obvious dog bite scar on her shoulder.

She isn't the only Walsh member with a dog bite scar. I wear mine with honor. I can only hope Justine does one day as well.

My eyes snap down to Justine when she rolls over with a groan.

"Justine..." Trey says, his tone authoritative but not overly commanding. "Can you open your eyes for me?" I smirk when she answers him with a grunt. It's early, and dawn awakenings have never been Justine's strong point.

"Justine..." Trey tries again. My heart pumps out a funky tune when Justine slowly flutters her eyes open. "Hey."

She's clearly dazed and confused but lucid enough to shuffle into a half-seated position. "W-W-What happened?" she stammers out, her two words expressed extremely slow.

"How bad is her head injury?" Agent Machini asks in a whisper at the same time I say, "You don't remember?"

Justine barely shakes her head when her eyes pop out of their sockets. I only just get the bucket Nero dropped off with the bottles of water under her chin before she brings up some funky-smelling chicken.

I inconspicuously nod when Agent Machini warns, "You need to keep a close eye on her, Maddox. Vomiting after a traumatic brain injury can be a sign that something more sinister is happening beneath the surface." She must hear the woosh of my head bob because her concern shifts into an interrogation not even two seconds later. "Where was she located?"

Unsure, I repeat her question to Trey. "Where was she located again?"

"By Interstate 95. One of our couriers thought he was seeing things."

"Hold on," Justine says between barfs. "I was found along a highway?"

Trey nods. "You were a few miles from the private airstrip you used last week. We figured that was the location Nikolai told you to use in case of an emergency."

Justine brushes off his claims by screwing up her nose. "Why was I on Interstate 95? Blaire and Rico's apartment is miles from there."

"Blaire and Rico?" Trey's tone echoes the concerning sigh booming through my ears from Agent Machini. She's as worried by Justine's confusion as me. "What do they have to do with anything?"

"We had dinner with them last night," Justine replies while staring at Trey like he's lost his marbles. "You know this because Nikolai called you on our way."

I plant my backside on the section of the couch not taken up by

Justine's tiny frame before gathering her hands in mine. "You had dinner with Rico and Blaire *three* nights ago. You've been missing ever since." She stares at me, but her mouth remains tightly shut, prompting me to say, "You're also in Vegas. Trey meant Interstate 95 on the California border, not the one in Florida."

"That can't be true," she murmurs, gently shaking her head. "You don't just lose three days of your life."

"She needs to see a doctor," Agent Machini recommends at the same time Justine requests to see Nikolai. "Where's Nikolai? He'll prove we were with Rico and Blaire last night." She drops her eyes to the slops of food in the bottom of the bucket. "That is the rosemary chicken Blaire prepared for us. She used herbs that would help my queasy stomach."

When she lowers her hands to her midsection to emphasize the reason behind her upset stomach, her pupils widen to the size of saucers. She's hammered by dizziness when she lifts the hem of her shirt. I'm bombarded with red hot anger. The bruise on her stomach is worse than first thought, and it's the obvious shape of a man's fist.

"J," I mumble under my breath when she leaps to her feet and races for a door I assume leads to a bathroom.

Trey must have been raised in a household without women. He doesn't grant Justine even five seconds of privacy. He's up in her business in an instant. "You truly don't remember, do you?"

She peers at him in the vanity mirror before shaking her head. "All I remember is having dinner. The rest is blank."

"She needs to be assessed by a doctor, Maddox. Please, I am begging you to get her medical attention now," Agent Machini says during my short walk to the bathroom.

Since I agree with her, I wordlessly give Trey his marching orders, scoffing when he instantly denies my request with a brisk shake of his head. I thought Landon was anal when it came to ruling the roost. Clearly, there's a new contender in town.

Confident he won't defy Nikolai's orders as well as he does mine, I switch on the faucet in the shower before spinning to face Justine.

"Why don't you shower while I get you something to eat? Once you've filled your belly and taken a nap, your confusion may lift."

"TBIs don't work that way, Maddox," Agent Machini grumbles in my ear.

I make a *tut-tut* noise with my teeth, warning Agent Machini to back the fuck up before I stick my head under the water pumping out of the showerhead.

When she gets the hint by replicating the sound someone would make while zipping their lips shut, I run my hand along Justine's arm. "We'll be just outside."

I'm planning to give Trey the same orders I just handed Agent Machini, but before I can, he's up in my face, spitting out venom like he's Justine's keeper. "What the fuck do you think you're playing at? She doesn't have time to have a nap. If she's concussed, the worst fucking thing she could do right now is sleep. Furthermore, she may be the only person who can tell us where Nikolai is."

There it is. The real reason for his seemingly caring composure.

"That's my sister in there," I spit out after hooking my thumb to the partially closed bathroom door. "Her well-being comes before anything and anyone."

"If you truly give a fuck about your 'sister'..." he air quotes his last word, "... you'd know that the *only* person she needs right now is Nikolai." He works his jaw side to side before asking, "Are you here for Justine, Maddox, or to claw your way into a sanction you have no right to be a part of?"

Hello, pot, I'm kettle. Nice to meet you.

It dawns on me that Trey has looked into me as closely as I have him the past three days when he asks, "Did you and Dimitri have conjugal visits during your four-year stint at Wallens Ridge State Penitentiary? Or did he have you suck his cock in front of everyone, so they knew whose bitch you were?"

"You're better than this, Maddox," promises Agent Machini when I fist Trey's shirt in preparation to knock his smug grin right off his fucking face. "More violence won't fix anything."

Since I agree with her, I try to release the black hatred charring my veins with words. "Shut your mouth before I shut it for you."

"I'd like to see you try, twat-face."

"Big breaths, Maddox," Agent Machini encourages when Trey pushes me away from him by shoving his hand into my face.

I'm at the end of my teether, about to blow my fucking top when Justine enters the room in nothing but a teeny tiny towel. "We were attacked, bombarded without warning. Men came from all angles. They were wearing balaclavas and knew things about Nikolai not many know."

"What type of stuff?" I ask at the same time Trey says, "Then what?"

Trey's influence over Justine is undeniable when she answers his question before mine. "A battle ensued. Nikolai and Rico were outnumbered, but they held their ground until..." air whizzes between her cracked lips when she rubs the bump I pointed out to Trey earlier, "... a man grabbed me. He was so large, he didn't need to extend his arm to hoist me from the ground."

"That's good, Justine. Keep going," Trey encourages, mimicking the recommendation Agent Machini whispered in my ear.

Nodding, Justine does as suggested. "Nikolai threatened him, told him he'd kill his family if he didn't let me go. That's when another man entered the equation." Her eyes flicker as she struggles to unearth her memories in the vault they hide in when they become too much to bear. "Maxsim. Nikolai called him Maxsim."

"Maxsim?" Trey asks, his tone making it obvious he's heard of the name before. "Are you sure?"

Justine bobs her head so fast, any concerns she has a head injury flies out the window. "If he's Alexei's son, then yes, I'm sure. They argued about Nikolai killing Alexei and how Maxsim was going to use Eli to take Nikolai's place."

"How did Nikolai respond?"

"Umm... he said he had changed the rules, that Anatoly's rulings were no longer relevant." She licks her lips in an endeavor to divert the focus from the wetness welling in her eyes. "His reply angered Maxsim so much he signaled for his goon to hit me."

As her chin quivers, she sits on the edge of a bed I'm shocked belongs in the bedroom of a mafia prince. It's the size of the one in my childhood bedroom. I never switched it out for a king because I like the way it couldn't force a massive gap between Demi and me.

I stop relishing the memory when Trey asks Justine, "Do you know what happened to the men Nikolai and you traveled with? Roman? Rico?"

She stops shaking her head when I add, "Dimitri?" I'm not being a snoop. I am testing the cognitive functions of her brain as per Agent Machini's request. She said if Justine has an undiagnosed TBI, her brain will repress information surrounding the time of her injury.

Agent Machini grunts out an impressive hum when Justine says, "Dimitri was shot."

I drift my eyes to Trey when he discloses, "Dimitri is under watch at an undisclosed location. He was found by the Feds surrounded by numerous deceased members of a Russian association. They're seeking the death penalty."

I keep quiet about his outdated information. Even a novice in this industry can tell when their integrity is being placed under the microscope. Trey has been testing mine for days, and Justine gives his a workout now. "What aren't you telling me, Trey?" His lips barely twitch an inch when Justine snaps out. "Don't lie to me, Trey. You know the consequences if you do."

Who the fuck is this woman, and what did they do with my sister? Feisty Justine is back, and it's taking everything I have not to welcome her return with a high-five.

The first half of Trey's disclosure I am aware of, but the second half is new. "Nikolai's DNA was found on the scene. A pool of his blood was located next to a man only known as a myth... *Ubiytsa.*"

"Killer," Justine and Agent Machini translate at the same time.

Trey nods. "Rumors are his father was a Ukrainian weightlifter and his mother an operative at the Russian soviet. With his childhood devoted to beating his mother's lineage into him, his seven-foot-eight height never matched the maturity of his brain. His mental capacity only reached that of a young teen."

"Was he the man who held me hostage?" Justine questions.

Trey nods for the second time. "We believe so."

Certain they've slotted the pieces of the puzzles together incorrectly, I seek clarification to their beliefs. "What are you saying? Nikolai killed a man, and in retaliation, he was killed?"

Trey's shrug forces Justine's throat to work through a hard swallow. "We don't know. Dimitri was the only man found alive."

"Because he was too injured to flee?"

Justine's face whitens when Trey shakes his head. "He was left as a warning. If this were a takeover bid, Maxsim needs the word spread that he toppled the king. Dimitri is his equivalent of a town crier."

"That makes sense," Agent Machini says at the same time Justine discloses, "But Maxsim didn't topple the king. Nikolai isn't dead."

When Justine sways like a leaf on a summer's day, I attempt to grab the tops of her arms. I say attempt because she pulls away from me before I can. "J—"

"No!" she screams, her chest heaving. "Nikolai isn't dead! I'd know if he were dead. I would fucking know it." She sucks in a quick breath before adding evidence to her theory. "I somehow got from Florida to Vegas with my life intact. That wouldn't have occurred without Nikolai's help."

"The Vasilievs used a subsidiary entity to bid on you last year," Trey discloses. "You're only alive because they see you as an asset."

"What?" Justine fires back, her one word breathless.

Trey steps closer to her, his eyes oddly nurturing for a guy who looks like he goes through women like underwear. "I'll call a physician to check you over. He's very discreet. I assure you, nothing you tell him will *ever* leave this room."

Sparks of the hormonal teenager I exchanged words every damn day during summer break fire through Justine's eyes when she shouts, "I don't need a doctor! I also wasn't *raped.*" Her last word is barely a whisper. "Nikolai would *never* let that happened. He'd kill any man stupid enough to get within an inch of me."

I want to pat her on the back for standing her ground, but I learned the hard way that stubbornness doesn't always equal honesty. "He couldn't protect you from the grave, J."

Her glare cuts through me like a knife. "Then I'm lucky he isn't dead, aren't I?"

With determination the strongest emotion on her face, she races to a dresser in the corner of the room. Trey's eyes snap to the ground within a nanosecond of her towel slipping off her body so she can yank on a pair of sweatpants and a plain tee.

Once she has her hair pulled out of the collar, she twists to face Trey. "Where are the men?" My feet barely budge an inch when she repeats, "Where are my men!" louder this time.

"They're in the den..." Justine is out the door before half of Trey's reply leaves his mouth, and even faster than that, he's hot on her tail.

"Go with them," Agent Machini suggests. "If Justine isn't going to prioritize her health, you need to do it for her."

Nodding, I take off after them because for once, Agent Machini is right.

My future needs me.

My past doesn't.

Yet.

36

MADDOX

*W*hile picking at the sandwich I delivered as an excuse for a breather, Agent Machini asks, "What is your gut telling you, Maddox?"

I breathe out the nerves twisting my stomach before shrugging. "I don't know. Justine is adamant Nikolai is alive. She says she can sense his presence."

We've been working on pinpointing Nikolai's location for the past couple of hours. Justine spoke with Ryan Carter, an old friend and detective at Ravenshoe PD. His story corroborated what Rocco told me during my trek to my room. Neither the FBI, CIA, nor any of the men in Nikolai's crew know where he is. It's as if he just vanished.

I arch a brow when Agent Machini asks, "Do you think that's hope talking or something much deeper?"

"If you're asking if my sister is psychic, I'd reply with a firm no, but the Walshs have good instincts. If she says she can feel Nikolai's presence, who am I to argue with her?" After dumping my backside onto the bed, I cradle my throbbing head in my hands. I'm so fucking tired, but I can't rest just yet. "I would have given anything to sense Demi four years ago."

When Agent Machini joins me on the bed, her thigh brushes mine. "You stopped feeling her?"

I jerk up my chin, untrusting of my voice not to crack if I were to talk.

My wordless response doesn't give Agent Machini the hint. She probes me like true FBI agents should. "When was that?"

I take a moment to contemplate before muttering, "The day after the accident." I stop, breathe out sharply, then continue. "I gathered the delay stemmed around Max."

My throat dries when I remember animal control dragging Max out of the emergency room at Ravenshoe Private Hospital. He was as inconsolable that day as I was. It took three animal control officers and a heavy sedative to get him into the back of the transport van and over a dozen security guards to hold me back when my begs for them not to euthanize him fell on deaf ears.

"He was a good dog. He was just misunderstood." Realizing I'm once again focusing on my past instead of my future, I drag my hand under my nose to ensure nothing gross is spilling before standing to my feet. "Anyway. I better get back to it."

My steps freeze partway to the door when Agent Machini calls my name. "Maddox." She waits for me to spin around before saying, "The wounds of our past are often the most beautiful part of us." She nudges her head to a book with a bright yellow cover on the coffee table her half-eaten sandwich is sitting on. It's a book called *Triggers* by David Richo. "I can lend it to you once I'm done, if you'd like? It will help you understand why your body responds before your mind has the chance to make sense of a situation."

I shake my head, grateful for her offer, but certain it isn't necessary. "I'm a Walsh. I think with my heart, leap in feet first with my eyes tightly closed, then pray like fuck my head will get me out of whatever situation my heart yearned. My life isn't close to what I had hoped it would be, but changing who I am won't fix anything. I'll still be here, and they'll still be up there, without me."

Needing to leave before she sees the wetness pricking in my eyes, I pivot on my heels and rocket out the door. Agent Machini calls my name again, but this time, I don't stop. I continue walking down the narrow hallways, mindful she means well, but I am over people believing they understand what I'm going through.

Right here, right now, there's only one person who has the slightest inkling of the pain I've experienced the past four years, but there's still hope for her. Nikolai could still be found alive. I can only hope it occurs before Justine collapses from exhaustion. Her speech is slurred, her skin is so blistered, her scars aren't visible, and she's barely touched the sandwich I delivered to her before Agent Machini. She's running herself to the ground, and I'm confident that would piss Nikolai off even more than the knowledge half of his crew is working against her.

"J, I really think you should lay down for an hour or two."

She continues scanning over a dozen reports a partner at her firm couriered here hours ago while briefly shaking her head.

"Will you at least see a doctor?" I lean closer to her. "It isn't just about you anymore, J. Your baby needs you too."

I can tell I'm getting through to her, but she's as stubborn as a mule. It's a Walsh trait. "Trey has arranged for a doctor, but you don't need to worry about that right now, Maddox. I need you to focus on the documents Carmichael supplied us. If Nikolai is being held captive, he's at one of those locations. Find which one it is."

After taking a seat behind a massive set of topographic maps, I push over the bologna and cheese sandwich in a silent hint she should eat.

She doesn't get my insinuation, but that could be more from Trey slamming his cell phone onto Nikolai's desk with annoyance rather than ignorance. "What did she say?" Justine asks Trey, clueing me into the fact he was speaking with a female.

I don't like being out of the loop, but Agent Machini had been locked in our room for hours by herself. Even with her jabbering in my ear the past three hours, I'm confident she was getting restless enough to call in backup. She should count her lucky stars that the Bureau went along with her story on how Agent Moses died. If they hadn't, and she was convicted for tampering with a crime scene, she would have joined me at Wallens Ridge.

Standard cops don't last there a week, so I doubt she would have made it a day. Criminals have a way of sniffing out law enforcement. Why do you think Nero placed two goons outside our room the instant we arrived? He smells a rat. He just has no clue not all the stench is coming from Agent Machini.

After scrubbing a hand across his bushy beard, Trey answers Justine's question. "Not much. She hasn't seen Maxsim in over a year. She rambled some shit about his wife leaving him when he impregnated his whore. I tuned out not long after that."

My lips twist when another two pieces of the puzzle slot into place, although I'm skeptical Maxsim knocked up one of his whores. India would never allow such travesty. She would have forced her to have an abortion before she even knew she was pregnant, but before I can announce that to Justine, she reminds me why our father always warned us never to piss off a pregnant woman. "Get Carmichael back on the phone. If Maxsim isn't operating on behalf of his family, perhaps he is working with someone else."

"Carmichael won't talk to—" Justine ends Trey's ramble by holding her hand out palm side up. Once she has his cell phone in her hand, Trey joins me in sorting through sales documentation for land Alexei, Maxsim's father, purchased before his death. "Have you ever seen her like this?"

When he nudges his head to Justine, I twist my lips. "Determined or…"

"Out for fucking blood," he fills in, laughing.

His chuckle doesn't last long. Not only is he quick to recall why our shoulders are butted together, but Justine also whispers a man's name that gains her the attention of the room. "If Vladimir were alive, do you think Maxsim would be desperate enough to work with him?"

Whatever Carmichael is replying has her desperate to swallow, but she continues with their conversation, aware it's more than Nikolai's life on the line right now. His reputation is also being tested. "But it's not entirely unthinkable. Right?"

Justine looks relieved.

It's closely tailed by confusion.

"What is it?" More heavy breathing, then another question. "To whom?"

I angle my head when a roared voice booms out of Trey's cell phone. I don't know who Carmichael is yelling at, but even from a distance, it's obvious he's pissed. "You did it again, didn't you?"

Justine's eyes ping between Trey and me when more shouting sounds down the line. "For fuck's sake, Jeremy! Did the loss of your finger not teach you anything? They'll kill you this time when they discover what you've done."

She's most likely recalling the numerous arguments her brothers have undertaken the past ten-plus years. You can't have four testosterone metalheads in one space and not expect things to get heated. But this is different. This is one brother stepping over another to better himself. That isn't how the Walsh brethren operates.

Justine's hand shoots up to caress the scar in her shoulder when Carmichael's attention shifts back to her. His voice is softer, meaning I can't hear a thing he says, although the hope it flares through Justine's eyes assures me it is good.

My intuition is proven right when Justine disconnects the call before suggesting we search the Kyle Cannon area.

Not even two seconds later, Trey points out the rugged terrain area on an aerial map before delivering bad news. "Except for a few housing developments, there's nothing out there."

"Carmichael said there's a dirt road hidden by bushes," Justine explains, her voice both breathless and pained.

After another brief search, Trey replies, "I'm not seeing any roads."

I can't help but smile when Justine gabbles under her breath, "Because most men can't locate their nose. Give it to me."

She drags the map to her side of the desk so she can slowly scan the page.

She's barely perused the landscape for two seconds before she asks, "What's this?"

When she highlights a shimmer on the map that could be mistaken for a droplet of grease if she had eaten anything I've placed in front of her the past four hours, my heart beats out a funky tune. It looks similar to the aerial shots Agent Machini has of Clarks, Nikolai's hidden base a couple of miles from here.

Even with my heart raging, I try to play it cool. "A dome?" I lock my eyes with Trey's before attempting to pull the wool over them. "What material was used to build Clarks?"

Assuming my knowledge of Clarks is part and parcel of Nikolai's offer for me to use both his crew and property to assert my final wish, not the slightest bit of suspicion is seen in Trey's eyes when he answers, "Anything we could get our hands on, but a majority of our supplies came from a decommissioned airstrip on the outskirts of town. Others were shipped in."

"Decommissioned?" I double-check while pointing out an obvious airstrip in the otherwise rugged terrain. "Or still in operation?"

Before Trey can answer me, Justine jumps back into the conversation. "Maxsim had to get me to Vegas somehow. What if he didn't use a commercial airstrip?"

Her theory is plausible, and I'm not the only one willing to back it. Trey leaps out of his chair before barking at his men to get ready for battle.

When Justine misses the 'men' part of his statement, Trey ends her endeavor to follow him out of the room in a way I'm reasonably sure he should protect his nuts. "No, Justine. Just because I didn't send you away with Kristina doesn't mean I shouldn't have. You can't come with us. It isn't safe."

Before today, I thought Justine only wore her victories on her body.

Now I realize she also wears them on her heart.

Trey straight up told her she isn't coming, but she ignores him like she did me when I attempted to chase Brax out of the hot tub with a loaded BB gun and a can of mace. She would have preferred to see his ass shot than give in to her overbearing brothers.

When it dawns on Trey that his aggressive stance isn't getting him anywhere anytime soon, he shifts on his feet to face me. "Talk some sense into her, *please.*"

"J—"

It's the fight of my life not to smile when Justine interrupts me before I get a single word out. "No."

Although I'm loving the rejuvenation of her backbone, part of me does wonder if she's walking into a tornado, like sirens aren't wailing in the distance. "Mom has been through enough—"

She cuts me off for the second and final time. "I feel for her, truly I do, but her pain isn't even half of what I'm being pelted with right now."

I've felt the same way for years. No one understands how much it hurts until you've experienced loss firsthand. It has you willing to face a disaster head-on because you know even if it does kill you, death may be the only way to ease the pain.

I realize that Agent Machini is still listening in when she suggests I lay things out in black and white for Justine. "Some women need statistics. Others need support. Justine needs both."

After inconspicuously nodding as if she can see me, I ask, "If you go, you could get killed. Do you understand that, J?"

She nods without the slightest pause for reflection. "At least I won't die a coward. Col stripped the life from my veins years ago. He made me hate everything I was and everything I had once hoped to be." Her pain is my pain when she whispers, "If I lose Nikolai, I will once again lose every part of who I am. I won't survive going through that again, Maddox. I was barely living before Nikolai came into my life, so I refuse to live a life without him in it."

"J..." I want to tell her my plans, to explain I understand *exactly* what she's feeling, but with this not being the time nor the place for a sibling heart-to-heart, I do what I always do when I feel snowed under. I shift the focus to anyone but me. "Dad is going to kill me."

When Justine nods, agreeing with me, I drift my eyes to Trey. "I'll keep her out of harm's way."

Trey chuckles like I sentenced my baby sister to death. "Do you truly believe you have what it takes to keep her safe? These men are like me... they don't have morals."

Once again, my hotheadedness gets the better of me. "Do *you* truly believe Justine would still be here if I couldn't protect her from men like you?" I step up to Trey like he's the enemy, and he's to blame for all the fucked-up shit India has done in the past almost four years. "I took one night off, and look what happened. Men trained to keep my sister safe didn't, yet you feel you have the right to judge me."

I stare at him in warning and threat. Then I stare some more when I realize it isn't arrogance projecting from his eyes. It's fear.

Fear for what has been.

Fear for what is happening.

And fear for what is still yet to come.

He knows a storm is brewing. He's just hoping like fuck he packed enough sandbags to see him through the deluge.

Our stare down ends when Trey shoves a loaded colt into my chest. "I don't have time for this shit. If you want to walk into your death head-on, who am I to stop you?" He drops his eyes to the semi-automatic weapon I angled away from him since the safety is off. "The safety is on the tang. If you don't know what that is, you shouldn't be carrying a gun." While I flick the safety back on, he slings his eyes to Justine. "If you so much as get a scratch on you, you're going to take Maddox's gun, aim it at my head, then fire. Do you understand?"

"Yes." I shouldn't be shocked by Justine's brisk answer, you do anything for those you love, even murder, but I am. She protected Brax the best she could when I threatened him, but the instant the first pellet left my BB gun, she was out of the hot tub and racing for her bedroom, leaving Brax alone with three of her older brothers. Today, she not only agrees to take down one of Nikolai's men if he doesn't follow her orders, but she also assures him she won't need to borrow my gun to do it. "But I won't need to borrow Maddox's gun to take you down. I'll use mine."

With confidence I had always hoped to see in Demi, Justine pulls open the bottom drawer of Nikolai's desk, then removes a Sig Sauer P365 Nitron. Memories of my time at the range with Demi pop into my head when Justine loads the ten-round magazine with bullets without the slightest shake to her hands. She weapons up like a pro, assuring me I'm not the only member of the Walsh brethren to classify a firing range as a date location.

Once Justine has her gun loaded, she walks out of Nikolai's office with her head held high and her heart on lockdown. Today, she isn't taking no for an answer, and if the groove between her brows is anything to go by, no prisoners either. My baby sister is on the warpath, and for the first time in my life, I'm not going to interfere with her reign.

37

MADDOX

"Not a scratch, Justine," Trey warns Justine just before he signals for his men to raid the compound I pointed out only twenty minutes ago.

The grass surrounding the dome-like building is waist-high, and the metal is rusty and old, but there are clear indicators that India has been at this site sometime the past year. Stacks of diaper boxes are under an awning on my right, and the men unaware of Trey's sneaky approach are using empty formula tins as ashtrays.

My wish to seek out more clues is ended by six men in Nikolai's crew circling Justine and me like we're royalty. They don't just block the view, they also stop me from utilizing a single ounce of the adrenaline surging through my veins.

It's like a real-life video game, except you can smell death as much as you can see it.

"Drop!"

The youngest man in a protective detail pulls Justine into his chest before he fires a single shot over her shoulder. I only just catch her when he flings her into my chest so he can kill another perp charging at her with a machete. His desperation to get to Justine without adequate equipment sets off alarm bells in my head.

To men in this industry, Nikolai is the prize gem. If you have him, you have the ultimate power. Only a woman desperate to be loved understands the true value of the queen. Without his queen by his side, the king is worth nothing.

"Wait!" I demand when Justine attempts to break free of my hold when the padlocked room we're slowly pacing toward comes into her view. "Let Trey clear the room first."

If India is inside lying in wait, I'm as sure as fuck not letting my pregnant sister enter the room first. If India wants to hurt my niece or nephew like she did my child, she'll have to get through an army of men first, but then I'll still be here, ready and willing to take her down.

Once Trey's men have the final two dozen men neutralized, he signals for Justine and me to follow him to the door Justine hasn't taken her eyes off for the past three minutes. From there, everything happens in a quick, mind-blurring ten seconds. The lock is popped open with a bullet, the door is kicked in by Trey's boot, then Trey is yanked into the room by a tattooed hand.

His feet dangle mid-air as a dark-haired man with biceps as big as my head squeezes the light out of Trey's eyes by a brutal clutch of his throat. I, along with several members of Nikolai's crew, aim our guns at the brute's head. He's lit up like a Christmas tree, the twinkling of red only fading when Justine steps into the line of sight of numerous guns.

"J!" I scream in frustration at the same time she yells, "Stop! He's one of us." She jabs her fingernails into the man's hands, pulling him out of his psychosis before she locks her eyes with his. "It's me... Justine." Not a single red dot highlights her back when she adjusts her position so he can see the honesty in her eyes when she assures, "We're here to help you. Where are Blaire and Eli? Where's your Kitten, Rico?"

Trey falls to the floor like a bag of shit when Rico releases him from his grip a mere second before I notice the chain dangling from his left wrist.

He isn't one of India's soldiers.

He's one of her victims.

My theory is proven without a doubt when his zombie-like steps to the other side of the room expose who he's endeavoring to protect. A woman and child are huddled beneath a soiled mattress. The faintest rise and fall of their chests reveal they're breathing, but no amount of sugarcoating will alter the facts. They are on death's door.

"Get the SUVs!" Justine demands like a real-life monarch before she joins Rico on his side of the room. "We need to get them medical treatment ASAP."

As Rico lifts the unconscious woman into his arms, I assist Justine with the little boy.

"It's okay," Justine assures Rico when his massively dilated eyes flicker in response to me touching his son. "We've got him."

It takes Rico a couple of seconds to gauge the authenticity of Justine's pledge, and even then, he not once takes his eyes off his son during our slow trek to the SUVs.

His panic is understandable. Gender or age wouldn't have mattered if my child had survived. I would have protected him or her until my very last breath.

Once we have Rico and his family loaded into the lead SUV, I lock my eyes with a pair peering at me in the rearview mirror. "If you see an ambulance, keep driving. I don't see any good ones coming out this far."

I wait for Rico to have his wife and son buckled in the safety of his arms before tapping my hand on the SUV's roof, signaling for the driver to go. I watch its dusty retreat for barely a second when a husky female voice whispers in my ear, "You did good, Maddox. I'm proud of you."

I assume the praise is from Justine, but my assumption changes when my glance over my shoulder awards me with nothing but bloody carnage. Justine is nowhere to be seen, and I'm too doped up on adrenaline to register the familiarity of the voice in my ear.

"Where's J?"

Trey stops barking orders at his men to answer me with a shrug.

"She was here a minute ago." He drags his head to the left before veering it back to the right. "She couldn't have gone far."

When his scan of the terrain comes up empty-handed, he instructs a man with a tattooed head to take the first load of men to Jim's before he tells Nero to find Justine.

When Nero jerks up his chin in understanding, Trey gestures for me to follow him inside. My throat works hard to swallow when he stops walking near a table brimming with pharmacy canisters. They all have familiar-looking labels.

"Do you know what's inside these?" He doesn't give me the chance to reply. He simply stares at me like I'm dog shit on the bottom of his boot while announcing, "Abortion medication." He points to each pill canister while naming them. "Cytotec. Mifepristone. Hemabate. Dinoprostone. And last but not at all least... misoprostol." My eyes jackknife to his when he mutters, "Your crew's flavor of the month." He bounces his eyes between mine. "Or should I say Dimitri's crew?"

I laugh off his claim Nikolai's disappearance is Dimitri's doing. I don't claim to know all of Dimitri's inner-workings, but there's no fucking way he'd join forces with India. He wants her dead as much as I do. Furthermore, excluding India's current scapegoat, Trey is the *only* man from her past still living. If this isn't a deflection of blame, I never loved Demi, and we both know that's my biggest lie to date.

Trey works his jaw side to side when I ask, "I never picked you for a pharmaceutical rep. What was your major in high school? Chemistry, or working out which abortion drug was most effective for teen pregnancies?"

It dawns on me that his temper is as short as mine when he pins me to the wall as Rico did to him earlier. He's a little taller than me, but we're of similar weight, meaning he can't get my feet off the ground as Rico could. He has to choke me the old-fashioned way.

"Do you wanna know how I know the name of those drugs?" he asks after tightening his grip around my throat like I don't have one of his guns shoved down the back of my pants. "I studied them in great detail after Duchess's pregnancy test came back positive because I know all about the sick shit the Petrettis are capable of. She's been hurt before. I won't have her hurt again."

He's choking me to death, suffocating me with his bare hands, yet my brain can only focus on his confession that his girlfriend is pregnant instead of the screaming demands of my lungs. His admission changes everything, and it has me wondering how deep India's ruse runs this time around. Could she be endeavoring to kill two birds with one stone?

"Where is she?" I ask, talking with the last smidge of oxygen in my lungs. "Where is Duchess?"

"Far away from the sick fucks you like to play with," Trey breathes out slowly, his grip tightening.

Realizing I'll never subdue a hothead with words, I jab my fingers into his rib before executing the move I did when Igor paralyzed me with a bear hug, except I don't throw my head backward this time around, I headbutt Trey right in the fucking nose.

He stumbles back with a roar before he rares up with his fists blazing. We both have loaded guns at the ready, but we're too amped up with testosterone for a quick, uncallous battle.

We want carnage.

Lots of it.

"You're a fucking dead man, Ox."

The scarce bit of air I sucked down when I loosened his grip on my throat is forcefully evicted with a brutal left-right-left combination to my stomach. With my focus on breathing, his right fist kisses my jaw without any deflection.

Demi would have chewed me out for that back in the day.

While hissing through a possible cracked rib, I retaliate to both Trey's aggression and the painful memory bombarding me by pole driving Trey onto the dirty, blood-soaked floor. His back colliding with the concrete makes the same *oomph* noise my mouth does when I put my weight behind my hits. I act ignorant to the damage he's doing to my midsection while slamming my fists into his face. I get in three or four decent hits before the ricochet of a gun stills both my heart and my fists.

When it happens another two times, I clamber off Trey and race in the direction the bangs came from while screaming Justine's name on repeat. "J!"

Trey's winded breaths expose he's hot on my heels. His speed is so fast, he almost beats me to Justine being rolled down the hill by a man spraying bullets at insurgents sprinting his way like their last gig was in Iraq.

The stranger seems to have a handle on things, but just in case, Trey takes down the final two men lurking in the rugged bushland before he aims his gun at the confused crinkle between my brows. With flaring nostrils and a red, bloodied face, he stares at me for several long seconds. His eyes belong to a murderer, but before they can execute his every wish, he slowly lowers his gun. I don't know if it's finally dawned on him that I'm not the enemy or if he's afraid what Nikolai's response will be when he discovers Justine was pinned to the ground by the crotch of a man with a thick Russian accent.

"If you want to make it out of today alive, Ox, stay the fuck away from me," Trey warns before instructing his men to search deeper into the woods.

Although he looks like he's still itching for a bloodbath, he shifts his focus to Justine instead of the carnage only one hundred feet away. He doesn't bombard her about her reckless behavior like my brothers and I would have when she was a teen. He simply relays his disappointment with the same smothering glare I'm giving her.

I'm still pissed at his insinuation I am anything like the fools India has at her beck and call, but no amount of anger would have me over-looking the respect he gives my sister. From the range of looks she's garnering from Nikolai's crew, she needs as many men on her side as possible. Trey isn't an idle candidate, and I'd rather Justine not be in this environment at all, but I realize now that trying to pull her away from Nikolai would have been the equivalent of me not reacting to a fifteen-year crush when Saint pulled his signature move on Sloane instead of Demi.

As Justine is aided from the ground by the dark-haired, Russian-accented man, Nero returns from the woods. "Any signs of Maxsim?" Trey asks him, hopeful.

A man with burnt orange hair a similar color to Justine's standing next to Nero shakes his head. "No, but I bet she knows where he is."

He yanks forward a petite woman so aggressively, she falls to her knees. She's shuddering like she is in an ice bath. Her scared response reminds me so much of Demi's state of mind when she stumbled out of her uncle's Audi. She's scared, but not all her focus is on herself.

"I don't know anything—" Her words are cut off by the butt of the ginger's gun impacting with her temple.

I'm tempted to pole drive him into the ground like I did Trey only moments ago, but Justine beats me to him. "Don't!"

He doesn't appreciate Justine's snapped command, but before he can announce his disgust, the dark-haired stranger growls something to him in Russian. I don't know what he says, I'm not fluent in multiple languages like Justine, but it has the ginger-haired man backing away from Justine in an instant.

After swallowing harshly, the brute who gets off on beating women mutters, "Nikolai's?"

"Yes," several men answer in sync.

The man was already in fear for his life. Now, he looks set to end it himself. I can't say I blame him. It will be less painful that way. I've seen how protective Nikolai is of Justine. It's another reason I'd never rib her about their relationship like Saint did earlier this week. Everyone has their place in the world. Justine's happens to be at Nikolai's side.

When the red-haired man withdraws toward the forest, Justine approaches the petite brunette. It's clear they've met before because Justine has barely reached her side when the cowering woman whispers something to her in a foreign language.

"Who promised you, Maya?" Justine asks, her tone oddly composed for how hard her chest is rattling. "Maxsim?"

Tears join the blood streaming down one side of Maya's face

when she nods. Her wordless confession sees Justine sucking in her first lung-filling breath of air since she woke early this morning.

After another three big breaths, she continues her conversation with Maya. Since they don't want their conversation overheard, they talk in a foreign language I believe to be French. Although I can't understand a thing they're saying, several names are distinguishable. The most prominent—Nikolai's.

"Nikolai? He was here?" In her shock, Justine expresses this question in English.

When Maya nods, Trey steps forward. "When?"

"*Il y a trois jours.*"

"Three days ago?" Justine half questions, half confirms. She chokes on her spit when Maya nods again. "Was he okay?"

I watch Justine for signs of distress when Maya's head bob switches to a shake. "He wasn't well," she murmurs, her accent an odd combination of Russian and French. "How do you not know that? You were with him. You were the last person to see him alive."

A combined hiss breaks the pin-drop silence surrounding Justine and Maya. Like the glares she's getting could get any worse, Justine is hit with a truckload at once. They're brimming with suspicion, and they have Justine responding in a manner she would have when she was a teen. "If I knew where he was, I'd tell you." She sneers at the men staring at her through narrowed, skeptical eyes. "I don't know where he is. I don't remember anything!"

When she clutches her head like her brain is about to explode, the voice I heard earlier trickles back into my ears. "She needs to be seen by a doctor, Maddox. Knocks to the head cause many underlining issues you can't see from the outside. If her brain is bleeding, she could suffer irreparable damage." Agent Machini stops to catch her breath before adding to her plead. "Please, Ox, I'm begging you to seek urgent medical attention for your sister now."

Although shocked the device I slipped into my ear hours ago is still functioning, unanimity is my strongest emotion. Justine is struggling, and as much as I wish the cause of her suffering would miraculously reappear, I know as well as anyone that the possibility of that happening grows less likely the longer he remains missing.

"It's me," I whisper when Justine stiffens from me curling my arm around her shoulders.

As I guide her back to the fleet of SUVs, I sling my eyes to Trey, where I wordlessly tell him Justine's help with his search is now over. She needs rest, and if Nikolai were here, he'd agree with me.

Trey looks more relieved by my decision than disappointed. After lifting his chin in understanding, he shifts on his feet to face the men snickering under their breaths. "Gather up any evidence you can before reconvening at Clarks." When the men's bickering shifts to a sigh, Trey says matter-of-factly, "The day is still young. We will not fall until Nikolai is returned. If you do, you will fall on his knife just as quickly."

38

MADDOX

$\mathcal{I}$t took the men not even five minutes to pluck every bit of evidence, equipment, and DNA-laced objects they could find in the old airport hangar. Once it was loaded into the final two SUVs, we commenced our ten-mile trip back to the Popov compound. Justine has been quiet the entire time. She's not exactly sulking. However, she is extremely closed-off.

The last time I saw her this reserved was when Demi and I visited her in the hospital after she was mauled. She tried to refuse us entry, but I stormed in with the hotheadedness of a bull, certain nothing I could see would have been worse than what I had faced only days earlier.

It kills me to admit that the damage the Rottweiler did to her body still haunts my dreams to this day. Justine has often said the surgeons stitched her back together like a patchwork quilt, and I'd be a liar if I didn't agree with her. She had hundreds of stitches, head to toe, but mercifully, her face was untouched. If you discounted the pain in her eyes when she's rugged up for winter, you'd have no clue of the horrors she had been through.

It was the same for Demi. She was so beautiful and so fucking strong, but no matter how brightly she smiled, the pain in her eyes never quit. It was there for the world to see. I just acted ignorant to it.

What I said to Agent Machini earlier was true. I wouldn't change Demi's past because the scars of her childhood made her the woman she was, but sometimes, I wish I could erase the hurtful parts. Then she'd still be the woman I love, but every time she looked at me, I wouldn't have to strive for ways to numb her pain. I could have been with her solely because I loved her, not because I wanted her to have a better life.

Memories of the last smile she flashed me stop clouding my thoughts when my head collides with the back passenger window of the SUV Trey is commanding. He had to veer to miss a dog sitting in the middle of the field.

"Damn dog. Get out of the fucking way," Trey shouts a mere second before Justine's neck cranks to the back window of the SUV.

She stares at the dog Trey narrowly missed for two heart-thrashing seconds before she screams, "Stop!"

Trey locks up the brakes, skidding us to a stop, and almost causing the cars following us to ram up our ass. I stop glaring at him in the rearview mirror when Justine throws open her door and clambers out. After spinning in a circle, she drags her wide eyes over the barren land surrounding us. Although I'm lost on what's caused the rapid shift in her demeanor, there's a fire in her eyes that can't be denied. She's clawing her way out of the deep dark pit Nikolai's disappearance forced her into. She is re-emerging from her cocoon for the second time, except this time, her metamorphosis is solely for Nikolai instead of my freedom.

After taking in a bullet casing shimmering in the low-hanging sun, she drifts her eyes between Trey and me. "There's a gorge somewhere near here. Nikolai is in that gorge."

Ignoring the disdained looks she's being hit with, she returns to the SUV to gather the map Trey dumped onto the passenger seat earlier today. After rolling the topographic map across the hood of the SUV, she points to an obvious elevation in the seemingly flat landscape. "Here. Our truck went over the edge around here."

Trey squeezes Justine's shoulder in thanks before ordering his men to return to the SUVs. Half follow his command. The other half are too frozen with shock to move. They're not immobile in awe of Justine's sudden recollection of events, they are stunned by the gall of a gangbanger with a tattooed cheek and a bad attitude. "Are you all fucking clueless? Can't you see she's taking us on a wild goose chase, hoping we won't realize she's orchestrated all of this?"

"That's enough, Ethan."

Justine swipes her hand through the air, cutting Trey off. "Let him speak." She bridges the gap between her and Ethan without the slightest shake to her strides. "Because they may be the last words he ever speaks."

When Ethan attempts to get up in her face, I step up to him, chest to chest. I'm not shocked when I feel Trey's shoulder butt against mine. He may hate sharing the same air as me, but he can set aside his disdain when it comes to protecting Justine.

His overbearing desire to protect her assures me he isn't working with India. I doubt he even knows her imprint is all over the evidence Nikolai's crew scrummaged from the hangar. I have every intention to tell him about her involvement *once* my baby sister's life and that of her child is out of danger.

But not now when Justine is being eyed like their thirst for a bloodbath won't be quenched until all the blood is drained from her veins. I can't change my past, but I can ensure my family doesn't suffer more than they already have.

With one goon subdued by a double dose of threat, Justine sets to work on getting the rest on board with her plans. "I get it, all right? You want your king back." When a collective hum sounds over the flat terrain, she adds, "So the fuck do I. That's what I've been trying to do since you found me. I don't want to take Nikolai's place. I want him to come home." She strays her eyes over the many pairs staring at her in shocked awe. "If you don't want the same thing, then leave, go, but be assured, if you do leave, you'll *never* be welcomed back. The instant I become Nikolai's, I become a bratva. That means I'm as much your family as I am Nikolai's. When one of us goes down, we all go down. That's the bratva way." She steps closer to the men now looking at her as if she is a true queen. "So you need to make a choice. Either fight alongside me to bring Nikolai home or walk away like a coward. Those are your only two options."

When the men break into a Russian chant, Justine re-enters the SUV. She appears composed, but I know there's more to the gloss in her eyes than bewilderment about how fast she got Nikolai's men on her side. She's in pain. I just have no clue if the pain is in her chest or her stomach. It could be a combination of both.

"One more stop." My murmur is in response to the sigh Agent Machini releases when Trey steers the lead SUV in the direction Justine highlighted on the map instead of the closest hospital, but Justine believes it's for her.

"He's there, Maddox. I can feel it." She squeezes my hand before returning her focus to scanning the scenery. I do the same.

Not even two minutes later, I point to an abyss in the land that looks similar to a gorge. "There!"

Trey slams on his brakes as he did earlier before he locks his eyes with Justine's in the rearview mirror. "Does anything around here seem familiar?"

When she exits the vehicle to contemplate his question, I mimic her movements. She appears confused, but I'm highly skeptical it's from a knock to the head. Her eyes are flickering like Demi's did when she struggled to remember Kaylee.

Before Justine can make a dent in her confusion, a teenage male shouts, "Over here!" He's standing on the very edge of the gorge, unfearful he might fall.

"He's here," Justine whispers after peering down the rocky cliff edge.

When she commences scaling down the rocky surface, the gent Trey introduced as Nikolai's Russian counterpart requests she be careful while Trey tells his men to gather any equipment needed to hoist Nikolai to safety if he's found.

I jump to the command in his tone like I'm one of his lackeys. My eagerness can't be helped. The same bristling sensation is in the air now as it was when I followed Demi down the alleyway siding the gym her uncle owned. Greatness is about to happen. I just really fucking hope Justine and Nikolai's story has a fairy-tale ending.

Loose rocks fall out from beneath my feet when I follow Justine and Trey's trek through the gorge. I'm not in the gorge with them. I'm following every step they take from above.

A couple of minutes later, I lose sight of them when they disappear under an overhanging rock. They soon emerge on the far side of the cave-like structure, but it's a struggle to keep watch via the naked eye.

When I instruct the two men next to me to move the SUVs half a mile up, they act as if I never spoke. I'm about to back up my claims with either my fists or the gun stuffed down the back of my jeans, but Asher beats me to it. After unholstering his gun, he pops a bullet into one of the men's knees. While one screams in pain, the other listens very intently to the words Asher is sneering at him in Russian. I don't know what he says, but it has the second man jumping to fulfill my demand like I'm a regal prince.

"Thanks," I say, a little unsure how to respond.

I once believe violence solved nothing.

Now, more than my morals are on the fence.

Asher twists his lips like it's no big deal before he shifts his eyes back to Justine and Trey. "If you have half the courage she has, you'll be an asset to Nikolai's team."

"I'm not looking for a team," I reply before I can stop myself.

He throws his head back and laughs as if I'm being funny. I'm not, but since now isn't the time to prove a point, I continue pacing along the gorge, seeking Justine and Trey.

"J..." My call echoes in the depth of the gorge, but I don't get a reply. After shifting on my feet to face Nero, I ask, "How deep is it?"

He shrugs. "No fucking clue." When his reply causes blood to drain from my face, he bumps me with his shoulder. "Don't get your knickers in a twist, Ox." When he snickers out 'knickers,' he nudges his head to the collection of fake tattoos I got earlier this week peeking out of the collar of my shirt. "Trey sent K away with Eight so his focus could be solely on Justine. He won't let anything happen to her. He can be a prick when he wants to be, but under the scruff is a real fucking softie." He chuckles like he's shocked by his own comment before adding, "If he weren't, he would have peeled your fake tats off your body with a knife. Not even real patriots cover themselves with that much home heritage." When I tug on the collar of my shirt, he chuckles even louder. "I look forward to hearing the story behind them, but for now, how about we keep our focus on the task at hand?"

"Sounds like a plan to me," I mutter under my breath, annoyed but also grateful he isn't going to drill me.

It takes another thirty or so minutes before we get word from Trey and Justine, but thankfully, it's good news. Nikolai has been found. He's pretty nicked up and sporting a broken leg, but he's alive, and to Justine and the men surrounding me, that's all that matters.

"Let's load up and head out before the po-po drop in for a visit," Nero commands while slapping my back in euphoria.

I return his gesture, my gratitude uncontainable. All I ever wanted was to do a bit of good for my community. Although I'm far from Ravenshoe, it's embedded in my sister's bones, so technically, today's victory places a favorable strike on my measly good versus evil scoreboard.

A couple of minutes later, while following Nero's command as if I'm one of Nikolai's foot soldiers, the unease in Agent Machini's voice pinches my eagerness. "I got word Maxsim has been spotted at an airstrip two miles from your location."

"Is he alone?" I ask, uncaring if I look like a mental patient to Nikolai's men.

As I dump a bundle of rope into the back of the lead SUV, she answers, "No. There are over a dozen women with him." My thoughts immediately stray to India, but Agent Machini is quick to shut down that thought process. "Every one of them are wearing white nightgowns."

"If India's surrogates are with Maxsim, India must be close behind. The women aren't Maxsim's property. They're India's."

Agent Machini's lack of communication frustrates me to no end, but I'd be a liar if I said I don't understand the reason for it. My brain immediately switches off when she advises me the Bureau is holding back on storming the private airport hangar Maxsim was sighted in because they believe India's arrival is imminent.

In under a second, I slot my ass into the driver's seat of the lead SUV, then take off like a bat out of hell. A handful of Nikolai's men gripe about my abrupt departure, but for the most part, my flee goes unnoticed.

Justine found Nikolai, so they'll have their happily ever after, but I'll never achieve mine if India slips off the radar for another four years. Dimitri's team has been hunting her for years. This is the closest anyone has got, so I can't act as if this isn't my only chance to exact revenge for the death of my unborn child.

"Send the location of the airport to my cell phone. I'll sync it with the Bluetooth in the Range Rover." When nothing but silence resonates down the line for the next several seconds, my anger gets the best of me. "Please, Macy, you know as well as I do that India won't get anything more than a slap on the wrist. You've given the Bureau enough information on her to arrest her three times over, yet they always come back with the same response."

"They need more concrete evidence," we say at the same time.

"Yes!" I shout while wringing the steering wheel. "So help me to stop that from happening again."

"I can't," she fires back, her words as loud as mine. "You're not a judge, Maddox. You're not a jury of her peers, so you have no right to trial her."

"She killed my baby! She has murdered countless other unborn children! She doesn't deserve to live."

"But you do, Maddox. You deserve the peace Demi has now, the harmony, but if you do this, you'll never have that. You will rot in jail for the rest of your li—"

The click that cuts off Agent Machini's reply is quickly followed by a unique accent. "A dirt road is coming up on your left. Take it. The airstrip is one and a quarter clicks down." Although Smith can't see me—*well, I assume he can't*—I lift my chin before pulling hard on the steering wheel. "Feds are swarming the west entrance, so I'll direct you to the east wing. I may lose you the closer you get. They have blockers in place."

"Lead me to India. I'll do the rest."

"Attaboy," Rocco cheers down my earpiece, wrongly assuming I'm on his team.

I'm not doing this for Dimitri or Nikolai.

I am doing this for me and my family—all of them.

As Smith and Rocco guide me toward the private airstrip, I search the cab of the Range Rover for a better weapon than the one shoved down the back of my jeans. India rarely travels alone, which means I need to weapon up.

I've only just pulled a machine gun off the back-passenger side floor when Smith demands me to brake. I lock them up so fast, I add to the bruises my tussle with Trey caused my ribs.

"What?" I asked, confused as to why I'm parked half a mile away from the woman they've been targeting for half a decade.

Smith clicks on his mouse a couple of times before informing me, "I piggybacked onto the satellite feed the Feds are using to track India's Benz. It isn't traveling toward the airstrip Maxsim is at. She's heading in the opposite direction."

What. The. Fuck?

After executing a three-point turn, I ask, "Has the Feds' cover been blown?"

The woosh of a headshake drowns out Smith's frantic tap on a keyboard. "I don't believe so. She sent correspondence to Maxsim saying she needed to tie up loose ends and that she'll meet him at Bora Bora within a couple of days." Smith curses under his breath before adding, "If the video file I extracted from her phone is any indication of who she's after, she'll only need one bullet to end two lives... perhaps even three."

I'm about to ask what the fuck he's on about, but before I can, my phone dings, indicating I've received a text message. I dig it out of my pocket so fast, I veer onto the wrong side of the road.

A head-on collision is the least of my problems when I watch the footage playing on the screen on my phone. It is of a pregnant lady being bound to a chair by two brutes. Balaclavas are covering their faces, and they've weaponed up like they're going to war. Although the female is conscious, the stream of red careening down one side of her head exposes she may not be for long.

"Jesus fucking Christ," Rocco and I murmur at the same time, revealing Smith is updating Rocco on the fly along with me.

"Who is she?" Rocco's tone indicates he's unaware of her identity, which is shocking since he seems to know everyone.

"Trey Corbyn's wife," I answer on Smith's behalf. I only saw the quickest glimpse of her profile when Trey carried her out of the Popov compound earlier today, but it was enough to make a positive identification. "He said he sent her away to keep her safe, so how the fuck did India find her so quickly?"

"Nikolai has a snitch." Rocco's swift answer reveals today isn't the first time he's contemplated this. "And if the niggle in my trigger finger is anything to go by, it could be the same man that's had Dimitri running in circles the past five years."

Smith hums out an agreeing murmur before announcing the feed India is watching is untraceable. "She's using a server similar to the one Vladimir used when he auctioned Justine. I need an invitation to log in, and even then, access would be limited."

"Hold on, what? My sister was sold?" Nothing but shock highlights my tone.

"To Dimitri," Rocco fills in like it's old news. "That's how Nikolai found her when Vladimir kidnapped her. I told you about this."

"Like fucking hell you did," I snap out, pissed as fuck but still primed with enough adrenaline from an earlier win to push it to the back of my mind. "We will have words about this later, but for now, can you send me India's current location. If she's anything like her file states—"

"She'll tie up the loose ends herself," Rocco interrupts, hitting the bullseye.

Like magic, the Range Rover's dashboard switches on, and a map of Las Vegas brightens the screen. "She's the orange dot. You're the blue," Smith advises before he continues tapping on his keyboard.

The several miles between India and me become less obvious when I plant my foot on the gas pedal. I race through the desert valleys of Vegas while racking my brain on what I plan to do when I reach India. No matter how strong my wish for revenge is, I can't sit back and watch India put another man through what I went through. Losing a child is hard enough, but when you lose the woman you love as well, grief alone destroys the strongest man.

It ended me.

I won't have it do the same to Trey.

My speed is so relentless, I'm shocked when my sail past a stationary police cruiser doesn't see me being chased down by blue and white flashing lights.

I discover why when Agent Machini exerts her frustration about a mass casualty shooting via Smith's microphone. "They were told to hold! How hard is it to follow orders?"

Smith may have blocked her from my feed, but he's keeping tabs on every word she speaks. Trust is no longer a strong point of mine, and it appears to be the same for Smith.

"Now we may never get her." Agent Machini's growl barely drowns out the line of police cruisers darting past me. They're lit up like a Christmas tree and driving as recklessly as me.

"Are they going to Maxsim's location?" I ask, unsure why I care but too curious to act nonchalant.

"Yeah," Smith replies casually before instructing me to turn left. I'd drill him for more information, but his next set of words keep my focus on the task at hand. "India has stopped at an industrial property half a mile up. Dim your lights."

It takes me a few seconds to work out how to do that. The Range Rover's headlights are automatic, and the sun has now set.

It dawns on me that Smith can see what I'm seeing when he mutters, "Now creep up a quarter of a mile before walking the last quarter," only a nanosecond after I switch off the headlights.

With a chuckle, Rocco says, "Look up and smile, big boy. The artificial intelligence they advertise to sell this pricy ride is what fucked society. Why do you think I love old-school cars? No automatic shutdowns, no sneaky pricks listening in on my private conversations, and my girl can suck my dick while I'm driving, and I don't have to worry about some sick fuck stroking his cock to her gagging on my schlong." Through the personal assistant bot mounted under the rearview mirror of the Range Rover, he sees me roll my eyes. "Don't be jealous, Ox. If you play your cards right, even I'd be tempted to suck your dick tonight."

I usually find crude humor entertaining, but now I understand Demi's frustration when I used it to deflect my anguish. It's frustrating not knowing what someone is thinking in general, much less in a dire life or death situation.

Rocco is still chuckling in my ear when I pull up a couple of blocks from the stationary orange dot on the dashboard of the Range Rover. After slipping my cell phone into my pocket, I toss open the door, then slide out, only curling back in to gather up the AK-47 and a cap. My looks have changed a lot in the past five years, but I'd rather be safe than sorry.

If India recognizes me, my plan will go to shit before it's even activated.

After I've lowered a cap to shadow my eyes, Smith's voice breaks through the silence teeming around me. He doesn't break out a comedy skit to deflect his nerves. He keeps things strictly professional. "The satellite imagery is poor due to a bad sensory angle, but I'm reasonably sure India is the sole occupant of the premises." He clicks a handful of times on his mouse before the hiss of a vacuum-sealed lock unlatching rustles through the dead quiet night. "The quickest access to the main hub of the property is via an industrial freezer on the right of the driveway. It should be coming up on your left shortly."

Although the freezer Smith referenced is the same size as the one at Petretti's, it doesn't take me long to realize it isn't used for the storing of food. There are two bodies, a handful of body parts, and buckets I'm not willing to look into to douse my curiosity.

This time around, the cat can die on his scratching post. I learned from the errors of my past. I won't make the same mistake twice.

"Which way?" I ask Smith when my trek through the freezer sees me confronted with a T intersection. Light isn't projecting either way, so I have no clue if I should go left or right.

Smith mutters, "Left," just as I'm blinded by a massive spotlight.

"Yippee-Ki-Yay, motherfucker. It's about time you showed up," Rocco greets before he turns on a fire hydrant full pelt to drench me from head to toe, drowning out Agent Machini's warning that I'm walking into a trap.

39

MADDOX

I don't miss Rocco's faint grin when I wiggle a finger in my ear to loosen the clump of water stuck in there. He's standing behind the monitor Dimitri's white face is filling, as dry as a fucking desert. I can't say the same. I'm so drenched, I left a puddle in my wake with every step I took down a recently burrowed mine shaft.

Trey's wife, Kristina, or affectionately known as 'K' to people in this industry, wasn't kidnapped by India or Maxsim. She was placed in 'a temporary restrictive hold' by Rocco and Smith.

Yes, that is how Rocco justified his first foray into a violence-against-women campaign. He's doing it for K's greater good. Unfortunately, I can't call him out on it. From what Dimitri, Smith, and Rocco have told me over the past hour, if they hadn't intervened, K would be on a shipping container along with Dimitri and his family as we speak.

India is so fucking desperate for an English heir, she's willing to take one who doesn't belong to her, but since K isn't as far along as Audrey was when India forced her to continue with their surrogacy plans as drafted, India was left with no option but to take K with her while relocating abroad.

Since she had to keep her plans of a British heir from Maxsim, she branched out to secure K through the same channels Vladimir used when he auctioned my sister. It took weeks of negotiations to reach this point, but the collection for K was organized for later today.

That's where I come in.

India knows Smith and Rocco. She interacted with them multiple times while endeavoring to sink her nails into the Italian Cartel. Although we've met in passing twice, once at the warehouse where I found the empty canister of misoprostol and the second time when she stood next to Col while Justine was being mauled, Dimitri isn't worried that she will recognize me. Since most of my free time in prison was spent in the yard, I bulked up. The sun faded the freckles I'm infamous for and added a heap of blond streaks to my usually reddish hair. When you tack those aspects onto the new stencils Tails added to my body three days ago, I still look like a Walsh, just one from the other side of the pond.

Dimitri could have hired any man for this job. Criminals would come out of the woods to be in his favor, but he knows this is as personal for me as it is for him. He got his daughter back. His son was heard in the background when we were speaking. I can't achieve the same outcome as him. India stripped me of the chance. She not only killed my unborn baby, but she also encouraged Col to punish Justine outside the extent of her so-called disrespect.

I couldn't come back from Justine's mauling. No matter what I did or how hard I tried to pretend I was okay, it fucked with my head so much, I made stupid mistake after stupid mistake. It was that recklessness that ended Demi's life. It was what ultimately took her away from me, so it's only fair India is prosecuted accordingly by me.

"All right, I'll do it." The casualness of my reply doesn't weaken its impact. Rocco slaps my back while Smith gets to work on finalizing details with India. All correspondence with her has been done through the dark web. We technically don't know it's her. The only time her identity will be proven is when she arrives here to collect K.

Rocco stops slapping my back mid-hit when Dimitri asks, "On what condition?" When I arch a brow, shocked at his ability to read me, a rare smile tugs one side of his lips higher. "You didn't gain Col's eyes just because you could fight, Ox. A gangbanger knows a gangbanger."

I brush off his claims I'm anything like him with a huff. My time at Wallens Ridge indicates I could make a killing in his industry if money was what my heart desired. Unfortunately, it isn't. Who it wants no longer exists, and neither will India by the end of today.

I cough to clear my throat of unwarranted nerves before stating my terms. "The women India is carting from country to country. I want them freed and returned to their families."

"It isn't as easy as it sounds." Dimitri's reply is for me, but his eyes are for someone he's peering at over his laptop screen. "Some of the women were sold when they were children. They don't even know their real names."

"But India would."

"She won't give you what you want, Ox," Rocco intervenes. "She isn't like the women you've met in this industry. You could torture her for hours, and she wouldn't speak a peep. She's fucked in the head."

Smith hums out an agreeing murmur for half a second before he races across the room. "There could be a way around her stubbornness." He spins around the prototype laptop he's been using to communicate with India for the past couple of weeks. "The site is impossible to hack, but if I were to log in directly via India's device, I wouldn't face so many issues." He taps his index finger on an icon at the top of their chat window that indicates India uses her cell phone for all correspondence. "If you keep her talking long enough, I could access her buried files with voice recognition. They may unearth the information you're after."

"Okay. I can do that."

I stray my eyes to Rocco when he asks, "Are you sure about that, Ox? I'd be tempted to shoot the bitch in the head on sight, and she didn't fuck with me like she did you and Demi."

Demi's name alone convinces me, much less peering at the grubby face of the first lady on a stack of photographs at my side. The information Audrey, Dimitri's first wife, disclosed to Dimitri exposes that the women aren't incubated with India's children the old-fashioned way. They're held down in dirty rooms on stained mattresses and violated by alleged health professionals like Dr. Franklin. As if that isn't bad enough, they're raped by the men India brainwashes to follow her scheme, then beaten until they miscarriage if their rapist forgot to use protection. They've endured hell, so I'm confident I can stand across from the woman responsible for years of torment for a couple of minutes to free them from more harm.

"All right," Dimitri says when he sees the truth in my eyes. "Let's get this wrapped up. India is scheduled to arrive within the hour. Once it's done, I need you to move onto that other task I assigned you before we left." He isn't talking to Rocco or me. His focus is on Smith. "I need it done ASAP."

"If it's there to be found, I'll find it," Smith guarantees.

Aware Smith won't stop until he finds what Dimitri is searching for, Dimitri shifts his eyes back to me. "Tell India I said hello."

It's wrong of me to smile, but I'd be a liar if I said my lips didn't hitch into a grin.

Fifty-three minutes later—*yes, I counted*—I lower a cap over my eyes, stuff a gun down the back of my pants, then back it up with a semiautomatic weapon. I never thought I'd contemplate killing another person, much less a woman, but not an ounce of guilt has thickened my blood the past hour. Dimitri laid everything out for me—how the Bureau has let India slip from their grasp time and time again, the number of victims she's amassed, and how she orchestrated Nikolai and Justine's disappearance.

Furthermore, just like she was responsible for popping the idea of Justine's mauling into Col's head, she did the same thing with Maxsim about having his goon hit her in the stomach.

India deserves to die. If admitting that makes me a monster, so be it. I'm at peace with my decision. I protected Demi as a child. I loved her as an adult, and I will honor her until the day I take my final breath. If that happens to be today, I'm okay with that as well. Death doesn't scare me. It's the prospect of living without Demi for eternity that scares me the most.

I'm dragged from my somber thoughts by Rocco squeezing my shoulder. "You good?"

I check that the magazine of my gun is loaded properly before lifting my chin. I feel like I'm dreaming, like nothing that is happening is real. I don't know if that stems from the fact my gut isn't twisted up in knots or the peace I feel knowing I've finally reached the end of the road.

The last five years have been fucking hard. Pretending you're okay when you're not is exhausting. I have so much more respect for people battling depression now than I've ever had. It's the biggest prison there is. There's no light at the end of the tunnel. No loosening of the cuffs. It's one dark hole after another.

Rocco takes a moment to gauge my real response before he hands me a bead listening device like the one Agent Machini gave me. "Keep her talking until Smith gives you the all-clear. If you do that, those women could be home by the end of the week." That lifts the fog by half an inch as do the words he speaks. "It will get better, Ox. It always does. You've just got to have faith the world couldn't be so fucking cruel."

After a second squeeze of my shoulder, he disappears down a dingy corridor that leads to a mine shaft. He wanted to stay close by, but we can't trust that India won't demand one of her men to search the premises before entering it.

To kill time, I walk around the large concrete and steel building, taking it in. It's kind of surreal learning this is the place my sister grew her wings. She didn't die here. She was reborn here. Nikolai saved her, and in thanks for his gallantry, Justine returned the favor. For someone who used to faint over a paper cut, I was shocked to learn she removed the knife that ended Vladimir's life from his chest. I guess I shouldn't be. There wasn't a single obstacle I wouldn't have scaled to save Demi. Even years after her death, I'm still leaping over those barriers.

I head to the front entrance of the compound when Smith announces a car is pulling down the dusty road. India wouldn't agree to come by herself, but she was stupid enough to agree to my demand that we exchange assets alone. Any johns in the car with her will be taken out by long-range snipers once I have India out of earshot.

"Stop right there," I say to the man flanking India's walk up the front stairwell, freezing both him and India in their tracks. "Raise your shirt... and your dress." I have to force my last command out of my mouth. I'm not interested in anything India is selling. I just don't trust her as far as I can throw her.

When they do as requested, I lock my eyes with India. "We agreed to be the only two people in attendance at the exchange." The accent I'm putting on is horrendous, but India doesn't seem to notice. She's too fucking high-strung to pay a bottom dweller gangbanger any attention. She only has the big fish in her sights.

"We did," she replies, her tone all pompous-like.

"Good, then tell him to fuck off and let's get down to business. I ain't got time for your shit, lady." Rocco's snicker about my impersonation is soft but unmissable. It's barely audible through the water still sloshing in my ears, though.

After a few seconds of deliberation, India signals for the brute to leave with a dainty wave of her hand. When he tries to cite an objection about her dismissal, her hand leaves a red imprint on his face. Her moods are worse than a schizophrenic—up and down like a roller coaster.

"Bag, shoes, and cell phone into the crate at the side," I instruct when she follows me into an old Popov compound. When she scoffs about my demand, I rip the goods out of her hands. "If you think I trust you, you've got another thing coming." Once I have the items where Rocco will have no troubles retrieving them, I nudge my head to the stairwell. "We have to go up before we go down." I step closer to her like I'm sharing trade secrets. "But you know that already, don't you?"

I wasn't lying when I said Dimitri told me everything. His stories included a confession about how India not only watched K be assaulted by Vladimir from a bunker hidden in the basement of this compound, she also recorded her abuse.

Those tapes were a major part of India's negotiation. If Smith hadn't located them, our agreement would have been null and void.

With the smile of a vindictive bitch, India whispers, "I'll never tell."

My teeth grit when she drags her fingernails across my pecs before she commences climbing the stairwell on our right, indicating she knows the way. "Were my specifications met?"

I lift my chin before joining her on the middle landing. "To the T." As the grate I dumped her personal goods in creeps across the room via wireless control, I show her the still shots Rocco took before conning me to be their lackey, then I move onto video footage. They expose how truly unhinged she is. She gets off on K's fear. I can smell how aroused she is, much less see it in her massively dilated eyes.

Once the faintest noise of rubber tires rolling over concrete is no longer sounding through my ears, I switch off my phone, stuff it into my pocket, then walk down a smoke-damaged corridor.

Partway down, Smith prompts me that he needs India to talk. She's barely said a handful of words to me. I jog to catch up with India. "What's with the mind games? I thought you wanted this girl for her kid?"

Her nose screws up from me referencing K as a girl, but she keeps her annoyance out of her tone. "If you don't make things interesting, Jamie, you'll live a very boring life."

She slips in my alias on purpose, hopeful it will have me on the back foot. What she doesn't know is Smith leaked my profile information on purpose to authenticate our ruse that I'm a bottom-dwelling gangbanger willing to do anything for a bit of coin. I did a brief stint in juvie when I was seventeen, have been busted twice for narcotics, and enjoy beating my misses on the weekends. As far as India is concerned, I'm the scum on the bottom of the ocean. She has no fucking clue she's even lower than me.

"Yeah, but what kinda thrill do you get witnessing carnage from afar? That would be like watching porn but never putting their actions into play. You get off on the idea of doing what they're doing, not that they're doing it to each other. Being in on the action is far better than watching it from the sidelines."

"That's true. Normally. But sometimes more important matters pop up."

"Like avoiding police raids at private airstrips?" When suspicion darts through her eyes, I'm quick to shut it down. "When I saw the broadcast on the news, I fucking knew it was you. You've got badass mafia chick stamped all over you."

I was hoping a bit of flattery would get her talking. Regretfully, it seems to have the opposite effect. "You've heard about me?" she asks, her tone snappy.

"None of it was bad," I reply, continuing my ruse that I find her attractive. In reality, she makes me want to barf. You can't have insides as ugly as hers and not see it when you look at her.

When I drag my teeth over my lower lip, she watches my teeth's rake before raising her eyes to mine. "What have you heard?"

I don't know whether to continue with the flattery or tell her what I really think, so I mix it up by giving her a bit of both. "That you don't stop stomping until you get what you want."

"That's true," she murmurs, her voice way too sugary for my liking. "So it won't be any surprise to you when I say there's been a change of plans." Wrongfully believing she's running the show around here, she plucks the revolver from the back of my jeans before she continues down the hall, barking out orders, "In approximately ten minutes, Trey Corbyn is going to walk through the doors of this compound." Just before she reaches the secret stairwell, she spins around to face me. "You're going to kill him."

Even with my stomach churning from her confession, I keep a rational head. "That wasn't part of our agreement. I got the girl you requested, so my job here is done."

I pretend to take a stumbling step backward when she murmurs, "Will that still be your answer when I offer you a million dollars?"

I thought she used sex to brainwash the men who jump at her every command. I had no clue she bribed them with money.

Silly me.

"You don't have a million dollars."

A ghost-like grin stitches across her face. "I did, but I don't anymore because I gave it to you." She nudges her head to the pocket I placed my phone in. "Check your account. I transferred the money on my way here."

I'm confident this is a test, and thank fuck Smith is as clued in as me. While I log into my online banking app, he checks the balance of the account we opened to authenticate our ruse. "There's no money in the account we set up. She's bluffing."

I give India a look, one that says I'd spit at her feet if I could. "You're all talk, lady. There ain't anything in my account close to a million dollars."

With a mocking grin, she slants her head to the side, then arches a brow. "There isn't? Hmm... perhaps you should check again?"

"What the fuck," Rocco murmurs in my ear when Smith announces the funds have now cleared. "She must have someone on the outside. I personally took care of the three johns in her car."

I bounce on the balls of my feet when Smith requests for me to stand closer to India to see if our connection picks up any interference. "Holy fucking shit. I'm a millionaire!"

Much to India's disgrace, I throw my arms around her neck and hug her tight. It isn't a long embrace, but it gives Smith exactly what he needs. "She's wired up. While waiting for the files in her phone to commence downloading, I'll backtrack the signal, but for now, keep her talking."

I inconspicuously nod before gesturing for India to enter the stairwell before me. "What exactly do I have to do for this money?"

Over the next five minutes, she discloses every sickening detail. How she's going to lure Trey to the dungeon-like room by playing old videos of K's assault. How she'll force him through a second game of Russian roulette, and that when she signals for me to enter the room, I'm to gun down Trey while she takes care of the man he entrusted to look after his wife.

"That's it? A straight-up mafia hit?"

While pushing video tapes into a set of old televisions outside the room K and Eight are in, she twists her lips. "Why complicate things with unnecessary details?"

The way she talks so nonchalantly about death agitates me to no end. She truly believes it's her right to choose who lives or dies. She's not God, and I very much look forward to announcing that to her. I just need Smith to hurry the fuck up.

Like he can hear my inner thoughts, he mutters, "I'm going as fast as I can—"

"But you're too fucking late," I mumble when the flash of headlights beams through a window above my head. "Trey is here."

"Fuck!" Rocco curses down the line while India drags a table into place for her Russian roulette game.

"I'm almost there," Smith promises as his fingers tap wildly on the keyboard of his multiple laptops. "Just a few more minutes."

"We don't have fucking minutes." When India's eyes snap to mine, I nudge my head to the room K and Eight are kept in. "Get them in here now."

I whisper in K's ear that everything will be okay while leading her into the room. She doesn't acknowledge me. With how quiet she is, it is as if she hasn't even sensed our presence. No whimpers escape her lips when I loosely tie her to the chair. She doesn't scream for help. She remains perfectly still, the tiny flutters in her baby bump the only indication she's alive.

As a shadow casts over the stairwell, I conceal myself in the dark nook in the far corner of the room. I'm tempted to end it all now, to take India down before she can harm another family, but no matter how many times my brain screams at me to curl my finger around the trigger, I can't. If I kill India for my own selfish reasons, I'll be trapped in hell for eternity. But maybe, just maybe, if I free the women who have been held captive for almost a decade, my good deed could excuse all the bad things I've done. My patience, my trust, and my wish to be with Demi again are all riding on that pardon. If I give that up, I will have *nothing* to root for, so for that reason, and that reason alone, I will follow India's plan until Smith tells me otherwise.

It only takes half a second for the videos India acquired specifically for him to rip Trey's heart out of his chest. While rambling incessantly, he fires at the televisions pushing him to the brink of insanity before he swivels on his feet to face the direction sniffling is coming from. K must have sensed his presence. She's no longer the zombie she was only minutes ago. Her chin is held high, and her chest is rising and falling in rhythm with Trey's.

I'm not sure if the gun India is butting against her ribs is responsible for that or Trey's roar. "What the fuck is your issue! Did daddy spoil his little princess too much she'd rather run his legacy into the ground than see it thrive?"

I miss what India replies. I'm too stunned by Rocco's announcement that there's a sniper dot on the back of my head. "Stay real fucking still, Ox. He's coming to you. He'll land at your six in five, four, three, two, o—"

The 'o' of one only just leaves his mouth when I ram my gun into the sniper's groin, spin around, snatch his rifle out of his hands like Dimitri did Rocco years ago, then smash my fist into his nose. When he stumbles back with a groan, I silence him with my boot. Since my headspace is a little better now than it was when Demi was locked in a room with her uncle, I only imprint my boot into his face once.

There's only one person I want to kill today.

This man isn't her.

"Fuck," I breathe out slowly when a bead-like device rolls from his ear. "He's wired."

"Could he be India's outside guy?" Rocco asks.

Even though he can't see me, I shrug before bobbing down to gather up the listening device. When I push it to my ear, shockwaves rocket through me. I recognize the voice on the end of the wire. It's Agent Machini.

"No one is to make a move until I say so. If you move before ordered, I'll expect your badge on my desk first thing tomorrow morning. Target is to be brought in alive. I repeat, India is to be brought in alive." She's either psychic or I breathe funny because I barely push out a shocked breath when her grumbly tone is replaced with a soft, pleading voice. "Maddox... is that you?" She must take my silence as a yes. "I need you to listen to me, okay? Your meeting with India is a setup. She knows who was behind the messages. Dimitri's crew is one of the loose ends she wants to tie. I need you to leave now. Seek shelter in the tree lines. I'll be there in a matter of minutes."

"I can't. It's too late."

Not just for India, but for me as well.

"It isn't too late, Maddox. It's never too late." She can say that because she doesn't know one of her colleagues is lying unconscious at my feet. Furthermore, I'm too deep in the dark to see the light at the end of the tunnel, and I'm too tired to search for it. "If you go through with this, you will start a mafia war. This is part of India's plan for world domination. She's pitting the Petrettis against the Popo—" Her words are silenced by the *doof* of a bullet zipping through a silencer.

"Agent Machini..."

Nothing but gargled breaths sound out of my earpiece.

She's either running or choking on her own blood.

"Macy!"

When nothing but sickening silence sounds out of the earpiece, I take my frustration out on the wall next to me. I get in two solid punches before Smith backs up her claims something is amiss. "The man lying unconscious at your feet is Special Agent Wraith Felix. He's been in the Bureau a little over four years. He's clearly rogue. I don't know any agents with 200K in an offshore account." After a handful more keystrokes, he advises. "His parents are Czech citizens. They live in the town the Dvořáks once ruled."

"Fuck!" I curse out while pacing back and forth. It's the only way I can think lately—by stomping out my frustration.

After a couple of seconds of contemplation, I ask, "How will this start a war?"

Rocco clicks the pieces of the puzzle together faster than Smith and me. "If India makes it appear that you and Trey took each other out, the Petrettis and the Popovs are required to intervene. The Popovs will retaliate on behalf of Trey, the Petrettis for you."

"But I'm not a Petretti."

"Empirically, you're not," Smith agrees. "But metaphorically, you are. Demi could change her name and her looks, but she would remain a Petretti no matter what, as would any child she birthed. Your baby may not have survived, Ox, but the rules we are governed by still acknowledge it. That child made you a Petretti."

Up until five seconds ago, I would have denied his comment. Now, I can't. Even if our child had all my features and my last name, he or she would have still had Petretti DNA. That alone makes me a Petretti.

I'm drawn from my thoughts by a furious growl. "*Fuck!*" Rocco grunts out with a roar when the obvious can't be denied for a second longer. We walked straight into India's trap." She played us like a fucking fiddle."

"*Tried* to play us," I correct, aware of what I now need to do.

India can't pit the Petrettis against the Popovs if she's dead.

"Pack up and go."

"No," Rocco immediately fires back. "If we leave, you'll be trapped here. We had the Range Rover towed."

The concern in his voice exposes he trusts Agent Machini's claim that the Bureau is only minutes away. It also reveals he is the man Demi believed he was.

It makes my decision to go it alone even easier.

"I'll do what needs to be done. You have my word."

"I don't give a shit about the mission, Ox. It can fuckin' wait. Although I want India to pay for what she's done, taking her down won't bring Demi back."

"I don't want to bring her back," I confess. "I want to go to her."

"Ox—"

"Just fucking go!" I scream when the anger in his voice switches to worry. "We don't have time for this shit now, Rocco. If you stay, we *all* go down, then where will that leave Dimitri's family?" I almost have him, so I'm certain my next question will get him over the line. "And what about your girl, Rocco? How do you think she'd cope seeing you locked up again?"

"Don't bring her into this," he breathes out slowly, his tone undeniably protective even with the sound of police sirens wailing through the air.

"Why? Because you know it will devastate her as much as it did Demi when I took the decision out of her hands. I fucked up that day, Rocco. I don't want to see you do the same, so go home to your family before you lose them altogether."

He curses under his breath two times before he demands Smith to pack on the fly. "We're going to talk about this, Ox. This ain't the fucking end of this conversation. Do you hear me?" When I hum out an agreeing murmur, he adds, "But if you're going down, can you take that bitch down with you?"

"It'll be my pleasure," I reply, smiling.

I wait for their frantic stomps to be drowned out by distance before checking that the safety on my gun is off.

Once I'm confident everything is ready to go, I re-enter the room India, Trey, K, and Eight are in. India appears shocked that I'm minus a bullet wound, but she plays it cool, confident in her ruse. "I don't want anything from you. You've done enough, now you can leave the rest up to us."

With a smile as hideous as her ugly insides, she nudges her head to me, hopeful Trey's tirade will end by him popping a bullet between my eyes. "You fuckin' piece of shit," he growls, convinced he's facing a rival instead of a comrade. "Not even your sister will save you from this. Do you hear me? You're a dead man walking."

While the stomp of Smith and Rocco's boots continue booming through the earpiece in my ear, I try to hint to Trey that I'm not his enemy. "Blood isn't always thicker than water, Trey. I thought you'd know that better than anyone." My gun is aimed at his chest, but he should pay attention to the words I speak the most. "I heard lots of stories during my time in lockup. Failed takeover bids. Men being brought back from the brink of death. Duchesses so desperate for a crown, they fucked with the wrong family over and over again."

I realize my act is up when India snaps out, "Wraith."

I don't mind. The sound of tires spinning over asphalt has overtaken the frantic beat of my heart. Rocco and Smith are in the clear, meaning I can now shift my focus to India. "I don't know what shocks me more, the fact you think I didn't scan the face of *every* person surrounding the cage my sister was mauled in, or that I didn't hear your disappointed sigh when Col agreed with the barter of my life for Justine's."

India's vindictive insides are displayed in the worst light when she compresses the trigger of her gun. The shock on her face when it dawns on her that the bullet chamber is empty is priceless. She was so hell-bent on seeking vengeance, she didn't bother to check if the gun she stole from me was loaded.

Shame on her.

The fact she tried to kill a pregnant woman without the slightest bit of remorse on her face sees me lifting the scope of my assault rifle from her chest to her forehead. You can't kill a heartless woman by firing at her chest. She'd need a heart for that method to work.

"You were so fucking desperate to be top dog, you didn't consider who you were taking down in the process."

She has hurt so many people—Demi, Justine, Trey, Dimitri, and me. She trampled us all because, unlike Demi, she didn't try to find her way out of the dark.

She let it consume her.

My finger stops shuddering around the trigger when Smith's breathless voice breaks through the drumming of my pulse in my ears. "What did you say that Agent's name was? Macy..."

I realize he isn't talking to me when Rocco answers on my behalf. "Macy Machini." He sucks in a sharp breath before breathing it out with a gargled denial, "No fucking way."

I'm about to ask what's going on, but thankfully, Smith chimes back in. "I cracked into India's phone. One of India's surrogates has the last name Machini. Kendall was abducted four and a half years ago from Miami. Her sister, Macy, has been searching for her ever since."

Goosebumps break across my skin as the final pieces of the puzzle slot into place. Agent Machini taking the wrap for Agent

Moses's death, and her desperation to bring India in alive was because she knew she'd never find her sister if India were dead. India would take Kendall's location to the grave. She was in a lose-lose situation. She either risked losing India or her sister.

That's all done with now. India can be sentenced for her crimes because Smith's confession advises he's hacked into India's phone. Her victims have been identified. They'll be home by the end of the week, and my return maybe even sooner than that.

As a video montage of my years with Demi rolls through my head, I lock my eyes with the woman who took away the one thing that would have tied us together for eternity, then speak three little words. "Dimitri says hello."

I wait for the video montage to reach the final smile Demi gave me before I compress the trigger on my assault rifle.

I feel no guilt when a bullet pierces through a crinkle in India's forehead.

No euphoria.

No victory.

Yet, I do feel at peace.

Agent Machini's warning about a mafia war rings through my ears when the slumping of India's body onto the stained concrete floor is quickly chased by Trey aiming his gun at me. I killed his enemy, but Smith was right, my unborn child tied me to the Petrettis for life, so it's only fair Trey sees me as one.

"I couldn't lure India out of hiding without offering up an incentive." I could rat Rocco and Smith out with me, but why would I? Their help has pushed me one step closer to Demi. I can't fling shit at them now.

Trey's words are hostile when he snaps out, "Admitting you brutalized my woman won't do you any favors."

"What would you rather, Trey? Your girl tied up and safe, or lying lifeless in a ditch with her stomach barren of your child?" He doesn't need to answer me. The expression on his face tells which way his pendulum swung. It went in my favor for once. "Yeah, that's what I thought." Some may call me a fool for lowering my gun, but they'd only be the people who believe death is scary. "If it weren't for Dimitri and me, she would be dead in four months." I motion my head at K partway through my reply. "Why do you think India wanted her brought in alive?"

Trey curls his finger around the trigger of his gun when I dig a sale document out of my pocket. It isn't for K. It's for Dimitri's first wife, Audrey.

"Who's Audrey?" Trey asks after taking in the name of the documentation I dumped on the table between us.

His eyes rocket to mine when I confess, "Dimitri's wife. Well, she was his wife before *that* piece of shit tested your theory that blood isn't thicker than water." The way I murmur 'that' leaves no doubt as to who I'm referencing. "Up until twenty minutes ago, Dimitri wasn't your enemy. I guess only time will tell where we go from here. Things get hostile when a mutual nemesis is eradicated." I inwardly curse my stupidity. I wasn't meant to say 'we.' I know where I'm going. I'm reasonably sure neither Dimitri nor Nikolai want to come with me.

Needing to leave before I instigate a mafia war instead of defusing one, I flash Trey a final smirk before spinning on my heels and walking away. He could shoot me in the back, but as I said earlier, death doesn't scare me. How could it when I've lived in hell for over five years?

Partway down the corridor, I disband my assault weapon before replacing it with a standard Glock. I'm not exactly sure how I am moving. My head is as hazy as fuck, and I'm shaking like I have the plague, but I continue putting one foot in front of the other until I'm outside the compound.

Some of the adrenaline keeping me moving disperses when I break through the dense bushland bordering the property. A sprinkling of rain has made the air extra fresh, but no matter how hard I try to fill my lungs with air, I can't. I've reached the end of the road, tired both mentally and physically, but instead of being granted the right to end things my way on my terms, I have to do it in front of a federal agent who doesn't know how to quit even while sporting a bullet wound.

Agent Machini stands a few feet away from me. One of her hands is aiming her gun at my head. The other is clutching her silky blouse that's now more red than white. She doesn't need to ask what happened to India. She can see the truth in my eyes. They have the same bleak, despondent haze they had when we crossed paths in the hallway at Wallens Ridge.

Furthermore, she sees me for who I truly am—a murderer.

"Get on your knees and put your hands behind your back."

Her anger propels her two steps forward when I shake my head. "I can't go back there. I won't survive it without her." I barely survived lock-up when Demi was at my side, supporting me. There's no way I could last decades there without her. I'd rather die. I just have one last matter I need to attend to first. "It isn't as you're thinking. Your sis—"

"Get on your fucking knees and put your hands behind your back!" Her anger is blinding her judgment as much as my grief is blinding me. We're both out of control. I'm just aware of it. Agent Machini isn't. "Don't make me shoot you, Maddox. *Please.*" Her last word is more a plea than a demand. It's as shaky as the hold she has on her gun while muttering, "I told you to stop. Why didn't you listen to me? She'll never be found now."

"She will be," I reply, my voice honest. "Kendall will be home by the end of the week. We found them, Macy. They're coming home."

She doesn't want to believe me. Years of disappointments have lowered her trust as much as it has mine, but there's an honesty in my eyes that will never dampen no matter how many people I kill. "You found her?"

"Yes," I reply with a gentle nod of my head before I fall to my knees, too exhausted to remain standing.

I'm so fucking tired.

So fucking empty.

It's time for me to go home.

"She's free, and now I will be as well."

"Show me your hands!" Agent Machini screams when I creep mine around my back to remove the revolver stuffed down there.

When I pull out my gun and butt it to my temple, she braces her legs at the width of her shoulders, screams my name in a long, mangled roar, then fires one time.

I don't know whose bullet takes me down first, but I do know one thing, whether in this life or the next, Demi's smile will always be my most favorite.

40

DEMI

One Month Later...

I place the book I'm in the middle of onto my bedside table before joining Max on the reading nook in the front window of our apartment. Considering the time of year, the weather is miserable. The wind is howling, and the rain is torrential. It's the perfect snuggling weather—*if I had a partner to cuddle with.*

While scratching Max behind his pointed ears that still seem a little saggy today, I take a moment to gripe about my years of celibacy. I'm not single because I am hideously ugly. The numerous dinner invitations I get every week assures me of this. It's more a personal choice.

I've not yet found a man who sparks an interest out of me. They're great for one date, but by the second date, I'm either bored as hell, or their arrogance shines brighter than the politeness they are cloaking it with.

Since I'd rather live alone with Max for the rest of my life than settle, I've done precisely that since the single motor vehicle accident that pinched my memories. I'm sure the right guy will come along one day, but if he doesn't, I am okay with that as well. I'm happy as I am, so I can handle a little bit of loneliness.

After taking in the way the streetlights make the rain appear more like sleet than droplets of water, I cuddle in closer to Max. "What's the matter, Maxxy? You've been extra moody the past month."

He's been sitting by the window for the past two hours, peering south. He's done it over a dozen times the past four weeks, but mercifully, today's watch is minus the whimpers he did the first couple of days.

I've had the vet out multiple times the past month. She assured me Max is fine. I wish I could express the same. Something is wrong with him. It just appears to be more mental than physical.

"Do you need to use the bathroom?"

When he flops his jowls onto my thigh, I take that as a no. He usually scratches at the door when he wants to go potty.

"What about a snack? I could fix you something."

My heart breaks when his big exhale rustles my nightwear. He never gives up an opportunity to eat. He must be truly miserable.

I snatch up the blanket from the sofa before requesting for him to scoot over. When he does as requested, I spoon him like it's perfectly normal for people to snuggle their dogs. Max doesn't mind my neediness. He's just as clingy. That's one of the reasons he keeps a good distance between me and any man who comes within a one-mile radius of me. He wants me all to himself.

The recollection of his protectiveness inches my lips into a smile. "What about a bacon sandwich. If my memory isn't failing me... which it does more than I care to admit... I'm reasonably sure Ben restocked the bacon before he left today."

Ben is the part-time sous chef at the café I own. He has the typical adventure-seeker look down pat. Brown, sun-dyed hair, crisp blue eyes, and a smattering of freckles dotted across his nape.

Despite Macy and Ben saying otherwise, I'm confident we met before my accident. There are too many familiarities about him for me to discount. It was those features that made us great friends the past four years. That, and the fact his girlfriend is my best friend.

We often gang up on him. He only retaliated with a wet tea towel once. His endeavor to protect himself saw his backside housing fifteen stitches.

"I wish I could understand you, Max," I murmur in his ear when his heart rate kicks up a notch. "It'd be a whole heap kinder to my heart if you could tell me what's wrong..." My words trail off when Max suddenly launches onto his feet. He barks at a car pulling in at the front of a motel half a block up two times before he jumps down from the reading nook and charges for the door. "Now you want to go potty?" I grumble more to myself than Max.

After placing a raincoat over my nightie, I snag Max's leash off the coatrack, then pull open the front door. "Max!" I shout when he races down the stairwell like a bat out of hell.

He leaps over the landing, squeezes through the doggy door not made for a dog of his size, then bolts down the street.

"Max!" I scream again while taking off after him.

It's late, and wild animals wander around these parts at night. He could be seriously hurt if he doesn't slow down.

"Oh my God, I'm so sorry," I apologize to the man Max has barreled over one block down from my apartment. "He isn't usually like this." I'm not lying. I was expecting the man's face to be a bloody mess. Instead, it's covered in the aftermath of Max's sloppy kisses.

The reason for Max's obsessive affection comes to light when I pull Max far enough away from the stranger, his face becomes exposed.

Holy.

Flaming.

Cupcakes.

An angel fell from the sky with the deluge of rain. Reddish blond hair, bluish-green eyes, and a jaw that would make sculptors envious, and don't get me started on the tattoos the fitted white shirt clinging to his fit body can't hide. He's gorgeous, meaning my tongue is hanging out of my mouth right along with Max's.

"That's fine," the stranger assures, serenading me with his scrumptious voice. It's a little moody, but that's understandable considering he was just knocked over by a smelly, wet dog who's eager for a second round. "I'm just glad he's friendly."

When I notice his bandaged hand, I tighten my grip on Max's collar with one hand before assisting the stranger from the ground with the other. I've barely curled my hand around his uninjured one when he pulls it back like he got zapped.

I can't say I blame him. There's some major voltage happening, and it isn't from the lightning breaking above our heads.

The man slants his head in a way far too adorable for anyone over the age of six before he slowly raises his eyes to my face. He drinks in the faintest scar running down the middle of my chest, my lips, my nose, and another unfavorable scar in my cheek before his eyes finally find mine.

"Hi,' I whisper, a little disappointed by the absolute shock in his eyes. I'm certain I look like a wreck. I'm wearing a raincoat over a granny nightie, but I was still hoping for a better response than a gaped mouth and massively dilated eyes. "I own a café around the corner. If you drop off your jacket tomorrow, I'll have it dry cleaned for you." His leather jacket doesn't look pricy. His ride, on the other hand, looks both classical and expensive.

As the stranger's chest heaves, he strays his eyes to the right. When I follow the direction of his gaze, I spot another equally attractive man. His tattoos are more colorful than the man standing across from me, and his eyes are entirely green instead of the greenish-blue combination the mystery stranger has, but his watchful stare doesn't do crazy things to my insides. His smile reminds me of the grin Ben gives me every morning when I gallop down the stairs of my apartment. To save on expenses, I converted the attic in the café to a loft apartment. It's cozy and perfect—just like this mysterious man.

I call myself an idiot when the man smart enough to stand under the awning to protect his clothes from the downpour jerks up his chin, summoning his friend.

"Sorry, you probably need to go."

"No," the handsome stranger shouts, startling me. It isn't a scared startle. I'm more pleased by his eagerness to keep me around than frightened. "I'm right where I'm meant to be."

After wiping the excitement from my face, I spin back around to face him. "Are you sure?" I query through twisted lips. "It's pretty wet out here."

"It is," he agrees, his shock lessening the longer he takes in my smile. "Should *we* seek shelter?"

Shockingly, I nod without the slightest bit of hesitation. It usually takes several invitations and multiple grovels for me to agree to an advance. I don't know why my defenses immediately dropped when our eyes locked and held. I just feel comfortable with him. Safe, which is weird considering I can't remember the last time I experienced fear.

"Do you want to... umm... come to my..." I point to my café, too chicken to formally invite him into my private abode. I hate making the first move, but there's so much chemistry brewing between us, I'd be a fool to ignore it.

After reminding myself I'm a grown-ass woman who can invite male guests over, I ask more smoothly, "We could grab a coffee at my café if you'd like?"

When he nods, I inwardly tap dance before shifting on my feet to face his friend. He lifts his chin when I do the same mute pointy thingmabob to my café.

My interests pique when Stranger Number Two shadows our walk instead of participating in it. His protective detail has me wondering if Stranger Number One makes a living with his deliriously handsome face. He's probably uber-famous, and I stupidly have no idea who he is. I prefer reading over watching movies. I don't even own a television.

Within a dozen steps, my curiosity gets the better of me. From what Macy has told me, that's a quirk I've had since I was a child. "Is he your bodyguard?"

When the stranger's reddish-blond brow pops in silent questioning, I nudge my head to the man maintaining an amicable yet safe distance.

Stranger One drifts his eyes in the direction I nudged before he returns them to me. "Ah... no," he replies, somewhat sheepish before he pinches his thigh. When his brutal nip does nothing more than crinkle his damp jeans, he says, "He's a... friend."

I drag the back of my hand across my forehead. "Phew. I was getting worried I was meant to know your name." Ignoring the stitching of his brows, I pat Max on the head. He's helming my walk like he usually does, but instead of standing in front of me, he's standing at the mysterious stranger's side. "This is Max..." I touch my chest. "... and I'm Demi. It's nice to meet you..."

After a couple of seconds of deliberation, he accepts the hand I'm holding out in offering before saying, "Maddox. I'm Maddox."

"Maddox," I murmur to myself, certain I've heard the name before but confident I could never forget such a handsome face.

I stop trudging through years of blackness that were once memories when we arrive at my café. When Maddox opens the door for me, Max bolts through like his chivalry was for him before he shakes his fur dry. I laugh at the mess he makes in the foyer—it was either laugh or cry, so I went for the one that's easier for me to pull off. I'm more a happy person than a sooky la-la, so laughing is always my go-to emotion—before gesturing for Maddox and his friend to take a seat.

"Would you like coffee or tea?" My heart patters in my chest when a brilliant idea pops into my head. "Or I could cook you something. I have everything you could imagine back there."

"Coffee will be great," Maddox's friend replies before he guides Maddox to a booth in the middle of the empty space.

"Great! Coming right up." I dart into the kitchen like bees are chasing me, except I don't race for the coffee pots. I bolt up the stairs like a madwoman to get changed. I'm not just wearing a grannie nightgown, my panties are from the same dreary collection. The waistband goes past my belly button, for crying out loud!

"Don't say a word," I say to Max when I re-enter the kitchen ten minutes later in a fitted dress with brushed hair and a dash of cherry-flavored lip gloss on my lips. "I dress like this every day. You've just never seen it because you're always walking in front of me instead of next to me."

When he raises a doggy brow, I stick out my tongue, double-check my bra is doing what it's meant to do, then burst through the revolving door of the kitchen like today is the first day of my life instead of the day I was born.

41

MADDOX

"*J*bet you're not pissed about me shooting you in the hand now, are you?" Rocco says with a snicker, his pompousness at an all-time high.

You didn't hear him wrong. Thirty-seven days ago, my gun, Agent Machini's gun, and Rocco's gun all fired at the same time. Agent Machini's bullet pierced through Rocco's shoulder. Rocco's bullet shattered multiple bones in my hand, and Rocco's perfect aim saw my bullet graze my ear instead of embedding into my brain as I had planned.

He shot me to save my life, and up until ten minutes ago, I hated him for it.

Now... now I'm beginning to wonder if my bullet did its job. This is heaven, right? It has to be. Demi and Max are here.

My theory would be more convincing if Rocco weren't here, though. I don't care how many times he denies it, that prick is going to hell when he dies.

Even Smith agrees with me.

When Rocco places a file down in front of me, it's the fight of my life to take my eyes off Demi. She's moving around the counter of a quaint café in a little unknown town in Montana, preparing coffee.

It's taking her longer than usual to prepare our order since her eyes continually glance my way.

I hope she doesn't think I'm a creep. I can't help but stare. For one, she's even more beautiful than I remembered, and two, she's meant to be a ghost.

I saw her demise.

She died right in front of me.

But I realize that isn't the case when my eyes drop to the paperwork Rocco set down. It's marked confidential with an official FBI seal. It's covered with handwritten text, but one name stands out throughout the scribble—Demi's.

"Terri Glouchester died three days earlier in a traffic accident. The scar you mistook for Demi's was from her autopsy. With her head angled to the side, and her clothing matched to what Demi was wearing, which you could get at any department store since all her funds went to Col, a mistake is easily excused."

I place my thumb over Terri's face before drifting my eyes to Demi. Their similar height and body shape give credit to Rocco's claim that the wreckage that claimed Demi's life was staged, but it doesn't explain everything.

"How did they know we were going to crash?"

My jaw ticks when Rocco says, "Because the airbags in the Buick we're set to go off once you were twenty miles out from the cabin."

"You set us up?"

He nods without shame, like killing enemies doesn't make me a murderer.

"Why the fuck would you do that, Rocco?" I lower my voice when my roar gains me Demi's attention. I want her eyes on me. I just don't want them to have an ounce of fear in them. She hasn't looked over her shoulder once in the last ten minutes. That was unheard of in Hopeton. "You're supposed to be our friend."

"That's why I did it. Demi was going away, Ox. They were going to pin a murder on her. I saw the shit that happens to those women in Wallens Ridge firsthand. I couldn't sit back and watch Demi go through that." He scoots to the edge of his chair, so I can see the truth in his eyes when he says, "I had planned to tell you what really happened, that her accident was a ruse, but then Demi's life ended for real."

I point to her standing mere feet from her, too shocked to talk.

She's right fucking there as healthy as an ox. *And oh so fucking beautiful.*

My eyes float back to Rocco when he mutters, "She isn't the Demi you remember, Ox. Her shell is the same, but her insides are completely different. There's no hurt. No pain—"

"No recollection of who she once was," I mumble when the truth finally dawns on me. I wasn't dreaming when Demi introduced herself as if she didn't know me. She was truly stumped. "Why doesn't she remember me?"

When Rocco attempts to hand me a thick medical file, I push it to his side of the table. "Give it to me in layman's terms, Rocco, because right now, I am still not convinced I'm not dead." I tried to end my life. I was prepared to die, and not even thirty days at a mental health facility could fully convince me I deserved a second chance, so why am I getting one now?

Rocco chuckles before relaying a whole heap of mumbo jumbo that pretty much insinuates that a brain injury saw Demi lose all memories of her childhood, her teen years, and the tumultuous yet beautiful year and a half we had together.

"So she doesn't remember anyone? Her dad? Kaylee... *me*?" I choke over my last word.

If I were honest, I'd admit I'm not overly worried about her forgetting me. Memories can be recreated minus the nightmares that taint them. If she doesn't know who I am, she doesn't know the lengths I went to make her mine. To her, I'm not a killer or a once-life inmate.

I'm just a man crushing on a beautiful woman.

It's kind of perfect when you truly think about it.

Rocco halfheartedly shrugs. "She knows of her dad and Kaylee, but they skimmed over the bad parts like how they died and why. Dr. Nesser believed Demi's mental stability was as important as her physical capabilities. When he noticed a drastic change in her temperament after hypnosis therapies, he realized unlocking her memories could be more harmful than her living without them." He licks his lips before hitting me with the big stuff. "He believes Demi did the same thing as a child. It's why she couldn't remember Kaylee." He leans in even closer to ensure his words are only for me. "Do you remember Demi telling you the story about how she ran after her father and Col got into a tussle at her family home?"

I jerk up my chin.

"Did she happen to mention she stumbled onto Kaylee's body?"

As I shake my head, my heart pains for Demi. That was years after Kaylee was taken. She would have been badly decomposed.

"After she came to—"

"She passed out?" I butt in, too shocked not to interrupt.

Rocco shakes his head. "She was knocked out by one of Col's goons." Air whizzes out of my nose as I struggle to keep my emotions in check. "But when she came to in the hospital, she had no recollection about anything that had happened that morning and many before it."

"So her dad protected her by keeping them locked away," I fill in, finally clicking on. When Rocco nods for the second time, I ask, "Is that why she doesn't know who I am? Are they saying I'm a bad part of her life?"

"No, Ox," Rocco replies without pause for thought. "I would have killed the fucker if he even hinted at that." His eyes reveal he isn't lying. "But I can understand how it would have been hard for them to explain how influential you were to Demi without introducing all the bad stuff. That's why they figured it was best to wait until you could *show* her instead of telling her."

"They?"

I assume he's talking about Dimitri and Smith but am proven wrong when he nudges his head to the sidewalk outside. Although her face is hidden by a large umbrella, Agent Machini has an identifying aura. It's been even more blistering since Kendall was returned stateside two weeks ago, and it could go head to head with Caidyn's natural charisma. He's standing at her side with begging, please-don't-kill-me eyes.

"They didn't want to keep this secret from you, Ox, but at the end of the day, they had to do what was best for Demi. She had to come first." I drift my eyes back to Rocco when he mutters, "Just like you needed time to get your head screwed on straight before I dropped this bomb on you. If I had brought you here the instant Smith unearthed Demi's location, you wouldn't have gotten the reaction you did from her because for some fucked-up reason, she finds this more attractive..." he whacks me in the chest, "... than this." He waves his hand over my face, doubling my smile.

I've endured blow after blow after blow the past five years, but all the sorrow lifted the instant Demi's eyes locked with mine.

She made me whole again.

"Will her memories ever return?" I ask after a couple of seconds of quiet deliberating.

Rocco shrugs, truly unsure.

His shoulders land back to the original spot with only a second to spare. Demi has arrived at our table with a tray of coffee. It almost topples out of her hand when she spots Agent Machini and Caidyn outside.

My emotions don't know which way to swing when Caidyn brushes off Demi's wordless invitation for him to join us with a shake of his head before he mouths to her that he'll see her tomorrow.

She pokes her tongue at him before she lowers her eyes to mine. They're grinning with mischievousness, but lust doesn't form in them until our eyes collide. "Don't pay him any attention. He's a little weird with out-of-town folk."

"Weird or jealous?" I ask Demi when she places a mug down in front of me.

While taking a moment to relish the jealousy in my tone, she adds a dash of milk and four clumps of sugar to the dark concoction steaming in front of me. Only once she has me on tenterhooks does she release my jealousy back into the wild. "Weird, of course. Ben is my best friend. We've *never* been like that."

The hardness her frisky wink causes the front of my pants won't stop me from asking, "Ben?"

Caidyn's middle name is Benjamin, so it would be an easy alias for him to pull off. It's also less obvious than Caidyn. If I had to pick a pseudonym for him to use, I would have chosen Benjamin.

Demi nods again before she serves Rocco his coffee. A hopeful grin tugs at my lips when she only plops two clumps of sugar into his mug. I always have my coffee with four clumps. Did she remember that, or was it just a fluke?

Eager to find out, I lock my eyes with Demi's, which happen to be slowly drifting over my face, before asking, "Would you mind cooking us something? We drove straight through from Vegas. I'm starved."

"I'd love to." Her smile is brighter than the twinkle her eyes got when she realized I caught her stare. It's amazing how sharing she is with her emotions now she isn't afraid to share them. She likes that she was busted ogling me just as much as I love that she can't help but stare. "Is there anything in particular you'd like to eat?"

I snatch the menus out of Rocco's hand before he can peruse them, then I shake my head. "No. We eat pretty much anything." I pause to give her the chance to intervene. When she doesn't, I add, "Except snails."

Her laugh, my fucking God, it's perfect. "You can be assured we will *never* serve snails here." My nostrils flare to suck in her delicious scent when she leans in close to whisper in my ear. "Unless he disses my cooking." She motions her head to Rocco. "Then he deserves to eat slugs for dinner."

I don't miss the quickest press of her thighs when I throw my head back and laugh. Rocco is positive the Demi standing across from me isn't the Demi from my dreams. I'm not convinced. In a way, this Demi *is* the Demi from my dreams because she's free like I always hoped she'd be. There's no fear in her eyes, no panic coating her skin. Her wings are fully expanded, and they haven't been clipped with carnage. She can finally fly high, and I'm going to do everything in my power to ensure she soars to her full potential.

While chuckling about the gaga gleam in my eyes, Rocco tosses a bundle of bills onto the tabletop before sliding out of the booth. "It looks like you have everything under control." He stretches, using the long day as an excuse to leave, so he doesn't appear rude to Demi. "Thank you for the coffee. I'll be sure to drop in anytime I'm in the area." After accepting an unexpected goodbye hug from Demi, Rocco lifts a gym bag my shock had me missing onto the tabletop. "Car keys, driver's license, passport, and anything else you may need is in here. If you need more, you know how to reach me." His tone makes it obvious the money puffing out the gym bag isn't a loan. It's mine to keep. Or should I say, *ours* since Demi is a part of the equation. "Take care of her, Ox," he murmurs before he stalks out of the café, leaving me alone with Demi and Max for the first time in years.

Only once he disappears into the dark night does Demi mutter, "He seems nice." She screws up her nose before blurting out something she would have never been game to say only years ago. "A little rough around the edges, but nice, nonetheless."

"He's okay in small doses, but I wouldn't recommend him to anyone long term." A tiny vein in her neck flutters when I slip out of the booth. She's standing so close our chests compete for space with every breath we take. "Can I help you cook?"

The eyes of the woman I love stare back at me for several heart-mending seconds before she dips her chin. "I think that would be nice."

Her breaths come out in a hurry when I cup her jaw, but she doesn't pull away. As I stare into her hurt-free eyes, I float my thumbs over the silky-smooth skin on her cheeks. I take my time assessing every perfect feature of her face, in awe of both her strength and her beauty.

Once I have every flawless detail memorized, I drag the tip of my index finger down her nose. It wells her eyes with tears in an instant and makes her words super croaky when she whispers, "We've met before, haven't we?"

I clear away the tears she releases without shame when I nod my head before saying, "Just now... outside in the rain."

After whacking me in the stomach, she giggles. She knows I'm being playful just like I know the best thing about memories is creating them.

Or in our case, recreating them.

I hope you enjoyed Maddox and Demi's story as much as me. The next book in the Italian Cartel series is Rocco. You can find his preorder here: Rocco

To stay up to date with my books, join any of the places below.
Facebook: facebook.com/authorshandi

Instagram: instagram.com/authorshandi

Email: authorshandi@gmail.com

Reader's Group: bit.ly/ShandiBookBabes

Website: authorshandi.com

Newsletter: https://www.subscribepage.com/AuthorShandi

ACKNOWLEDGMENTS

This page is always super hard for me to write, and this month, it is even harder. During the writing of this book, Chris's dad's blood cancer turned terminal, and his uncle, Chris's dad's eldest brother, health took a turn for the worst.

As I am writing this, we laid Chris's uncle to rest yesterday and his father will be farewelled in what I am sure will be a fitting ceremony on Sunday. It has been a terrible time for the Boyes family the past couple of weeks. I've kept working, because fortunately for me, this is how I escape the bad and relish the good. This book made me cry—a lot. But that's okay, sometimes it's good to let the deluge out. Despite wishing otherwise, we can't always live in a world full of rainbows and sunshine. Besides, there isn't rainbow without a storm, and I like them enough to put up with a couple of dark clouds.

But if you are struggling to find the light at the end of the tunnel like Maddox, don't hesitate to reach out for help. Message me, drop me a PM, or write a post on my wall. I'd rather hear your thoughts than lose the ability altogether.

We're in this together.

Shandi

PS: I want to send a special thanks to Tam for promoting the shit out of Ox in my readers group and on TikTok. It makes me immensely happy that you connected with the story so much. Now to find a thousand more readers just like you xx

ALSO BY SHANDI BOYES

Perception Series

Saving Noah (Noah & Emily)

Fighting Jacob (Jacob & Lola)

Taming Nick (Nick & Jenni)

Redeeming Slater (Slater and Kylie)

Saving Emily (Noah & Emily - Novella)

Wrapped Up with Rise Up (Perception Novella - should be read after the
Bound Series)

Enigma

Enigma (Isaac & Isabelle #1)

Unraveling an Enigma (Isaac & Isabelle #2)

Enigma The Mystery Unmasked (Isaac & Isabelle #3)

Enigma: The Final Chapter (Isaac & Isabelle #4)

Beneath The Secrets (Hugo & Ava #1)

Beneath The Sheets(Hugo & Ava #2)

Spy Thy Neighbor (Hunter & Paige)

The Opposite Effect (Brax & Clara)

I Married a Mob Boss(Rico & Blaire)

Second Shot(Hawke & Gemma)

The Way We Are(Ryan & Savannah #1)

The Way We Were(Ryan & Savannah #2)

Sugar and Spice (Cormack & Harlow)

Lady In Waiting (Regan & Alex #1)

Man in Queue (Regan & Alex #2)

Couple on Hold(Regan & Alex #3)

Enigma: The Wedding (Isaac and Isabelle)

Silent Vigilante (Brandon and Melody #1)

Hushed Guardian (Brandon & Melody #2)

Quiet Protector (Brandon & Melody #3)

Bound Series

Chains (Marcus & Cleo #1)

Links(Marcus & Cleo #2)

Bound(Marcus & Cleo #3)

Restrain(Marcus & Cleo #4)

Psycho (Dexter & ??)

Russian Mob Chronicles

Nikolai: A Mafia Prince Romance (Nikolai & Justine #1)

Nikolai: Taking Back What's Mine (Nikolai & Justine #2)

Nikolai: What's Left of Me(Nikolai & Justine #3)

Nikolai: Mine to Protect(Nikolai & Justine #4)

Asher: My Russian Revenge (Asher & Zariah)

Nikolai: Through the Devil's Eyes(Nikolai & Justine #5)

Trey (Trey & K)

K: A Trey Sequel

The Italian Cartel

Dimitri

Roxanne

Reign

Made in the USA
Columbia, SC
19 October 2022

69744127R00196